PRAISE FOR DE

Havoc

"Deborah J Ledford's *Havoc* releases the latest chapter in the harrowing story of Taos officer Eva Duran and her latest quest for justice. During a significantly dark day in the Pueblo community, Ledford tells the story of Officer Duran and a wide community of characters who somehow balance their duties to solving a devastating crime in their community and maintaining traditional obligations with pride and dignity. Ledford juggles these details with a heightened sense of knowledge and research and creates a significant and accomplished portrait of contemporary crime fighting in tribal communities."

—Ramona Emerson, author of *Shutter*, Edgar Award nominee, longlisted for the National Book Award and PEN/Hemingway Award

"*Havoc* is a crackerjack crime novel that got me at page one and had me reading as fast as possible. My favorite kind of story: gripping, fast moving, and emotionally involving with characters I truly cared about. A winner!"

—Christopher Reich, *New York Times* bestselling author

"Atmospheric, poignant, and set in the Taos Pueblo, Ledford's tribal police officer Eva 'Lightning Dance' Duran doesn't flinch in this dark, twisting tale that's riveting from the first page. A fantastic second book in this new series from a master of crime fiction."

—Jamie Freveletti, award-winning and internationally bestselling author of the Emma Caldridge series

"*Havoc* encompasses the elements of a thriller that I look for: a no-nonsense, relatable heroine who gives as much as she takes; a book that's as much about the characters and what they're going through as about the crime; and a story that weaves in culture and representation of its setting—the Taos Pueblo reservation. Deborah Ledford lays out a multifaceted plot that is thoughtful and compelling, giving us multiple perspectives that only elevate an already propulsive plot. All I can say is applause to you, Deborah."

—Yasmin Angoe, author of acclaimed *Her Name Is Knight*

"A pitch-perfect sequel for fans of Eva 'Lightning Dance' Duran, who is back seeking justice for her Taos Pueblo community after violence strikes and a dark conspiracy must be unraveled."

—Vanessa Lillie, author of USA Today bestseller *Blood Sisters*

Redemption

"*Redemption*, by Deborah J Ledford, gets under your skin. Fresh and ferocious Native American deputy Eva 'Lightning Dance' Duran never lets up in her quest woven through the Taos Pueblo land. Atmospheric and awash with color, customs, and ancient ways. I loved this."

—Cara Black, *New York Times* bestselling author

"Deborah J Ledford has artfully woven the voices of multiple characters connected to the Taos Pueblo to create a pattern of stories that illuminate the challenges as well as the enduring power of Native American women. The rhythm of daily life is evident in Ledford's lovely, intimate prose. I eagerly await the new adventures of Eva Duran, who will, no doubt, unearth more mysteries in the buried layers of New Mexico."

—Naomi Hirahara, Mary Higgins Clark Award–winning author of
Clark and Division

"*Redemption* is a page-turner! I loved reading about sheriff's deputy Eva Duran and her battle against dark forces on the reservation. Sharp characters, a great setting, and a plot that keeps you guessing. A riveting thriller that hits hard and keeps you hooked."

—David Heska Wanbli Weiden, Anthony and Thriller Award– winning author of *Winter Counts*

"A riveting tale of murder and intrigue on a Native American reservation from an immensely talented voice in crime fiction. Deborah J Ledford has created a page-turner featuring an unforgettable hero in Eva 'Lightning Dance' Duran."

—Isabella Maldonado, *Wall Street Journal* bestselling author

Snare

"White-knuckle suspense at an electrifying pulse."

—*Suspense Magazine*

"*Snare* is a gripping read that won't be easy to put down."

—*Midwest Book Review*

"Ledford, who is part Cherokee, shows enormous empathy and insight. Despite many obstacles, Katina battles her demons and reclaims her spirit power in time to confront her tormentors in a harrowing finale. *Snare* is a well-deserved nominee for the Hillerman Sky Award."

—Steve Schwartz, Poisoned Pen Bookstore review

Crescendo

"Inola Walela becomes the avenging angel of death, leaving no stone unturned in order to bring justice for one small boy in this knife-edge drama. Walela's search brings her closer to the truth in a cataclysmic chaos of events. Following in the footsteps of J. A. Jance, the police procedural genre has birthed a new author to follow. In *Crescendo*, Deborah J Ledford raises suspense to a higher level as she intertwines her Cherokee heritage with her writing, exposing all of us to her award-winning style."

—Suspense Magazine

"Since I read the first book in the series, *Staccato*, I've loved the character Inola, a Native American cop who's constantly having to prove herself to her police department colleagues in the relatively backwoods town of Bryson City, North Carolina. In spite of her stubborn nature, her inability to communicate with those she truly loves (Steven and her grandmother Elisi), and her insistence on going out on her own despite obvious dangers that threaten—you can't help but love her. Tough, focused, and smart, she's everything you'd want in a heroine."

—Midwest Book Review

Causing Chaos

"Standing round of applause for this dynamic blast of a thriller."

—Suspense Magazine

HAVOC

ALSO BY DEBORAH J LEDFORD

Eva "Lightning Dance" Duran Series

Redemption

Smoky Mountain Inquest Series

Staccato

Snare

Crescendo

Causing Chaos

Short Stories

Screaming Horses

El Dragón

Sighted Brother

The Spot

Cuba Bound

HAVOC

DEBORAH J LEDFORD

THOMAS & MERCER

Text copyright © 2024 by Deborah J Ledford
All rights reserved.

Published by Thomas & Mercer, Seattle

www.apub.com

Amazon, the Amazon logo, and Thomas & Mercer are trademarks of Amazon.com, Inc., or its affiliates.

ISBN-13: 9781662510458 (paperback)
ISBN-13: 9781662510441 (digital)

Cover design by James Iacobelli
Cover image: © Justin A. Morris / Getty Images; © Jesus Giraldo Gutier / Shutterstock

Printed in the United States of America

To the spirits who guide us and never let go

CHAPTER ONE

His heartbeat thundered in his chest while he checked the Breitling moon phase watch. 8:01. His breaths were rushed and trapped in the plastic Guy Fawkes mask that hid his identity, scalp itching under the cheap shoulder-length dark wig. He envisioned the tellers stocking their drawers for the Friday payday crowd that would arrive to cash checks, and to handle tourist transactions throughout the day.

The 3D printed Glock knockoff in his nitrile-gloved hand felt like a toy in his grip as he tucked his body flat against the alley wall outside the Taos, New Mexico, bank. *Lightweight but deadly when loaded*, his business partner had assured him. He didn't trust that the thing would even work, but the untraceable firearm would be a bonus if he had to actually fire it. He tapped his free hand on the SIG Sauer P238 Micro-Compact at the back of his belt for just in case.

After one final set of deep breaths in and out, he disassociated completely and rounded the corner. One quick glance verified that no one stood in his path. He kept his head down as he strode to the entrance. He swung the door open, stood there for an instant as he scanned the area and confirmed he would not encounter a security guard or any customers. Optum lifted his gun and charged to the long counter.

"You know what to do," he hissed.

The three female tellers froze. Two immediately raised their hands. The other took longer so he swung the handgun. He stepped to within a few feet and trained the barrel on her forehead until she also complied.

Optum stared at her, mesmerized by the Native woman's face free from makeup, which allowed her true beauty to shine. He glanced only a moment at the name tag pinned to her blouse that stated LILY. An unfamiliar floral scent, tinged with a hint of her fear, wafted to him. Long silver-and-turquoise earrings hung to each collarbone. She flicked her eyes on his own, then kept them on the gun. Her open hands trembled, and her bottom lip quavered. Slow tears tracked down her cheeks. He licked his lips, wanting to taste her skin the color of rich hot chocolate.

Focus! he reminded himself. *You can play later.*

He pulled a canvas tote bag from under his hoodie and tossed it to the middle cashier, took a step closer as each of the women stripped their drawers. He lost track counting after nine stacks of bound twenties and easily another few thousand in loose bills as they were stuffed into the bag.

"No hundreds," he snapped when one of the women reached to add those to the bag.

His own words screamed in his head: *Too much time. Get out!*

Sweat dripped off the bottom of the stifling mask. An annoyance more than a concern. Whatever residue landed on the counter and floor couldn't be traced because he'd never been arrested and his actual identity wouldn't appear in any law enforcement database.

He swung to the sound of muffled voices at the front entrance. Lunged forward and snatched the bag as two cops in uniform entered. One man, one woman, wearing big smiles, exchanging banter. He tucked behind a pillar and chanced a peek. It took only a moment for the female cop's demeanor to change. Maybe she noticed the wide eyes of one of the tellers, or felt something in the air. She took in her surroundings, lowered her hand to the holstered gun at her hip—a real Glock for sure. The male cop took a step closer, to-go cup raised midway to his mouth.

Before her Glock cleared leather, he pointed his own firearm at her and squeezed the trigger. Again. And again. Four pulls. No roar of a gunshot. Nothing but a feeble *click*. Frustrated, he stuffed the worthless piece in the front pocket of his hoodie, then reached for the reliable firearm.

The male cop dropped his cup and went for his weapon. As soon as the gun cleared its holster, he took a step toward Optum and slipped on the spilled coffee. The cop's arms pinwheeled a few times, comical spins that Optum would have laughed about if not for the dire circumstances. The cop finally lost his footing completely—airborne for a moment— then his body thudded, face up on the floor.

Optum whipped his SIG Sauer free. In smooth calculated moves, he dove for another pillar, hid behind the column and lowered to a crouch. He raised the handgun, aimed the sights at the other cop, who had her gun pointed at him. He held his breath, steadied his arm and eased the trigger back. This time a satisfying *crack* deafened him. He fired again. Crimson spewed from an area outside the safety of the cop's Kevlar. He hoped for a neck shot or scalp graze. Lots of blood to keep her partner and the others occupied.

As he sprinted toward the exit a *pa-kaaw* roared. The door shattered, raining a sheet of glass that clattered and danced as shards hit the floor. He ducked, tucked his shoulders to his ears and crouched as he raced outside, took four strides and rounded the corner. He kept running, actions on autopilot as he envisioned the necessary steps of his getaway.

He had spent the previous two days before the heist canvassing the area and he knew precisely where to turn. He bounded through a row of tall hedges to catch his breath. Adrenaline coursed throughout his entire body as he stripped off his gloves and mask, thoroughly wet from his perspiration. The wig came off next, then he added everything to the bag crammed with money. He pulled the Glock replica from his sweatshirt and glowered at it. The time wasted brandishing the damned thing could have cost him not only the money but his life. The rush had been worth the risk.

He resettled the SIG in the waistband at the middle of his back and took only a moment to check his watch. Two minutes. He smiled, pleased by his achievement. Continuing down the alley, he took another shortcut that led to an adobe-walled strip of stores and art galleries.

Hidden birds chirped and joined undecipherable conversations as he wove beyond a three-tier fountain where a group of people dressed in T-shirts emblazoned with New Mexico destinations and products waited for breakfast tables.

As he took another turn, he swept off his hoodie to reveal his own touristy shirt. He slowed his steps and walked along the sidewalk that paralleled the Paseo del Pueblo Sur two-lane, already packed with cars forced to travel well under the speed limit.

He held an unrushed pace and kept his attention turned to gift shop windows that exhibited trinkets, artwork and southwestern items. The wail of sirens assaulted his ears, growing closer with each heartbeat. He spotted two SUVs—Taos Police Department emblems on the doors, emergency lights flashing—turn and then disappear from view.

Relieved to see the Historic Taos Inn sign ahead, he warned himself not to rush. *Almost there.* He made his way to the back of the hotel, where a parking lot housed dusty cars.

Sweat ran a path down his spine as he reached in his jeans pocket, took out a key fob and headed for a nondescript white sedan. He slid behind the steering wheel, tossed the tote bag to the passenger's side floorboard. Taking no time to rest, he fired up the engine, and then inched out of the lot to join the vehicles driven by tourists and frustrated locals who traveled along the main road that ran through the heart of town.

Traffic and his nerves eased once he passed a sign that stated TAOS PUEBLO 1 MILE and he continued on US Highway 64 until well out of the city limits, and then made a left at the first traffic light in miles. He monitored his speed and kept going west for five minutes, then turned on a dirt road across the street from the Taos Regional Airport.

Optum approached a salvage yard that contained at least a hundred cars in various stages of disrepair. He had yet to see a single worker the seven times he'd visited the location to research his getaway, and this time was no different—no one stopped him as he passed the main building and searched for an empty slot.

He parked at the outer perimeter, between two sedans that looked much like the beater he had purchased for cash a week ago, took up the tote bag, then pulled the lever to send the driver's seat all the way back. He used the hem of his shirt to wipe down the steering wheel, turn indicator, door and seat handle.

Out of the vehicle now, he ran the entire drive through his mind to make sure he hadn't forgotten anything. "All right. We're good," he whispered and made a beeline for another row of vehicles, eyes trained ahead on a pristine sterling gray 2003 BMW Z4 Roadster.

Now snug and safe inside his cherished Beemer, Dream Red seats cocooning his body, he replayed the morning's events. All had gone as planned . . . except for those two damned cops showing up. Then he had to shoot one of them. He shrugged. *Oh well. Not my fault.*

He reached behind the passenger seat, pulled a leather duffel bag from the footwell, unzipped the bag, removed a shirt and a pair of loafers, then buttoned the long-sleeved J.Crew oxford over his T-shirt. He felt more like himself after he kicked off the scuffed sneakers and slid on the buttery leather Manolo Blahniks.

Next, he took up the tote bag, sorted out the bound cash from the loose bills, put the stacks in the duffel and zipped it shut. He reached in the bag for the only remaining item and scowled at the useless plastic firearm. He popped open the glove box and tossed the thing inside, then stowed his SIG in there too.

Adjusting the rearview to see himself, he ran steady hands through his light-brown hair, winked one of his bright-blue eyes, lit up his face with a trademark smile, nodded. "And now, on to phase two," he said to the reflection.

The vehicle rumbled to life and he approached the way he came in, eyes forward, never even looking at the building where, again, no one came out. He thought about next steps. The loose cash he would keep. The bound bills—no doubt sequential and traceable—would be held by his partner. Let him take the risk in case the desired results went to hell.

Already anticipating the Bloody Mary and beer he would savor for an hour, while relaxing in front of a fire at what had become his favorite local breakfast joint, he made the return trek to the city of Taos, where havoc now reigned.

CHAPTER TWO
EVA

Taos Pueblo tribal police officer Eva Durand tapped the toe of her black tactical boot, hooked her thumbs on her duty belt studded with sheathed law enforcement implements, and did her best to rein in her impatience. A breeze kicked up and her hair, pulled back in a tight ponytail, slapped her lower back as she stood seven feet away from two bear-size men—indistinguishable except for the color of their shirts. The twins stood next to each other, shoulders slumped, heads bowed to the dirt drive in front of one of six nondescript mud-colored HUD houses of identical exteriors, provided by the government for cheaper housing on reservation lands. They had so far answered her barrage of questions and more than a few reprimands without words, instead offering their customary grunts or shrugs.

She considered activating the body camera clipped to the front of her Kevlar vest so she could one day show them their behavior and shame them into being better Pueblo men. This type of call from dispatch to the same location, involving the same men, had become the norm since the first female Taos Pueblo police chief pinned the badge on Eva's uniform a year ago. A hamster wheel routine involving the twins that never seemed to be resolved, yet often amused her. At times, by the end of the negotiation the two had forgotten what even caused the per-usual harmless initial ruckus.

Both shared a reputation as troublemakers and often slackers, but the entire tribe also knew the brothers could be relied upon to help at the mere suggestion of a request or need. The last remaining master craftsmen on the rez, they were able to build anything tasked to them, wire an entire house in a weekend, cut and stack three cords of wood in an afternoon.

"Here we go again, boys. These disturbance complaints are getting to be a habit. Your neighbors worry that you're gonna hurt each other for real. How many times do you think you can get away with this before I lock you in a cell? Maybe I should go ahead and tell Chief Lefthand her cousins have been at it again."

Both younger men looked even more remorseful. Many on the reservation had trouble picking out Paco from Navi, but Eva had known the Barboa twins all their lives—poured out their beer as teens, kept them from inflicting bodily harm as they roughhoused while she baby-sat them as youngsters, bathed and swaddled them as infants. She gazed at a birthmark that resembled a dime-size cloud below the left earlobe of the twenty-five-year-old who stood closest to her, then flicked a laser focus on him. "Paco, I don't want to come back here ever again."

Paco reared back and Navi said, "Nailed you, brother."

"Talking to you too, Navi."

"Yes, ma'am."

Eva turned to where a much older woman stood looking out from the front window. One bony hand clutched the lapels of her sweater together, and she held the other to her mouth. "You've scared your auntie. Again."

Both men followed Eva's gaze and looked even more contrite. They waved to their elder, draped their arms around each other's shoulders, beamed wide smiles. The woman shook her head and stepped away from the glass.

"Just messing around," Navi said. "Nothing for Auntie Anita or anyone else to be scared about."

"Right," Paco said. "Sometimes we get a little excitable, that's all."

"And that excitement turns to yelling and then pushing and then fists will fly," Eva said. "Navi, you still have a black eye from the last time I was out here."

The twin sporting the faint injury touched the area and winced. "Doesn't hurt."

"That's not what I'm talking about."

"Didn't mean to do that," Paco said, cheeks tinged red from embarrassment. "He turned the wrong way and I popped him good."

"Yeah, you did."

They both giggled and Eva had to force herself not to smile at their typical kid-like behavior.

"Listen, you've got to move on, now. Isn't there somewhere else you can be?"

"What time is it?" Navi asked.

Eva checked her wristwatch. "Little after nine o'clock."

Both men looked at each other, wide eyed. "Uh-oh," Navi said. "We're late."

Navi put on a puppy-dog face and implored, "Lightning Dance, Auntie was gonna drive us to work, but she's gotta be mad seein' you out here. Can you give me a ride?"

"Me too," Paco said, same hard-to-resist expression.

"All the way to Sabroso's? No. That's twenty minutes from here. I need to stay on the rez in case other earth-stopping calls like this one come in," she said, her tone sarcastic and overdramatic.

"I'm gonna be late for work," Navi said.

"Me too," Paco parroted.

"Lamb and Hatch chiles demi-glace are on the menu today," Navi tried. "The place is gonna be slammed."

"Please," both begged in unison, sounding more like little boys than grown men.

Their big brown eyes landed on her until she sighed and said, "Fine." She hitched her thumb toward the official DPS four-door pickup truck. "But you have to ride in back."

The brothers turned to the unit, assessed the mesh cage that separated the front seats from the back, shook their heads. "Nuh-uh," Navi muttered. "Nope," Paco replied. "We're good," both said together. Open hands raised to shoulder level, they took a few steps back.

A high-pitched three-tone alert screeched from Eva's cell phone tucked in a sheath on her belt. Before she had a chance to check the screen, the handheld radio emitted a similar tone.

She released the mic clipped at the shoulder of her uniform, plunged the push-to-talk button. "Duran here. Go ahead, Dispatch."

"Urgent assistance requested by Taos PD, Duran," the excited voice through the speaker said so loud Eva reared back.

"What've you got?"

"Robbery in progress. Shots fired. Taos PD officer down. Alvarado Bank, on Kit Carson. All law enforcement alert—city, county, and us."

"No shit?" Navi said, wide smile exhibiting perfect white teeth.

Eva cut her eyes at him and took a few steps away for privacy. "What can you give me?"

"Nothing to confirm at this time."

"Suspect or vehicle description?"

"Nothing to confirm at this time," dispatch said again.

"Very helpful," she muttered.

"Chief Lefthand says to stay vigilant for suspicious vehicles crossing the reservation boundary."

She clicked the speaker mic and said, "Copy. On my way to the village's north entrance. ETA two minutes."

"Copy. I'll post Cruz Romero on the south end."

"Duran, out." Eva let out a relieved breath. No one would get past her, or her partner in law enforcement, and life.

"We could help," one brother said, voice excited as he bobbed up and down on the balls of his feet.

"Yeah, let us help," the other chimed in.

"We'll *stay vigilant for suspicious vehicles*," Navi said, mocking a spot-on imitation of the dispatcher's voice.

"Uh—no."

They all turned to the slam of a door, followed by a stooped elderly woman, ring of keys jingling in her clutch. She glared at her nephews a moment. Then she grinned at them, and all looked to be forgiven.

"They won't give you any more trouble, Anita. Right, boys?"

"Right," Paco said, trying to take the keys their elder refused to relinquish.

"Sorry, Auntie," Navi said, opening the driver's door of a battered Toyota.

Eva rushed for her vehicle, simultaneously slamming the door and firing up the truck's engine. She glanced in the rearview mirror to see the twins waving away the cloud of dust that billowed from the tires.

CHAPTER THREE
KAI

Kai "Single Star" Arrio tried to hold pace alongside his constant companion, a Belgian Malinois he had been working with for over a year.

When he stopped, Shadow halted. Still, ears up, tongue out, head high, eyes flicking from his master's face to the tennis ball launcher in his hand, muscles coiled and ready to spring the moment Kai issued the call to action. The young handler didn't coax with treats. Didn't need to. The search and rescue animal in training was motivated by praise alone—and the reward of his favorite tennis ball, now wet and dripping slobber from the previous retrievals.

Kai winced as he held the skanky ball with his thumb and middle finger, then snapped it in the ball launcher. "Good boy, good boy. That's a good boy."

He rubbed the dog's neck and ears and thumped his side with an open hand seven times. Shadow let out an ear-piercing *yip*, then spun around and around, yipped again, thrashed his thick tail side to side.

Kai lunged a few quick steps back, wove, turned one way, reversed the movement. Shadow mirrored every maneuver, pinned so close to Kai's thigh he could feel the canine's body heat through his jeans.

"Sit."

It took a moment for Shadow to settle for the command. Tongue lolling, he panted, muscles tensed, ready for another sprint.

"Waaai-t," he said, drawing out the command. The dog's body vibrated in anticipation.

The early-morning sun warm on his back, a breeze kicked up, and Kai flared his nostrils to catch the scent of sagebrush, and wildflowers—blooming a last gasp before early October's first freeze in less than a month—that dotted the expansive property. The view ahead of him, flat plains of the reservation that butted up to the Sangre de Cristo Mountains, unobstructed by a single building.

The calm lasted only a few minutes before his mind began to race, as it far too often did. Even now, a full sixteen months later, Kai would break out in sweats whenever his worst awake and asleep nightmare came back to jolt him—of his mother missing for twelve days. His grief and abandonment so profound he had somehow found himself sitting on the edge of the railing along the Gorge Bridge, looking down at the over-six-hundred-foot drop to the Rio Grande below his dangling feet. His mother's best friend, Eva Duran, had come to his rescue that day, and later saved his mother from the certain death three of her friends had not been fortunate enough to escape.

He stopped and turned around, to the sprawling ranch-style house of his mother's people for generations where he and his mom now lived with his uncle, and thought of Paloma inside. She rarely left except to tend to her favorite horse at the twelve-stall barn, nicer than most local homes. His mom refused to talk about the heroin addiction that had been at the center of her kidnapping and what must have been a harrowing ordeal as she realized each of her friends had been murdered during their captivity. Just as Shadow had helped him recover, he supposed the shark-gray stallion helped her. Still, he wished she spoke even half as many words to him as Mako received.

Kai was okay with her isolation though—at least he knew she was safe. His own healing had been because of Shadow and knowing that his mother was off the drugs that had imprisoned Paloma's body and mind for years, and free from the woman he considered batshit crazy who had scooped up his mom hoping to "cure" Pueblo women of their addictions—a different kind of imprisonment, but every bit as traumatic to her soul.

Although they had both been told by the tribe's healers that sharing their ordeals with each other would release the demons and help them move on, mother and son continued to carry too much shame to even hold each other's eyes for more than a few moments at a time. Evasion and ignorance, even before the ordeal, had often been the former champion hoop dancer's go-to, and the brilliant student had learned these traits well from her.

Patience, Single Star. White Dove needs time to heal, his uncle Santiago had told him whenever his elder noticed the shunning. All Kai did and didn't do to find his mother still haunted him and he often wondered if Paloma even knew the depths he and Eva and Cruz Romero had reached to bring her back to them.

Now frustrated, Kai raised his arm, readying to catapult the ball. Shadow remained seated, crouched low. "Steady." The canine held his position. *"Go!"* This time Kai chucked the ball as hard as he could, aiming for the chicken coop a few yards from the house.

Shadow burst forward, paws barely striking ground, rocketing ahead. Kai winced as his companion reached the small-scale version of the main house, where Rhode Island Reds and Lohmann Browns scattered and protested, wings flapping as they leaped clear and then strutted and clucked their surprise.

Shadow dropped the ball and, nose to the ground, proceeded to make a wide figure eight traverse that tightened with each revolution. Kai recognized the behavior—trouble on the horizon—and started to sprint toward the dog.

Finally homing in on one area, Shadow stopped and started digging.

"No, no, no," Kai pleaded.

Dirt flew from his front paws, plumes of dust and clods flicked behind him. Pebbles dinged the ground when they landed three feet from the dig site.

"Stop," Kai commanded. And when Shadow didn't comply, he said "Enough," his tone firm and no-nonsense this time.

Shadow halted his aggressive behavior, swiveled his head, then his body to face the stern command, sat. Ears up and alert, he waited for the next instruction.

"Nice," he whispered. "Good boy."

He turned to the house and spotted his uncle Santiago on the porch, stance wide, one boot holding the screen door open, arms folded tight against his chest. Kai didn't have to imagine the scowl his elder never tried to hide. He sighed, dreading the reprimand he would surely receive as soon as they returned to the house.

Kai knelt to inspect the hole Shadow had accomplished. Seeing nothing unusual at first, he sifted through a handful of dirt. The second scoop revealed the hidden treasure the dog had unearthed. Kai showed the Malinois a toy soldier, scuffed and faded. Shadow yipped, head snapping upward, but he remained in a seated position.

"What is it with you and plastic?"

Another yip followed.

Buying time, in no hurry to join his strict uncle, Kai brushed off the dirt-crusted soldier on his jeans, attempted to straighten the bent rifle barrel, with little success. He reached for the leather medicine pouch he always kept in his hoodie pocket and dropped the little man inside to keep company with his other treasures.

"Well, let's get this done with." Shadow whined, dropped the rest of his body flat to the ground, laid his snout on his paws. "Hey, it's your fault we're in trouble."

The dog twitched his tail, sweeping dirt back and forth, and Kai swore the Malinois gave a mischievous grin.

CHAPTER FOUR
NATHAN

Nathan "Little Bear" Trujillo stood in the line of kids from his third-grade class. He held his best friend Betty's hand, still a little nervous about being on his first school trip. His teacher had told them they would be going to Santa Fe and everyone had looked forward to the field trip for weeks.

It felt strange being away from the reservation. Before he went to sleep last night, his mom cried a little and his dad told him to be brave and to have fun. Maybe his parents didn't miss him too much. And he tried to have fun.

His stomach growled and he wished he could take the peanut butter sandwich and chips from his backpack his mother had put in there before he got on the bus that morning. He patted his front pocket to make sure the dollar she had given him was still there so he could buy a drink. He hoped they had orange pop somewhere in the museum full of Indian stuff he'd never seen before.

He liked the rows of arrowheads in a glass case best. He imagined himself on the reservation with a bow made just for him, arrowhead on one end of the arrow, feathers on the other, pulling back the string and letting it fly. Maybe even sitting on the pony his friend Kai Arrio let him ride a few times.

Nathan's class went to another room. This one had pictures of plants as well as fake ones behind big tall glass. He pointed to one, then another, naming each one for his travel buddy and best friend in his class.

"You're so smart," Betty said.

He felt his cheeks burn. Kai was a tall guy, older and way smarter than him, and would know what to say back. Nathan shrugged at the compliment and looked away to hide his embarrassment.

Betty lurched forward, head snapping back, her braid like a whip.

"Watch it," another kid said.

Nathan turned to see who had pushed his friend. Robby Sanger. The bully in his class. Bigger than all the other kids because he had to take the third grade over again. Mean and awful, especially to the Pueblo kids. Nathan's stomach dropped and he didn't feel hungry anymore.

"Knock it off," Nathan said under his breath, trying to be brave but not wanting to get pushed. Or worse.

Robby leaned in close. "What'd ya say, Indian boy?"

"Nothing," Nathan muttered.

"Liar." Robby took hold of Nathan's wrist and dragged him away from the group of schoolkids and the two adults who were supposed to be watching them. No one but Betty saw Nathan being pulled around a corner. He tried not to show her he was scared. But he was.

Robby held on so tight Nathan couldn't feel his fingers. He yanked and turned and pulled and tried to wrench his arm away. Then he grabbed the other kid's pinkie and bent it back until Robby let out a yelp. The bigger guy let go of Nathan's wrist, made a fist, and threw a punch. Nathan's head snapped like Betty's did and he was too stunned to move. Didn't feel a thing. Then he tasted blood, reached up to touch his lip, winced when he wrinkled his nose.

"Ha!" Robby put up both fists and danced from one foot to the other, ready to hit him again.

The making fun of his friends from the reservation needed to end. And Nathan knew how to stop it. He kept looking at Robby when he took off his backpack, unzipped the top, brought out the one thing he didn't ever want to use again. The thing he had hidden from his parents and everyone who had asked about it—even Kai's friend, the lady police officer who worked to keep his people safe.

He gripped it with both hands, pointed in front of him like he had been taught from the bad guys last year.

"Nathan, don't!"

He thought the voice belonged to Betty, but the ringing in his ears sounded so loud he wasn't sure.

"Whoa, whoa. Wait a minute." Robby opened his hands, raised them, took a few steps back. "I'm sorry. Sorry-sorry-sorry," Robby said, tears and snot running down his face. "Please . . ."

"What's going on over here," an adult's voice boomed from behind Nathan.

He cut his eyes to the voice. Whispered his own apology to his mom and dad, and Kai, and anyone he'd ever met.

Closed his eyes for what would come next.

It didn't take long.

CHAPTER FIVE
EVA

For a full hour Eva had fumed beside her Taos Pueblo PD truck, where she'd allowed only a few cars and two pickups to pass. If she didn't recognize either the driver or a passenger, she instructed them to turn around and head anywhere but where she held position.

There had yet to be a sign of any truly suspicious vehicles, and no one had halted, U-turned and sped away at the sight of the official vehicle, so there she stayed, waiting for something—anything—to happen.

Her former job as a Taos County sheriff's deputy had required her, along with two dozen of her colleagues, to patrol and answer crime calls for her area of the county. Most of her day was spent driving her assigned region, sitting so long behind the wheel of the SUV her legs would tingle when she slid out of the seat at the end of a shift. But at least she'd felt satisfied she made a difference representing the law.

Her current position required her and only nine other fellow officers to cover 110,000 acres and three thousand people of her community. A daunting task she tried not to think about too much. She loved being a tribal cop, protecting and looking out for her fellow Pueblos, but patience continued to be the most needed task to master.

She hadn't become a cop to stand around and wait while law enforcement officers from every local agency actively participated in an investigation. A crime as brazen as a bank robbery involving shots fired and an officer down, deemed all LEOs necessary—tribal, city, county, even FBI as soon as that team could get to the area.

As she readied to say *Screw it, I'm outa here,* she turned and spotted a whirl of rising dust, indicating a vehicle headed her way. She crossed her fingers that this would be her replacement so she could at least try to get in on the action of tracking the shooter. She knew people on the Taos city police force. They would put in a good word to their sergeant. Surely they needed all the help they could get.

A DPS pickup that matched Eva's drew close, then pulled up behind her own, and she headed to the driver's open window, where Ernie Mateo sat behind the wheel.

He hooked an index finger to the frame of his sunglasses and slid them low on his nose to reveal the sharp eyes of the skillful hunter she knew him to be. Each season, for the past decade, he could be counted on to score the first elk or deer for his wife and three children—always unselfishly offering his neighbors the extra meat. "Any action?" he asked.

"Nuh-uh. You?"

"Nope. Typical. If the offender's Pueblo, no way he'd head home."

"Usually, but I'll keep my eyes peeled. Never know, you know?"

"I hear ya," he said.

"Any word on the officer?"

"Nuh-uh. Female is all I heard." He must have read her shocked expression and added, "You know her?"

"Probably."

"Chief said you can head out," Mateo said, tone soft.

"Did she say to where?"

"Wherever, I guess. Said your shift is over." He reseated his shades and nodded a confident shake of his head. "Better go before she changes her mind."

"All right. Thanks, Ernie," she said, confused, actually only a few hours into her shift.

She figured this to be an unspoken approval from her boss to do whatever Eva felt best. The current chief, a former tribal cop, often baffled Eva. Their sense for each other and mutual respect had come easily and quick, not merely because both were women—Eva never wasted her supervisor's time, submitted precise reports, followed through on every request, excelled at de-escalation tactics. In return, from the chief, she received the choice calls and investigations, often alongside Cruz Romero as an added bonus.

Eva relaxed a bit as she hurried back to her vehicle, having no doubt nothing vital would get past the capable Mateo. Belted in, she turned the key to the powerful V-8, crossed beyond the reservation's boundary line, mashed the gas pedal as she hit solid ground of the paved road.

A glint of sunlight through the windshield nearly blinded her. She flicked down the visor and took in a deep pull of sage-tinged air that had grown crisper the past few mornings. Change in season evident, she remembered the harsh winter from last year. Temperatures had plummeted, snowfall exceeded depths of five years previous. People of her community, stuck inside, made domestic calls more hairy for her fellow LEOs. No one happy for months. She hoped the first frost would hold off for at least a few more weeks.

As she headed the direction of town, she thought of her options. Check on the wounded Taos police officer came to her mind first. No name had been released, but Eva knew there were only a few women on the city force. She had her suspicions, and if she was right, the cop's partner would be waiting as close to Nadine Tallow as permitted.

An endless line of brake lights met Eva the moment she took the curve of the two-lane road on the way to the heart of the city. At a complete stop, one forefinger tapping the steering wheel, her left heel jiggling on the floorboard, she muttered curses and refrained from hitting the siren and flashers to life.

Although early, and the Friday morning before the three-day Labor Day weekend, tourists crowded the sidewalks along the main thoroughfare. Not a single New Mexico license plate adorned the vehicles of various makes, trucks, even a few RVs that made getting across town a maddening experience. Good for the local business owners, not so much for a cop anxious to reach her destination.

Her anticipation ratcheted up as she crawled closer to the location where the robbery occurred. She looked down the street and craned her neck, unable to see the structure due to at least a dozen official vehicles, all parked disorganized and haphazard, reminding her of little boys' abandoned toys. She resisted the urge to cross the police tape and take a look at the active scene being processed—the sight verified her involvement was not necessary, so she proceeded onward.

She flicked on her blinker and turned left, where back roads of the neighborhoods would provide a faster route to the hospital south of the historic district. The shortcut, known only to locals, would trim a full ten minutes off the trek.

She buzzed by her own two-bedroom rental and cast a quick gaze to the fence post, thinking she might spot the magpie she'd named Rio that greeted her every morning and evening. But she received no spirit animal mojo as she blasted past.

After a few near-misses and tapped brakes, she turned at the Holy Cross Hospital entrance and parked close to the emergency bay, where an ambulance remained, back doors wide open. Anticipating what she might encounter, she tightened her stomach muscles and picked up her pace. One glance confirmed her suspicions. Blood-soaked gauze on the floor of the unit. Lots of it. She lowered her head to concentrate on her footsteps.

She thought about going through the doors marked AUTHORIZED PERSONNEL ONLY, then decided she didn't really want to be that close to the chaos behind those doors. Instead, she went around the building to the main entrance, and made a beeline to the waiting area.

Eva stopped when she caught sight of Taos police officer Andrew Kotz. He stood rigid, back close to the wall, hands clasped together, looking forward. She focused on his duty belt, Glock stripped from his holster, and realized he must have taken at least one shot at the time of the offense. Relinquishing his service weapon would have been necessary for the ongoing investigation, especially if it turned out Kotz had hit the perpetrator, or an innocent bystander. The thought of either possibility again made Eva queasy.

Kotz didn't seem to sense her until she stopped a few feet away. Finally he turned his head, eyes wide and bloodshot, face ruddier than usual. He let out a heavy sigh and made a move so sudden she thought he would lunge to hug her. Then he seemed to realize the need to be discreet and professional.

She stepped back from the smells that emanated from him. Old coffee, sweat. The faint but distinctive metallic oxidation of iron—spilled blood—verified by the rust-colored swirls that remained on his hands and neck. All pungent, especially the fear.

Investigators from his department would need the uniform, now considered evidence. It wasn't her place, but still she asked, "Want me to find you a pair of scrubs so you can get out of those clothes?"

He stared at her, unblinking, either ignoring the offer or unable to register the words.

"Is it Tallow?" she asked.

He nodded, gritted his teeth so hard his jaw muscles bulged before he said, "Thanks for coming."

"Who else has come by?" she asked, already knowing the answer—his entire force would be out looking for whoever shot their police officer and risked the safety of anyone in the vicinity.

"I screwed up, Eva," Kotz said, ignoring the question.

"What do you mean?"

"It's my fault she's here. When I realized what was happening, Nadine already had her gun out. I reacted, but slipped. Ass to the ground when the shots went off. She dropped. Just dropped. I got one round off, then . . . I ran to her, instead of after the gunman."

"She's your partner. It's a natural reaction to render aid."

"We shouldn't be working together. We're not objective. Nobody knows . . . But still . . ."

"Andrew, everybody knows."

His shoulders slackened and he dropped his gaze to the floor a moment, then lifted his tear-filled eyes to her. "I love her, Eva. More than anything or anyone I've ever known. Now I might lose her. Probably lose my job too."

She pointed to a row of plastic chairs lined up against the wall. "Come and sit with me," she said, figuring he had been standing since they'd wheeled Officer Tallow in.

Kotz collapsed in the closest seat and she sat down beside him. In an effort to comfort, she placed her hand on his shoulder, then took his cold hand and held it tight. Kotz returned the squeeze, and it felt like he didn't want to ever let go.

"Am I interrupting?" a man said in a low tone.

She recognized the voice right away and turned to see Cruz Romero standing an arm's length away, wraparound sunglasses hiding his eyes, feet planted in line with his shoulders, arms crossed tight against his Kevlar-covered chest.

Eva couldn't read him as she usually could and wished he would remove his shades. She wasn't sure if he was upset about her tenderness toward Kotz, or if something else bothered him. He wouldn't leave his post and go off the reservation unless an urgent matter caused him to find her. The day had barely started—surely the situation they were already dealing with couldn't get even worse.

But in their line of work, of course it could.

CHAPTER SIX
CRUZ

Taos Pueblo police officer Cruz Romero tamped down his annoyance as deep as he could manage. The sight of Eva comforting her former lover had flipped a switch, as it sometimes did when he caught the two of them together. Although displeased by the private moment the two shared, Cruz reminded himself not to show his frustration or any hint of jealousy. He and Eva were in a good place now and he didn't want to spook her. They'd broken up as often as they'd been together. He wanted their relationship to stick this time. To last. Forever.

He unfolded his arms and stuffed clenched fists inside his uniform pants pockets, but Eva would have already identified his stick of dynamite behavior. Every single time his anger bubbled, she'd catch his slight before he even said a word and find a way to extinguish the potential fire before the flame even ignited. A talent. Also maddening because he had yet to figure out her tells after more than thirty-five years.

When she had turned her head to see him standing there, she'd let go of the city cop's hand. Cruz softened when he noticed how torn up the other man looked—realized the need for Eva to comfort the man. Thought about what he must be going through. Imagined for a moment

Eva atop a gurney on the other side of the doors. The brief image almost dropped him to his knees.

Before any of them could react, a commotion stirred at the reception desk, where the volunteer spoke to two suited men, hair buzzed tight to their scalps, one talking far too loud.

Kotz stood and straightened his posture. Eva sighed and got up from her chair. Cruz looked over his shoulder. "Feds," all three said together.

"They got here fast," Eva said.

"Must be stationed in Santa Fe," Cruz supposed.

"Shots were fired. ATF will probably be here next," Kotz said, talking low and fast.

The sound of heels hitting linoleum pounded toward them.

"Shit. Here they come," Eva whispered. "Quick—who are we looking for? What did he look like? *Was* it even a *he*?"

"Ninety seconds, two minutes max is all I had, but male, for sure. Five-eleven. Black latex gloves, one of those weird masks—you know, white face with black eyebrows, mustache, strip of a beard." He used the tip of a finger to indicate the sharp lines of where the facial hair would be.

"Guy Fawkes mask," Cruz said. Eva raised an eyebrow and looked impressed, not the first time he'd surprised her with his eclectic trivia knowledge.

"Yeah, right, that kind. Black long-sleeved hoodie, long dark hair—"

"Native? Or Hispanic?" Cruz snapped.

"I don't know, Cruz."

Kotz turned a terrified glance to the feds striding faster now that they had acquired their target. "I'm really toast now," he muttered.

"You knew they'd be coming," Eva said. "Be cool. Stay on point. Answer only the questions they ask—don't offer anything else."

"Got a lawyer?" Cruz asked.

Kotz shook his head, eyes going wide. "Never needed one before."

Eva reached out and gave the city cop's arm a squeeze. "Want me to stay?"

"Sergeant said he's on his way, but that was half an hour ago."

A voice boomed, "Officer Kotz?" The shorter of the two men flipped open a leather cover to expose a badge and FBI credentials. He flicked his eyes on Cruz, then Eva, and said, "Let's find a private corner."

The fed's silent partner stood so close and invasively to Kotz that Cruz thought the younger cop might bolt. But he held it together and Eva raised a thumb and pinkie finger to her ear, mouthed *Call me*. Kotz gave them an imploring look before the three rounded a corner out of view.

Cruz led the way out of the hospital and kept quiet as he ran through his mind how he should tell Eva the worst possible news he had volunteered to give.

"Why are you here, Cruz?"

He was there for a reason. One he didn't want to speak out loud, the reality too horrific for mere words to convey. Eva wouldn't want him to hold the revelation from her a moment longer, so he prepared himself for any reaction that might come his way.

He dropped the professional demeanor he strove for while in uniform, took off his sunglasses and looped them on his duty belt, eased his expression. Then, unsure why, he held out open hands palms up—maybe to catch his best friend if she faltered. "Chief Lefthand needs you to know something."

"She sent you? Why didn't she just call?"

"I offered. Figured you might be here."

He stayed silent a beat, searching for the proper words to release to the universe that would forever alter the paths of those who received them. Words that would need to be said over and over until the entire community received the heartbreak.

"What is it?" She lowered her eyebrows—an annoyed frown he knew well. "Tell me. You're freakin' me out."

"It's about Nathan Trujillo."

"Little Bear?" When he didn't continue, she took a step, close enough for him to inhale the hint of her sage and lavender shampoo. "What's happened?"

"Nathan and his third-grade class went on a field trip to a museum in Santa Fe this morning and . . ."

"And . . . ? *What?*"

"A security guard saw our boy take a gun out of his bag . . ."

He paused so long Eva grabbed his arm. *"Tell me."*

"Eva, the guard shot him. Little Bear is gone."

She lowered her head, shoulders, hand. Whispered over and over, "No, that can't be."

He couldn't bear to see her in distress. She looked completely unable to fully process what he had told her. The sorrow just beginning to settle in. He had only received the news from their chief twenty minutes ago and the cloud of doom grew darker as he watched her struggle.

He reached out and tipped up her chin to force eye contact. "We'll get through this. His parents need us to be strong for them. I'm going to notify Gabriel and Pabla now."

"We should both go," she stated, confident, resigned.

"You're sure?"

He could tell she wasn't, but nodded anyway, probably already pained by what would surely be the young couple's reaction to losing their cherished son and only child.

"I'll meet you at the Trujillos'," he said. "Go to Santiago's and pick up Kai."

"Kai?"

"He's been there almost every day for a year now—helping the little guy get over what he went through. Take the dog, too. Shadow will be comfort to his folks."

"Right. Good idea. I need to go there anyway to tell Santiago about Nathan."

Cruz smirked. "What're you, a comedian now?"

Eva tilted her head, confused.

"He would have gotten the call before Chief Lefthand. Hell, *he* probably told *her*."

CHAPTER SEVEN
TOMÁS

Tomás Salas swept the already pristine floor of his two-car garage detached from his house, waiting for the alarm on his cell phone to alert him he needed to get ready and head to the high school. He kept his workspace tidy at all times in case a bolt of inspiration needed to be captured before the thought dissipated, or completely disappeared. Household items were stored on a rolling rack tucked to the shortest wall of the rectangular space, storage boxes on shelves along one of the two long walls, a row of seats he had removed from his van so he had more cargo area against the last. The rest of the area acted as his home office.

He appreciated his job teaching biology and was always proud of his students and their accomplishments, especially his star former pupil, Kai Arrio, who currently attended the Taos campus of the University of New Mexico. No one believed the kid would even survive what he had faced throughout his high school years, let alone flourish—except Tomás. Salas had immediately recognized the young Pueblo's innate abilities and unparalleled knowledge identifying local flora. If Kai could retain his focus and not allow his traumatic homelife to kill his dreams, he would be a celebrated rising star in an industry hungry for new blood and innovative notions. Of this, the mentor was certain.

But Salas yearned to be done with the students, bureaucracy, time away from his real work. He looked at the only item atop a long work-table in the middle of the space and smiled at the first 3D creation he had printed three years ago. He was hooked as soon as he'd watched, fascinated by the printer head that moved back and forth at a furious pace, layer by layer building the beginner's-level print of the black palm-size miniature tugboat.

The new hobby captivated his every spare moment. At first he spent hours searching for online software to print whatever he could think of. Knockoff movie figurines, intricate fidget spinners his students were fascinated by. Then an elaborate medieval-themed chess piece set that made him want to learn how to master the game. Nighttime dreams of what else he could build energized his waking hours and stayed with him until he sketched out the designs.

He set the broom aside to straighten a storage box marked CYNTHIA on one of the organized-within-an-inch-of-its-life Gorilla Rack storage unit shelves. He hadn't uttered his wife's name for almost six months, when she had packed up the choicest of their stuff and the cat that hated him. Without a word to him, she just drove away as he watched her back out of the driveway, from the very spot where he now stood.

For years before she fled, he had tried everything he could think of to appease her. Accomplished everything on her endless, flat-out absurd honey-do lists without complaint. Went with her to art galler-ies, of which he figured there must be seven hundred in Taos alone. Didn't complain when she spent twice the normal amount at the organic-everything market rather than shop at the perfectly fine big-box store. Worst of all, he agreed to her healthy food kick, even the daily bran muffins—disgusting things that grew in his mouth as he chewed each bite.

He thought of the sawdust-posing-as-food torture, shuddered, then reached inside the Little Debbie box his wife would have fainted over if she'd found him with, dug out the last treat, opened the crinkly cellophane, shoved half of the entire Star Crunch cookie in his mouth and closed his eyes to savor an ideal balance of chocolate, caramel and crunchy rice. The perfect breakfast.

Although he realized his ex hadn't really been listening to him much for months before she gave up on him, Salas continued to be baffled about her leaving. Had yet to receive a note or text or phone call or email of explanation. Still called out "I'm home" when he returned at the end of the school day. He stroked his mustache and beard, which had become increasingly bushy, feeling no real need to pay attention to his appearance now that he was alone. Oh well, he figured, now he could devote his entire attention to his pet project—the reason she had probably actually left him in the end.

A three-succession knock on the garage door threw Salas out of his reverie. A Pavlovian response immediately followed, knowing who would be visiting—unannounced as usual, which unnerved Salas because he liked to be prepared for the infrequent meetings. He nudged his glasses that had slid down his nose back in place and swallowed the treat as he rushed over, tapped the opener push button mounted near the door, waited for it to whir open. Beyond his twelve-passenger van in the driveway, he spotted the familiar vintage dark-gray BMW sports car, top down to show off the red leather seats, parked at the curb in front of his house.

Simon Optum, the polished younger-by-a-decade man Salas had befriended at a home renovation show in Albuquerque three years ago, ducked through the opening, carrying a leather duffel, his knuckles white from grasping the bag's handles so tight.

Salas's investment partner and self-proclaimed entrepreneur said, "I took a chance you'd be here."

"Biology labs instead of classes today. I don't need to be at the school until one o'clock."

The other man scrunched one eyelid almost closed. "This school business isn't going to get in the way once our project is up and running, will it? I'm going to need everything you've got soon."

"No, no. I'm completely focused. You never have to worry about me."

"Didn't say I was. Just need you to stay sharp, my man." Optum smacked Salas on the back, an openhanded slap that jarred him off balance.

Salas sniffed the air, then stepped closer to Optum. He smelled of beer, and . . . "Do I smell gunpowder?"

"Target practice with one of your guns earlier today."

"You shot it?" Salas said, anxious to hear about the firearm's accuracy.

"Tried to. Piece of crap, by the way. Failed. *Four times.*"

"Where is it? I'd like to figure out what malfunctioned so I can adjust the printing parameters in the software."

"Don't worry about it. Probably operator error. I'm not much of a gun guy."

Optum took the black tugboat from the table and Salas bristled, worried his partner might pocket the item, never to be seen again. The man tossed the miniature vessel in the air and caught it in his palm one, two, three times, then turned it over, brought the little craft close to his face, and said, "Cute."

Salas held out his hand to take the little ship, then put it in his pocket and redirected the conversation to what he really wanted to know. "When will your investors deposit the money? I need to get going on this because I found the perfect piece of land on the reservation to start the first house. The Vulcan printer from ICON in Texas is the ideal equipment." The tactic seemed to have no effect engaging his partner, so Salas pushed a bit harder. "I heard a construction company in Santa Fe is looking to buy some of the same equipment. We don't want them to find out about our plan and steal our idea . . . right?"

"I do hope you're not trying to pressure me, Thomas," Optum said—the English language pronunciation, rather than traditional Spanish—his voice on the edge of a growl.

Salas raised his hands, an attempt to defuse the conversation that had taken an awkward turn. "No, no, Mr. Optum. I don't mean to push. Not at all."

"Good. That's good. You need to understand that the *idea* is the easiest part of the puzzle to solve. Money is the challenge."

Salas wanted to shout, *Easy? You have no idea how much work and time I've put into this, you little shit.* But he held his tongue and let the other man continue his chiding.

"Takes finesse. Experience." He scanned Salas head to toe and back again. "Style, and class."

The slow burn of embarrassment crept to Salas's cheeks. He tugged down the hem of his T-shirt that no longer quite covered his stomach. Tried his best to hide his disdain as he took in the other guy's fancy button-down shirt, and the extravagant shoes that probably cost more than a month's worth of groceries for a family of six.

"Patience," the other man continued. "I'll be meeting with the entire group next month."

"Next *month*? I thought you said everyone was already—"

"Two are flying out from Copenhagen. The houses are very popular over there, so these guys will be able to advise us."

Salas tried to hide his frustration when he said, "I don't actually need any advice. I've spent three years figuring all of this out. All I—we need are funds to carry out my proposal." Salas went to one of the storage racks, selected one of twenty rolled-up full-size blueprints, spread the precisely designed specs out on the workbench and ran a loving hand over the printout. "This one will be first. Nine hundred square feet—"

"Two bedroom, one bath, decent-size kitchen and dining area," Optum interrupted. "I've heard your pitch before. Save the speech for the investors." He dropped the duffel on top of the drawing, putting an end to the discussion. "I need to head back to Chicago. Keep an eye on this for me until I get back, all right? Put it somewhere safe and forget about it."

Salas nodded, eyes on the bag, wondering what could be inside.

"Don't open it." Optum pointed a finger and jabbed Salas's chest with it. "Hear me?"

He nodded again.

"I need you to say it, Thomas."

"I won't open it."

"No matter how much you want to."

But now that's all Salas wanted to do. "I promise," he said.

The other man stared at him. Didn't blink. Didn't avert his gaze.

Tomás's eyes burned as he warned himself not to glance away. *He's looking for loyalty,* he told himself. *Don't look away until he does. Don't do it, don't do it, don't—*

Optum winked, slapped Tomás on the back again. "Excellent. Get ready, partner. Success is coming! We're gonna be so stinkin' rich."

Then the CFO to their not-yet-official company turned and headed for the garage door, jogged to his sports car, fired up the powerful engine, and *poof*—he was gone.

Salas stood there long after the BMW sped away. Replaying the conversation, he took the little boat from his pocket and absentmind-edly stroked the first 3D printed item he had customized. He turned it over, looked at his personal logo etched on the bottom, and smiled at the tiny face of a fox staring back at him.

After a few more minutes, he pushed the button to close the garage door, and when it hit the floor he slid the lever at the bottom of the track for extra privacy. Then Salas returned to the rear of the space, took hold of the storage unit that held the household products and rolled the shelving unit to the right, only wide enough for him to open another door and enter the gap sideways.

The mechanical whirs, cooling fans, and occasional high-pitched whines comforted him as he took in the surroundings warmed by spin-ning motors. He surveyed the four long tables, where a dozen 3D print-ers, each fed by a roll of black filament, worked full-speed to generate replica Glock-style gun frames and their various parts.

Salas crossed to a separate workstation and sat on a stool that creaked from his weight. Out of habit he clicked the remote's power button for the twenty-four-inch television on the table, already tuned to the local station to keep him company while he worked. Then he opened the lid to a laptop and brought the screen to life. He accessed and reviewed the computer file he had customized, and searched for any glitches he may have created that could have caused Optum's printed gun to misfire.

Of course, the somewhat slick operator out of Chicago could have been lying. For sure, Salas smelled spent gunpowder on the man's clothes. If the printed gun didn't fire, why would that be?

Less than a minute later, he found the anomaly—a glaring error he was surprised he hadn't caught. Fingers hovering over the keyboard, he considered what to do. For a full minute. Another more.

The knockoff guns had been a profitable venture he hadn't expected. At first he sold them one at a time, then seventeen months ago he made a small fortune selling thirty pieces to someone. He heard later the guy was a now-deceased drug dealer.

He no longer had to make any actual deliveries, now that a bulk customer had found him. Salas would go to the agreed-upon drop-off location arranged via a burner phone, leave the goods and take the stack of money in an envelope waiting for him there. Deal done. Easy.

Every time Tomás sold a round of the Glock knockoffs, he told himself it was for the greater good. His only financial option if Optum couldn't pull off what he promised about the investors. The end-game of producing affordable housing would wipe out any previous wrongdoing.

He shrugged, moused to the line of code, eliminated the flaw, tapped in the revision, saved the file.

The businessman he'd been making the replicas for only used them for training purposes. More like a movie prop. A toy. Harmless.

He almost convinced himself.

Almost.

CHAPTER EIGHT
EVA

Eva rehearsed in her mind at least twenty times what she would say to one of the most prominent council members of her tribe as she drove to his sprawling property that took up numerous plots of land on the reservation. Santiago Mirabal, known as "Hawk Soars" by their people, older brother of her best friend and uncle to one of her favorite people on the planet, would need to be the first of the community to advise, guide and instruct what the next steps relating to Nathan Trujillo should be.

She needn't have bothered preparing. Santiago stood on the long porch of his ranch-style house, arms crossed, tapping an impatient rhythm on the planks with the sharp toe of his cowboy boot, as if he'd been expecting her for hours.

"Are you here about Nathan Trujillo?" Santiago asked the moment Eva slid out of her vehicle.

She reared back. "How do you know this? I found out . . ." She glanced at her watch. "Half an hour ago."

Santiago tsked—his standard nonverbal communication—but of course he knew, as Cruz Romero suspected. Probably the first person called when the teacher in charge of the field trip realized the fallen child's identity. The Pueblo people held few secrets from each other. Eva would have to react quickly to keep ahead of rampant gossip. She figured the moment "Nathan" and "dead" publicly left the first person's lips, word would spread quick as a flash of lightning.

"Do you think Pabla and Gabriel know?" she asked.

"Doubt the news has reached their area of the rez."

Eva secretly hoped the young parents had already found out about their son. That she wouldn't have to be the one to deliver the devastating information. Words that could never be taken back. A cruelty the tribal cop would forever be associated with every time the couple encountered her.

"I'll pay for transport, no matter the cost," Santiago said.

"Should someone from the tribe go get Nathan?" Eva asked.

"Already got a man lined up. Cleared it with tribal government." Santiago waited a beat, eyes watering. "The boy needs to come home," he said, voice thick with tears.

Eva averted her eyes to allow him privacy to return to his usual indifferent attitude. "Where's Paloma?" she asked.

"The barn. Always at the barn."

"What does she do out there?"

"Hangs out with the horses mostly. Keeps everything in order. Rearranges things. Driving my stable manager Tommy crazy. She even hung up some pictures in the tack room."

She found the particulars amusing and thought he might chuckle, but he didn't. She bit back her laugh before she said, "Sounds like she's helping out. That's good, right?"

"More like hiding out." He held up his phone. "I'll make some calls tomorrow to make sure my guy doesn't run into any body blocks while he's in Santa Fe."

The screen door shut and Eva took that as her cue to move on. To conserve her energy for what would surely be a long day, she decided to drive to the barn, as impressive as the main house.

Eva pulled up short when she found her friend in the aisle between the double row of stalls, where she brushed the tallest and widest Arabian stallion Eva had ever seen. Paloma "White Dove" Arrio cooed to the giant—rhythmic tones so low Eva didn't recognize the tune. Paloma wore her dark hair that reached her waist pulled back in a tight ponytail that mimicked the horse's as her movements swayed.

"Hee-yah-ho," Eva said, the Tiwa greeting.

"Hey." Paloma kept her attention on the horse, one hand on a curry brush, the other hanging on to the gray mane.

Movement caught Eva's attention in one of the stalls. She frowned, recognizing one of the Barboa brothers. When he turned she caught the birthmark below his left earlobe. Paco, she now knew. When he'd asked her to take him to work, she assumed it would be the same place to drop off his brother, at the high-end restaurant north of the rez.

Paco kept glancing their direction, but averted his gaze—didn't wave or greet her with his usual charming boyish grin—whenever Eva tried to catch his eye, as if avoiding her.

"When did the Barboa brothers start working here?" she asked Paloma.

"I've only seen one." She shrugged. "Started about a week ago. He's only here a couple hours a day. Santi's deciding if he should hire him."

"They're usually inseparable. That's Paco."

Eva noticed that Paco spotlighted his attention on Paloma, even raked hay over his shoes a couple of times, and she realized the younger man had a crush.

"Here to ride?" Paloma asked, redirecting Eva from her amusement.

"Uh—no. I'm not getting on that thing."

"How can you still be afraid?"

"'Cause I almost got killed by one of them."

Paloma chuckled, turned, finally gave Eva her eyes and the smile that captivated those privileged enough to observe it, including the Navajo man who had helped create their son.

"You were ten."

"That thing bucked me off—"

"And you landed on your feet! Couldn't believe it. You were so pissed. Stormed over to that pony, stood in front of it, eyes all squinty.

Put up your fists . . ." She doubled over laughing, then wiped her glistening cheeks.

"I would have punched him, too."

"He knew that, for sure. Remember what he did?"

"No. I've blocked that all out."

"He took a step toward you and rested his forehead on yours."

"That never happened."

Paloma stabbed the brush at Eva. "It did. You may have purged that part of the memory, because it's sweet and tender. But I haven't forgotten. Neither has Santi. Ask him, he'll tell you. He'd never seen anything like that happen, still to this day."

"Now you're just makin' shit up."

"Nope. Time for you to make up with the four-hooved creatures. Get over it."

Those final words stopped Eva cold. The three words she knew rankled Paloma most. Four syllables uttered so many times by strangers, friends, family after the death of her beloved husband, Ahiga, and the end of her dancing career.

"Let's go to the village next Monday. It'll be Labor Day—there could be dancing on the plaza," Eva tried, ready to receive yet another rejection, as the hundreds before.

"No. I don't want to be around anyone. Don't want to see them stare or point and whisper. 'There's that loser. Used to be big-time on the rez. Remember all the sashes she won, how she was the best hoop dancer in four states? Bet she's still doing drugs. Got our girls killed.'" The mocking, high-pitched tone, face twisted in disgust, caused Eva to rear back.

"People don't think that."

"Everyone thinks that," Paloma muttered.

"You haven't been off the property for months now. The more you isolate yourself the harder it will be to adjust. Let's go out, visit some people, make some new friends."

"I don't deserve friends. I don't even deserve you."

Tears sparkled in Paloma's eyes and Eva cautioned herself not to approach. "You can't get rid of me," she said. "I'm not going anywhere. And I'm not letting you go."

Eva clenched every muscle, hoping her friend's reply would not wound her heart more than she already had.

"Yes, you will. Everyone does."

The accusation stung. A rebuke Eva didn't deserve, and still she stood there, holding back instead of defending herself. Wondering if she would ever have the right to do so. Her friend, more of a sister, had been through multiple lifetimes of horror and anguish. And now Eva was about to deliver another blow to her Native sister's already fragile psyche.

"Listen . . . there's bad news."

Paloma's strokes halted. She stood there, fluttered her eyes closed. "Do I need to know?"

"Yes. I don't want you hearing from anyone but me." Eva stepped closer to her friend, who looked reluctant to move away from the animal's support. "Nathan was shot."

"Nathan? Is he all right?"

Eva shook her head.

"No," Paloma whispered, shoulders drooping as she clasped the curry brush tighter. "On the rez? His house? . . . Did it happen at school?"

"No. Santa Fe, during a school trip. I don't have many details right now."

"Have you told Pabla and Gabriel?"

"Heading to the Trujillos' next. Cruz is meeting me there."

"You should take Kai," the boy's mother said.

"Cruz and Santiago suggested the same thing. I don't think it's a good idea, Paloma. Death notifications are disturbing. Traumatic, sometimes. He might not get over it."

"He's a man now. We can't protect him from everything. Not even a parent's grief. He'll take Shadow. The three became good friends. Spent a lot of time together. Kai was teaching Little Bear about the plants. He'll want to go."

Eva considered a moment, then nodded her agreement. "Is Kai around?"

"He's working on his secret project." Her friend hooked a finger and Eva followed her to the last stall of the barn.

Kai Arrio, known as "Single Star" to their people, college freshman, biology phenom, had his hands in a rectangular glass terrarium long as a car. Eva recognized most of the vegetation as indigenous to the area, but didn't have a clue what the rest could be.

"Why is it secret?" she whispered to Paloma.

"Because it's not ready to share with anyone yet," Kai said.

Kai's Belgian Malinois and constant companion stood alert next to his human. The four-footed creature pranced over and sat in front of Eva, tongue lolling, tail sweeping a clean spot on the floor. Animals were not her forte, and every time she encountered one, she didn't quite know what to do. Fortunately the not quite a pup anymore sported a red harness emblazoned with DOG IN TRAINING on one side, SEARCH AND RESCUE on the other, and a black-embroidered patch that stated DO NOT PET.

Kai looked up, no doubt happy in his element. "What's up, Eva?" he asked, voice pleasant and carefree for the moment.

"Could you and Shadow take a ride with me?"

CHAPTER NINE
CELIO

Celio Novar was bored. So bored. No friends. Nowhere to go. No place to be until his biology lab started in a couple of hours. He absentmindedly stroked the buzz cut at the top of his head, soft and fuzzy. Like the baby chicks that hopped around in a crate at their neighbor's house. Eventually, they would get big enough to lay eggs, and later would be traded at the meat cutter and processing place north of town.

The strokes soothed him as he sketched a precise pencil drawing from memory with his other hand—a navy warship—into his well-worn spiral notebook. The one he kept at home, hiding his secrets and thoughts—good and bad. What made him mad or sad.

Some pages featured his grandma's recipes of his favorite foods. She would even let him help her cook sometimes, especially near Christmastime when she would need to make hundreds and hundreds of her famous tamales for her neighborhood customers and sell to the fancy organic market they couldn't afford to shop at.

Now the thought of the masa delicacies, shredded beef, corn, green chile, monterey jack cheese, and his favorite red chile pork made his stomach growl. He rubbed his belly, which stretched out his black XL sweatshirt, and adjusted the elastic waistband of the matching sweatpants—clothes he thought of as a uniform that hid a build that often confused people. Made them think he was much older until he turned around and showed his baby face and innocent expression. Although sixteen, most people were shocked when they found out he already had a driver's license and regularly drove his abuela to her doctor appointments and picked up her medication at the drugstore, sometimes twice a week.

Celio and his brother, Manuel, had lived at their grandmother's house ever since their parents had left. First his mom, five years ago, then their father about a month later. Manny thought their dad, who threw fists more than compliments, killed their mother, then ran off when the cops came around asking questions. Celio didn't know for sure. Would probably never know. People long ago had lost interest in finding out, even their abuela, who never mentioned her daughter's name and now called the boys her own.

As he thought about his constant worry, Celio shaded areas of the drawing, the final step that made the picture even more realistic. He needed to find a way to stop the kids at school from picking on him. All he *really* needed was to figure out the final steps of his plan, which had started when his brother had gotten him into something Celio wasn't sure he could get out of. Wasn't sure he wanted to, either.

He wondered how much longer it would take for his brother to tell him to pick up more of the 3D printed handguns. The deliveries had come more often lately. The envelopes of money to replace the box of fake pistols thicker than the one before.

Manny had told him a bunch of times that the firearms didn't work. More of a prop like in the movies. But Celio figured that was a lie—otherwise why would the transactions need to be so secret? More like covert missions than a harmless trade of plastic for money every time he made a run.

He understood the power—even if the guns didn't fire, they were useful. Maybe that was the point. Not to be used for any real violence, but to scare and intimidate to get what someone wanted, without putting anyone in any real danger.

And the more he came into contact with the plastic pieces, the more he wanted one for himself. He got the allure. Like the candy he was addicted to. Just holding one made him feel good all over. Satisfied. And powerful for the first time in his life.

An obsession had started. Now all he had to do was figure out how to take one of the fake Glocks for himself. He could give back some of the money in the next envelope Manny gave him—maybe no one would notice just one of the guns missing.

"All I need is one," Celio said, playing out in his mind what exactly he would do when he made that one his own.

CHAPTER TEN
EVA

Kai took the news about his young friend better than Eva expected. Tears didn't come right away, but Paloma's son had lived through so much turbulence and change and disappointment over the past few years, and she wondered if he had become wary of showing outward emotion in front of people. She never knew when the tenderhearted young man needed comforting, or even how to react when he did. He was the closest to a nephew she would ever have, but he was not hers—not completely. Eva had learned to stand back and let the young man's mother take point now that she was healing and felt more confident about being the parent rather than the one who needed parenting.

Although there was a deep connection between the two, Eva often worried what to say to Kai whenever they were together. Silent most of the time, but when he forgot his shyness the dam burst and he would hit her with a flurry of questions and explanations and clarifications, leaving her stunned by his brilliant mind.

She spent too much time alone. Didn't socialize with her colleagues. Women in cackling groups baffled her. Men often either leered or ignored her completely. So she felt more comfortable in her own home, Cruz beside her a few nights a week, and visits with Paloma when her friend was up to it.

While the dog investigated the dirt and trees near Eva's vehicle until Kai instructed him to do his business, Eva thought about her knack for reading criminals and suspects within an instant of laying eyes on one, but the young man before her remained a mystery. Much like his uncle Santiago, she was rarely sure if a storm brewed just under the surface. His suicide attempt sixteen months ago haunted her to this day. Visions of him sitting on the railing of the Gorge Bridge, Rio Grande roaring below—distraught about his missing mother and furious that no one believed his assertions that she was in danger—wrenched Eva from her nightmares while asleep. And when awake, the memory would wash her body in sweat if she allowed her mind to spin.

In an effort to ease the kid so he wouldn't get too lost inside his head, she said, "Cruz is meeting me there. You don't have to do this, Kai."

"Yeah, but I want to." He picked up after Shadow, tossed the plastic poop bag in the garbage bin a few steps away. "Shadow and I have been to the Trujillos' a lot since all the bad stuff happened. They know us. We can help."

He opened the passenger's-side back door and pointed. "Up!" Shadow leaped and landed in a seated position. Eva slid behind the wheel and turned to watch Kai as he took a strap from his back pocket and proceeded to clip the safety restraint to the headrest's bar, then snapped the end to Shadow's harness ring. Eva swore the Malinois looked like a happy prisoner behind the barrier.

Per usual, Kai didn't say a word the first few minutes on the road to the reservation house where Nathan Trujillo had been born and lived all of his too-few years. In an effort to hold back her sadness, she tried for a conversation.

"How do you think your mom is doing?"

"Better. Not as many bad dreams. She used to wake up screaming. Scared the crap out of me. Hasn't happened in a while."

"You two still all right at your uncle's house?" she asked. "Is he being reasonable?"

47

"Most of the time. Mom stays in her room a lot. Or out in the barn with Mako. I don't see Uncle Santiago much. School and research and dog training takes up most of my time. He's pissed at Shadow though."

"Uh-oh. Why?"

"He keeps digging behind the chicken coop. Gotta be twenty holes now. Drives Santi crazy. Says I need to be more firm. *Make* him know who's in charge."

Eva swung her gaze to him for a moment. "You mean hit him?"

"No! No, course not. 'Firm reinforcement' is what he calls it. More leash work and stricter commands. Thing is, he finds something every time. Shadow's always right." The dog keyed on his name and cocked his head. "Aren't you, boy?"

Kai pulled the familiar leather palm-size medicine bag from his hoodie pocket, untied the drawstring, fished something out and held the item up so she could see it without taking her eyes off the road. "Plastic is like crack to him."

She cut her eyes to a scuffed and faded toy soldier, posed on one knee, rifle barrel bent at an angle. "No way! Haven't seen one of those in forever. I bet that's Cruz's. We used to play with toys just like that, where the chicken house is now. What else has your dog found?"

"A couple race cars with rubber wheels. Lots of Lego pieces. Even a little giraffe."

An ear-piercing high-pitched yip filled the cabin, as if to confirm the treasures. Eva flinched, let out a surprised yip of her own, winced, stuffed a finger in her right ear. "What the hell, dog!"

Kai reached back and wiggled his fingers through the mesh to pet the Malinois. "Inside voice, Shadow."

The dog let out a soft guttural *woof* and Kai chuckled.

Four more minutes of silence felt appropriate as they drew closer to the turnoff to the Trujillo property.

She let out a relieved sigh when she spotted Cruz parked on the street where Nathan's family lived. He raised a single finger from his hand that clutched the steering wheel. She did the same. She passed his tribal PD pickup and he pulled out behind her.

After the short drive farther, she parked in front of their destination. Eva took hold of Kai's wrist, and said, "You've got this."

He nodded, got out of the truck and released Shadow. The dog must have sensed his master's apprehension as he tucked in close. Eva wished she had her own dog for comfort while she waited for Cruz to join them, then they all approached the house.

The front door opened before Kai had a chance to knock. "Well, hello," Nathan's mother said. "Come in, come in." Pabla Trujillo stepped aside and motioned for everyone to enter.

Cruz held Eva's eyes. They gained courage from each other a moment, then crossed the threshold.

Eva noted that the woman looked considerably better now that she had recovered from her kidnapping along with her husband, with Nathan left to his own devices during the weeks they had fallen prey to the drug dealers who had taken over their house. She sat on the couch that had been replaced, thanks to Santiago, along with every other piece of furniture in the two-bedroom house in an effort to purge the darkness of the evil men who had died in the residence.

Nathan's father rounded the corner and crossed to shake Cruz's hand, then Kai's, then Shadow's. Gabriel beamed at Eva, and said, "Is it my birthday?"

Taken aback by the humor, Eva wasn't sure if she should laugh.

"You've missed Nathan," Pabla said. "He's on a trip with his school class."

"I know, ma'am."

Pabla reared back at Eva's formal tone. "Ma'am? Since when do you call me . . ." Her words trailed off. She straightened her back, thinned her lips, as if sensing her world leaned over the edge of forever altering.

Kai released Shadow's leash and the dog eased to the woman, sat before her, raised his head, gave her his soulful eyes. Pabla stroked his face with both hands over and over as she cooed, "I've missed you."

"I have difficult news," Eva said, knowing how to start, but unsure how much to reveal.

Gabriel sat down next to his wife and placed his hand on her knee. "What is it? You're scaring us."

"It's about Nathan. There's no easy way to tell you . . . Nathan has passed."

Gabriel chuckled, looked from Pabla to Eva to Kai and back to Eva. "Passed what?"

"The body of your little boy is in Santa Fe. He passed on."

"Did you say 'body of our little boy'?" he asked.

"Yes. I'm so sorry, Gabriel. Little Bear is no longer with us."

The father turned to the boy's mother, who kept her attention on the dog that continued to be there for her. "I don't understand."

"He was shot—"

"Stop. Just stop." Gabriel sprang from the couch, stormed to Eva, stopped three feet away and stared at her, his expression turning from anger to disbelief to shock in the moments it took to reach her.

"He's dead?" Pabla managed, her voice trembling.

"I called your auntie, Pabla," Cruz said. "She'll be here soon."

"This can't be," Gabriel whispered over and over.

Eva knelt down in front of Pabla, so close to Shadow she felt warmth coming off of his body. "Do you have a recent photo of Nathan?"

The young mother nodded, stopped petting the pup, reluctantly rose from the couch, and disappeared down the hallway.

"She won't survive this," Gabriel said in a low voice.

"She's a strong woman, Gabe," Cruz said.

"Not without Nathan. He is her purpose."

Eva glanced at Kai. Face pallid, watching only his dog, teeth clenched so tight his jaw muscles bulged. She sent him supportive thoughts—to keep it together—*hold in your emotions, they are the ones to be comforted. Don't let them see that you are breaking inside.*

As if the young man caught her mental warning, he took in and released a deep breath, then snapped his fingers for Shadow to approach, pointed to Gabriel. Shadow responded to the signals, padded to the grieving father, sat down and leaned against the man's leg. Gabriel absently stroked the dog's head and his demeanor visibly eased.

At that moment, Eva thought the Malinois would be an ideal support animal. Then again, he already fit that description. The creature had helped his companion through some very dark times.

"Everyone will help her," Eva offered, going to Gabriel, then taking his hands in her own. "And you. Like before. Your sufferings brought the whole tribe together. Made us *all* stronger. We'll be there for both of you again."

"Hope you're right, Lightning Dance," he muttered.

His wife returned to the room, a picture frame held to her chest. She reluctantly handed the photograph to Eva.

"I promise to take good care of this," Eva said, looking at the memento.

She remembered when the picture had been taken. At a medal-pinning ceremony at the community center. Nathan's reward for being the warrior in the face of immense danger related to the murders of three Pueblo women. The tribe's governor and war chief had even been there when the newly appointed Taos Pueblo Police Department chief pinned the gold medal topped by a ribbon of the blue, tan and green colors that represented the Taos Pueblo flag.

Eva mustered every bit of fortitude she could call forth. All she wanted was to flee the comfortable little house, now tainted by agony and suffering once again. She gave Pabla a supportive squeeze to the shoulder, and the same gesture to Gabriel, and assured them she would return soon.

Cruz walked with Eva to her vehicle. "I'll stay until family gets here," he said.

Eva nodded her appreciation. "Gonna be a long day."

They both watched Kai throw a tennis ball to arc high into the air. Shadow sprinted, tail and ears straight back as he raced to retrieve, and then returned it for another round. Cruz looked reluctant for the carefree moment to end. He leaned in and she thought he would kiss her—but Kai called out and killed the moment.

"Can you come over here? Shadow's being weird."

Eva and Cruz approached where the dog worked around a simple wooden cross angled at the head of a mound of dirt. Shadow's attention remained on the ground, nostrils flaring, as he turned around and around, then seemed to grow wary as he keyed in tighter. Then the dog stopped his curious behavior, sat down and looked up at his handler.

"Strange. He does that when he's found something plastic, but he'd be digging like crazy if it was."

Shadow lay down, paws on the ground, entire body pointing to a particular area.

"He found something, for sure," Kai said.

"Drugs buried by the dealers?" Eva said. "Something like that, maybe?"

"Doubt it," Kai said. "He's not trained on drugs. Just the basics right now."

"Black powder?" Cruz offered.

"Maybe. He's done some of that for his nose training."

Cruz and Eva shared a look. She thought of the procedural implications a moment. She had no grounds to get a search warrant, wasn't sure she needed one.

"That's Bonkers's grave," Gabriel said, coming up behind the group. "Nathan's dog."

"Could it be bones?" Eva asked.

Kai shook his head. "No cadaver training, either."

As if fed up with waiting for the humans to decide next steps, Shadow shot up from his prone position and started to dig and dig. Frantic, unrelenting, focused motions.

"Shadow, *no*," Kai shouted.

Cruz grabbed Kai's arm when the handler made a move to control his dog. Although Eva didn't quite approve of Cruz's reluctance to intervene, the dog's actions released them from personally tainting potential evidence.

"Probably just a toy soldier," Kai said, then whispered more to himself than the others, "*Please*, be a toy soldier."

The Malinois continued to rake loam away until the hole reached two feet deep. The sound of a crinkle made them all curious enough to step closer and Eva could see thick plastic, being shredded by claws.

"Stop him, Kai," Eva said.

"Back. Release!" Shadow reluctantly abandoned his find, circled Kai, then sat down at his trainer's side.

Cruz knelt down and looked closer into the hole.

"Careful," she warned. "Might be something other than a dog's bones down there." She pulled two sets of latex gloves from one of the compartments on her duty belt, handed one pair to Cruz and struggled on the others. Next she took out her phone, selected the camera function, focused on the hole, then nodded for Cruz to proceed.

She took a succession of captures as her partner pulled out what turned out to be a garbage bag, careful not to let the contents tumble out from the ripped gaps.

"What did he find?" Gabriel asked, a nervous tinge to his voice.

Cruz untied the knot at the top of the bag and opened it wide to expose the contents. He whistled as Eva gaped at the sight so shocking it locked the breath in her chest so long she staggered back a step.

"Yep. Plastic," Cruz said as he held up the frame of what Eva recognized to be a replica of an actual gun pinched between his thumb and index finger.

"Why didn't Shadow find these until now?" Eva asked.

"We never came over here," Kai said. "Nathan was usually at the Red Willow Center when I saw him. And his mom or dad would drop him off at Santi's barn a lot."

"Nathan doesn't like to remember how Bonkers died," Gabriel said. "Always gets sad when he comes here to visit . . ." The young father dropped his chin to his chest and muttered, "*Didn't* like. *Got* sad."

Eva placed a supportive hand on Gabriel's arm, her heart breaking in tandem with his at the thought that now everything related to the boy would be stated in the past tense.

"Your monster deserves steak tonight," Cruz said.

"Who is the best dog in all the world?" Kai shouted. The Malinois jumped up, spun in a circle, sat in front of his handler, yipped his reply. Kai ruffled the dog's neck. "Shadow is! Good boy, good boy, good boy."

"*Really* good boy," Eva said as she crouched to take a closer look.

CHAPTER ELEVEN
SIMON

At precisely noon Liam O'Banion, a.k.a. Simon Optum, as well as thirteen other aliases, checked out of his suite at the El Monte Sagrado. He had enjoyed each of his stays at the Taos resort where sunlight winked between the leaves of massive trees and would miss the immaculate grounds, precisely groomed foliage, the scent of fresh pine in the air. He registered all of this, thinking how much several of his ladies—including the twelve-year-old daughter he rarely visited—would enjoy the flowers of every color in terra-cotta pots and along the sidewalks that wound through the high-end ten-acre property.

He tossed his suitcase of essentials in his Beemer, brought the engine to life and pulled out of the lot, wondering when he would return. If he ever should. The various trips seemed to be more frequent and longer. Anxiety had begun to wear on him whenever he opened his eyes in the morning and realized he wasn't at his main home base in Chicago. Found himself having to think hard for a minute to get his bearings before he slid out of bed.

He had so many counterfeit driver's licenses and IDs and tales behind each identity that lately he'd had to double-check which state he woke up in to remind himself which story he was hiding behind. He thought to himself that one less place of lies to keep in his head would probably be a good thing.

It was a long drive back to the Windy City so he had plenty of time to ponder the next elements with his clueless partner, far more suited to play teacher than entrepreneur home builder. He would have Salas establish a formal corporation next month so that all financials would appear legit. A lot of his boss's money would be run through what would incrementally become a large-scale venture. Tens of thousands, maybe hundreds of thousands—hell, why not millions—could be laundered.

The possibility bloomed and his heart thudded a quick beat, which grew even more rapid when he approached the street that led to the bank he'd hit earlier that morning. He craned his neck to get a better look. Yellow police tape remained strung across the road and a police cruiser, parked sideways, denied entry.

He thought about the night before when, always the cautious criminal, he had pulled on nitrile gloves, scrubbed a toothbrush dipped in bleach over the entire 3D printed handgun and ammunition to be sure any possible fingerprints or DNA residue would not be traced to him or Salas. Then he had loaded the rounds into the magazine and assembled the gun as Salas instructed. Maybe he hadn't paid good enough attention to putting the thing back together but it turned out to be a useless hunk of plastic.

He knew that timing was crucial when it came to pulling off a perfect crime, essential to stick to every step and movement he rehearsed in his mind for multiple hours, sometimes days, before he initiated his fully formed plan. One second off, a single deviation from the intent, and you're fucked. The fake gun could have cost him way more than time.

He smiled. Because that was the fun of it. The rush. The adrenaline pump. The not knowing if he would survive the transgressions.

The teller's face came to him in a flash. "Lily," he muttered. Yes, he felt regret for the terror he wielded, especially over the young, darker-skinned women who in other circumstances would want to spend time in his bed. But that was part of the allure too.

He thought of how good he'd become at pulling off robberies. How he intuitively knew what to do and say and act and react. At first he hit convenience stores late at night. A couple of grocery stores. Now six banks. He had thirteen identities to care for and feed. Each had different characteristics and personalities, from custom-tailored suits to a mechanic's overalls.

And the women. So many wants so they would satisfy his needs. The phrase *Nothing's for free* came to his mind—no truer words when it came to the stunning ladies who brought him joy and ecstasy if the timing and proper playtime of dinners followed by clubs where they danced for hours worked for their schedule. Only then would he get what *he* wanted.

And although Optum took down mid-six figures a year from his overall Chicago boss, he could never have *too much* money. But if said boss ever found out his extracurricular activities . . . well, Optum never let that thought stay in his head for very long.

He often wondered if the act of stealing was what really got him off. Quenched his desires. That maybe he should stick exclusively to this art. Forget the women dotted around the nation. Quit lighting money on fire just to get laid and feel important. Build up the funds and pick a Polish bride as two of his cousins had.

Then the vision of gorgeous Gloria in Lincoln, Nebraska, flashed in his mind. Her long blonde hair streaming over her chest to barely conceal gorgeous tits, long legs open and waiting, red-painted fingernails stroking exactly where he wanted to be. He adjusted his crotch to ease his growing erection and thought no more about merely one woman to fulfill his desires.

He turned on the radio to get his mind off the cravings of his plaything. Already tuned to a local station, he caught the end of a news story about the bank robbery. If the press could be believed, the cop still hung on after heroic lifesaving measures and surgery to repair the gunshot wound that had nearly taken her life.

Didn't matter to him whether the cop lived or died, but he supposed her surviving would be less of a risk to him if he were to ever be implicated in the robbery and assault. *As if.* He smirked. *They'll never catch me.*

He glanced at his reflection in the rearview, beamed his trademark smile, then said, "Yes, you're that good."

Less than a mile outside the city limits, traffic started to back up on the two-lane. He drifted over the lane markings to see what caused the holdup and a car laid down on his horn and nearly took off his sideview mirror as it sped past.

"Fucking hell," he muttered, tweaking the wheel to get back in his lane.

He crawled a few car lengths ahead, stopping every minute, and still couldn't see what lay ahead. After a bend in the road he spotted two white SUVs, marked SHERIFF on the front quarter panel, parked at an angle, which allowed only one car from either direction to proceed. Two cops, hands on the butts of their holstered guns, spoke to drivers, and then waved them to move on one after the other.

Nervous sweat trailed down Optum's side. He considered turning around, going a different direction, not chancing being questioned, but he didn't want to look suspicious and have one of those cops or others nearby run him down and take him in for evading police questioning. Run his prints that didn't match anyone alive. Do a computer search on his fake driver's license. Or worst of all, discover the multiple other identifications inside a hidden custom-made compartment in the trunk. Silly, he thought, probably wouldn't happen—but why risk it, right?

And so as he waited his turn, he ran through answer options in his mind. He panicked when he wasn't positive he had ditched the wig. Certain about the mask and hoodie, but how would he explain a fucking wig that matched the description of the bank robber if it was somewhere in the vehicle?

He closed his eyes tight and replayed his actions after he'd finished the job. Hoodie off after the mask and gloves, then put inside the bag with the money. But what about the wig? Had he ditched that along with everything else in the dumpster behind the hotel's restaurant, stinking like it hadn't been emptied in a week?

His thought right then was to get the hell out of there. Turn around and go back to the city he had grown attached to. The crisp clean air, amazing sunsets and those spectacular clouds. And vistas that went on forever. Real-ass Mexican food, not the wannabe shit at home. The high-end resort where everyone treated him like the big shot he was.

Most of all he would miss the money he'd left behind. But even that would be a good thing. Someone would find the stacks bound in straps that obviously came from the Alvarado Bank in the high school teacher's possession. The robbery and shooting case would be closed. He would be free and clear. Salas might snitch, but authorities wouldn't find Optum. Maybe.

Then again . . . that damned wig.

Taking the only risk he was willing to entertain, he waited for the car in front of him to crawl ahead and for the cops to look away. He performed a three-point turn like the master driver he prided himself to be, kept his speed under the limit, and considered his options.

CHAPTER TWELVE
EVA

Eva felt all eyes on her the moment she walked through the front entrance to the Taos Pueblo Police Department. She carried multiple clear evidence bags containing the items recovered at Bonkers's grave—empty trash bag that had contained everything they found, plastic gun knockoffs, and loose rounds of ammo that clinked as she swung her arm.

She approached Leandro Ramirez, who shared duties as a detention officer, occasional dispatcher, and evidence room manager. One of Eva's favorites on the force, he had been the toughest exterior to crack, but when she found out he crafted knives as a hobby, she brought him a few turquoise stones and long obsidian arrowheads from her grandfather's collection. After that, he insisted she call him Lenny—an honor, according to a few of her astonished coworkers.

Lenny's head lowered to take in the contents in her hands, and his eyes danced as she grew closer to the locked mesh doors of his domain. He pulled a key from the retractable key holder secured to his duty belt, flicked the dead bolt, hitched his head for her to follow.

"Chief's checking on a frequent flier in detention," he said. "Should be here soon. Let's get started."

Eva hoped the troublemaker locked in one of the cells was not Paco or Navi. Or both. Although the twins were always respectful to her, they had been known to push the limits of her fellow law enforcers over the years.

Standing at the long worktable in the middle of the room, Lenny wriggled all of his fingers, prompting her to hand over the bounty. He laid out the items, arranged them in a single row, then inspected each firearm bag one by one, making sure each barrel was locked in the back position to ensure the weapon held no round, and zip-tied to keep the trigger from firing.

Each bag crinkled when he smoothed out the plastic to note the evidence registration numbers for each Glock replica on a log sheet, and then searched for serial numbers—of which he didn't find a single one—and proceeded until everything was cataloged. He signed his name, provided his badge number, dated the bottom of the document, then slid the paper for her to do the same.

She wanted to think about anything other than Nathan and his destroyed parents and what the young couple would face in the days and years to come. The disturbing thoughts kept crowding her mind so she looked for a distraction.

Curious, she took in the surroundings she rarely spent much time in. Floor-to-ceiling shelving units housed evidence boxes stacked in rows. Precise handwritten names, dates the items were cataloged and case-closed date, as well as record numbers in thick black Sharpie allowed the searcher to quickly access items secured from crime scenes on the reservation. The volume of names she recognized surprised her. She even remembered some of the newer cases by the victim/offender dates.

She started at the top row and scanned left to right, then when she'd finished taking in those she assessed the next wall of items she'd never paid any attention to before now. The bottom two rows were marked by different handwriting, the oldest dates so far, ink slightly blurred and fading. Eva's eyes halted on one of the receptacles. She stared, glanced at Lenny, who remained busy with the loot she'd brought him. His attention remained averted so she took a step closer to the curiosity marked:

LEFTHAND, ANGEL SIMONE

Eva had a feeling the date held some significance, but the detail hid beyond her memory. She couldn't pinpoint why and tried to remember more about the Lefthand family, if any tragedy had befallen anyone close to the chief. Nothing came to mind.

Eva had been on the tribal force for only one year, and her boss had been sworn in three months prior to that. She wondered how the other woman, ten years younger than herself, had endured the resistance she had surely met on a daily basis starting out. Cruz had told her the prior chief had been particularly hard on the only two female officers on his force at the time, dispatched them to the most difficult crimes—alcohol disturbances, domestic calls, always for rape investigations—and never cut them any slack, sometimes insisting they pull double shifts. Lefthand's colleague bowed out after a few weeks on the job, but Lefthand wouldn't quit.

As if her boss knew she had been thinking about her, the first female to be appointed tribal police chief entered the room. "Lenny, give us a minute."

He gave an apprehensive look at the evidence on the table, and didn't look happy to relinquish his post, but picked up the log sheet, exited the room and closed the door behind him.

"So," Lefthand said. "Guns. Go."

Eva didn't hesitate and rattled off the recovery details. "Yes, ma'am. Ten 3D printed guns . . . well, mostly partials. Three fully assembled. Also two handguns—real ones—stinking of gunpowder. Most likely not cleaned after they were fired. And eighty-five loose nine-millimeter rounds."

"What else can you tell me?"

"Very little, other than that. The three drug dealers who took over the Trujillos' house didn't survive, and now Nathan is gone too, so there's no way to verify the firearms are linked to the offenders."

"We've got nothing?"

"Might get lucky with fingerprints?" Eva said, more of a hopeful question than a statement, knowing the difficulty in pulling prints from plastic.

Her boss picked up the bag containing the loose ammunition. "Maybe on the rounds."

Eva took a deep breath and clasped her hands together, nervous to ask what she had been considering the past few hours. "I've been thinking about something."

The chief dipped her head, once, indicating Eva to continue.

"Think I could go to Santa Fe? Be an escort to bring Little Bear's body home? While I'm there I could talk to Alice Jones."

Chief Lefthand showed no reaction, and held the pose so long Eva thought her boss might not recall the woman currently in a Santa Fe prison awaiting trial for the murder of the drug dealers who had taken over the Trujillo family's house.

"Interesting request," the top cop said.

"Jones might know—"

Lefthand raised her index finger, and Eva halted her words. Her commander stayed quiet so long Eva was sure her idea would be shot down. Instead, her boss nodded—one uptick of her chin—silent interest. "Think she'd talk to you?"

"Oh, yes. She'll talk."

Eva knew the narcissistic murderer would open up. She also knew the interview could go sideways, or wouldn't prove helpful. The psychopath—determined to be a hero without consideration to the lives taken, nor to those who survived, still dealing with the aftermath—lied all the time. Every word offered would have to be vetted and verified. Still, Eva thought the murderer might light a beacon on an element they hadn't yet considered.

But time was not on their side. One cop down could enable the bank robber to slip through the already wide loop of law enforcers in pursuit, and finding out what Alice Jones knew about the fake guns wouldn't even necessarily be helpful.

"I hear Santiago Mirabal made Nathan's arrangements," Lefthand said, voice tight and tinged with annoyance.

At first Eva reined in her surprise. She assumed the body-retrieval assignment would have come from her chief. Now she figured Santiago must have pulled strings, gone above her rank, cleared the task with the tribe's governor or maybe even the war chief—made arrangements without Chief Lefthand's blessing. Had been forced to go along with the decision. No one could refuse Santiago Mirabal. Even the one who wore the shiniest badge.

"No secrets on the rez," the chief said.

"Is that ever a *good* thing?"

Always diplomatic and professional, no response to Eva's direct comment followed. Instead, the chief said, "Better stay put. I'll need everyone on point. Lots to plan for."

Disappointed, but understanding, Eva nodded in agreement, unsure if her fellow Pueblo sister meant preparing the rituals for the little boy being brought home to the sovereign land of their people, or the possibility of the need to keep peace as their oftentimes impatient people waited for answers about his death.

Lefthand scanned the table, taking in each firearm. Shaking her head, the woman in charge went through the door and left Eva alone with the disturbed aura that remained in the area. She locked her attention on the arsenal atop the table, convinced the items were the source of her discomfort. Despite her relative youth, Lefthand hadn't appeared rattled in any way. Eva knew the chief had big power. Unflappable, calm energy.

Eva strove to assume the same bearing and attitude—needed the self-awareness the chief radiated in order to confront the danger and darkness Eva felt certain she'd encounter during the investigation.

She would need the confidence. The entire force would.

CHAPTER THIRTEEN
SIMON

It took Optum longer than ever before to arrive back in the heart of town. He flailed an annoyed arm a dozen times to get slowpokes and lookie-loos to finally find their gas pedals as he crawled toward and then past the bank robbery site.

Frustrated, nearly out of smokes, he spotted the Allsup's Convenience Store sign and turned into the parking lot. He killed the engine, got out of the BMW, head down, thinking about next moves and if he should check back in at the resort.

Someone bumped into him and he almost tripped on the step near the entrance. He frowned, about to hurl his customary insult, raise a fist if necessary—stopped his words from flying out of his mouth just in time.

A woman turned around and his scowl melted away. Native, in her twenties, flashy earrings peeking from her long dark hair gave him a smile. "Sorry about that. Didn't mean to cut you off."

He matched her grin. "It's all right. I should have used my blinker."

The other woman giggled and covered her mouth with her hand.

He rushed ahead, held the door open, swept his arm for the women to go ahead of him. "Here you go."

"Thanks," the first woman said and linked her arm to her companion's. They dipped their heads together, and whispered shared words he couldn't hear.

He stayed an aisle behind them when they stood at glass-front coolers and scanned the rows of colorful drinks.

Another woman joined the two. "Did you hear about Lily Bernal?" she asked the others, eyes wide, anxious to spread the gossip.

At first the girl's tone caught his interest—then the name Lily gained his full attention. Curious now, he stood as close as he dared.

"No. What?"

"She was working at the bank. The one that got robbed this morning."

"No!"

"Yeah, Littlefeather's a teller there."

"Is she okay? Did she get hurt?"

The other woman shrugged. "Dunno."

"We should go see her."

"Yeah, maybe she'll tell us what happened."

"No, just to make sure she's okay."

"You're right. You know me—just wanna know all the facts so I can be ready if she needs me."

"Uh-huh," the other woman said, her tone unconvinced.

"What?"

"You and your mom are the biggest gossips on the rez," she said, laughing.

The other women joined the amusement. "Truth," they said together.

Optum kept one customer between him and the Indians as they stood in line. Purchases in hand, they rattled on about what they would ask the bank teller.

The ladies waggled their fingers to him and he returned the gesture when they exited the convenience store. He plucked out one of the bundles of flowers from a bucket near the checkout counter, told the clerk which cigarettes to pull from the display, added a pack of gum, paid and hurried out the door to his car.

By the time he started his engine, the first two females he encountered, now in a white sedan, pulled from the lot and made the quick turn to one of the two main roads that led to the Taos Pueblo village. Optum had always wanted to take a tour of the ancient dwellings, but never found the time during his brief stays in Taos.

"I've got nothing but time now," he muttered as he glanced at the flowers on the seat beside him.

The less-than-two-minute tail on a dirt road ended when the sedan parked in a lot marked for visitors. Optum swung into an empty slot, watched the two women get out of their car and say a few words to the Indian boy who sat on a folding chair at the mouth of the parking area.

He kept his head down, held the flowers low so as not to draw any attention, took rushed steps to catch up to the women.

"Five dollars," the kid said.

The command stopped Optum. He whirled to the voice.

"To park."

He reached in his pocket, took out the thick fold, considered giving him only two singles, then decided he might piss off the kid and that he probably shouldn't draw any attention to himself. He peeled off a five, handed it over, took long strides to make up the gap to the others.

The houses were spaced far apart and he thought for sure someone would call him out, be told to get away from there, he didn't belong. Then the two turned to a path that led to a house the color of mud set back from the road. Plants in a big colorful pot placed near the front door painted sky blue indicated a proud female lived there.

He recalled Lily. The welcoming smile on her face at first, followed by a frown of confusion as she looked at his masked face. Then the terror as he raised the useless pistol. He willed away the erection growing in his pants.

He tucked behind an overgrown hedge that hid him from the street but still allowed him to hear hushed voices. The door opened to reveal a woman. He recognized the teller right away and replayed her name in his mind a few times, liking the sound of it in his head.

The woman didn't welcome the others inside her house. She stood there, arms crossed, blocking entry. Her head bobbed as she answered the questions with nods instead of actual words.

"Are you sure?" one of the visitors said.

Lily nodded.

"We could bring you some food," the other wannabe guest said. "Grandma's gonna make bread and stew tonight."

A shake of the head this time.

"Well . . . okay. Guess we'll go."

Firm nod this time. The door closed.

The rebuffed women didn't notice him or even turn his direction as they hurried off, voices now a little loud as they talked over each other, both of them sounding embarrassed and mad about being turned away.

He forgot the women in less than a moment. He waited a full ten minutes to make sure no other visitors would approach the house. Worked over in his head the flattery and wooing conversations that had been successful for him in the past. He needed a quick connection. And a safe place to hide out while the shitstorm settled in the city so he could make his final escape back to Chicago. What better way than to kill a day or two with a new conquest?

Optum stepped from his hiding spot, straightened his collar, ran a steady hand through his hair, raised the flowers.

He strode to the door, and put on his most charming persona no woman had ever been able to resist.

CHAPTER FOURTEEN
TOMÁS

Tomás followed his former student, impressed by what he'd seen so far of the property. He'd never been to this part of the reservation and he kept looking around, awed by the tractor and farm equipment that looked showroom immaculate, not a bit of dust on the paint or windows. A strip of lush grass wide enough for four horses to sprint as far as a football field surprised him the most. The emerald color popped against the afternoon's deep-blue sky and he imagined riders on saddles vying for position until they crossed the finish line.

"This is a very impressive ranch, Kai," he said as they approached an imposing barn up ahead.

"My uncle doesn't mess around."

"You're not kidding."

They made a turn, walked beyond a massive open doorway and started down a long breezeway bookended by at least a dozen horse stalls. Hay dust tickled his nose when he raised his head to take in the exposed rafters as high as he could glimpse in the darkness.

"I hope this isn't a bad time," Salas said.

"Naw, it's all right. I've been wanting to show you this."

They approached the end stall and Kai motioned him to enter the open area. The floor had been swept clean and there was nothing in the enclosure but a glass aquarium almost as long as the six-foot-long wood stand it sat upon. Instead of fish swimming in water, the glass panes held plants.

Salas recognized each young seedling from those found at his favorite spot on the reservation—where he took classes, and Kai sometimes met him, to study a multitude of indigenous flora all in one area. Those had been some of the teacher's favorite times. Alone, teaching his star pupil. Passing on the knowledge he didn't think anyone but himself cared about. Until this special, alert kid came into his classroom.

From the first day, ten minutes into the class, Kai shot his hand to the ceiling and asked question after question. The pupil had been the first to express interest, so hungry to learn he filled up an entire notebook of chicken scratches in the first week.

"Fine job, Kai. Really good presentation. Scarlet globemallow's difficult to propagate away from its originating soil. The hound's-tongue, too." He leaned in closer. "Wow—fourwing saltbush. These are all remarkable specimens. Is this for one of your university assignments?"

The younger botanist's expression dropped from pleasant to remorseful. "I'm . . . was working on it with someone."

"Oh? Do I know who?"

"No. Someone from my tribe."

Sadness vibrated from Kai and for a moment Salas thought the young man might break down. He turned away to provide some privacy and caught movement in his peripheral vision. A woman dressed in a white flowing dress held the reins to a huge gray horse that followed. Head lowered, her lips moved as the pair slowly walked his direction. He couldn't make out the quiet words, and he wondered what she could be saying to the stallion. Wanted nothing more at that moment than to have her speak that privately to him.

"Who is that?" Salas asked.

"My mom. Paloma. You've never met her before?"

Salas shook his head, unable to stop looking at the woman. Captivated by her dark waist-length hair, almost iridescent in the late-afternoon sunlight, reminding him of the magpies that flourished at that favorite research spot on the reservation. "She never attended any of the parent-teacher functions."

"No, she wouldn't have done that," Kai said. "Too much going on in her life to be much of a parent back then."

Salas had made a conscious effort to avoid the news about what Paloma Arrio had suffered almost a year and a half before. And didn't rely on gossip about her drug-abuse years before that. He knew she was once a celebrated dancer for the tribe, that she was the sole survivor of a crash that killed her husband and two other Pueblo dancers. Instead, he had turned a deaf ear so he could be impartial for Kai. To be there without the knowledge that could compromise how he would respond if the boy ever came to him for advice. But he never did. It made Salas a little sad that the young man didn't feel close enough to trust his advice on such personal matters. Even so, they remained friends even after Kai graduated and went on to excel at the local branch of the state university.

Salas asked questions, tried his best to remain interested, nodded his head as the young naturalist explained the reasoning behind the vegetation choices. He recommended advice on which types of flora would need more room between others in order to flourish in the tight space. Offered what he believed the water-to-dry-days ratio should be.

Every time the boy looked away, Salas turned to the beauty, who had tied off the horse outside the farthest stall. She brushed the stallion, oblivious to everything but her task.

He waited for the right time to ask for a proper introduction. Mouth dry, tongue thick, perspiration trickled down Tomás's back and he didn't dare raise his arms in case his shirt's armpits were embarrassingly wet from nervous sweat. He ran a snippet of dialogue through his mind that didn't sound too inane, turned his attention back to Kai for a moment, then back to his mother. Who no longer stood there. The horse remained tied to the stall door, but she seemed to have vanished.

A thought came to Salas, one that suddenly became insistent. "Do you like living here?"

"Yeah, I guess."

"But you'd like a place of your own, right? For you and your mom?"

"Yeah, that's probably not ever gonna happen."

"It could though. I've heard a lot of your people have land, handed down or gifted to family members, some for generations, but it's too costly to build on the property."

Kai nodded. "Lots of people want to but can't come up with the money. Anyway, only a couple carpenters around here can do that kind of work. Anyone who can put together even a freakin' birdhouse have moved to Santa Fe or Albuquerque."

A glint lit up Salas's eyes. "I want to show you something."

Salas reached into his pocket, took out his favorite small-scale 3D printed model, twice the size of a piece from a Monopoly game, he always had on him. A talisman that kept him focused on his end goal. He handed it to Kai and said, "I'm going to manufacture these. Affordable housing on the reservation."

Kai frowned, looking confused as he rolled the toy-size house in his palm. "Plastic houses?"

The mentor beamed at his former student, hands on his hips, legs wide—a superhero pose. "No, this is just the model. The process is called 3D printed structures. Houses made by machine. Made of concrete."

Kai continued to look skeptical so Salas spoke faster, added excitement to the presentation. "Your people need houses and don't have enough qualified people to build them. My idea solves that problem."

"Yeah, but how are you gonna actually get this done? Don't you need equipment? And money?"

Salas waved a hand, as if swatting away a non-problem. "Working on that right now. Entire communities are being built this way. I'm telling you, this is the future of housing, especially for disadvantaged areas, like reservations."

Kai reared back. Salas hadn't intended the statement as a diss, but the boy looked uncomfortable. Worried he might be losing the one person who could actually help him get started working with the Taos Pueblo community, he eased his tone and leaned in closer, kept his voice low and confidential. "Imagine it, Kai," Salas said. "Solid housing on every reservation in the nation. That's my commitment. To start here and then approach the other Pueblo tribes in New Mexico. And the Navajos in Arizona! So many Natives are living in desperation there. Imagine what a new life they could lead if they didn't have the worry of not having a solid structure to protect them from the elements."

The young man looked intrigued after Salas's last comment. Kai returned his smile and held out the house, but Salas waved it away. "Keep it. For luck. Help me visualize the real thing. We can manifest together!"

Salas couldn't recall a single thing Kai talked about by the time he returned home. All thoughts remained on the first woman who had caught his attention since his ex handed him a menu at what then became his favorite diner. He married her four months later.

The funk of depression evaporated at the possibility that lightning could strike again.

CHAPTER FIFTEEN
PALOMA

Paloma Arrio, known as White Dove by her tribe and former fans, had searched everywhere in and around the barn she could think of for Kai and his Malinois companion. She had heard him talking to someone in the stall where Kai kept his selection of plants, but by the time she had used the bathroom in the tack room, the visitor had left and she still had no idea who the voice belonged to.

Figuring Kai must be back at the house, she gave a stroke to each of Santiago's collection of horses, issued a few promises that she would be back with apples for them and Mako soon, then made her way from the barn to the main house.

Although her steps and movements had become more fluid and less painful over the months of intense physical, mental and chemical rehab, she found the progress to be far less than she'd expected or hoped for. Still, she kept going. Retrained her mind as she worked her body. She could now go hours without suffering cravings.

Paloma felt a presence and the tormenting essence dropped its shroud. She halted. Shuddered. Balled her fists. The aura so profound it threatened to take her under, suffocate, drown her in evil. The sweet scent of Johnson's baby shampoo the nurse practitioner who had kidnapped her would wash her hair with nauseated Paloma. Tug of one hundred brush strokes she administered every night tingled her scalp.

Swooned from every hit of the drugs that would flood her entire being every day and night of her captivity.

She shook her head back and forth, waist-length hair whipping side to side. *No. Stop. Leave me.* She imagined a brilliant white light in her mind's eye, high up and to the right, filling the outline of a doorway. She shouted the silent command, *Go.*

The evil showed itself, grew bigger, bolder.

Go!

White Dove held her resolve, palms stinging from her fingernails biting the skin. She simultaneously expelled a puff of air, placed stiff hands on her chest and forcefully brushed off the remnants of the haunting. The vision spun, then floated closer to the doorway, as if being beckoned to the light. The apparition turned, glanced back a final look, wavered, hesitated its advancement, then swooped for the light.

Paloma slammed the door shut, trapping the specter, forbidding further access.

After a moment, the trembling ceased. No further troubles followed. It took a few minutes to catch her breath, reset her composure. She felt a little shaky by the disturbance but confident enough to carry on.

Paloma found her son in his room, which years ago used to be her younger brother Sky's domain. She smiled thinking of Sky atop a crazed bronc, agile body and raised arm flailing as he fought to stay atop his mount until the eight-second buzzer resounded his victory. Also stung by the rodeo bug, their other youngest brother, Sol, soon joined Sky on the circuit. Five years ago now. She hadn't seen them since. Lately they had expressed the possibility of a return for a visit now that she was "cured"—a term that left her baffled. She often wondered if anyone who had endured what she'd dealt with could ever really be *cured*? Not her. Not yet anyway.

She reached the open door and Kai turned to her before she said his name—a talent her oldest brother Santiago called "radar" because the boy always seemed attuned to his mother. *Turn your radar on,* would be all Paloma ever needed to think if Kai got lost in a crowd or was late for dinner as a little boy.

He must have sensed something in her demeanor. Worried brows knitted together as he said, "What's wrong?"

No point lying or evading because, like her best friend Eva, she knew he would keep pestering for an honest answer. "Got jumped a minute ago," she said.

He somehow turned even more pallid and took a few steps toward her. His dog Shadow followed, attention alternating between the two humans as he searched for clues how to react. Kai absently stroked the dog's ear. Her boy's already dark eyes had turned black.

"Did you banish it?" he asked, voice a little frightened.

After her troubles, once she'd healed a few months and eventually became willing to ask for help, Torrie Lujan—so old no one actually knew his age because he had outlived so many—had taught her the banishment "trick" that had worked better than anything she'd tried. She wasn't the first to wonder if the Pueblo man held shaman powers. When asked if he did, the ancient elder's already deep wrinkles would crinkle at his eyes and mouth, amused by the assumption. *"Mee-be. Been many years on this earth. Seen ever-ting. Ever-ting and more. Got nowhere to be. Time to listen. Heard every story from every man, woman, child. Warrior, midwife, politician, gravedigger."*

Their people would tell him he should write a book. Teach the world about all he'd learned, which brought even bigger grins and adamant refusals. *"Their mysteries die with me."* Most likely the reason Pueblos of every age talked to the wise man. Secrets. Held by one man alone. The single person who could be trusted not to gossip.

"I did," Paloma said. "All good now."

Kai released a deep breath and the light returned to his eyes. He returned to studying the piles of clothes laid out on the bed.

"Are you going somewhere for a week?" she asked, doing her best to hide the amusement from her voice.

"Can't decide what to wear for the vigil."

"Hoodie, jeans, white T-shirt, belt, sneakers." Paloma pointed out each item as she identified them.

"Yeah, you're right. Why change perfection." He turned his head and gifted her with his cherished smile.

Worn out from the long walk, she tried to hide her limp as she went to the bed, picked up the nixed clothing, then crossed to the dresser.

"What's up?" Kai asked.

Hesitant to tell him what had been on her mind, she said, "Will you be all right? You know . . . seeing Nathan tomorrow?"

"Not looking forward to it." His head snapped up and he turned his full attention on his mother. "Will you be all right?"

Apprehension tapped in her chest. "Yes," she said, turning away so he couldn't see her nervous uncertainty. "It'll be good for you to be there for the Trujillos."

"Thought it was for Nathan."

"Yes, but Pabla and Gabriel need you most." She looked at Shadow, lying a couple of feet from his person. "And Shadow, too." The dog swished his tail at the mention of his name. "A lot of our people will be there tonight. Promise you'll be careful to guard your heart."

Kai chuckled. "You make it sound like we'll be seeing bad Pueblos."

Paloma had seen "bad" people. Spent too much time around them. Nearly killed by more than a few. "Not bad. But some may not be for-giving. Because of me. And what happened."

Although the tribe had seemed to forgive her, Paloma still felt shame when one of her people stared at her too long, spoke in whis-pers, avoided her gaze. Probably nothing to do with her, but the dis-comfort to be around more than a few people at a time continued to hang over her.

Her abandonment behavior toward her only child stopped further words. Over and over, Kai had promised he'd forgiven her too. She'd had a sickness, he knew. But the wounds still needed healing—for him, and her.

"Do you want to do something?" he asked. "Go somewhere?"

Reluctant to answer, she looked way so he couldn't read her again, and said, "No, I should stay here. Get my head around what's to come for the next couple days."

"Well, I know where you'll be. You're gonna wear out the brush on that gray of yours."

She chuckled, left the boy alone, and began the trek back to the barn to continue the steps she had been rehearsing ever since she'd received word about Nathan's death. A celebration and feast would already be in the planning stages. Special, like the boy lost to them forever.

As the former reigning hoop dancer, celebrated in four states, a slew of award sashes hidden in the back of her closet, she needed her moves to be perfect. Respectful of the life lost. Her own rebirth rising from the dancing flames, fueled by the loss of the little bear who would dance no more.

CHAPTER SIXTEEN
EVA

Paperwork all caught up for the day, waiting for word about when Nathan Trujillo's body would be delivered back to his parents, her mind kept turning back to the boy. Heart heavy, feeling more exhausted than the early evening hour warranted, she hung up the keys to the official pickup and pulled out the set for her 2000 Land Rover Discovery Series II she fondly called the Beast.

Head on a swivel, she drove US Highway 64 toward her favorite Mexican restaurant, paying attention to each driver who approached and then whizzed by, wondering each time if they could be the elusive bank robber every LEO in the state by now searched for. Not that she knew what one would look like. She hadn't encountered that type of crime over her entire eight-year career for the sheriff's department, first as a dispatcher and 911 operator, working her way up the ranks to deputy, and certainly not during her yearlong stint so far as a tribal cop.

Five minutes later, comforting aromas of chiles, beans and chimichangas from the deep fryer met her as she stood at the hostess station waiting for her order of enough food to stuff four people. Stomach growling, she texted three words to Cruz.

TAMALES FROM ORLANDO'S?

His reply came almost as fast as she sent the message.

WHEN AND WHERE?
GRANDPA'S IN 20.

A thumbs-up emoji popped on the screen and she smiled, anticipating his company as much as the food.

She caught excited snippets of chatter about the bank robbery and what they would do with the money if such a feat could be pulled off, but overheard not a single concern about the cop shot or sympathy for the terror the tellers must have endured.

Then she grew sad and tired and upset. To keep her mind from spinning, she took out her phone again and tapped a text to Officer Kotz.

CHECKING IN.

Bubbles below her message appeared for a moment, then his reply came through.

FEDS SUCK
YOU OK?

No reply came to that inquiry.

NEED ANYTHING?
MY LADY TO BE ALL RIGHT

Her heart sank, feeling his pain.

BE STRONG. I'M HERE FOR YOU.

Nothing else followed from him and she figured he would provide more details when he felt level enough to share.

She closed her eyes and imagined the wounded officer lying on a hospital bed. Surely IVs had been inserted. Gauze covering the surgical site. Cannula in her nostrils to maintain the oxygen input level. At least one machine monitoring vitals. Or maybe worse—intubated and in a medically induced coma. Her hunger dissipated, as if in sympathy for Nadine Tallow's unknown condition.

Stop, she warned herself. Hoping for a successful distraction, she turned to look at the patrons at the nearby tables. She recognized a few locals from her community and wondered if they knew about Nathan yet. Again her mood plummeted and she felt more tired than if she'd run a marathon.

"Duran," a voice called out, rescuing her from the gloom that threatened to ruin her evening.

She took the take-out bags, thanked the hostess, palmed a ten-dollar bill to her favorite waitress as she walked past, then strode toward her vehicle, doing her best to ignore the raucous beer and margarita crowd at the outdoor tables.

Secured inside the Beast, the rich aromas of her favorite foods made her stomach growl. Her appetite returned as she pulled out of the parking lot.

Again she searched. Always searching. For answers, reasons, motives of why people did what she'd often heard them proclaim to have no control over.

Unsure of what she would find. If anything at all.

CHAPTER SEVENTEEN
TOMÁS

Tomás dropped to his couch, careful not to dump the lava-hot double-serving bowl of microwave mac and cheese topped with sliced vienna sausages on his lap. Once settled, he took up the TV remote and clicked on the local channel broadcast out of Santa Fe.

He tuned out one annoying commercial after another while he waited for the evening news to come on, blew on a steaming forkful of cheesy goodness. He popped the bite in his mouth and thought about the impromptu meeting with Simon Optum. The demand for him not to open the leather duffel continued to worry Salas. Anything could be in there, but he didn't dare pull the zipper and look inside. The guy probably had a camera hidden in there, just waiting to catch Tomás in the betrayal. Unwilling to face the consequences, he pushed the bag from his mind and settled back on the couch cushion.

He still puzzled over Optum's parting shot, *We're gonna be so stinkin' rich.* Salas didn't want to be rich. He wanted a successful venture. Sure, extra funds would be helpful, but what he craved, anticipated, needed most was to see his paper drawing and software designs come to life. Full-scale size. The perfect structure being produced, efficient machines churning out precise rows of cement that rose to the deep-blue New Mexico sky.

The final intent, to hand the keys to the one person he wanted to express gratitude to most. Kai Arrio. The biology student had been one of the brightest lights that shone in what had been much of his entire miserable life.

Salas tried to be reasonable about Optum's plan of how the evolution of Tomás's mastermind intent should evolve. Patience at the top of the list. But it had been three years since he first pitched the idea to his partner and all he'd received so far was promises. No paperwork—the businessman didn't want to risk any tax consequences. Nothing but a handshake to seal the deal—no LLC structured, again to dodge potential tax repercussions. No actual percentage breakdown when the venture became fruitful—maybe a fifty-fifty split. Probably not, Salas figured, after Optum's diatribe about how little the idea meant to the overall success.

What Salas had done to get this close to completing his goal was a different matter. Something he shushed away the second realization started to creep in. The printed gun frames and parts that made them complete units. And profitable. Although a danger, for sure, on so many levels.

Now that he'd had time to think, he felt a little better about himself that the gun hadn't worked. Four misfires, according to Simon Optum. A complete failure. Which meant, more than likely none of the knock-offs were viable. Maybe he should make sure they never would be. It would be easy to re-alter the software fix he'd made that morning. But doing so would put him in danger—one pissed-off buyer and he'd be out of business . . . or worse.

The dead drug dealer and his minions came to Tomás's mind. The press had reported that 3D printed guns had been found at the location of the deaths. That their killer had been put away and probably would never get out of the Santa Fe prison. But what if the press got it wrong?

Maybe the cops changed the story. Hid the truth so they could catch the actual murderer.

"The shooter could have used one of my guns. I'd never know," he muttered to himself, his mind beginning a spinout that sometimes took hours to talk himself down from.

That moment, the newscaster's voice halted his dark thoughts.

"In Taos this morning, a police officer was shot during a bold robbery at Alvarado Bank on Kit Carson Road."

The scene cut to video footage of police vehicles parked up and down the Taos street, yellow tape creating a barrier that blocked off the end of the road.

"There are no known suspects and the single gunman remains at large at this time."

Tomás wasn't sure why, but an ominous feeling overtook him and for a moment he forgot how to swallow the congealed pasta in his mouth. Hands shaking, Tomás set the bowl down, reached for the remote, turned up the volume.

"Also related to Taos this morning," the anchor continued, "a tender age boy from the area was fatally shot in Santa Fe while attending a school field trip at the Museum of Indian Arts and Culture. Due to the child's age, we will not be revealing the victim's name. No charges have been filed against the museum's security guard. We will keep you posted about this unfortunate shooting when we receive more details."

He stood up and started to pace. "No. Can't be related," he muttered to himself. "Can't be. They didn't report anything about 3D guns during either news story. You're just being paranoid."

He raised the remote, smacked his forehead with it a few times, continued his spin around the tight area in front of the TV set.

"There's no way. No way."

His guns didn't work. Optum had been certain on that matter, and clearly pissed off about it.

But if even one *did* happen to work . . .

"No. Stop it. Just stop. This has nothing to do with you." Salas shook his head and dropped back to the couch, took up his bowl, clicked to a different station. Moments later, he tuned out the raging what-ifs and lost time watching the DIY show demonstrating examples of different flooring types that would be perfect for his showcase house on the reservation.

CHAPTER EIGHTEEN
CRUZ

Cruz crossed the reservation in his official vehicle as the sun dropped lower in the western sky, calmed by the scent of sagebrush and sights of flowering plants in the occasional yards he passed. He savored this favorite time of the day, and favorite season, before the cold set in and drove most people inside and made his job even more challenging. He accelerated the pickup in anticipation of sharing tamales and time with his favorite person, thinking what could be better?

The only thing he didn't look forward to was the sight of the remains of Eva's grandfather's house. The burnt-out shell always reminded him of the arson cases he had investigated in the past. No one had died during the actual fire, but he and his colleagues assumed three Pueblo women had spent their final days and moments there. Where Paloma had nearly perished as well. An unseen fist squeezed his heart every time he imagined their fear.

After the final turn, he spotted Eva's Rover ahead. Back door open, she sat on the bumper, legs swinging in the dead space above the ground. He considered stopping to watch her awhile, but she raised a white bag and his mouth salivated knowing the goodness that awaited.

He tried to avoid taking a closer look at the charred two-by-fours stripped of drywall. The caved-in roof that littered the foundation. The only things recognizable the toilet and cast-iron bathtub in the middle of the rubble. Nothing salvageable—not even the beehive fireplace in the corner of the front room where as kids he and Eva and Paloma had roasted marshmallows on sticks her grandfather would carve to fine points for them.

Eva had often told him this was where she had spent almost every single good memory, growing up beside her grandpa. He knew she didn't plan to continue living in the city of Taos, didn't want to rent a place from someone else, that she needed to be closer to her work and people on the rez. He wanted to help her, even had a lockbox full of tools in the back of his truck, flat shovels to scoop up the mess, jugs of water ready to quench thirsts and wash away muck and maybe even tears.

The rebuild would be emotional. Nothing would be the same as what had perished in the flames. He figured maybe that was why she had waited to get started. She could be as stubborn as him and he knew that pushing her risked driving her away. She needed time to figure out when the universe was ready to show her a sign to get started. So he waited. Something he was very good at.

He parked beside her ride, got out of the DPS pickup and approached her. Six-pack of Bow & Arrow Native Land in one hand, two bottles of orange pop in the other. She teared up—he hoped only because she was touched that he would remember Kai had once told them that was little Nathan's favorite drink.

Comfortable in their relationship after knowing each other since toddlers, silence was their primary mode of communication. He popped up to sit beside her and tried to be patient while she took her time digging out to-go containers. She handed one to him and they waited a beat, then simultaneously cracked open the lids, closed their eyes, breathed in deep.

Both uttered a drawn-out *"Ahhhh."*

The beer, kissed by a hint of blue corn, complemented the Mexican food to perfection and Cruz relaxed for the first time all day.

He finished his three tamales in the time she ate one of her own, then gave her the puppy-dog eyes that got her every time. She slid half of a cheese enchilada to his plate and he winked at her.

After they scraped their containers clean, bagged the trash, polished off their beer, Cruz opened the orange soda. Yet to speak a full sentence, they clinked the bottles together, toasting the boy's memory, continued the silence so they could replay fond memories of the young Pueblo as they sipped the drink so sweet his teeth tingled.

"How's Kotz?" he finally said. "Partner's still alive, right?"

"Yeah, he would have mentioned that when I texted him. He didn't offer much. Said 'Feds suck.' That's it."

Cruz couldn't recall a single time he'd had a halfway decent experience dealing with a governmental agency when they had been invited on the reservation to assist in an investigation. Everyone became suspicious when the black four-by-fours, windows tinted so dark no one could see in, driving way too fast on the dirt roads of the sovereign land arrived. Never fewer than three massive SUVs at a time, four agents or investigators to a vehicle. All "experts" in the field of evidence gathering, computer programs that required special clearance to access, spouting lingo that meant nothing to the tribal cops.

The assistance often turned contentious and Cruz didn't remember any cases solved due to their efforts over the years. The missing women and teens continued to be missing. Pueblos raped, beaten, sometimes murdered by outsiders trespassing on the rez never arrested.

"He's not wrong about the feds," he said through gritted teeth. "Heard anything else about the robbery?"

"Guy's still in the wind, far as I know."

"Feds'll be pissed about that."

"Think they'll want to talk to the Trujillos about Nathan's death?"

Cruz blinked hard a few times. He hadn't considered that to be a possibility. "Prob'ly not. Sounds like there were enough bystanders to corroborate. There's no doubt the security guard shot Nathan. Also no doubt Nathan pulled out what appeared to be a gun."

"Think that's true?" Eva asked in a low voice. "Wouldn't be the first time a brown kid was falsely accused of something."

"Lots of witnesses."

"Yeah," she whispered, regret in her tone.

He wasn't sure if he should tell Eva what else troubled his mind. Didn't want to wreck her day further. The phone call an hour ago had been a surprise, about a favorite cousin and good friend. Someone he and his brothers would do anything for. Lily Bernal. The smart but unconfident girl who still shied away from praise. She had never had a steady boyfriend that Cruz could recall. Didn't frequent bars in town or hang out with more than one friend at a time—if at all. He knew she preferred her own company at her little house on the rez, where she lived alone.

Curious if Eva already knew the detail, thinking maybe she had heard something he wasn't yet aware of, he decided to say, "Lily Bernal was one of the tellers at the bank."

Eva whirled to stare open mouthed at Cruz, obviously shocked by the revelation. "Littlefeather? Is she all right?"

He shrugged. "Her brothers and uncle will be out hunting."

"Yeah, that's what we need. Vengeful relatives."

She stared out at the horizon awhile and he thought that might be the end of their conversation that had barely started. Then she surprised him when she said, "Did she tell you anything helpful? Maybe a description? Direction where he went? If it was a man?"

"She's not answering my calls. Sounded like the feds pressed her pretty hard at the scene. Prob'ly doesn't want to talk to any more cops."

"She's your cousin. Family. Should we go see her—not in uniform?"

"Pretty sure her house is full of people by now. Don't want to push it. Sure as shit we don't want to be hit with a thousand questions about what's next and why haven't we caught the asshole who terrorized our girl."

"We can't catch a break today," she muttered. "How are the other tellers doing?"

"They're not from our community. Don't know. Shook up as Lily, I bet."

Eva lowered her head and crossed her arms high against her chest. "I don't want to talk about this stuff anymore."

"Me neither."

They swung their legs in unison, eyes forward to watch the sun sink lower to the horizon.

After a few minutes he changed the subject to one he was curious to hear about. "Decided what you want to do with the place?"

She shrugged. "Rebuild. The foundation is still sound."

"Sure you want to do that? Spirits and all?" He pointed ahead. "Maybe start over at the edge of the property line?"

"The water well wasn't corrupted, so that'll save me some bucks if I don't reroute any pipes. Anyway, right here is where Grandpa chose. His is the spirit I don't want to upset."

Cruz knew all about distressed spirits. Had been chased by more than a few over the years due to his reckless or thoughtless actions. "I can get a group together. We'll have everything taken down and hauled away in a weekend. Everyone will want to help. We can make it a celebration."

Eva smirked. "Celebration of what?"

"Getting beyond a truly shitty situation."

"It really was. But I'm not beyond it. Not even close. I think about what happened here every day. Thought I wouldn't. That the memories of all the good times living here with Grandpa would drive away the darkness."

"Gonna take time," he muttered.

She released a drawn-out sigh. "I'm not sure if I can keep doing this."

Dreading the worst of what she could say, Cruz held a breath so long his lungs burned. Fearing she meant she wanted to end their relationship, he said, "What do you mean?"

"I don't want to ever have to tell a family their child is dead. Never again."

"But you know we will," Cruz said.

His love lowered her head and nodded, hair draping forward to hide her expression and maybe the tears that rarely fell down her perfect cheeks.

They sat in silence for a while, then he said, "The driver is supposed to be at the Trujillos' first thing in the morning."

"He'll need the burial clothes. I'll meet him there. Wanna make sure they're all right too. Kai and Shadow will go with me."

"Kai and the pup will be good company."

She gave him a sidelong glance. "The chief already knew Santiago set up the preparations."

He didn't tell Eva that he had been the one to tell Lefthand about the arrangement, or that Santiago felt it would be best for the heads-up not to come directly from him. Cruz wasn't sure if his current lady knew how close he and his previous partner had actually become, when they worked together on the force a few years ago, before Lefthand was appointed chief of police. Sure as hell he didn't want to chance squashing the good place they were with their relationship. Didn't want the risk of his apparently unwarranted envy about her and city cop Kotz to blow back on him.

"I'll meet you there, in case the driver has any questions," he said.

Her feet hit the ground and she prepared to leave. It might not have been the right time, but he needed to gauge her heart before he left. "Your folks are still in Santa Fe, right?" he asked, hoping he hadn't reopened a wound.

Eva's body tensed beside him. He wondered if the parents she hadn't seen in years ever scratched at the back of her thoughts, if now they would be all she could think about.

"Wanna ask the chief again to be the escort?" he asked. "Maybe you could see your parents while you're there."

"No point wasting time on them," she snapped.

"Right," he said, but he didn't think she sounded at all convincing.

CHAPTER NINETEEN
TOMÁS

Tomás thrashed the sheets, tried to get comfortable, failed for a full hour before he gave up on sleep and went to the kitchen to pour a glassful of soda and grab what remained of a bag of barbecue potato chips.

He sat in the dark at the table, opened the lid to his computer, signed on, then searched for updated articles and YouTube videos related to 3D home building. He watched a few but found it impossible to focus. The news reports of the bank robbery and death of the boy from Taos kept niggling at him and he couldn't turn off his brain.

Then Kai's mother Paloma crowded his thoughts, bringing him welcome relief from his unease. Now that he had seen her, he regretted all of the missed opportunities to get to know the most stunning Pueblo woman he'd ever encountered, who had been absent from all sixteen parent-teacher meetings throughout Kai's high school years, as his student.

He sighed, closed the open tabs to his housing sites, typed PALOMA ARRIO DANCE in the search bar, waited as hundreds of options loaded, clicked on the clip noting the highest number of views.

He sat back and watched, unsure if he took a breath or blinked the entire three-minute dance segment. He hit the play arrow again. His heartbeat thrummed with the drumbeat, heel of his foot keeping time.

The filming angle wasn't tight on the three women featured, but the dancer in the middle resembled Kai so he kept his full interest on her.

Riveted, he watched the moves and after the tenth viewing he had memorized the entire routine. Feathers and beads and bells, all of the sights and sounds resonated deep within him.

He had attended a few of the public powwows on the Taos Pueblo in the past and now wished he had paid more attention. Maybe he'd even seen the woman the announcer called "White Dove" dance at one of those events.

Another plan evolved, bloomed, the vision so clear. The house he would build first. He could almost smell the air tinged with smoke from the fireplace that awaited them to discover in the front room. The one for White Dove and her son. He'd always wanted to be a father. And what better child than Kai? Well, not a child—but even a young man needed a role model. Being his mentor had been his greatest achievement as a teacher.

He had never been struck numb by a woman such as Paloma Arrio. Not by passion—not yet. He knew how to wait, to be patient, to be ready. Most likely more of a dream. But why not reality? They could be a family.

The urgency to officially get started on the new life that awaited prompted him to take action. A need as raw as any he'd felt before. He took up his cell phone and dialed Simon Optum's number. After the sixth ring the connection went to voice mail. Only a high-pitched tone. No prompt to leave a message. He frowned, looked at the phone, confused. That had never happened before. Although the man never picked up the phone as soon as Salas called, he could rely on the confident man's voice leaving precise instructions to leave a message. Tomás sent a text next.

HOW'S THE INVESTOR MEETING SCHEDULE GOING? DO YOU HAVE A DATE YET?
WHAT CAN I DO TO HELP?

He hit the blue arrow to send and waited. And waited. Five minutes, ten.

Again, he tried:

?????

The man from Chicago had always been quick to answer his texts until now—had often told Salas, *No matter what time, hit me if you have any questions or come up with something helpful for me to sell this idea to investors.*

Salas frowned, eyes on the phone, waiting for the dancing bubbles to assure him an answer would be forthcoming.

The need to rest took hold. Too exhausted to rise from the chair, he laid his head on his crossed arms atop the table, reached over and tapped the keyboard to play Paloma "White Dove" Arrio's video again. His eyes fluttered closed, a smile on his lips. The dancer whirled and spun and dove in his mind as he drifted off.

Joyful for the first time since he could remember.

CHAPTER TWENTY
SIMON

Simon Optum stood on Lily's front porch, door open in case the woman called out for him. Optum checked his phone and thought about calling Salas, who had left ten voice mails and twice that many texts—all ramping up in intensity as the hours passed.

In too good of a mood to be bothered with his freaked-out partner, instead he lit a cigarette and replayed his achievement that had gotten him to where he now stood.

Wooing the Indian woman had been one of his easiest victories to date. He figured she must be pretty desperate to completely lose herself in a total stranger. Then again, how could she refuse?

As she'd opened the front door, he raised the cheap bouquet of flowers and gave her his most charming smile. She fawned over them, as if they were long-stem red roses. He gave her the whole "Sometimes it's easier to talk to a stranger" bullshit, spoke real sweet, put on his patience hat.

When he'd made it inside the house, she offered him coffee and he pulled out her chair at the kitchen table and insisted he'd make a pot for her. It didn't take long for her to tell him everything about the robbery. How she was so scared and ashamed that she didn't even try to stop the man with the gun because she'd completely forgotten about the panic button right under the cash drawer. She could have saved that cop if she'd done what she had been trained for. She didn't want to see anyone close to her because they would know what a failure she was.

After she settled, exhausted from her distress, he laid it on thick— told her all the crap he knew would calm her down. The syrupy bullshit to make her trust him and believe he was there for her. Promised her she was safe. He wouldn't let anything happen to her now. He would stay close and protect her.

He held her as she cried, then sobbed, then screamed—enraged that she'd had to go through this, and worried about the cop who may or may not be dead.

And then she kissed him.

Urgent and needy.

And *then* . . . the quickest lay agreement in history.

He let out a satisfied sigh and considered going back into the house to go another round. But first he needed to move his vehicle. He glanced at his Breitling. 11:52. He convinced himself it shouldn't be a problem, if he kept to the shadows.

No lights lit up the windows of any houses as he walked past and he only heard a single dog bark, thankfully from inside one of them. He halted his slow pace every time he heard an unfamiliar sound, then proceeded on at an equally measured rate.

He tucked up tight to a long fence at the edge of the street and soon made it to the intersection that led to the ticket booth and the little shack at the edge of the parking lot. Anxious to see his vehicle, he hurried up, took the final turn, and was almost blinded by a bright light atop a pole in the middle of the lot.

Even approaching midnight the area still held a lot of cars and it took him a minute to locate his BMW, dwarfed by a mud-caked jacked-up pickup truck. He heard an engine, took a few steps back and tucked between a thick row of hedges that reminded him of his hiding place right after the bank robbery.

An old Land Rover pulled to the edge of the lot and parked, then a female dropped from the seat to land her cowboy boots on the dirt.

He froze when he realized the woman wore a cop uniform. Taller and leaner than Lily, this woman looked fit and capable. He stared at her, intrigued by her confidence and purpose.

He must have made a sound because she turned around—the metal badge glinting from the streetlight. Optum swore she looked right at him. He held still as sweat trailed down his sides and he forced down a sneeze from the dusty foliage.

Finally she stepped deeper into the lot, lifted a portable radio in her hand, and said, "Dispatch, I've got eighteen vehicles at the visitors' lot. Probably here preparing for Nathan Trujillo's vigil, but we should keep an eye on them. All have New Mexico, except one. BMW late-model two-door, silver, no body damage, Illinois plates."

Then the woman cop rattled off license plate numbers as she assessed each vehicle—including his own—and waited for a response.

"Got it," the tinny voice replied. "Chief said to head home if you checked in. Big day tomorrow."

"Copy. Duran out."

The woman cop lingered, giving his sterling Beemer way too much attention. He gritted his teeth the entire time she made a full circle around the car, looked in every window, even under the vehicle. He thought for sure she would reach for the door handle to see if it was unlocked—like cops in Chicago would do, with or without cause—and was surprised when she didn't.

Something about the woman cop troubled him. Maybe her self-assurance, unafraid to be on her own in the dead of night. But when she'd looked his direction he swore she knew he was there lurking. Not someone. The man who had caused a lot of trouble for cops and had vanished into thin air. *Him*.

The cop surely hadn't actually caught sight of him, but Optum felt trapped. And seen. Like never before. He should get in the car, leave everything at Lily's behind, drive the opposite direction from the cop, go to the main road and get the hell out of the whole damned state. But now the tribal department was on alert about the cars in the lot and his might be identified if he risked leaving the reservation.

He chuckled and waved away his unwarranted apprehension as he jogged to his car, anticipating Lily's warm naked body in the bed where he would join her in a few minutes. He feathered the gas pedal so the powerful engine would only purr rather than roar, and accelerated just enough to coast all the way to Lily's without hitting the brakes.

He parked behind the house, got out, and pulled at the shirt stuck to his back soaked with nervous sweat. Confident no one would spot the Beemer from the street, Optum lit another cigarette.

But he didn't relax because he knew, for the first time since he could remember, he might have a formidable adversary.

And now, she had his plates.

CHAPTER
TWENTY-ONE
EVA

Eva woke an hour before dawn. With a mug of fresh-brewed tea in hand, she went over the list in her mind of what to prepare for that day, and hoped she hadn't forgotten anything.

Dressed in jeans, button-down shirt, well-worn cowboy boots, hair loose and flowing to her waist, she had considered wearing her uniform—to show respect for the Trujillos or anyone else she might encounter—but decided not to emphasize her position as a tribal cop until she was officially on duty to keep watch over the upcoming vigil.

Keep it light, she reminded herself, then promised herself she would try. In case anyone needed a reminder she wasn't to be messed with, she tucked her badge wallet in her back pocket.

She wished her friend and former mentor Dr. Tavis Mondragon had been the medical examiner appointed to perform the autopsy in Santa Fe. He would be honest with her and let her know if something seemed off about what caused Nathan's fatal injury. Any hidden evidence she should be aware of. But when she called to request his assistance, as he had last year, he informed her the district attorney in Albuquerque had tied him up with a particularly tricky quadruple homicide.

Her nerves ruffled at the edges as she thought about what could go wrong—lack of communication being first. Outside agencies weren't always forthcoming when dealing with the tribal community. Almost as if her people were considered a different species. Mysterious and clandestine. She could only hope the representative of the tribe would be able to carry out his instructions and bring Nathan home as soon as possible.

Attending to the final vigil and burial tasks meant she could be away until late that night or maybe even through the next day. She made up the bed and went to the kitchen, where she emptied the water kettle, downed the last of her lukewarm tea, then unplugged the television set in case one of the area's all-too-often power outages occurred.

As she zipped up her jacket and locked up the front door, Eva's thoughts kept drifting to Nathan. Memories of watching the little boy play with Shadow in the grass pasture by Santiago's barn, Kai showing him how to discern one plant from another, Cruz's smile as he watched along with her. Iridescent black flowing hair, somewhat feminine features, but all boy inside and out—a fearless kid who could race and maneuver his BMX bicycle faster and more daringly than anyone twice his age.

She couldn't share any of this with Paloma, who had kept her distance from Nathan, still shamed by what Little Bear must have witnessed while she did whatever it took to feed her addiction when she bought and used drugs at the Trujillo house while the dealers had set up their operation there.

The brisk morning air stung her cheeks as she made her way to the Beast. She inhaled the fresh scent of pine, surprised by the faint cloud that drifted from her mouth when she exhaled. At the Rover, she opened the rear compartment, removed the clip holster that contained her Glock and two loaded magazines from the bag. Then she unlocked the built-in gun safe bolted to the floor near the door, and secured her weapon inside the steel case.

The magpie Kai had named Rio, closest thing to a pet Eva had, swooped overhead, landed on the fence post at the edge of her drive, greeted her with its high-pitched squawk as it did every morning and evening.

"Keep an eye on the place, Rio," Eva said to the bird.

As if in understanding, the bird let out an earsplitting screech and flicked its tail at her as she pulled out of the driveway, unsure when she would see the winged creature again.

CHAPTER
TWENTY-TWO
KAI

Saturday's early-morning dawn met Kai as he sat beside his uncle Santiago on the front porch of the family home. He huddled in the heavy jacket over his hoodie. The temperature had dropped overnight and Kai tucked in tight against the warmth of Shadow, who sat between the men, eyes ahead, tongue lolling, clouds of steam bursting from his mouth with every huff.

Kai absentmindedly stroked his companion's back and kept thinking about his first sighting of Nathan Trujillo. On his motorbike late one night, the headlight had hit a dark figure on the rez, too small for a man, too big for a coyote. The being sprinted across the road and vanished, as if an apparition had crossed his path. The second time was when his mother's and the little boy's nightmare ended—when Nathan's parents had been released from their captivity in the Trujillo house.

After the ordeal, Kai checked in on Nathan every day. They spent endless weekend hours deep on the reservation, where Kai would teach his unofficial pupil all about the plants and how they could save, or take, lives.

Kai wasn't sure how his days would be without the company of the kid he'd been mentoring. The little brother he never had by blood.

Would never have again by friendship. As if knowing he needed a little reassurance, Shadow leaned in shoulder to shoulder, dipped his snout under Kai's neck and nudged him for a snuggle.

Santiago hadn't said anything since they took their places outside, then the floodgates of conversation flung open, his uncle asking questions as fast as Kai could answer them. *He's nervous,* Kai thought. Then he wondered if he should be too.

The time spent with his uncle usually didn't include talking, and never senseless banter. Santiago's all-business, show-them-nothing personality could be off-putting, but after spending more than a year living together, often never leaving the property except for classes, Kai knew the tribal councilman wore his aloofness as armor.

"If we run into any obstacles getting Little Bear home, would you be willing to go with Eva to Santa Fe?"

Kai frowned, confused by the request. "Yeah, sure, whatever Eva needs."

"Probably won't need to, but you and Shadow would be good company to her."

"Maybe I could meet her parents."

Santiago did a slow pivot of his head to look directly at Kai. "Who told you about them?"

"Mom did, a while back. I don't remember them at all."

"Been gone a long time. Way before you were born."

"Did you know them?"

"Thought I did. Her dad was my high school track coach. We were tight. Taught me a lot. He was training to qualify for the Olympic team." Santiago lit up a rare smile. "Man, he was fast. Supposed to bring home the gold medal to the tribe. Make everyone proud."

His uncle rarely shared anything about his past. Kai gave him his full attention, anticipating what would come. "Yeah? Did he make it on the team?" Santiago shook his head and Kai leaned in closer. "What happened?"

"Eva." His uncle halted a beat. "Never saw Benito run again. Stopped coaching. Started learning how to sculpt and throw the clay. His dad was not happy."

"What was her name? Eva's mom."

Santiago raised an open hand for Kai to stop talking. "We don't say her name. Don't ask."

"Okaaay . . . What was she like?"

The man reverted to his usual stern bearing. "We never got along. She didn't like Paloma either. Don't know why, so don't—"

"Don't ask," Kai interjected. "Got it."

"We all loved Eva's grandpa like he was our own. He was her real family. All she ever needed."

"I get sad for Eva sometimes. Her grandpa died a long time ago. Who does she have now? For family."

"Us. She has the three of us. And Cruz." He reached over and playfully tried to pinch Shadow's tongue between his fingers. "And this guy here."

Up until last year, only his mom was good enough for him since his dad died. Considered to be a smart kid throughout school, he didn't have many friends. And like Eva, he had no siblings and figured that was why they made a good team.

"Why did her parents leave like that and never come back?" Kai asked. "Were they disenrolled or banished or something?" he joked.

"Something like that," his uncle muttered, which left Kai even more puzzled.

"Really? Are you saying—?"

Santiago sliced the air with his hand. A karate chop of finality. His uncle's thundercloud energy ramped up around him and even Shadow whimpered, puzzled by the switch in the human's attitude.

Although intrigued and a little nervous about knowing something he shouldn't, Kai stopped his inquiry. For now.

"I'm not sure why I'm going to the Trujillos' this morning."

"For Little Bear."

"Yeah, but . . ." He almost said, *The boy's dead so why does he need me?*

The look of concern left his uncle's expression. He reached over and draped his arm over the dog and squeezed Kai's shoulder. Kai froze, unsure how to react to the unaccustomed act of affection.

"Your friend's spirit will be scared. Being there for his parents is the first step to their healing. Whenever you can, assure Little Bear he'll be all right. That nothing and no one can hurt him now. That he is coming home. Home to his parents, those who love him, the people of our community. To the spirits who will guide him for now and forever."

When Santiago's voice cracked at the end, Kai looked away, too shy to show his shared grief.

Kai felt honored as he sat beside the wisest man he had ever had the privilege of finally getting to know. Proud of his bloodline and heritage, due mostly from what he had learned from his uncle—excited about what he would be taught in the future now that both had cracked open their wounded hearts.

Santiago pointed at a whirl of dust that rose to the lightening sky. "Here she comes," he said. "Blasting down the road like the daredevil she's always been."

Kai nodded, unsure if he really wanted to rush to the next phase of his life journey—the first steps for a dead boy's return, the raw emotions of his people when they gathered to receive and lay the boy to rest, the experience of the heart-shattering mourning of the parents he had grown fond of. He hoped he would not break in front of any of them.

But if he did, Kai now knew Santiago "Hawk Soars" Mirabal would understand. And be there for him.

CHAPTER
TWENTY-THREE
EVA

Eva pulled up in front of Santiago's house, where two men sat on the porch, Shadow between them. Kai waved when she got out of the Beast and the Malinois leaped the three steps to land on the ground and bound her way—a sideways gait of excitement, whipping tail, lolling tongue, body vibrating under his red training harness.

"Hey boy! Ready to go for a ride?"

The Malinois yipped, did three spins, and raised his paw for her to shake. Eva laughed, appreciating what would probably be the single light moment of the entire day.

She turned to Santiago. He didn't rise from the step, didn't even raise an index finger on the hand that rested on his knee. She gave him an upward nod and waited for the wave for her to join him, but it never came. He looked as grave as she felt.

She opened the Rover's back passenger's-side door and Kai snapped his fingers, pointed to the seat, and said, "Up." Satisfied the dog was secure, Kai got in the passenger seat.

"Will he be all right back there?" she asked, sliding behind the steering wheel.

Kai pivoted his torso to look at the dog. "You're good, aren't you, boy?"

The dog yipped and Eva felt certain she would never get used to the high pitch that pinged around her skull every time he let out his distinctive racket. She rubbed her right ear and winced.

"Shadow!" Kai said. "You're being too loud. Apologize."

The dog lunged forward and licked the full length of Eva's face.

"Gross," she said. "I don't know which was worse." She chuckled and wiped away the slick streak with the cuff of her sleeve.

Kai giggled and pulled his companion's face to his own, mashing their foreheads together. "You called him *my* dog yesterday. He's not mine."

"What do you mean?"

"Santiago is listed as his owner and trainer. It's an accreditation thing. The handler has to be certified for the dog to be classified as an official search and rescue animal. I'm not."

"Well, maybe you should work on that. You're really good with him."

Kai shrugged one shoulder, then went silent. She hoped he was considering the suggestion.

The next moment he looked a little wide eyed and couldn't seem to fit the latch plate of his seat belt into the buckle. Nervous about the unknown journey ahead, she supposed.

She waited until the *click*, then when she felt his anxiety fade, asked, "You ready?"

"Let's do it."

She studied him for a moment. His resolve did not falter. She fired up the powerful engine, waved to Santiago and proceeded the way she came.

Not a single word had been traded for a full five minutes and Eva felt the need to make sure Kai was coping all right with what could be a whirlwind of emotions. Hoping to get a conversation started, she decided to start with something generic, and said, "How's school?"

"Good," he said. "How's policing?"

"Good."

Again, the compartment fell silent a full minute before she said, "Whew! Glad we got the hard talk out of the way." She chuckled and glanced at Kai, who remained stone faced.

She gave him a cautious look. "Do you wanna talk about Nathan?"

He shrugged. Not a yes. Not a no.

Unsure if she should push, but fearing he would shut down entirely if she didn't, she said, "Paloma mentioned you were teaching him about plants."

"Yeah, a little bit. That terrarium I've got going, I started it for the Red Willow Center—for kids being tutored there so I could point out the cool plants around the rez. Hopefully get them interested in how they grow. But Nathan really liked learning and he listened to me—I mean really listened. Decided I'd gift it to him after the plants got bigger and stable enough to move to a new environment."

"Nathan probably appreciated spending time with you as much as finding out about the plants."

"I liked it too. We were tight. Like he was my little brother."

Kai went silent and even Shadow seemed sad.

After a few minutes, Kai surprised her when he said, "I think my high school biology teacher is crushin' on my mom. I asked him to come over to see the terrarium. Thought he'd like it. Takes up a lot of space so I keep it in the barn. Mom was there, 'cause you know . . . she's always there. Thought Mr. Salas was gonna faint when he saw her. Wouldn't stop staring at her. Totally distracted." He chuckled. "I think he forgot how to talk."

"Really? Would that be weird—the two of them maybe together?"

"So weird. Nothing will ever happen between them though."

"Why's that?"

"He'd have to get past Uncle Santiago."

"Yeah, probably right. Not happening anytime soon."

"Or ever," he said.

"Does it worry you that Santi is so protective of her?" she asked.

"Sometimes. But she needs protecting. Maybe always will."

"She's not a broken bird, Kai. She might surprise you both."

"I'd like that."

Kai reached in the pocket of his hoodie and took out the leather medicine bag he always kept with him, ran the fringe stitched at the bottom through his fingers. Eva had noticed him do this many times over the past months. An action that soothed him and seemed to keep his mind on track. She often thought of getting one made for herself and considered what she would put inside. Her grandfather's pocket watch for sure, maybe one of Rio's feathers, something treasured and gifted to her from Cruz and Paloma—there were many of those after over thirty years of friendship.

Kai's voice snapped her from her reverie. "What happens next?" he asked.

"Hopefully there won't be any issues releasing Nathan's body. Don't know how the autopsy turned out. Or if it's even happened yet."

"Do you think Nathan's death is suspicious?"

Eva didn't share what she immediately thought—that a brown kid's untimely death would always be suspicious until proven otherwise. Instead, she took the middle road and said, "Haven't heard much of anything at all. Playing the waiting game."

The statement seemed to placate the young man. They went quiet again and Eva thought about the possibilities of what she and her colleagues might encounter. If there would be a formal investigation into the boy's death. If they would release the body of Nathan to the Pueblo driver's custody, or if it would needed to be held as evidence. So many possibilities to consider, and no guarantee of learning crucial clues to her many questions.

Or maybe to receive any answers at all.

CHAPTER
TWENTY-FOUR
SANTIAGO

Santiago sat at his kitchen table looking out the floor-to-ceiling wall of windows that allowed an unobstructed view of the endless pristine mesa and the Sangre de Cristos. He glanced at the two cell phones side by side, a leather-covered notepad open to a sheet of jotted notes. Pen in hand, he considered what else he would need to attend to so his driver wouldn't encounter any delays or hitches while picking up Nathan Trujillo in Santa Fe.

Certain he'd thought of everything, which included making the most important phone call necessary to assure cooperation, he rose from the hand-hewn hardwood chair, knees popping as they always did when he sat too long, cursing the days as a much younger man that left his body creaking from injuries working the horses and careless stunts showing off for the women he wanted to impress.

His main concern was timing. Ideally the tribe would be able to hold the viewing ceremony that night, and perform the burial the following morning. But he was all too familiar with bureaucracy and he figured he might need to make another call to his politician contact if the transport man ran into a situation.

He closed the notebook, pocketed the cell phones and left the kitchen. For a reason he'd yet to pinpoint, his thoughts kept returning to Eva's parents. He'd been taken by surprise when Kai asked if he'd known the couple who hadn't returned in more years than Santiago could remember. He'd pushed their memory aside, and refused them space in his heart or soul.

He had been the one to tell Benito and Marcella to leave. *Go now,* he had warned that night when the entire world shifted under the threesome's feet. *Take what you can, I'll get the rest to you. Call me when you've found a new place.*

But they never did. Never reached out. Disappeared before any actual trouble could come their way. And it would, if they were ever to return. No one forgot on the rez. Tales, actual or made up, had a way of simmering, never truly erased. And over the years, as a high-ranking councilman, it had become his responsibility to remember former indiscretions so the past would not come back to haunt the present. And remind others of the consequences if punishments were not imposed. Eva's parents had yet to meet their judgments and face their penance.

He shook his head, knowing that he would need to step in. Drag the couple back to the reservation if necessary. Be the responsible party before the newly appointed tribal police chief, now privy to cold case files, got the itch to thoroughly investigate a case so raw the elders banned mention of the victim's name tied to the injustice.

He stood on the front porch, figuring Chief Lefthand had her hands full at the moment—bank robber on the loose, shot city cop, security team to assemble for Little Bear's vigil and burial.

"That'll keep her busy," Santiago muttered, unsure if it would be enough to divert the focus of the most dedicated, laser-focused law enforcer he had yet to meet.

CHAPTER
TWENTY-FIVE
EVA

They had encountered no vehicles on the rez road the entire eight-minute drive to their destination that early in the morning, and Eva was surprised by what she saw after she took the final turn. Just as Santiago promised, a gleaming black hearse waited in front of the Trujillo home.

A Native man unfamiliar to Eva, nearly bursting the seams of his black suit coat, stood at the rear of the Cadillac XTS. Foreboding and forbidding, he reminded Eva of a sumo wrestler awaiting instructions.

"Nice ride," Kai said, impressed. "Way to be, Uncle."

She slowed down to a respectful speed, and parked next to Cruz's TPPD truck near the front of the Trujillo house. She keyed on six older Natives huddled together—all dressed in traditional garb and draped in colorful shawls of high-ranking tribal members, hair wound in tight braids that trailed down their chests, heads bowed.

Nathan's parents stood at the open front door. Gabriel's arm draped around Pabla's waist, the grief-torn mother holding a short stack of neatly folded clothing. Burial clothes, Eva realized, and her heart stuttered as she imagined the little body dressed in the coverings.

Paco and Navi Barboa stood a respectful distance from the councilmen. The twins kept close together, Paco wiping away his tears with a blue bandana, a red one clutched in Navi's fist.

"You've got this, Lightning Dance," Kai said, the same words Eva gave him the day before, offered with twice the conviction.

She let out a ragged breath and prayed he was right.

The group of men stepped aside to reveal a rectangular rough-hewn wooden box. A low rumbling hum resonated from them.

"Did you know there would be a coffin?" Kai asked.

"No. Thought the driver would only be picking up Nathan's clothes." She nodded to the twins, who had yet to raise their heads. "Paco and Navi must have worked all night," Eva said, awed.

"It looks so tiny," Kai said, his voice soft and young.

"Nathan was small for his age."

Cruz stepped to the Rover and opened his arms, an *Are you coming?* gesture. She let out a relieved breath seeing him there, having her back as he always did. He would know she'd be nervous about encountering the grieving couple again, would offer to be the intermediary if necessary.

"You ready?" Kai whispered.

Eva smoothed her hair, took a deep breath, opened the door. A burst of wind caught her clothes as soon as her boots hit the dirt. She tucked a lock behind her ear and took cautious steps toward the group. No one said a word.

As she stepped closer, she caught sight of the design of a small bear's paw—the symbol of the boy's Native name—burned into the wood, above where Nathan's heart would be when placed inside the box. She trapped a sob in her chest.

Two men could have managed the load, and yet each knelt, lifted, and then all six as one, they raised the impossibly small box and carried it to the back of the awaiting hearse. The driver opened the rear door and the men slid the four-foot-long coffin into the cargo area.

Eva went to Nathan's parents, grateful they didn't ask her anything because she felt certain she wouldn't be able to speak beyond the lump lodged in her throat. She took the bundle of clothes from Pabla. The deerskin soft in her palms felt light yet substantial, beads flashing their colors, even in the dim early-morning light.

"Do you want Kai and Shadow to stay with you?"

Both shook their heads in unison, but Eva waited a beat to make sure they wouldn't change their minds.

"Be strong," she whispered to the devastated parents.

Impossible, she knew, but the customary words issued to those grieving would be expected. She carried the coverings to the driver, then returned to her vehicle.

Cruz sidled up next to the driver's side door. She belted herself in the seat and he closed the door. "Gonna be a long day," he said.

"We'll have to split up. Double-triple duty for everyone."

"Wish we could stay together today."

Eva squeezed his hand on the open window frame. "I'll miss you too, Wolf."

And she would. At least Kai and Shadow would be there to remind her to stay focused, be the Pueblo the tribe would want representing the community as they put the young Native to rest. Keep her from being so nervous about the upcoming events so that Paloma's son wouldn't be.

She hoped she could pull off the undertaking. A confidence she didn't quite feel.

CHAPTER
TWENTY-SIX
CELIO

Lost in his thoughts, focused on the scratch of pencil on paper, an urgent knock at the door startled Celio nearly out of the chair. He angled to see behind him. The door flung open and there stood his brother, filling up the doorway.

Hair styled short, no gel or product, no beard or tats, Manny didn't look like a threat while he stood inches away, big smile and bigger laugh, making a stranger feel at ease . . . as he pickpocketed his mark's wallet. Or broke into a vehicle within seconds to steal valuables hidden under a driver's seat and in the glove box. Maybe even poach the car too and drive it to the salvage yard near the Taos airport so he could strip it for parts to sell at an ask-no-questions shop in Española.

Manuel Novar had style, and a reputation, and rarely if ever got caught. He worked to maintain the cool and smooth outward appearance. But Celio knew the anger that boiled inside. Too well. He had the scars and broken bones to prove he always needed to be alert around his brother.

The house felt smaller when bigger-than-life Manny entered a room, but Abuela, who spoke no English and cooked three hot meals every day, thought both of her grandsons were perfect in every way. Celio knew otherwise.

His older brother had always been a troublemaker and now there were two others Celio had to worry about. The last couple of months, Manny was always joined by an Indian dude Manny called Tomahawk, and a guy who had a straggly beard that reached his chest, secured by a rubber band midway down, and smelled like stale cigarette smoke from a room away. Celio was pretty sure Cal was in love with Manny, who was clueless to the guy's stares—always watching, right next to the ringleader everywhere they went. The threesome made up a chilling group who wore their testosterone as if it were a matador's cape.

The man, who said he used to live on the reservation outside town, had been crashing with them for a few months now, but Celio didn't know him at all. The guy hardly ever spoke, and when he did it was only to ask his grandma a question. Celio didn't want to be jealous of the guy, who didn't seem to have any family, but he didn't like to share his abuela—not even with Manny.

As usual, this morning, Celio felt an urgency coming off his brother in waves. "Need you to call the guy for a pickup," Manny said, tossing a stuffed envelope on the bed. "A dozen tonight."

Celio slumped his shoulders, tried to be covert as he slid the notebook into the open drawer beside him. "'Kay. I'll let 'em know. Can you pay me this time?"

The older brother thrust a finger out and pointed. "I gave you that dirt bike. It's better than money. Don't think that's for free."

Yeah, the one you stole from that druggie guy, Celio thought but didn't dare say out loud.

"I don't . . . I just wish you'd pay me something. You're not doing it for nothing, right? I'm taking all the risk—"

Manny stormed across the room, grabbed the neck of Celio's shirt, jerked him from the chair to face his fury, raised his arm and backhanded the younger brother, catching his cheek and bottom lip. Celio wasn't sure what surprised him most—the viper-fast movements and strike or the loud smack of skin hitting his own.

Manny raised his closed fist, waved it an inch from Celio's nose. "Disrespect me again and you get a real beating. ¿Entendido, pedacito de mierda?"

Celio understood. And he wasn't a little piece of shit. His mother had told him many times before she left that his name meant "heavenly" and that she loved him more than anyone or anything else in the universe. His grandmother adored him too. Celio brought both women's faces to the forefront of his mind for support and tried not to cry.

"Call. Now," Manny roared, stormed to the door, shouldered past the Native dude who had probably watched and heard everything. The door slammed shut and Celio breathed out a sigh of relief to be alone again.

Celio got it—as a minor, if he got caught, he might end up in juvie, but not prison. Manny had already been locked up. Swore he'd never go back. So the younger Novar would be sacrificed if necessary. Celio had no delusions about that.

The realization stung him every time he thought about taking the fall for someone who didn't even appreciate what was at stake for him. The threats coming from his brother made it that much more painful. Celio could lose what little he had. A chance as the first person in his family to go to college and eventually make a salary. Legit money. Health care for his grandma who needed new knees after standing for twelve hours at a time cooking the delicacies locals craved.

He wanted to be a chef one day. To make his mother's mother proud. Not a cook at a fast-food place. A real restaurant. Tablecloths and stainless steel knives and forks kind of place.

First he needed to survive. And to do that, he needed to protect himself from the assholes who bullied him at school—called him fat and useless and a beaner. His ears burned and he clenched his fists thinking about the students, some younger than him, who picked on him endlessly. If they had known who his brother was they probably would leave him alone. But Celio wasn't a snitch. And anyway, Manny and his two thugs were the ones who could do him the most harm.

He picked at an inflamed cuticle with his ragged fingernail until a spot of blood bubbled from the wound. The sharp hurt there eased the ache in his cheek and his lip and his heart. A release, if only for a minute. He ran his tongue over his lip and tasted iron as he thought about his situation.

An idea came to him he couldn't believe he hadn't thought of before. No one but Celio and the man who made the guns knew about the secret drop-off location. Celio made sure of that. Never told Manny, who didn't want to know. *Plausible deniability,* his brother had told him. Showing off like he was some TV lawyer or something.

He took up the envelope, peeked at the thick stack of twenties inside. Thousands of bucks. Thought about taking the money. Run. Get on the dirt bike and go. Leave the assholes to the assholes. But then what would his abuela do? What would she think if her other treasure in life disappeared? He could never return. Ever. And so he sighed, resigned to the fact he had nowhere to go and no future. Only the here and now.

He turned his attention to what had brought him to what had now become his job. It hadn't been hard to find a place for the drop-off and pickup location even his brother's *pendejo matones* didn't know about. Five minutes from the high school and six minutes the other direction from his house, the abandoned hotel had been closed for years. Fencing wrapped around the entire property, but Celio had no trouble cutting through the chain-link off to the farthest side, away from the street.

He had often spied on the gunman, who would park at the burger place right next door, and no one would know he had actually slipped through the cut fence and jogged around back to replace the cash envelope with a box of plastic guns everyone seemed to want.

And really, all he needed was *one* of those pistols. To keep his tormentors away. Help show him a little respect. Shut them all up. Even his brother if he had to.

Yeah, Celio thought. *I could do that.*

He took the notebook out of the drawer and started drawing again. Guns this time. One after the other—realistic down to the custom stippling on the grips, just like he had seen in real life every time he picked up a delivery.

Then he wrote out the name of the man who made the knock-offs. Over and over, hoping the repetitive spelling of the name and the motion of his pencil scratching paper moving up his hand, arm, shoulder, neck, would burn into his brain.

Satisfied his plan would work, he took out a flip phone from his pocket and tapped out a text to one of the two numbers saved in the burner.

CHAPTER
TWENTY-SEVEN
TOMÁS

As Tomás tried to come up with an excuse to offer Paloma Arrio for his visit, he stacked twelve 3D printed and assembled handguns inside a box. His eyes landed on the bag that Simon Optum had instructed him to keep safe and hidden. Again he fought the urge to tug the zipper and look inside. The man's warning boomed in his mind and he told himself to let it go. Not worth getting caught betraying the man's trust.

Salas tucked the box under his arm, secured the secret room's door and squared the rolling shelves against the wall. Confident everything was in order, he ducked under the garage door, tapped in the security code on the exterior module mounted beside the door. After the garage door closed behind him he jogged to his van, then stowed the box in the back. As he slid behind the steering wheel, he thought about the text that had come in an hour ago.

Although the drop-off wouldn't be until after dark, he wasn't sure how his time together with Paloma would go. Maybe she would want to accompany him for coffee, or lunch—or best of all, a nice dinner. He'd always wanted to go to the fancy Sabroso Restaurant, order the bison burger he'd never had the opportunity to try. Kai had shared elk stew a cousin had made for him during lunch break one time—other than that, he'd never eaten exotic game of any kind.

He decided a conversation about cuisine would be a perfect start in getting to know each other. "Who doesn't like food?" he said to himself as he reached behind the passenger seat, found what he craved, opened the box, dug out a wafer cookie stuffed with peanut butter and covered in chocolate, bit off half the treat, closed his eyes and imagined feeding the lovely lady the other portion.

He put the twelve-passenger van into reverse and waited for a slow-moving Ford to pass, then maneuvered the tight neighborhood road that met the main street. That would take him to the north entrance that led to the Taos Pueblo reservation for another ten-minute drive.

Unlike yesterday afternoon, when he'd arrived at the vast single-level house, he didn't see the gigantic pickup truck he assumed belonged to Kai's formidable uncle. Salas had never met the man but knew of his reputation on and off the reservation. A successful businessman who had traveled to Washington, DC, to speak for the tribe and help pass legislation, even raised a boatload of money for his community, if the news reports could be believed.

He decided to head to where he'd first caught sight of Paloma and took in the green trimmed grass of a white-split-rail-fenced pasture, where a few horses grazed. The spread reminded him more of a Kentucky farm than the high plains of northern New Mexico. He wondered how many wells it took to keep that part of the property looking so lush, then spotted windmills that dotted the acreage, multibladed rotors spinning in the breeze.

Right at 9:00 a.m., he parked at the barn's opening and became a little nervous that he might have arrived too early for visitors.

Then he saw her.

And she smiled at him.

And he knew. His purpose, destiny, reason why he'd had to wait so long for his life to actually start.

He realized that Paloma "White Dove" Arrio hadn't been ready. Until now.

CHAPTER
TWENTY-EIGHT
EVA

Eva had almost made it to Santiago's house when her cell phone rang. She glanced at the handset that announced DR. MONDRAGON and excitement tapped her chest. She pulled over to the side of the narrow road and told Kai, "Gotta take this."

"Shadow could use a run." He got out, released the Malinois and she watched them trot to the flat plain.

She clicked on the phone and smiled. Her forensics mentor when she was a university student, he had become a close and trusted friend over the years.

"Thanks for calling me back, Tavis. I know you're slammed—"

"Anything for you, Eva. You're most likely curious about the young Pueblo," he said, getting right to her concerns.

"I realize this is a big ask. Anything at all you can share?"

Eva imagined him sitting at his desk as he stroked his always-trimmed beard, thinking about how much he could and should share with her. The silence unnerved her, but she knew he needed the time to process, think of the ramifications. She crossed her fingers, hoping he would lean toward her favor.

"You should have the forensic form in your inbox."

She closed her eyes and silently thanked the universe, and Mondragon. "You know me too well," she said, grateful for the fact.

"Best for me to be hands off on this one," the medical examiner said. "Unfortunately this case isn't assigned to me."

"I understand what you're saying, Tavis. Thank you."

The moment the connection ended, she accessed the email tab on the phone, clicked on the message, waited for the attachment to download. Screen so small, she had to zoom in on the image and move it around to comprehend all the details.

A whimper escaped as she took in the injuries stated on the body intake form.

DECEDENT: NATHAN TRUJILLO. MALE. EIGHT YEARS OF AGE. NATIVE AMERICAN. BULLET WOUND TO UPPER LEFT QUADRANT OF CHEST. COLLAPSED LEFT LUNG. NASAL FRACTURE. RIGHT DISTAL RADIUS FRACTURE.

Impossible words made real now that they had been assigned to a case.

She bit the inside of her cheek, willed her eyes not to fill with tears. Kai and Shadow both turned around, as if sensing her distress. They hustled to her before she had a chance to wave them over.

"My shift doesn't start until later," she said. "Let's hang out some more."

"Sure. Whatcha wanna do?"

"Let's go to the village," she said. "See if anyone needs anything before Nathan gets here."

"All right. The shops should be open soon." He opened the door for Shadow, then got in his own seat. "Maybe we can find something for the Trujillos."

She tuned out her surrounds and allowed Nathan's injuries to crowd her thoughts as she pulled onto the two-lane track. Before long the boy would be placed in the wooden box crafted exclusively for his small frame. Her body involuntarily shuddered as she imagined the sight.

She looked over at Kai and thought about all the adversities the young Pueblo had already overcome. And of the future he was destined to face and conquer. Paloma's son would experience the opportunities Pabla and Gabriel's boy never would.

Crime had been her primary focus for more than a decade. Her profession, her life. Some investigations had been standard, other cases yet to be solved. But the biggest atrocity she had faced so far was the death of the child who would never grow up to be as tall and wise and gentle as the young man seated next to her.

She pictured the absolutely fearless Little Bear on a BMX bike racing on the rez.

And her heart broke all over again.

CHAPTER TWENTY-NINE
CRUZ

Cruz Romero let dispatch know he would be on personal time for the next hour and drove beyond the reservation's boundary line. The traffic was light for ten in the morning and Cruz made record time driving through and beyond town as he made his way to Holy Cross Hospital.

Unsure whether he should be doing what he'd planned, he pushed aside his apprehension. He didn't really want to get to know the man and his girlfriend, but his curiosity about why Eva had been attracted to the very Caucasian, meek, insecure boy-cop Andrew Kotz captured all reason and he found himself turning into the hospital parking lot.

He did feel bad for the guy. Tried to imagine Eva getting shot. How would he react? Out-of-his-mind worried, no doubt. Eva might be pissed about him being there, but it might also buy him points for her to know he had reached out, offered words of support. She would want to know if Kotz needed anything, so he added that to his list of inquiries.

Inside the main entrance, he placed his forearms on the information desk, flashed a smile, and leaned in toward a woman, VOLUNTEER stamped on a metal tag clipped to her shirt. "Could you tell me where I can find Police Officer Tallow's room?" he asked, voice smooth.

She tapped a computer keyboard and told him a room number. He thanked the younger woman, made his way to the bank of elevators and pushed the button for the proper floor. He walked out to a standard pod unit, nurses' station and command center in the middle, carpeted corridor wide enough for several people to walk next to each other, doors to patients' rooms in the outer ring.

He spotted Kotz at the farthest corner. Dressed in street clothes and tactical boots, he sat in an uncomfortable-looking chair outside a closed door. Elbows on his knees, hands cradling his head, Eva's friend looked beyond sad, maybe even in mourning. Cruz's heartbeat pounded. He halted, apprehensive that a death notification had just been delivered.

Cruz eased forward, as if confronting a skittish colt. "Hey, Kotz."

Kotz flicked his head upward, blinked a few times as if unsure about who stood there. He got up slowly, faced Cruz, didn't say anything.

"Thought I'd check on you."

"Oh. Thanks."

"Why are you out here? Is she sleeping?" Cruz prepared himself for the worst possible answers.

"Tests. So many tests."

Cruz let out an imperceptible breath, relieved he wouldn't have to comfort the stranger. "Can we do something for you?"

"'We'?" Kotz asked.

Cruz shrugged. "Me. Eva. Need anything?" The man remained quiet so he tried again. "Anyone you want me to contact?"

"Nadine's parents are on a cruise. Somewhere in Portugal. They're trying to get here. Don't know when yet."

"How about your people?"

"I told them I'm fine. They don't know who got shot . . . I don't think."

"Ah, man, you better get on the phone. Wouldn't be fair to them to find out about it on the news if some jerk-ass reporter leaks the names."

Kotz nodded. "Right. You're right." He took out a cell phone from the thigh pocket of his cargo pants and raised it. "Do you mind staying in case they bring Nadine back? I don't want her to think no one's here for her."

Uncomfortable about the request, Cruz shifted his weight one foot to the other. He'd never actually met the shot cop. Didn't even remember her first name until Kotz spoke it. Still, he nodded and took up watch at the door beside the chair where Kotz got up from.

The other officer's voice muted, then disappeared as he rounded a corner.

Less than a minute later, a monotonous squeak caused Cruz to face the noise growing louder and soon a hospital bed steered by a man in scrubs rolled into view. As they came closer, Cruz assessed the cop who had become the victim of a cowardly crime. To his knowledge no one yet had any idea when or if the case of the near-deadly assault would be solved.

Clear tubing from an IV bag hanging at a pole attached to the bed frame ended at the top of Tallow's hand. He winced at the sight of the inflamed and bruised area where a needle stuck into the vein. Locks of long blonde hair fanned out over the unsubstantial pillow. Her eyelids fluttered open and she hit him with the bluest eyes he had ever seen.

Unsure of what to say he merely waved. She lifted her unobstructed hand and wriggled her fingers. A connection had been made. *Now what,* he wondered, feeling a little nervous to be alone with the woman he didn't know at all. *Say something.*

"Kotz will be back in a minute."

He opened the door and the hospital worker pushed the gurney through the opening, centered it in the middle of the private room, parked the head of the bed against the wall, then left without exchanging a single word.

"Andy's making a phone call. I'm sure he'll hurry."

She let out a squeak of a laugh. "Andy," she croaked, voice soft and low. "His mother calls him that." Her face lost all the slight humor. "She'll be worried. Likes me for some reason."

"Probably because you like her son."

"Not because he loves me?"

"Means more that you appreciate her boy. Does for my people anyway."

She raised her eyebrows, as if she'd learned something for the first time.

He noticed a straw stuck inside a pink pitcher, reached for it without asking if she wanted the water, and held it so she could take a sip.

"Lifesaver."

"My goal in life."

She chuckled again, smiled so wide a dimple drilled the right side of her mouth. "Mine too. Until now."

"Don't give up, Officer Tallow. We need good cops."

"Good cops don't get shot."

"Bullshit. They get shot every day. Difference is you're not dead."

Kotz flashed past the open door. Cruz heard his boots thud against the floor and then halt. The officer entered, red faced, chest rising and falling. "Sorry. Sorry. I tried to get back before you."

"It's okay, Andrew. Officer Romero has been keeping me company."

"Feel up to telling me what happened?"

She hit him with those blue eyes. "Depends. Are you asking as a colleague? Or are you just curious?"

He almost said *Both*, but figured he should stay professional. "Fellow cop."

"Romero, we've been through this a hundred times with our department," Kotz said.

"Maybe something will kick loose the hundred and first."

The city officers looked at each other a beat before Kotz said, "We came in as the robbery was in progress. Suspect had his gun out and up. Tallow saw him first."

Kotz had referred to his partner as a cop would, by her last name, and Cruz knew to proceed as a law enforcement officer rather than as someone merely listening to a story. He took a notebook and pen from his cargo pants pocket and flipped to a blank page.

"Notice anything distinctive? A limp, tattoos? Wearing a mask, but maybe eye color?"

Kotz's mouth dropped open. He looked out at nothing, thinking, then said, "Blue. His eyes were blue. Almost as light as Nadine's." He turned to his partner. "I was so worried about you I must have forgotten that until right now."

Cruz jotted down the detail and added,

MOST LIKELY NOT HISPANIC OR NATIVE.

Kotz took out his phone. "I need to let our sergeant know so he can add eye color to the BOLO description." He left Cruz and Tallow alone but within eyeshot from the corridor outside the open door.

"I didn't have time to see his eyes," Tallow said. "Definitely wearing a long black wig though."

"Try to remember his voice. Accent of any kind? Did he stutter? Hesitate?"

"No. That fucker knew exactly what he wanted. He exhibited zero fear or conscience."

Cruz wished, as he had since the incident, that the TPPD had access to the investigation files to fill in the blanks, but knew that would most likely never happen.

He thanked Tallow, and as he left, clipped Kotz on the back, then hustled from the hospital.

As he strode to his vehicle, he texted Eva.

SHOOTER = BLUE EYES

Her reply came back as soon as he tapped the little blue arrow to send.

THEY'RE HIDING SOMETHING HERE.

He realized she had sent a cross text the same time as his own. Appreciating they were still in sync, even from all the way across town, he sent his reply and then waited for her to take in his information.

DON'T TAKE ANY SHIT FROM THE LOCALS
BLUE EYES??? HOW D'YA KNOW?
KOTZ

He waited for the phone to vibrate in his hand.

CHAPTER THIRTY
EVA

Eva had parked in the Taos Pueblo village lot assigned to tourists when Cruz's text came through, moments before the one she'd sent him.

Kai and Shadow turned around and looked at her from outside the vehicle. He opened his arms and Shadow yipped. She held up two fingers and he gave her a thumbs-up, then approached the volunteer in charge of taking parking fees.

She leaned back in the seat and hit the icon to call.

"Hee-yah-ho," he said.

"Why are you talking to Kotz?"

"Hello to you, too."

"Not the time, Officer Romero." She got right to her first annoyance. "Kotz. Talk to me."

"All right, all right. We had a friendly chat, the two of us and Tallow. That's all. Thought you'd appreciate me checking in on the shot officer . . . And your friend."

"And finding out what no one else has."

"Yep. Blue eyes. Andy called his supervisor. It'll be on the BOLO by now."

"What are you thinking?" she asked.

"Offender most likely isn't Hispanic," he said.

"And not one of us . . ." She hesitated, because anything could still be possible. Although she could think of more than a few mixed-race Natives who had light-green eyes, she had never seen anyone from their community with blue eyes. "*Probably* not one of us," she amended.

She went quiet and listened to birds chattering in a willow tree beside her vehicle as she pondered what she and her team should do next. The death of Little Bear in a different city deemed a tribal police investigation moot. But surely there was something they could do about finding the bank robber who continued to terrorize the community, on and off the reservation.

As so many times before, Cruz seemed to read her, even from the other end of a phone line. "Seems like things are boiling up," he said.

"What do you mean?"

"Just a feeling."

Cruz had the best intuition of any LEO she had ever met so she didn't negate his statement, or lessen whatever they unearthed could mean—for the investigation, or those involved.

"Let's talk to Lily Bernal," he continued. "See if Littlefeather noticed the robber's eye color to verify."

"We need to be careful, Cruz. The bank robbery isn't officially our case. The feds won't want us doing anything that could harm their investigation."

"Okay. Let's give it a day. And I'll let her know you and I should be there if the feds show up to question her again."

She watched Kai greet and answer visitors' questions as they got out of their cars. The respectful young man gave them his best smile, pointed across the street to the building where they could purchase tickets to tour the ancient village of her people.

He caught her looking at him and whirled his arm for her to come on. Shadow did a triple spin, hunkered down, popped up. She got out of the Beast and started toward the impatient duo. "Haven't told the chief yet, but I spoke to Dr. Mondragon," she said, voice low so Kai couldn't overhear her. "Nathan had other injuries besides the gunshot. Broken nose and wrist."

"Hmm," Cruz hummed. "You thinkin' maybe Nathan was assaulted first?"

She hadn't actually thought that but now the possibility got her feeling his assessment might be spot-on. "We should talk to his classmates. He would have been assigned a field trip buddy. They're supposed to stay together."

"School bus got back last night. I can reach out. See who made a statement. The families will want to know their kids are safe. Good excuse to talk to a few of them. I'm on it."

"Thanks, Cruz. I'm at the village with Kai. Talk later."

Eva tapped the end call icon and scanned the parking lot as she walked. She didn't see the distinctive BMW and turned her thoughts to the diagram Dr. Mondragon had sent, now burned in her brain. She recalled the details without having to refer to the photograph of the one-sheet.

The report's information bothered her. *Why would Nathan have fractures to his nose and wrist? Maybe how he fell after being shot by the guard? Probably dead shortly before he hit the ground? Most likely cracked his wrist when he stuck out his hand to catch himself? Broke his nose after landing face first?* But Cruz's idea of a possible altercation before the shooting also made sense to her. She might never know for sure.

She would do all she could to follow whatever evidence she'd be privy to, and find the truth about what led up to Nathan Trujillo's tragic demise. The little boy no longer had a voice so his body would have to provide answers. She was certain Dr. Mondragon would be her ally with that. And if it was determined something had actually happened to the boy before his death, someone needed to speak for him.

She reached Kai and his Malinois and he asked, "You good?"

Still distracted, she nodded and the two sprinted ahead, leaving Eva to think about the bank robber who had terrorized her hometown and its residents and visitors—fully in her investigatory sights now too.

The offender could be hiding out on the reservation—maybe taken in by an unsuspecting elder welcoming a visitor inside their home to pass the hours. Eva often felt her Red Willow people were too trusting, probably due to the necessary interactions with tourists that kept the financial wheels turning.

A burst of chilly wind nearly spun her around. She drew her jacket tight against her body and looked up at Pueblo Peak. The race against Mother Nature a yearly dance, snow would dust the mountain, then the entire reservation before too much more time passed.

Eva shook her head, thinking about yet another unknown to deal with. She needed answers. Before the first snowflakes fell.

CHAPTER THIRTY-ONE
SIMON

Simon Optum pulled the bank teller closer to him, snuggled her neck, smiled when Lily purred. The bed springs screeched and she giggled so he spooned her tighter and bounced again. He was happy to make her laugh. Better than the tears that had sometimes taken him hours to chase away.

Everything had come to a stop for Optum. No schedule to keep, nowhere to be, no one to see. A mini vacation he could get used to. He gave merely a brief thought to the outside world—had no idea whether the bank robbery was still hot news in the area, or if a different crime had taken interest away from his bold accomplishment.

Optum knew he should check in with his boss. Too many days without a phone call made the old man nervous and he didn't want one of his colleagues to come looking for him. That would be bad. For everyone, because bodies stacked up whenever that had happened the few times he'd ventured out on his own too long over the years.

"Don't think I've ever slept this late," Lily said, snapping him from his notions. She made a move to pull away from him.

"No, stay . . . This is nice," he pleaded, stroking her black hair, which smelled earthy and held a hint of some sort of flower he didn't recognize.

"I'm so hungry," she said. "And thirsty. Let me fix some eggs and green chiles."

Optum's stomach growled when Lily mentioned the offer of food. She giggled her little girl laugh and he joined in her delight—not a fake amusement. Her quiet way of being had lulled him the entire twenty hours he'd been alone with her. No senseless chatter, or high-pitched cackles, or endless questions he normally would have to endure. The Indian woman had barely spoken actual words to him, instead communicating with her body and the dark-brown eyes that didn't look away. He'd lost himself in that gaze. He realized she had charmed him.

"You won't need to go to the store, will you," he said—not a question, and more of a suggestion than a command.

"No. There are enough staples to last weeks, if you don't mind canned milk in your coffee."

"I don't mind at all," he said, actually minding very much.

"Do you like elk? Think I'll make stew for tonight."

His stomach rumbled again. From hunger or revulsion, he wasn't sure. He pulled a comical face, and said, "Sounds great."

She stabbed his side with her elbow. "You'll love it."

She got out of bed and kept her back to him, shy, even after all they'd done together, each starved for more. She put on a robe draped on a chair in the corner, gave him a sweet smile, closed the door behind her.

She left him alone, where he stayed under the warm bedding. Taking Lily on the road with him crossed his mind. He'd be less suspicious with a woman in the passenger seat.

It'll probably take me a few more days to make her all mine, he thought. He set his sights on two days. A challenge. She wouldn't even need to know what was going on while she waited in the Beemer as he instructed cashiers to strip money from their registers when he crossed over state to state.

He'd figure out what to do with sweet Lily the bank teller along the way.

He had two options. Set her up at his Lincoln Park condo . . . or find an exclusive spot in the desert, where nothing but the coyotes and vultures would find her bones.

CHAPTER
THIRTY-TWO
CRUZ

Cruz Romero had been a peacekeeper as far back as he could remember. Even as a kid he could calm down screaming children fighting over toys. During his teen years he talked men and women out of their car keys before they made drunken mistakes. As a young adult he brokered deals acceptable to both parties, and dispatched bullies with a fist if words didn't work.

After high school he washed dishes at the only Tiwa restaurant in the region, led tours on the village explaining the basic tribal traditions and history of his people for groups of visitors from all over the world. Most challenging were his seasons spent as a guide for hunters and anglers, where he would lead outdoorsmen to the choicest spots to bag deer, elk and trout. He even worked on a hotshot crew one harrowing summer—and still experienced occasional nightmares of flames licking at his boots from that terrifying experience.

He didn't have an eye for or interest in creating art and collectibles, so in his early twenties decided policing was one of the only other options that would allow him to work on the reservation, stay on the only land he knew or wanted to know. Turned out all his past experiences were training for his current job as a law enforcer.

After fifteen years on the tribal force, some saw him as a lackey, even his brothers saying more than a few times, *You've been a cop forever. Why aren't you the police chief yet?*

He didn't want to be chief. Bureaucracy and politics didn't suit him. He would leave that to those who chose to change the world. Cruz only wanted to watch over his small corner of the universe he called home. He would be a patrol cop and investigator for as long as his boss and the tribal council would allow.

But he never expected to have to question a child about the death of a classmate. A trauma they might never outrun. Certainly never unsee.

He arrived at the Red Willow Center before noon, where women, men, children, elders, aunties and uncles, and some older siblings of the kids who had been on the field trip with Nathan buzzed around the meeting hall. The community outreach facility staff, primarily volunteers both Native and non, looked harried and bewildered as they tried to allay fears while simultaneously tending to the youngsters who might or might not have witnessed anything disturbing during the altercation that had taken their classmate's life.

The war chief, in agreement with the tribe's governor, had encouraged parents of the Pueblo children of Nathan's class to attend counseling sessions and an art therapy class at the facility, but he didn't expect to encounter so much chaos.

Of course everyone would want answers, and a crowd had the school principal cornered and peppered him with questions. Cruz spotted one of his fellow tribal officers and covertly gave him the okay signal. His colleague returned the gesture, indicating he had everything under control over there.

At the opposite end, Cruz counted seven boys and girls he thought looked to be Nathan's age gathered around a long low table that held a scatter of crayons, colored pencils and artwork scrawled by young hands and imaginative minds. They sat on miniature chairs, intent on drawing, ignoring the hum of annoyed voices that rose and fell in waves.

He pocketed his wraparound sunglasses, and recognized a volunteer who taught art classes at the center. "Hey, Carla. I'd like to talk to one of the kids about what happened to Nathan. Think that'd be all right?"

She looked more worried than when he approached, but issued a name and pointed to one of the girls at the table.

"Need to clear it with the parents. Could you send them over?"

The worker peeled away and Cruz approached in slow steps, glanced at the drawings, looked for violence or other disturbing images—relieved to see no depictions of blood or a dead person on any of the sheets.

A couple who reminded Cruz of the Trujillos—arms around each other for comfort or maybe support—approached, eyes on one girl in particular.

The male Native introduced himself and his wife and stroked the long hair of the little girl. "This is Betty." She turned her tiny face upward. "This nice police officer wants to ask you some questions, okay?"

The mother chimed in, "We'll be right here."

The couple stepped back and Cruz considered one of the empty pint-size chairs, assumed the damage he would do to it, and opted for the floor instead. He sat cross-legged next to Betty, took up a fresh sheet of paper and brown pencil and started to sketch the view from his house—the field that led to Taos Mountain.

The young artist slid him a daffodil-colored pencil, its point nearly worn down to the wood. "Needs yellow."

"You're right." He took up the implement and added sprigs of flowers to his landscape. "Much better."

She gave him a thumbs-up and continued her masterpiece.

"I like your drawing," he said.

She issued him a satisfied nod and patted her animals-in-progress. "Ponies. My favorite."

He had little experience questioning, or even dealing with, young children. Left that to others on the force who had kids. But the tiny lady beside him presented herself as an old soul. Eva would probably tell him not to talk down to or baby the youngster.

Betty rescued him from overthinking when she asked, "Are you a real policeman?"

"I am."

She nodded again. "You want to talk about Nathan." Not a question.

"Were you and Little Bear friends?"

"Best friends," she whispered.

Hands still working his drawing, he glanced at her. Bottom lip jutted out, a teardrop slid down her cheek and dropped to bloom a circle on her paper.

Cruz noticed that none of the other kids paid any attention to him, or to Betty. She looked small for her age, even smaller than Nathan, which was what probably drew them to each other. "Did you sit together on the bus to Santa Fe?"

"We always sit together."

"And walked with Nathan during the tour at the museum?"

She didn't motion or reply this time. He worried about pushing too hard. Thought about calling the worker over to give him a pointer or two.

"Is Nathan in trouble?" she asked.

The question cracked Cruz's heart. He realized the girl's parents hadn't told her about her friend's death. "No, no, don't worry about Little Bear."

She continued to draw, strokes slower, lines more firm.

"You're not in any trouble either, Betty."

The little girl leaned close to Cruz and whispered, "It was Robby. He's mean to us little kids. Always pushing us around. Calling us bad names."

Cruz scowled, eyes thinned as he took in one kid after another around the table. "Which one is Robby?"

"Not here. He's not one of us."

"Did he say something mean to Nathan?" She shook her head and he tried again. "Who was he mean to?"

Another headshake. No reply.

"It's okay. You can talk to me. It's my job to keep you safe."

She looked at the kids. No one looked back. "Can you keep a secret?" she whispered.

"Yes."

"He was mean to *me*. Said I was stinky and dirty and poor."

Under the table Cruz squeezed his hand into a fist, wanting nothing more than to punish the cruel kid who hurt the tiny Pueblo's feelings.

"Nathan pushed him away from me and Robby grabbed his hand and hit him in the nose."

She went silent and stared off as she rocked lightly back and forth in the chair to calm herself.

"What else happened?"

"Nathan got away and took something out of his backpack."

"What did he take out?"

Betty shook her head, reluctant to continue, tears now flowing down both cheeks.

Cruz sensed her parents' anxiety but needed a little more time. He scooted closer, gave her his full attention, said in low soothing tones, "We're almost done, Betty. Be brave a minute longer. For Nathan."

She turned to Cruz. A slow movement that reminded him of an owl. Affect flat when she looked at him. "A gun. He pointed it at Robby and then there was a man and then . . . *Boom!*" she shouted.

Cruz flinched at the loudness of the word, an auditory shock after her hushed tones.

The room went quiet. Everyone turned in Cruz's direction. The dad maneuvered himself to block Cruz from further access to his daughter.

"Thank you, Betty," he said. "I'm proud of you. Stay strong."

He got to his feet and slid on his sunglasses—an attempt to hide his shock about Betty's revelations. He nodded to the volunteer and his fellow officer when he exited the space. In the main corridor, he took out his phone and tapped out a text to Eva.

NATHAN STOOD UP FOR A BULLIED LITTLE GIRL BEFORE SHOT.
WARRIOR TO THE END.

CHAPTER
THIRTY-THREE
EVA

Eva reread Cruz's text and tried to hide her tears from Kai. She should call her partner and find out exactly what the info meant, but now that she had stepped on sacred land she felt the need to focus on herself. If only for a short while.

She closed her eyes, counted her footfalls for a full minute, knowing without seeing where her steps would lead. She felt the vibrational power that traveled through the soles of her boots, up her legs, torso, arms, ending at her fingertips and crown of her head.

When she opened her eyes she saw Kai nodding, big smile on his face, and she knew they had shared the emotional visitation of the spirits that watched over them.

She patted his shoulder, a silent confirmation, and they walked beyond another curve. The first sight of the ancient *Hlauuma* and *Hlaukwima*, North and South Houses, was revealed, and as always, a gasp caught in Eva's chest. The ancient, mud-covered honeycomb of separate private homes within the two multiple-storied houses often filled her with wonder. Her breath halted, as if witnessing the sight for the first time.

They crossed the narrow footbridge to the less busy South House, and the gentle babbling of the Rio Pueblo stream, which split the path between the dwellings, eased Eva's taut nerves.

Kai snapped an upward tic of his head. "Hey, isn't that Ricky Soto?"

She turned to where he indicated and recognized one of the less-celebrated jewelry makers, whose talents deserved more recognition.

They approached the always-shy Pueblo man, who sat alone next to the structure. A traditional rug woven in the turquoise, tan, blue, white and green colors of the Taos Pueblo flag was spread out in front of him, where exquisite silver and beaded goods nearly covered the entire design.

"How's business, Ricky?" Eva asked.

The Pueblo a few years younger than her grew animated at the sight of his visitors. He popped from his cross-legged position and clapped his hands a few times. "Eva! Single Star! Can't believe it. Haven't seen you two since I can remember."

"You've got some nice stuff," Kai said. "Sold much today?"

Ricky raised an open hand and rocked it back and forth.

Kai knelt down and examined the perfectly lined up rows of goods. Silver jewelry and chains glimmered and beaded cuffs exhibited pleasing arrays of color variations.

Eva admired the pieces, each design unique and captivating.

Kai pointed to one of the pieces that melded stamped silver and rows of beads. "How much for that one?"

"For you, little brother, twenty bucks."

Kai blew out a puff of air. "Worth lots more than that." He reached into his pocket, withdrew a fold of bills, stripped off five twenties, and handed them to the jeweler.

"Dude, that's too much."

"Nope. Wrap it up, Ricky."

He smiled and proceeded to polish the silver of the bracelet, careful not to displace any of the beads in the middle of the cuff.

"How'd you get so flush?" Eva asked, impressed by the generosity, and the amount of money Kai had been holding on to.

He shrugged. "Uncle Santi pays well to muck out his stalls."

Ricky wrinkled his nose. "Not a fair trade."

"I don't mind. Get to spend time with my mom. And Shadow loves to watch the horses."

"Young dude and his dog," Rick said. "Doesn't get much better than that."

Shadow alternated his attention as each person spoke, convincing Eva, not for the first time, the smarter-than-usual canine followed every word of the conversation.

The artist dropped the trinket inside a black velvet bag, tied the drawstrings and handed it to Kai. "Why are you here?" Ricky asked Eva.

"Nathan Trujillo . . ."

The Pueblo's expression plunged from happy to sad in a blink. "Yeah, I heard. Damn shame."

Ricky cast his attention left, then right and Eva sensed he might have something to share about the incident. She hitched her head, beckoning him to follow. "Lots of ears here," she said. "Kai will watch over your treasures."

"You bet. Let's see if I can sell something for you."

Eva took a few steps away so they could speak more privately. A couple and their young daughter stopped in front of Ricky's display, close enough for Eva to listen in on the conversation that soon became a negotiation.

"Can I pet your Hündchen?" the little girl asked.

"No, Bärchen, the doggie is working," the very tall man beside her said.

Shadow yipped, did a quick spin, sat, panted. The little family laughed.

"What does 'bear-chin' mean?" Eva heard Kai ask the mother.

"Little bear."

Eyes wide, face losing a shade in color, Kai shot Eva a look. Verification from the universe they were on the proper path. She returned his shocked expression.

The daughter curved her back, curled her fingers into claws, wrinkled her nose to show her teeth, growled. Held the attitude a moment. Then squealed in excitement.

"She's obsessed with them lately." The father patted his daughter's shoulder.

Kai seemed to recover when his four-footed companion nudged him. "Shadow likes you. He'll let you pet him if you want," he said, apparently unable to resist the sky-blue eyes and tiny hands clasped to her chest.

The enchanted little girl dropped to her knees, lined up her nose inches away from Shadow's, stroked the top of his head gentle and slow.

"His name is Shadow."

"I'm Maggie."

"What do we do when we meet someone, Shadow?"

The dog raised its front left paw and the little girl giggled. She took it in both of her hands and they shook, then she said, "Are you a real Indian?"

"Shush, Maggie. That isn't polite," the father said, a mortified expression on his face.

"I actually *am* a real Native American. I live not too far from here." Kai pointed to the north.

"We live in Berlin," Maggie said. "That's in Germany."

"Well, I'm glad you came to visit Shadow, Maggie. He doesn't like everyone. You must be a very special and magical person."

"Yes, I am!" the girl crowed. Shadow yipped. The family laughed again.

"Did you make this beautiful jewelry?" the woman asked, tucking a lock of blonde hair behind her ear so she could admire the pieces.

"No, ma'am. My cousin, Singing Elk, made all of these. He's over there." He snapped his chin toward Ricky. "That woman he's talking to wants to buy everything. She's trying to make a deal right now, so if you see anything you like . . . might want to let me know."

The woman's eyes went wild as she whipped her head to the man, who automatically pulled out a wallet from his front pocket and fished out a credit card.

Kai clicked his tongue. "She's gonna pay all cash."

The woman let out a slight guttural sound, crossed her arms tight to her chest, sneaker tapping the ground. He accordioned open the money compartment and nodded, which prompted the woman to kneel down, point at items for Kai to pick up as she scanned the multiple rows of jewelry, until the man returned what appeared to be their secret code of tapping feet. She selected one more item, stood up, turned to Eva and gave an apologetic shrug.

Carrying out the show full circle, Eva held out her open arms wide, a *What are you doing—those are supposed to be mine* motion.

Kai proceeded to tuck the ten items into separate drawstring velvet bags, handed the treasures over to the woman, took a few business cards from a stack on the table and gave them to the man. "Singing Elk can ship anywhere. Tell your friends!"

"I have a *lot* of friends," she said, taking up most of the remaining cards.

Ricky looked much more relaxed when Eva led him farther away for more privacy and she asked the first question that burned in her mind. "What have you heard about Little Bear, exactly?"

Ricky winced, reluctant to answer. "I don't know if—"

"Seriously, bro. Santa Fe cops here aren't telling us anything," Eva interrupted. "The Trujillos are hurting. You want to give Pabla and Gabriel some peace, right?"

"Yeah, for sure. But what if—"

"No one will know. I promise."

"'Kay." Ricky darted his eyes all around to make sure no one listened in as he said in a quiet voice, "What I heard is that our little dude took out a gun from his backpack and pointed it at another kid.

Security guard at the museum pulled his own gun. Nathan must've panicked or something. Didn't drop the stupid thing. Guard shot. Only one bullet but it did the trick."

"I know all of this. What else can you tell me?"

Ricky waited a beat. Another. Then he leaned in and said in an even softer voice, "Here's the thing . . . The gun wasn't real."

"What do you mean, not real?"

"Plastic. One of those printed things that keep poppin' up all around Taos. Couldn't fire even if Nathan wanted it to."

Eva thought about the bag of guns Shadow had dug up at Nathan's house. No telling how many others had been scattered around the property, or maybe even inside the Trujillos' house. "Oh no," she whispered. "You're sure?"

Ricky nodded. "My contact is straight up. He was there. One of the chaperones from Nathan's school."

"Think your guy will talk to me?"

"He's scared. Really scared. Only told me because we're buds. Local cops told him they'd lock him up if they found out he talked to anyone about it."

"Is he still in Santa Fe?"

"Don't know. Called him again last night and earlier today. He's not picking up."

"This is bad."

"Yeah. He said people around there are flippin' out—not just Natives. Whites, Hispanics, everyone is pissed. That guard's in hiding. They wanna string him up."

"Because of Nathan being a Pueblo?"

"Nope. Because he's a . . . was a kid."

"Nathan wouldn't want that. Neither would his parents."

Ricky shrugged. "What're you gonna do? Dead kid and guns. Happening too much."

Shadow and Kai bounded over and he handed Ricky a thick fold of bills.

"*Daaamn*," Ricky said, playing out the word. "This is more than I've made in a month. Two, maybe."

"We had fun, didn't we, Shadow?" Shadow wagged his tail. "Better get over there. That woman's probably telling everyone she passes to check out your stuff."

Eva pointed and Ricky turned his attention to the people bent over his blanket, five, then eight shoppers, crowing *oohh*s and *aahh*s. "You're the best, Single Star. Seriously, bro. Come back next week. Later, Eva." He hurried over to his spot behind the goods and started a sales pitch, confidence renewed.

"Ready to head out?" Eva asked Kai.

"Yeah. What's next?"

Shadow pranced beside his master, head on a swivel, missing nothing. Eva noticed that Kai did the same and she pondered who taught the other to be so vigilant all of a sudden. Were they subconsciously pinging on a feeling rather than an actual object or person? Maybe they sensed a hesitation in Eva.

She didn't want to involve the young man and his dog in the "next" and didn't know if she wanted to go down the path either.

CHAPTER
THIRTY-FOUR
CELIO

Celio took his time eating the lunch his grandmother prepared for him—chicken, beans and cheese quesadillas, the tortillas shining from butter grilled in a cast-iron skillet. He chewed slower than usual, careful not to reinjure his lip.

His abuela sat at the table next to him, tears swimming in her eyes, clucking over her *nieto* and scolding the abusive one under her breath—a rattle of soft Spanish. Celio appreciated the support. They needed to stay close. Stick together with the hope one of them could talk the lion down when he started to ramp up again.

She feared the rage too. Had begged Manny not to strike her when his anger roiled if she didn't fix a meal fast enough or get out of the bathroom or forgot to buy him his favorite chips. The silliest things could set his brother off, then cause him to throw a glass or toss a plate across the room, while spit flew from his mouth as he hurled accusations. Then he would cry and apologize and promise he would be a better man. After a day or two the cycle would start all over again.

Bad enough that his classmates bullied him relentlessly, now he had to worry about his own shared blood turning against him. Celio couldn't stand too much more. Always scared, snapping awake at unfamiliar sounds in the night, flinching at loud unexpected noises. Even his favorite foods and candy didn't work to placate his nerves like they used to.

He couldn't figure out what had caused the shift in his brother's weird temper. He had been his usual self until a few months ago. He suspected the mood swings had to do with the guns—maybe too much pressure being the middleman. Hopefully not drugs, although that wouldn't surprise Celio. The Indian guy Manny hung with always had a blank look plastered on his face and never showed emotion. Ever. And the other buddy couldn't hold a thought in his head more than a minute, so he probably took stuff too.

After Celio finished his meal, washed the dishes, thanked his grandmother and kissed her goodbye, he packed the envelope of cash, water bottle and a few packages of M&M's from his private stash in his backpack. Then he put on his helmet with the shield that completely hid his identity and got on his dirt bike.

He threaded his way beyond town, sticking to side streets and neighborhood roads so the noisy motor wouldn't draw attention in case any cops were close by. The Kawasaki's plates and registration belonged to a dude named Santiago Mirabal, and that wasn't going to change anytime soon.

He took the first entrance off the highway that led to the Pueblo reservation, then followed the tracks left by other bikers. He accelerated when dogs in the yards of the few houses he passed barked and chased after him, but otherwise kept a slower pace so he wouldn't stir up too much dust or cause the annoying revving noise of the engine.

A few minutes later he reached the destination he had been to half a dozen times before. Unsure why at the time, during his previous trip with his teacher, he had paid close attention to each curve, landmark, unique tree or bush that led them to the location.

Completely lost, he made a wide figure eight to see where he went wrong, spotted the massive rock that looked like it had dropped from the sky, and knew which direction to head. Closer now, Celio thought maybe his teacher would be there already, but he didn't see anyone bent over studying the ground. During biology lab yesterday, Mr. Salas had told the class he would be right here today if anyone wanted to join him to study how the plants evolved or died off as they prepared for the fall season. Where was he?

He sent up a prayer that the man would come soon. To please, *please* let him be able and willing to help. Celio added mention of his abuela, thinking God probably gave her preference in the prayer department. She always talked to Him, worked her rosary beads hours at a time. Never missed Sunday morning or Wednesday evening Mass.

He laid the motorbike flat, took off the helmet, wiped his sweaty face with his sleeve, then removed his backpack and scrunched down behind a cluster of bushes he knew from Mr. Salas's teaching to be sagebrush. Heart beating fast, perspiration trailing down the middle of his back to absorb in his waistband, he kept watch for the long van that had delivered him and his class there for the outside-school field trips.

While Celio waited, he replayed something his brother told him soon after the gun pickups started. *I got my eyes on you, hermanito,* Manny had said, eyes glittering. *Even when you think I'm not there . . . I'm always lookin'.*

The words didn't make Celio feel safe. Instead, the statement felt like a threat. A warning not to screw up or try anything outside his brother's instructions. Which was why he'd wound up on the reservation, waiting for the man only he knew would deliver the guns as soon as it got dark enough tonight to sneak there without being noticed.

He touched his cheek, still tender from his brother's strike. Laid fingertips on his hurt lip and winced. Anger, outrage and humiliation smoldered, ashamed by the disrespect his brother had issued. Celio decided, if he could find the courage, he would take care of his brother first.

Frustration rumbled from Manny nonstop lately. Anything and everything seemed to set him off. Just thinking about the red-faced, teeth-bared, wild-eyed beast of a man no one dared to cross brought a shiver down the length of Celio's body. He had begun to carry his dad's old knife in his back pocket just in case. The blade was only three inches long, but would probably be enough to stop his brother if Celio couldn't talk him down or get away fast enough. He hoped.

He took a drink of water, ripped open a bag of candy, crunched the first piece, went for another—green, his favorite—taking his time for the entire disc to melt in his mouth before he popped in another one.

Already bored after ten minutes, he dug out a notebook and handful of colored pencils from his backpack. He loved the feel of a fresh spiral pad, smooth and blank and ready for his words or sketches. A blank slate for his imagination to flow. The only time he felt whole. When he could tune out everything and everyone, especially his own racing thoughts that would often spin around a racetrack of doom at lightning speed.

He drew the foremost thing on his mind. Anticipation building after each stroke of the pencil, he imagined the feel of the gun in his hand. Magazine full of ammo, ready to fire. Raising it, finger on the trigger, one eye closed to aim the sight. All the things the hundred or more videos he had watched ingrained in his mind, practiced in front of the mirror, fingers simulating the weapon.

Soon he would have one of his own. No longer the drop-off and pickup person—now the customer. He had already peeled off five twenties from Manny's envelope, and had another sixty he had saved from doing chores and helping out his neighbors.

His strokes became harder, thicker lines denting the paper.

He would pay whatever it took to bring the treasure home. Home to Manny. For the next time the enraged bull of a brother came charging at him or his abuela. For the last time.

CHAPTER
THIRTY-FIVE
TOMÁS

Tomás Salas drove the long passenger van, bumping in and over divots in the nonexistent reservation road as he steered his van, then parked on the flat plain, careful not to trap crucial flora under the wheels.

He slid from behind the wheel, opened the rear double doors, leaned against the bumper and reveled in his favorite place, even more so now that his plan had been formulated. Salas envisioned where he'd build the house for Paloma, Kai and himself. The ideal placement of windows that would allow the best breezes to cool the rooms. Which angle the view of the Taos mountains would be most dramatic from, on a porch that would wrap around three of the exterior walls.

He lifted his face to the sun and took in a deep breath. The aroma of sage, soil and the cleanest air he'd ever experienced brought back pleasant memories of all the classes he had assembled here over the years. Where he would turn his mind as he doodled new floor plan designs while his students took tests or fulfilled their lab time requirements.

He had been coming every Saturday the past few months to clear his head and get his mind off the pressures of waiting for Simon Optum to get the investors' money together. He even told his biology class every Friday in case anyone wanted to join him. None of them ever did. He'd never encountered anyone during his times there. Even his best student, Kai, seemed to have lost interest in the place.

His former student's terrarium project came to his mind and he decided to look for a specimen or two he hadn't seen in his protégé's collection. Always prepared, the biologist reached in the cargo area and took out a pair of work gloves, short- and long-handled shovels, and two plastic buckets, set them next to the van, then started a slow tour of the area in search of distinctive plants.

Still glowing on the inside after his private time with Paloma Arrio when she crept into his thoughts, he walked the approximate dimensions of his House Design Number Three. "Yes. Right here will be perfect."

He thought he heard someone call out his name. Frowned when he saw no one. Stood still as the voice rang out again, louder this time. A figure walked in his direction. Dark hood up on the hoodie, dark set of sweats, dark sneakers—standard attire for a teenager—could be male *or* female. They obviously knew him, but Salas grew wary and formulated in his mind what to say if he needed to justify being this far out on a secluded part of the reservation. He had permission from the tribal authorities, but the actual proof of the clearance from the tribal government office was framed and hanging in his study at home.

"It's okay. It's me." The figure pushed the hood down to reveal his entire face.

Salas recognized the person now. "Celio?" he asked, confused. A sophomore from his third-hour biology class, who never raised his hand or participated beyond what was asked of him. Kept his head down, usually sketching in his notebook. Talented, actually. As he recalled, no parents in the house, raised by his grandmother and one older brother.

Salas looked beyond his van and did a 360-degree survey of the area. No car anywhere, but he did see the handlebars of some sort of bike behind some sagebrush. He took a few steps and spotted KAWASAKI printed on the side of the lime-green cycle.

He was shocked to see his student, who looked younger than his years. His weight had increased over the months and Salas suspected his homelife might not be stable.

"You said you'd be here today."

Salas smiled and opened his arms. "Here I am."

The young man leaned against the oxidized maroon hood of Salas's van. "I always liked this place."

"How long have you been waiting?" Salas approached the boy, who held his place at the vehicle. "You shouldn't be here alone."

Salas noted the black eye the sixteen-year-old tried to conceal as he stood in profile. But the kid couldn't hide his split lower lip.

"I wanted to see you . . . ," the student said.

Celio's words trailed off and Salas followed the boy's upward gaze, to the formations that reminded him of whipped cream clouds spewing from an aerosol can.

"Why did you come here, Celio?"

"Please, Mr. Salas. You gotta help me. They won't leave me alone." He gathered the cuff of his sweatshirt and wiped away snot from his nose. "I'm scared all the time. They're gonna kill me, I know it."

Salas patted the air, an attempt to placate the kid. "Hang on, Celio. Tell me what's going on. Who are you afraid of?"

"Can't tell you. Bunch of guys. Pickin' on me all the time."

"I'm glad you came to me, Celio. Let me take you to the police. I'll stay with you and make sure they help you."

"No! No cops. My brother will find out and he'll do worse than this."

Salas pointed to the lip that oozed blood. "Your brother do that to you?"

"Doesn't matter," the kid raged. "The only way you can help is to give me one of your guns."

The kid's statement, calm, matter of fact, no hesitation at all, sounded so odd and out of the blue that Salas let out a confused chuckle. But Celio didn't smile. His expression turned hard, dark eyes darker than before. Salas knew the kid was not kidding. The blood rushed from his head, legs went numb and threatened to buckle.

"I don't know what you mean," he lied, hoping the boy didn't hear the tremble in his voice.

The kid's tears dried up as quick as he'd shed them. He had been faking his terror. The teacher's mouth dropped open, gaped at his student while he tried to think of what to say. "I don't have any guns." He tried not to look at his van. "Who told you that?"

The kid shrugged, gave him a smug grin, playing with him, Salas realized.

"Tell me."

"You don't know what the person you're selling them to is doing with them, do you?"

His student watched for a reaction. Salas had nothing to offer because he had no idea.

"I do," Celio said, an all-knowing, snide expression on his face. "You really think your guns are for classes and target practice?"

Again, Salas tried not to look at his van, where the dozen Glock counterfeits—assembled, oiled, ejected magazines ready for loading—were stored in the back, awaiting the upcoming transaction.

Celio blew out a puff of air, then winced and touched his wounded lip. "Surprised you haven't figured it out by now. They're all over town. Probably in Albuquerque by now. Maybe Texas. Arizona?" He shrugged. "Who knows?"

The claim stunned Salas and he didn't know how to respond.

"Shit. You're stupider than me, *Tomás*." The boy emphasized the Spanish pronunciation, then rattled off a string of what Salas assumed to be expletives and disparagements that made him glad he didn't comprehend his father's native language.

Salas had never seen or heard the boy lash out. Brain fumbling, he wasn't sure what he should say to calm him down.

Before he could come up with anything Celio reached behind his back, whipped his hand forward, arm extended. He flicked his thumb and a knife's blade shot outward.

Salas raised his open hands to his shoulders. The blade looked to be only a few inches long—probably not long enough to kill him. Maybe. "Whoa, hang on."

"Go to the back of the van," the kid said, voice flat, menacing. "I know that's where you keep them for the drop-off at the hotel."

Mind spinning, hands still up, Salas took slow steps toward the rear of the van, shocked that Celio knew about the clandestine location. Unable to come up with a single convincing thought, he reached beyond the open doors and slid the box toward him. Celio stood close, blade now pointed at the ground, intrigued as he watched Salas unfold the cardboard box's flaps.

Salas dug out the first Glock knockoff that hit his fingers, clasped the grip tight in his hand as he held it out for the boy to see.

"Where's the magazine and ammo?" Celio asked.

Salas assumed the student had researched the internet for proper lingo, or watched cop shows like his students talked about before classes, maybe his brother had taught him. Unsure if he should comply, Salas studied Celio for a bit. Knew no way in hell could he give the minor the gun.

The kid held his stare. Determined and firm about his decision, he aimed the knife at his teacher's gut—and Salas knew there would be no talking the youth out of what he yearned for. No changing of a mind that shouldn't even know about the weapons.

He wished now that he had marked which versions were in the box. He knew for certain half were freshly printed overnight. The others were created and assembled from previous batches—firearms that had the misfire glitch. Buying time, he studied the firearm, although the flaw he'd fixed wouldn't be visible.

Salas let out a resigned sigh, took up a tote bag that clinked when he reached inside and took out an empty magazine and handful of loose rounds of ammunition. The teacher smelled the nervous sweat, and maybe fear coming off the kid's body when he took a step closer, mesmerized by every action as Salas loaded the magazine, then slapped it home inside the butt of the grip.

"Have you ever fired one of these before?"

"Nuh-uh. Watched lots of YouTube videos though."

"Not the same. Especially the sound. The discharge is really loud. Deafening if you don't wear ear protection." He dug out a pair of gun muffs from the tote bag, but the kid didn't go for them.

Instead, Celio held out one hand for the replica, his knife with the other. Reluctantly Salas handed over the firearm. The kid pocketed the knife, then hefted the gun. He pulled back the barrel, loading one of the bullets in the chamber. Then, finger inside the trigger guard, he raised the fake Glock at Salas and smiled.

Salas batted the barrel away. "Don't point it at me, idiot!"

A switch seemed to flip in the student's eyes. It happened in an instant. From awe to fury. "What did you call me?"

"Nothing. I didn't mean anything—"

"*Idiot*. You called me an *idiot*. You think I'm stupid, too, huh?" He tapped the barrel against the thigh of his jeans. "You're just like everyone else. You don't give a shit about me. You just want money." He raised the gun, pointed it at Salas's face ten inches away. "Well, I don't have any money because they steal it from me. Even my brother doesn't pay me for doing the pickups. Manny takes all the money. Well now I'm gonna steal from you."

Salas lunged for the gun. Grabbed the barrel with his left hand, trapped Celio's hand on the grip with his right.

The kid's mouth dropped open, shocked.

For a brief moment Salas thought that would be it. Celio would back off, let go, relent, get on his motorbike and go, he would get in his van and drive off, Tuesday after the holiday they would see each other again at school, neither would mention a single thing about the incident.

Celio lunged this time.

Too stunned to react, Salas almost lost control of the weapon. He squeezed and wrenched his hand. But the kid had leverage and bulk on his side and within seconds overwhelmed Salas, trapping the teacher's finger inside the trigger guard.

The two continued to battle for the weapon. Salas gritted his teeth, grunted. Sweat ran into his left eye. He blinked over and over to clear his blurred vision.

"Let go, Celio. This isn't safe," he said through gritted teeth.

"*You* let go."

The teacher realized he had only a moment to react. He released one hand, lurched, spun, tucked the boy's back to his own chest.

Surprisingly strong, the kid thrashed, tried to wrench free.

Salas grunted, planted his feet, held on.

A thunderous *crack* made everything silent but the ringing in his ears.

Shocked, Salas released his hold. Celio took a staggering pace, turned around and looked at his teacher.

The boy held his breath, gritted his teeth, face turning red from the strain. A vein popped out on his forehead. Eyes wide, filled with tears. A scream gurgled in his throat. He gagged. Deep crimson rushed from his open mouth.

"Oh, god," Salas whispered. "No, no, no."

He rushed forward. Caught the student. They both hit the ground. Salas leaned against the rear tire, pulled Celio to his lap and rocked the boy in his arms. Dared to look down at the thick pool of blood increasing on the ground beside them.

"Why, Celio?"

"You weren't gonna give it to me. I need it. *Please.*"

"You need an ambulance. You're gonna be all right. Let me get my phone." Salas started to rise, but his student grabbed his arm, winced from the sudden movement.

"No. Don't leave me."

Salas matched the boy's panting breaths, tried to keep from looking anywhere but at the blood that grew wider. He leaned closer and whispered, "I would have helped you."

"Only losers ask for help."

"That's not true. Everyone needs help sometimes."

"Even you?" the boy asked, sounding younger than before.

"Absolutely. A lot. You even helped me once. Do you remember?"

"Nuh-uh."

"After class last month. I couldn't find my keys. You asked what I was looking for. I was upset and frustrated. I knew there was no way I'd lost them because I had them when class started. I searched and searched." Salas knew he rambled far more nonsensical information than necessary.

"Don't remember that," the kid said, voice slurred, eyes fluttering closed then back open.

"That's okay. I do. I know you're a good person, Celio."

He felt his student slipping away and held him tighter, bent low to his ear and said, "How did you know I have guns?"

"I do the money drop and pickup. Manny set it up with the gun shop guy."

Salas searched his mind for who Celio could be talking about. He didn't recall anyone by that name from his classes. Then he remembered. "Manny. Is that your brother?"

Celio managed a nod.

Salas knew of the older Novar, thankfully never one of his students. A troublemaker throughout high school five or six years back. If a fight broke out on campus Manuel Novar could usually be to blame. Taunting younger girls and the Native kids was sport to the six-foot-four imposing Latino. Salas had never once witnessed him in a good frame of mind or with a smile on his face.

"Manny won't give me a gun. It's an important job," Celio continued, his voice growing fainter. "Dangerous, too. I should have a gun. Right?"

"Who else knows?" Salas asked.

Eyes locked on his own, the boy didn't respond.

"Who else, Celio? Does your brother know who I am?"

Celio's eyes fluttered.

Salas shook the boy and he winced. "Does he?"

Still no response. A minute later, Celio whispered, "I'm sorry, Abuela." Then more pronounced to Salas, he said, "Tell Manny . . . Tell him I did good . . . I—I didn't cry . . ."

The weight in Salas's arms grew heavier. The boy's every muscle slackened. Words stopped.

Breaths slowed, stuttered a few faint gasps.

Light in the eyes unfocused, dimmed, glazed over.

The gun slipped from his relaxed hand.

Then nothing more emitted from the boy who would never become a man.

CHAPTER THIRTY-SIX

EVA

Eva felt odd as soon as she dropped off Kai and Shadow at his uncle Santiago's house. The Pueblo kid had become a trusted companion when they'd spent time together over the past year. Throw Cruz into the mix and they became a bold foursome along with Shadow, exploring pristine lands as they shared adventures all over their territory. Cruz had taught the boy how to fish, and Eva—the better shot—took over target practice. Much like the company he kept with the Malinois, she knew Kai appreciated their experiences together, forming a strong and reliable bond.

She had a feeling the rest of the day would be a long one so she decided to take a break before she got back to patrolling. By now she'd hoped to hear back from Dr. Mondragon or her chief or even Santiago about whether the vigil would take place tonight. She hoped so—it had been well over twenty-four hours since Pabla and Gabriel had seen their son. It was time to say goodbye.

The midafternoon had already started to cool down as she went in search of Paloma and she thought about the long line of her people who'd be standing out in the cold to pay last respects to Little Bear. A lot of firewood needed to be cut and stacked in piles beside the bonfires that would shoot firefly sparks to the dark sky throughout the night.

She picked up her pace when she made the final turn to the barn and spotted Paco Barboa raking outside the structure's opening.

"Hey, Eva," he said, eyes on her, still pulling the rake.

"Paco. Will you be here much longer? We're gonna need a lot of firewood to keep folks warm at the village. It'd be great if you could help out."

"Yep. Gotta finish out the hour here, then Navi and me are on it."

"Good man." She patted his shoulder as she passed.

Hay dust tickled Eva's nose as soon as she entered the breezeway. As most times before, she saw Paloma, who brushed and talked to her other best friend, tied up in front of the middle stall. The animal, appropriately named after a shark, swished his tail and munched the tufts of hay in a container lashed to the rail.

"Thought I'd find you here." Eva settled on a bench beside Paloma and her horse. "How are you feeling?"

"Fine."

"Always 'fine,'" Eva whispered.

Paloma halted the brush but didn't respond. She sat down beside Eva and stroked Mako's leg as he continued to chew.

They sat in their customary silence as long as Eva could bear. Then she leaned forward so she could watch Paco. He glanced in Paloma's direction and raked hay over his boots. Eva chuckled. "Paco can't keep his eyes off you."

Paloma tsked. Flicked her hand, a move much like Mako, who swished away a fly. "He's a boy."

"Paco and Navi built Nathan's casket. Handy with his hands." She waggled her eyebrows.

Paloma issued a scalding look.

"No? Well, how about that biology teacher? Kai said he's taken more than a little interest in you too."

Paloma let out an exhausted sigh. "I don't need another man in my life. Plenty enough with Kai and my brother, and Cruz. I've become too dependent on them. And you. It's time for me to look out for myself."

"Didn't mean to upset you," Eva said. "Thought seeing you would be a distraction, and I hoped you wanted some company. These cases are filling my mind up. Bank robber, 3D guns that keep showing up. Nathan's death. Just wanted a break for a while. You know . . . to sit here and smell the horse shit." Eva snapped her chin to Mako, who flicked and munched. "Watch you brush a bald spot on that demon-hooved creature."

Eva gave her a little grin, but Paloma didn't join her in the amusement.

"Have you come here for advice?" Paloma asked.

"Well, yeah," Eva said. "I always want to hear what you have to offer."

"All right, fine." Paloma slapped her hands on her thighs. "Not everything is your responsibility. You don't always have to be right, Eva. Sometimes you just have to be. And no one expects you to solve everything. Some things . . . or people . . . aren't meant for you to fix. Don't need to be fixed at all. We have to find our own way."

Eva let out a nervous chuckle. "Sounds like you're talking about you and me. Are you angry with me? Should I leave?"

"No. But I need you to stop treating me like a suspect you need to figure out every time I see you. I'm not going to slip. Not going to use again. I see what I have and what I lost. There's still lots of healing to do, but I'm focusing on the right now. And whatever will come. When I remember what I've done to the people I care about . . ."

Eva's worry escalated when Paloma shut her eyes tight and shook her head, stopped her movements, took in a slow breath and let it out even slower. She wasn't sure if she should reach over and attempt to comfort the clearly distraught woman.

On the edge of panic, Eva made a move to stand up—race to Paco and tell him to watch her while she ran to get Santiago.

Finally Paloma lasered her full attention on Eva. "I only want to go forward now," she said, voice determined and confident.

Tears burned Eva's eyes.

"I don't mean to hurt you, but I'm done with the coddling and everyone treating me like a skittish colt."

The realization appeared to have surprised Paloma as much as it did her. Her friend looked lighter, brighter, and unashamed for the first time in years. Unsure how she had arrived at this point at that moment, Eva didn't want to analyze the breakthrough—was merely happy her friend had come to the decision on her own.

Paloma straightened her back, neck, shoulders, as if preparing for Eva to lash out. "You always have an opinion. What do you think about that?" Paloma snapped, confidence and finality in her tone.

After almost an entire minute, Eva said, "I think I'm gonna like the new Paloma 'White Dove' Arrio." She smiled and nudged her friend's elbow. "I think you will too."

CHAPTER THIRTY-SEVEN
DAMON

Damon Sandoval sat on a folding chair in Manny Novar's grandmother's backyard, knife in one hand, six-inch-square piece of a willow tree limb in the other. Eight completed carvings of miniature bears and foxes sat in the pile of shavings. At first the task had been a hobby to pass his many hours of free time, but now he used the pieces to barter for food, and sometimes he'd make a little money from tourists buying gifts for their youngsters.

He had lost more jobs than he could remember since he'd been fired from the Taos Pueblo PD eight years ago—or was it ten. Twelve? He stilled his blade and tried to remember the year he had been disenrolled from the tribe. Shamed by everyone he'd ever known. Nothing but backs turned to him. An embarrassment to the tribe and his police force who stole evidence and tried to sell the items online. Even his family had cut him off completely.

He'd been squatting way out on the rez when he first met Manny Novar. Camped out near the stream for water, nothing but an old tarp lean-to for shelter, warming up canned food over a small fire every night for weeks.

That first encounter, Damon had waited outside the smoke shop begging for single cigarettes, hoping someone would be soft enough to give him an entire pack. Some tourists handed him a few dollars but he couldn't go inside or the owner would call the cops or run him off. Then Manny and Cal drove up, took mercy enough to toss him half a pack of American Spirits and started asking about the casino down the road.

Damon knew all about the casino from his aunties back in the day, who spent nearly every Tuesday through Thursday there—had told him about the best machines, which dealers were friendliest, best times to lay down your money or push the buttons.

Turned out Manny was a pretty good gambler once Damon shared his betting secrets. Weeks turned into months and the Spanish guy's wins turned less than his losses, tenfold or more. He'd had to borrow money from the man he picked up the fake guns for. Big mistake.

Damon knew Manny owed the gun shop guy tens of thousands of dollars, borrowed at a high rate he hadn't worried about—at first. Huge debt that Damon was sure the dude had no way of paying back. All because of the casino on the Pueblo reservation Damon had introduced him to. And now Manny couldn't even try his luck there since the three were now banned because Manny lost his temper a few months ago. Damon could have told him that would happen—shouldn't have grabbed the bolo tie on the blackjack dealer, pulled him close, threatened his mother if he didn't start dealing him decent hands.

Manny's volatile moods often unnerved Damon, which surprised him because nothing much got under Damon's skin. He'd had to step in a few times when Manny raised his fist to his grandma. Unacceptable. And he hit the kid Celio. Too many times.

Letting the abuse go without stepping in shamed Damon. He knew he should intervene. And lately he wanted to leave, just get the hell outa there, but he had nowhere else to go. In return for a spot on the floor to sleep, he kept the trees and bushes trimmed, took out the trash, and did the chores the other boys didn't want to do. Anyway he liked being around Manny's grandma. Missed his own. Did everything he could to protect her. The woman was always kind, smiled at him, let him watch her in the kitchen and help with chores. Celio usually helped prepare the meals, but Damon showed her how to make frybread, and made notes in his head so he could cook for his woman someday. If he could find one that would have him.

Manny kept Damon on edge, a constant annoyance, and he had to take all the shit thrown at him. Pretend his insults didn't matter. To always follow and never take the lead.

"One more time," he said to himself, the knife carving deeper than he intended. "Call me Tomahawk one more time."

He calmed himself, didn't let the fire of rage ignite. Too soon for that. He needed to sit in the quiet and think. And carve. And think some more.

A few people on the rez still talked to Damon. Most were as bad off as him, couch surfing and unsure about when they'd get their next hot meal, but lots of gossip still came his way.

He did have one particular ace in the hole. One he held on to. A secret he hoped he would be able to play soon, because Manny wasn't only a hothead. The dude was unhinged and standing on the edge of a very tall cliff. Another big loss and the big man would topple.

He smiled, allowed himself a satisfied grin as he raised his head to the magpie that landed on a fence post and chattered at him.

Then Damon would take over. Run the fake guns and whatever else the distributor wanted. Be the muscle with a brain, unlike Manny, who never thought a single step ahead. All he needed was to find out who the mastermind actually was. To figure out how to play Manny Novar. Trick him if he had to.

His knife hand halted as a thought came to him. Maybe the kid Celio knew who the kingpin was. Now he wished he'd become closer to the younger Novar. Too late now—the boy was way smarter than his older brother and would be suspicious if Damon pushed too hard.

Nope. He decided it was better to wait. Let the universe guide him.

"Patience," Damon reminded himself, speaking to his knife. "Soon it will all be yours."

He turned the wood creature in his hand. Gripped the knife's handle. Ran the blade across the neck of the statuette, its head landing on the top of his well-worn boot.

"And then they will *all* pay."

CHAPTER
THIRTY-EIGHT
SANTIAGO

Santiago had in mind something he wasn't certain he could pull off. But he would. Always. Whatever his fellow Pueblos needed. There would be no more waiting. Keeping his people at the mercy of others had to stop. He had decided that Nathan "Little Bear" Trujillo needed to come home. Tonight.

As a former member of the war council, he had met numerous high-ranking government officials of various agencies around the state, as well as visiting different tribes to meet with their council members. At the height of his reign he had journeyed to Washington, DC, to successfully finalize negotiations of the initial Abeyta water rights settlement in 2006. He and his team had become heroes when they returned home—celebrated with a feast and an unprecedented festival on the plaza in front of the *Hlauuma*, North House, at the village.

During that ceremony, a new warbonnet was placed on his head by his mother. Replete with eagle feathers fashioned from his former headdress, fresh beads featuring the Taos Pueblo flag colors stitched on the headband. Tears had streamed down her proud face as he bent low to embrace her.

He and his Pueblo contingency had also traveled to many states, where they would express the need to keep their tribe—and all tribes—self-sufficient. Exhausting and often soul-crushing experiences, except for the relationships he had cultivated. Such as the one friendship he cherished beyond all others from that time.

He picked up his phone and redialed the same private number from earlier that morning.

Two rings later, a friendly laugh came over the line. "This can't really be you again so soon."

"Afraid it is."

"What do you need this time?" the low rumble of the senator's voice said.

Santiago settled into the silence for a moment, then said, "One more favor."

"Already pulled a big rabbit out of a deep hole. Let's see if I can continue the streak."

"The boy—"

"Nathan Trujillo."

"Yes," Santiago said, appreciating that the legislator remembered the fallen youngster's name. "I want him brought home, today."

"Big ask, Santi. The medical examiner might not be ready to release him yet."

"Understood. But I need you to make this happen."

"Done." No hesitation.

Santiago let out a relieved breath. "Thank you."

"How would it go for me to attend the funeral?"

"Not advisable. My people might misunderstand."

"You could explain—"

"No. Better there's no outsiders, even though you've helped my people more than they will ever know."

"I didn't help you for political favors."

"Yes. I know. You are a true friend."

"Come out and visit. You stay put too much. Julie would love to see you again."

"Bring her riding next time you're in Taos."

"Even better! She'd do that in a hot minute."

"Found a prized stallion for Paloma. She might let your wife play with it."

The laugh again over the cell phone made Santiago smile—he figured probably the last light moment he would have for the days to come. Again he issued his gratitude for the undertaking he alone would not be able to accomplish and clicked off the connection.

Next he called the Trujillos and let them know Little Bear would be with them before the sun fell beyond the horizon. The mother's grateful sobs nearly broke him and he cut the call before his own emotions had a chance to release.

The last reach-out would prompt everyone on the reservation to action, much earlier than expected. The heat over pots of already-simmering meat and stews would need to be raised to lessen cooking times, and wood cut to feed fires for light and heat inside the mourning house and outside for the overflow of people waiting to extend their respect. Bakers would spread the word to each other to light the *horno* ovens to bake the bread and pies the moment he hung up.

Most sacred of all, the private first-floor dwelling within the North House would need to be prepared right away. All furniture removed, dirt floors swept, tables and folding chairs set up along three of the walls, power strips running from a generator for the array of slow cookers that would contain the food to feed those who would line up to be served the traditional feast of beef and pork chile dishes, beans, and casseroles. He hoped someone knew the boy's favorite treats and would think to bring them in his honor too.

He walked through his house, down the hallway that led to the five bedrooms, and entered the door at the farthest end of the corridor. Santiago made an effort to keep his vision trained forward so his attention wouldn't stray to the bedside table on his mother's side of the mattress. He knew the book she had been reading the night she died would still be there, bookmark covered in kittens stuck between pages thirty-two and thirty-three. His dad's table held a stack of years-old fish and game magazines, articles dog-eared, pages crinkled from rereading over and over. Always learning, both of them.

Nothing had changed in this room. Maybe never would. Bed made, as if waiting for them both to return for the night's slumber. Dresser, nightstands and lamps wiped clear of dust once a week. Their sanctuary all the years they were married, until they passed on—cherished mother first, then father not even four months later. Santiago felt their presence every time he opened the door and stepped over the threshold.

Although it was the biggest bedroom in the house, Santiago didn't have the heart to disassemble the sacred space, where his parents would often escape long before dark to spend time with only each other. So many memories he couldn't bear to put in boxes, stored away, possibly never to be opened again.

He went to the ancient cedar chest his grandfather had made eons ago, opened the lid, inhaled the faint wood scent that had lingered after so many decades. He removed each piece respectfully, one tightly folded blanket after another, then a supple leather miniature-size outfit he recognized from a few pictures of him being cradled as a baby in his mother's arms. A pain of loss caught in his chest. He set the clothing aside and dug out more items.

Sadness crept in when he didn't find what he was searching for. Santi couldn't think of anywhere else the piece would be. Resigned that the search was over, he put back the coverings, careful not to wrinkle the tight folds. He gasped when he caught sight of the edge of a design and familiar colors.

"Thank you, Universe," he muttered, unfolding a frayed and faded wool blanket. Five feet long and half as wide, the red, black and white traditional weave had been created by his grandmother and gifted to her daughter the morning Santiago "Hawk Soars" Mirabal entered his existence as a Taos Pueblo member, screaming and scrunch-faced, fists whirling, head covered in the longest black hair anyone had ever seen— if the stories of his first breaths of sweet New Mexico air were true.

Because the blanket was the first covering to touch Santiago's skin moments after birth, his parents had kept the blanket tucked away all these years, intended for their eldest son's last moments of his final time above the earth. But Santiago wanted the tiny warrior's protectors to know that one of the highest-ranking members of the tribe felt the boy was deserving of the cherished contribution.

After he replaced the rest of the items and closed the lid, he took the blanket to be added to the collection of other items for Little Bear's vigil, which would begin at sundown.

In preparation for the boy to rest on the blanket Santiago had planned to gift to the family, he'd first have the *cacique* bless the cloth that would hold the boy in the embrace of their people, the spirits, Creator, universe. For the end of time.

CHAPTER THIRTY-NINE
EVA

Eva wanted nothing more than to be deep in the forest right now. Imagined red willows swaying, the scent of pine sap wafting in the breeze, hidden birds chattering, coyote howls in the darkness come nighttime—and so she drove there. Where she was certain to be alone.

She needed privacy to try what she had in mind. Although Chief Lefthand had denied her request to go to Santa Fe to meet face to face with Alice Jones—who was currently serving time in the women's ward at Santa Fe's correctional facility, awaiting trial for various felony charges including kidnapping, manslaughter, and the first- and second-degree murder of seven people—her boss didn't say Eva couldn't try for a phone call reach-out.

Eva's nerves jangled as she thought about the admonishment she'd receive if her supervisor found out she had straddled the line of approval. *Only a little,* she assured herself.

Afraid she might talk herself out of it if she thought much longer, she got out of the Beast and settled on the trunk of a fallen pine. After a few cleansing breaths, she sent up a silent prayer for strength. Reminded herself not to become emotional. Tell the prisoner nothing. Let *her* do the talking.

Eva pulled out her cell phone, dialed the number saved in her contacts, waited for the proper channels to approve the request. She centered herself, prepared for whatever would come her way. Asked her grandfather for courage and patience. Sadness enveloped her when she didn't feel the warmth of his essence beside her, or even in the surrounding trees.

As she waited for the jailhouse supervisor to either approve or deny the call with the prisoner, Eva ran options through her mind of how the conversation might go. She didn't want to spend any excess time that could give the inmate the opportunity to manipulate the discussion to *her* private wants. *No chitchat. Nothing personal. Don't let her in.* She replayed the inward instructions over and over.

Then the voice Eva never thought she would hear again before her court case said, "Deputy Duran. So nice to hear from you."

"Officer Duran."

"Oh, a demotion? I'm sorry to hear that." The Texas-accented voice on the other line actually sounded quite pleased.

"No, tribal police officer now."

"How wonderful! I'm sure your people are very proud to have you working for them instead of for outsiders."

Eva had forgotten the Texas twang of Alice's voice, more of a high-pitched chirp that became more animated as her tales expanded to full-out lies. *Stay impassive,* Eva reminded herself, unsure now if she should have made contact with the woman who had caused so much turmoil and sorrow.

"Why are you calling, *Officer* Duran?"

"Let's talk about guns."

Eva imagined the woman's elation when she said, "Oh, I know a lot about guns."

"What do you know about 3D printed firearms?"

"They use them as props for movies and TV."

"Untraceable, look realistic . . ."

"Good for criminals, I suppose."

"Did you ever encounter any when you were in Taos, or on the reservation?"

"No."

The answer came too quick for Eva's liking. "Are you sure? Three were recovered from the house where you shot the drug dealers."

"Allegedly," Alice replied, voice dripping with smugness.

"Right. Allegedly shot them. Think about this for a minute, Ms. Jones."

"Alice, please."

"Ma'am, we're attempting to figure out how a death occurred. A young Taos Pueblo boy. Eight years old."

The declaration seemed to capture Alice's full attention. Eva figured she must have raised the handset closer to her mouth, voice distorting as she asked, "Which little boy?"

"Nathan Trujillo. The child you met at the house where you killed the drug dealers." Silence followed and Eva realized her mistake. "Excuse me . . . Allegedly killed the drug dealers."

"Oh yes, we were very good friends."

Eva knew the woman lied. Had encountered Little Bear only twice. The boy had been insistent about that when questioned after the investigation had wrapped up.

"You didn't know him," Eva said, attempting to keep her voice impassive. "You might have met him, but you didn't know him. Not what a special and kind little boy he was before those men corrupted his family and took over their home."

"I took care of that for him. And for his parents."

"Right . . ." Eva imagined Alice reveling in being a hero. "Allegedly."

"Exactly," Alice said.

Eva waited a full minute, her intent to fully draw the former nurse practitioner in. Then she asked, "Do you remember anything about the boy having a gun?"

"Yes, of course . . . The first time I met him he had a plastic gun. It looked real. He said he needed it for protection. Was that a 3D gun? Is that what got him killed? Did he point it at the wrong person?"

Eva evaded the direct questions. She needed to be the one in charge, and had questions of her own. "You said you and the boy were friends. What did you two talk about?"

"I tried to help him get away from those bad, bad men, but he ran off."

"And you left him there. You must have known that was no environment for a child. You could have called the tribal police."

"They were horrible men," Alice said, ignoring Eva's statement.

"Deserved what they got?" Eva asked, goading the woman so she could ask her final questions.

"Allegedly."

"Three innocent women's lives were also taken by your hand."

Another pause. "Again—allegedly. And four drug dealers . . . Allegedly. You're welcome."

Eva assumed a smile lifted Alice's lips. Creepy. Masklike. She ignored the dig and uttered one of her own. "*Apparently* you didn't read the black box warning listing the side effects of the buprenorphine. That the drug can be fatal if too high of a dose is administered intravenously."

"How would you know about that?" Voice hard and challenging this time.

"Did my research. You obviously didn't."

"I don't appreciate you focusing on my failures."

"I don't appreciate you killing my people."

This time the woman did not indicate a hint of evasion. "Is the boy really dead?"

The inquiry confused Eva. Could the psychopath truly be concerned? "Yes."

"Time to call my lawyer," the woman said in an upbeat singsong voice.

Doom flooded over Eva. She wasn't sure what yet, but she had a sense she'd missed something. Or caused something. Something that would bite her and not let go.

"Why do you say that?"

"Little Nathan is the boy who told you and the other officers that I shot those very bad men. He was the only witness. Now there's no one to testify against me."

Eva clenched her stomach muscles tight so she wouldn't spew the bile that threatened. "There's no refuting. Even without firsthand testimony. Gunshot residue doesn't lie."

"I'm a gun enthusiast. Did some target practice earlier that morning. Did any of your people check the boy's hands after I was arrested?"

Unable to verify or deny for certain, Eva felt the blood rush her head.

The woman let out a cackle of a laugh. "Didn't think so."

The line went silent, but Eva swore she could hear the other woman's brain ticking over the line.

"Yes, it's all coming back to me now. I must have blocked out the memory. Devastating. Horrifying to see a small child lift a gun, point it, shoot one man after another. I'm tellin' you I couldn't move I was so shocked. And scared." Eva imagined the act. Innocence personified. "I'll never get over it in all my life."

"Unbelievable," Eva whispered. All she could manage.

"I believe my chances of acquittal are getting better and better. Please give my condolences to the little boy's parents. Such a loss."

Eva waited a few beats. Got hold of her emotions. Steeled herself. "There's no denying you killed three Native American women. You will spend the rest of your life in prison for that."

"Maybe. Maybe not. Did anyone actually see me do anything but try to save them?"

The line went quiet again, Eva figured probably so Alice could cunningly wait for her adversary to take in the entire shift of the conversation. Then she twisted the knife in Eva's gut deeper. "How is White

Dove? Does she talk about me? Is my cure still working? Please tell her she's welcome and that she can come and see me."

Eva couldn't help but gasp. She gripped the phone so hard her hand went numb.

"Anytime, Officer Duran," Alice shouted. "Her boy too!"

Eva ended the connection but could still hear Alice Jones's demented laugh resonate all around her. She cursed herself over and over. Until a court date was set, the killer might not have ever found out about Nathan's death and what that could mean for the upcoming trial . . . if not for her.

Shame and regret smoldered and she found herself sitting in her Rover without realizing how she'd made it there. Blind to everything but the ball of rage that had sparked—for Alice Jones, the circumstances around Nathan's death, her inadequacy as a representative of her police force, Little Bear's family.

Rage that could cost the dismissal of at least four of the murder charges against Alice Jones.

And Eva's badge.

CHAPTER FORTY
CRUZ

Cruz supervised the closure of the Taos Pueblo to tourists and made sure no vehicles remained in each of the visitors' parking lots. He had been surprised, but not shocked, when Eva called to let him know Nathan was coming home.

He didn't tell her that word had already spread, prompted by Santiago. He had never seen his people work so fast as teams shuttled chairs and tables, picked up every bit of trash on the plaza, swept the North House entrance of the private house where Nathan's vigil would be held. A generator had been placed and tested to provide power for basic lighting and to plug in the slow cookers inside the electricity-prohibited ancient dwelling.

A pickup inched toward Cruz, bed stacked with firewood, the precarious load taller than the truck's roof. The window buzzed down and the twins, Navi and Paco Barboa, waved in unison.

"Nice ride, Navi," Cruz said. "Did you steal it?"

The brothers' chuckles sounded a bit devious and they didn't answer yes or no. Cruz figured the odds were fifty-fifty. And splitting that much wood took great effort as well. The twins were fast and capable with an axe, but this fast? Cruz couldn't be sure. The temperature had dropped ten degrees in the past hour and the night promised to be a chilly one. The twins would be kept busy tending to the many fires throughout the night to keep those paying their respects warm. He waved Navi onward without further questions he didn't want the answers to.

He checked his watch and figured he had a good seventy-five minutes before the hearse carrying Nathan would get there. He'd need to be on point as lead security for the wake in a few hours. Keep the visitors moving, elders and families with infants and toddlers allowed to pay their respects first and to fill their plates with the prepared feast of the boy's favorite foods. But before any of that happened, Cruz needed a shower, a fresh uniform, and a little privacy before he faced hundreds of his people.

He informed his team he would be back in an hour and took the shortest route to his house on the rez. He parked in front of the white three-bedroom, two-bath structure he and his brothers had built ten years ago, and wanted nothing more than to sit in one of the rockers on the wraparound porch, enjoy the breeze, watch the sunset from his unobstructed view to the west. Crack a beer, wait for Eva. They could both forget the day together. Not even having to say a word as they held hands and rocked and sipped and watched their world turn golden to rust to black to a million stars their only view.

But duty called and time to rest would be many hours in the future. Anticipating the water pelting his skin, he stripped as he entered the house and beelined for the shower. He thanked the universe when he found a fresh uniform in his closet. He wove his still-wet hair into a tight braid, then secured the keepers of his duty belt to his personal belt, took the Glock from its holster, ejected the magazine to check the loads, eased back the barrel to confirm a round in the chamber, slapped the clip back in the handle.

He thought about what awaited. Many tears would fall during the upcoming viewing. Everyone beyond sad, even those who didn't know Little Bear feeling touched. A soul taken too soon. One who would never receive a blessing in his appointed kiva. No first hunt. No learning from elders' spoken stories passed down one generation after another.

And more trauma to be endured at tomorrow's burial lay ahead, where only close members of the family and those specifically chosen by Pabla and Gabriel Trujillo would be permitted to attend the ceremony. Which mean bruised egos and hurt feelings for those Pueblos being left out. He knew of many relationships, some lifelong, that had been severed over being unintentionally snubbed. His people were proud and some felt tears should be shed alone. Their mourning private. Most would accept the decision and stay away. Some would never understand and be waiting at the graveyard gate, expecting the parents to allow them entry to sacred ground.

More ancient traditions would follow, each as important as the other. Adhering to the customs and traditions was paramount during these occasions. The entire community would be watching, most importantly the Pueblo's governor and war chief and their staffs, as well as the entire tribal council. One misstep and Chief June "Bobcat Leaps" Lefthand could be ejected from her position.

So many were shocked that a woman had been appointed chief and probably some felt that it would not be so bad to see her gone. It would open the door for Cruz to step in—no training needed. But the boots-on-the-ground officer in Romero didn't want that. He was loyal and supportive, wanted his Pueblo sister to succeed.

And he didn't want to be chief. He would save that wish for Eva Duran when the time came for Lightning Dance to step up.

Now ready for security detail, he said to the mirror, "Show nothing, Wolf Song. Stoic Native Face, Officer Romero."

He would be vigilant. For what he wasn't sure. He sent up a call to his watchers—to keep him safe. To please help him hold his own emotion at bay, eyes clear, so that others might grieve.

Cruz took up a case of orange pop from the kitchen counter and headed for his official vehicle. Calm, centered, now ready to face his people.

CHAPTER FORTY-ONE
DAMON

Damon Sandoval watched as Manny paced the floor in the front room of his grandmother's house. Cell phone pinned to his ear, the guy had grown more stressed as each hour passed without word from his brother.

"I know, man. I hear ya," Manny said into the mobile, voice high and tight. "Tell him I'll have the guns by midnight . . . Yeah, I know it'll cost me . . . Tell him I got this. No problem. 'Kay? You'll tell him? . . . Okay, okay—midnight. Tell him we're good."

He clicked off the connection. His hand shook so bad it took three tries to pocket the phone. "That guy's boss isn't fuckin' around," Manny said. "I'm talkin' former marine sniper, take-no-prisoners shit. We gotta get those guns. Tonight!"

He pulled out the phone again and hit the redial for Celio's number. Fifteenth time. Again the canned answer. "Fuck! Where the hell are you, Celio? You'd better not be ditchin' me. I need those guns! You gotta get them for me."

Manny ended the call and glared at Damon. "What?"

"Maybe you're scaring the little dude."

"Mind your own business."

"This is my business, bro. I'm here to help. So is Cal. We got your back."

"Yeah, I know. I appreciate that, man. But only my blood brother can help me right now."

The phone in his hand vibrated. His eyes went wide when he recognized the number. "Ah, shit," he said, then swiped the screen to deny the call.

Seconds later a signal dinged, indicating a voice mail had been left. Damon knew that Manny didn't need to listen to the message, left by the actual man who paid for the knockoff guns—instead of an underling this time—bitching about the expected delivery that might be late because of Manny's little brother. That he was truly toast now that he owed the gun runner so much money to keep gambling. No way in hell to pay that back. Unless he robbed a bank, and that already happened so the cops would have hard-ons about anyone else pulling a gun in public. Shoot first. No questions. None of them could risk that.

"Maybe we could rob something," Cal suggested.

Damon knew firsthand that both convenience stores at the edge of town did big business. Lots of tourists buying snacks and drinks, mostly with cash instead of a credit card. Yeah, Allsup's would pay out as good as the slots once did. Still, the risk was too high. Damon figured someone would recognize him and he'd wind up in prison and everything would be for nothing. He talked himself out of the risky plan as fast as the thought popped into his mind.

"Naw, man. We just gotta get those guns," Manny muttered.

Damon grinned, his lips turning up higher and higher until Manny said, "What? Did you think of something?"

"If your brother doesn't show . . . I know where we can get some of those guns."

"The ones Celio was picking up? You know who makes them? Where the drop-off is?" Manny stepped closer after each question, eyes pleading for more information.

"Nope. Other ones."

Damon went silent to draw out the suspense.

Manny looked ready to launch at him, claws out. "Tell me!"

"The tribal police department evidence room."

"How do you know that?" Cal asked.

"Once a tribal cop, always a tribal cop. Still know people over there."

Damon knew Manny had nothing to lose. The gun dealer already had buyers waiting for the product. Celio might be too scared to make the pickup, especially now that he'd taken the money—hell, the pissant could be anywhere with that much cash. Twenty-four hundred dollars was a lot of scratch for a kid.

"Damn," Manny said. "You might be useful after all, Tomahawk."

Damon glared at Manny. "Told you not to call me that anymore." He kept his voice soft to enhance the ominous undercurrent.

"Sorry, sorry, man. I'm sorry. Didn't mean no offense." Manny held up his open hands. "How would we get the ones you're talkin' about?"

"Simple. Everyone will be at the vigil tonight."

"What the fuck are you talkin' about?"

"A Pueblo boy got shot dead. The tribal bosses won't allow his corpse to be off the rez much longer. Bet you a hundred the kid's death-watch will start after sundown tonight. Tomorrow at the latest. I've got someone who will tell me when for sure. Whole damned tribe will be at the village for hours. All the cops too."

Manny smiled. Slow. Menacing. "I knew I kept you around for something, Tomahawk."

Damon turned his back on the disparagement. The rage he knew well simmered. A slow, constant heat. Vengeance on the edge of a furious roil that would not be denied much longer.

CHAPTER
FORTY-TWO
EVA

The moment Eva received a text from Santiago that Nathan's funeral coach had crossed over the sovereign boundary line, she and Kai and Shadow raced to the Beast and sped to the street that led to the village.

She parked at the edge of the road, not far from a portable barrier that crossed the width of the thoroughfare and denied further access. Eva waved at two Pueblo old-timers who stood guard in front of the barricade. Both veterans wore military uniforms and garrison caps, ribbons and metals affixed to their left breasts.

She spotted the black Cadillac that traveled at a respectful speed. She reminded herself to breathe as tears wavered her vision as she thought of the child in the wooden casket—already worried about his parents' reaction when their son arrived at the home assigned for his viewing. Where the entire tribe would gather as soon as the sun sank below the plain.

Kai had slid low in his seat, eyes forward, shoulders up, chin tucked in the neck of his hoodie. Shadow rested his snout on his companion's shoulder, as if to keep him in place as much as for reassurance.

Close enough to see now, Eva watched the massive driver, who kept his hands at ten and two on the steering wheel, attention forward—stoic and professional as the first time she'd laid eyes on him.

The hearse stopped and the veterans moved the barricade, then flanked the vehicle, at the driver door and the passenger doors. In unison, they straightened their backs and shoulders, stood at attention, raised their right arms, snapped bladed hands to their foreheads. Held their salute until the funeral coach passed.

"Respect," Kai muttered. "Nathan would have liked that."

Eva didn't want Kai to be thinking of his young friend as if he was already gone. Not yet. Not until after the vigil and the burial and the mourning process. Only then would Nathan "Little Bear" Trujillo truly be gone to them.

"I'm sure he does," she corrected, as if the boy had personally witnessed the send-off.

As soon as the Cadillac passed, Eva turned the Beast around and followed. Farther ahead, a rope now blocked the main unpaved visitors' parking lot entrance, and a portable sign stated, PUEBLO CLOSED FOR PRIVATE CEREMONY. NO VISITORS. As with every traditional burial ceremony, men would be assigned to wave away each unauthorized vehicle, offering no explanations to the disappointed tourists.

Kai pointed to the massive pickup truck parked outside the barrier. "Uncle Santiago's here already."

Eva knew he would be, watching over every aspect of the upcoming ceremony. Making sure everything and everyone had been taken care of, in his stern and hands-off yet supervisory manner. Had probably checked on Pabla and Gabriel Trujillo a dozen times to make sure they were prepared, told them what to expect, explained the traditional steps of the process ahead—from tonight's viewing throughout the night, tomorrow's burial, and the following bereavement period. The young couple would undergo countless passed-down rituals to be certain their child's spirit felt loved and cared for.

The air hummed louder as they came closer to the ancient origin of the land of their people, centering Eva. They drove the main dirt track that led to the village, then she came to a halt in a dirt lot adjacent to the reservation's original graveyard. This would be as far as their vehicles would be allowed to travel on this day.

The cemetery, filled to capacity and restricted to new burials in 2017, contained faded and crooked simple white crosses that marked burial sites inside the crumbling three-foot-tall adobe wall that surrounded the area, including ruins of the original church on the sovereign land. Believed to have been built in the early 1600s, only a portion of the San Geronimo de Taos remained. As always, Eva cast a look to where her grandfather's cross had been before it had fallen—the loss still fresh whenever she thought of the day of his burial.

Eva and Kai simultaneously released a sigh of relief when they saw Cruz appear from around a corner. Dressed in his uniform, hair in a traditional braid, he hustled to them, then leaned his elbow against the open window frame, whipped off his sunglasses, held Eva's eyes a long moment, then beaded on Kai's gaze, did the same for Shadow. Seeming satisfied they had survived the day's journey so far, somewhat spiritually unscathed—he slid his shades back on and opened the driver's door for Eva.

Kai took hold of her arm as she readied to leave the vehicle. She waited for him to speak, didn't want to rush anything with him from this moment onward until the entire mourning period had ended.

"I don't think I can do this," Kai said, eyes on the medicine bag in his hand.

"It's okay, Single Star. Nothing is expected from you. Do only what you're good with."

"Thank you," he whispered.

Shadow leaned forward and licked the side of Eva's face. She didn't mind it at all this time.

Cruz had taken a few steps toward the awaiting hearse and turned back, cocked his head, arms open wide in a *Well, are you coming?* gesture.

Santiago came around the corner and walked toward them, as if he had sensed his nephew's distress. Kai got out of the Rover, released Shadow, then approached his uncle.

Santiago raised his eyebrows and Eva shook her head. Their silent communication conveyed, he said, "Let's get you home for a while."

"Okay," Kai said, sounding dejected, yet relieved.

"I'll check on you later," Eva said. "Thank you for spending time with me."

The young man nodded and started for Santiago's truck, head down, hands stuffed in his hoodie pocket.

"I appreciate all you did to make this happen, Santi," she said.

"It's my job."

"No. It's really not. But I'm glad it was you who stepped up." She leaned in and hugged the bear of a man, held him tight for a moment. "Kai did really well. Shadow too. The pup really helped us out the past couple days. He deserves a treat tonight. The most special you've got."

"That dog I gave away for free?"

"*That dog* has found crucial evidence and may have even saved someone from finding the guns. And he was a comfort to Kai. The Trujillos too. He's a canine hero."

Santiago let out a loud sigh. "All right. I'll pull an elk sirloin out of the freezer."

"And one for Kai. Probably won't eat it, but he needs to know you care about him too."

"He doubts that?"

"No—I . . . I didn't mean it that way. Just . . . Jeez, Santi, why do you have to make everything so hard?" She squeezed his surprisingly solid biceps. "Lighten up, big man."

He remained stone faced, gave her nothing. Too exhausted to argue or attempt to sway him into a better mood, she started to walk away.

"What you've done, Lightning Dance . . ."

She whirled on him. "What, Hawk Soars? What have I done?"

"More than you will ever know." He thumped his chest three times with a closed fist.

His sincere appreciation touched Eva. Embarrassed by her overreaction, she returned the heartfelt gesture and took steps toward Cruz.

"What was that about?" he asked.

"Santi being weird again."

"Nothing new. You ready for this?" Cruz asked when they reached the long black vehicle.

"Nope," she said. "Let's go."

CHAPTER
FORTY-THREE
KAI

Kai didn't turn to his uncle, who sat behind the steering wheel and
fired up the pickup's engine. Didn't want to see the disappointment on
the man's face for not being strong enough to complete what had been
expected of him.

But instead of recriminations, Santiago surprised him by saying,
"Your mom is waiting for you. She made our mother's famous potato
salad for tonight."

Kai reared back. "Mom? Cooked?"

"Yes. It took a while."

Kai let out a chuckle, imagining his mother figuring out the steps
to prepare the side dish he had been told everyone looked forward to
for every celebration and festival and powwow until his grandmother's
death.

As usual, silence followed as they inched respectfully down one road,
then another. Santiago took a less-traveled route and Kai figured something must be coming. That his uncle needed time to find the words.

"I've spent much of the day with the Trujillos," Santiago finally
said. "Nathan's parents appreciate you being like a big brother to Little
Bear."

"He was a good kid. Really thought he would take after me. Finish school. Go to college. Maybe we'd go into business together one day. He was fascinated by the greenhouses at the Red Willow Center. Wanted to preserve cuttings from every plant on the rez to make sure they didn't disappear."

"You can still do that, Kai."

"Better with two."

Kai had been working on something during the return trip from Santa Fe he wanted to ask his uncle. He never knew when he would get uninterrupted time with the man, so he went ahead and said, "How do you deal with your anger?"

"Deal with it?" Santiago shrugged. "More like, live with it. Lotta stuff makes me angry. Furious sometimes. People off the rez don't understand us. Pueblos fighting against one another over simple and sometimes irrelevant issues. Too much drink. Not enough money. Violence against the women. That's why I got involved in politics. Defending our people's rights, battling injustices. Be a peacemaker when I can be. Or when they let me. Some people don't listen, never will."

Santiago glanced over at him and Kai turned his head to look out his window.

"Why are you asking?"

"I get mad when I think about what happened to Nathan. And what those other kids who saw him get hurt are going through now." He took out his medicine pouch and ran the bottom tassels through his fingers. "Makes me wanna find that guy who shot Nathan and . . . I don't know what."

"End him?"

Kai whirled his attention to Santiago. "No!" Then he rethought his quick answer. Took some time to ponder if he actually could. "No," he said, less force in his voice this time.

"Because you are your mother's son. Your father's too. Even after all Paloma went through, she has forgiven. The drunk driver that killed

Ahiga and her friends. The people who took advantage of her when she couldn't make the right decisions. Alice Jones. Me."

Santiago's words halted but Kai had learned over the months to wait out the silence because more might come. His uncle cleared his throat and Kai knew another story would be presented.

"I've done regretful things in my past, as a young man," Santiago said. "Unforgivable if the indiscretions were to come out. One of the reasons I'm so private, and live in the power of knowing what others don't. Probably made me hard, always having to stay on my toes. Vigilant not to say too much so others don't ask questions. Because of that, I held anger in my heart much of my life. It kept me grounded. Focused. Determined to make something of myself. More than I needed to be. But I'm older now and don't have the patience for my impatience." Santiago chuckled, surprising Kai with the unaccustomed humor.

"Yeah, but you're still cranky sometimes."

Kai's kidding smile dropped from his face as soon as his elder cut his eyes at him and gave the smoldering look that always made Kai feel five years old.

Santiago turned back to the windshield. "Lots to be cranky about nowadays."

"For sure."

"Learn from my mistakes, Single Star. Don't let your fury get in the way of being happy. People have always been afraid of me. To this day, half the tribe are too anxious to approach me—think I know too much about everyone, that their secrets are mine to keep or share depending on my mood or how I'm treated. Been in a lot of fights with bucks who want to take me down. Kill my drive. Smash my power. Crush my soul. Destroy what they think is my empire, like I'm some mogul they see on TV."

Santiago went quiet again. Kai felt his uncle's distress and for the first time understood the man better. He imagined his uncle's loneliness must feel much like his own.

"Why are you telling me this, Uncle?"

"Be like me. But don't be me. Too lonely. When you're ready, find someone who makes you as happy as Paloma made Ahiga. That Navajo adored your mom. For now, surround yourself with good people—like Eva and Cruz—keep them close."

"It's been good hanging out with Eva today. Thinking maybe I'll become a cop."

"Absolutely not!" The force of Santiago's two words resonated in the truck's cabin. "You are a botanist. You will be a teacher. And a healer."

"I'll be poor."

"And happy. Don't worry. I've made seven lifetimes of money. You'll never have to worry about getting all the toys you want. After I'm dead and gone."

"That's not what I want. Things don't interest me. A car would be nice though." He beamed a big grin but Santiago didn't take the bait.

"The dirt bike not good enough for you?"

"It's great! I love it. Mom, not so much. I'm careful and take the back roads and wear a helmet, but she worries I'll get hit or forced off the road, or who knows what else."

"That's her job now. She's missed years of your life. Bound to go overboard about some things."

"Tonight's gonna be brutal."

"You don't have to attend. The Trujillos will understand."

"I want to go. And I will. Maybe when there won't be so many people."

"We'll figure it out. Go late in the night if you want."

"Thanks, Uncle."

"Paloma will want to be there with you. And for you. Me too."

Kai couldn't find the words to convey his gratitude. He swallowed a sob before it emerged, anxious he wouldn't be able to hide or stop his feelings.

"Any news about the bank robber?" Kai asked.

"None that I've heard. No sign of anyone suspicious reported on the rez."

"What about the lady cop?"

"Stable. She'll be all right."

Kai wondered how Santiago knew information about people and events, even those outside the rez boundary. He knew the tribal council member had contacts all over Taos and the state. Some of them high up in government, although he didn't know who exactly. The man continued to be a mystery and Kai reveled in any details his uncle shared. He drank in the refreshing ice-cold water of information, sweet and satisfying as sips from the Rio Pueblo de Taos stream that ran between the North and South Houses in the village.

"And the guns? The plastic ones, like Shadow found. Any ideas where they're coming from?"

"That's a question for Eva and Cruz. Tribal police don't keep me in the loop as much as other members of the tribal council."

"Think the feds will come around to the rez?"

Santiago strangled the steering wheel. "No point. They won't find anything. Bank robber's long gone."

"Yeah, but the guns—"

"Enough, boy," Santiago snapped. "Too much Eva-time. Sounding like a cop."

"See. Cranky."

Kai caught the slight twinge of a smile on Santiago's lips. Then, in a blink, his uncle reverted to the Stoic Native Face he wore so well.

CHAPTER FORTY-FOUR
EVA

Eva and Cruz waited beside the black Cadillac parked at the mouth of the path that led to the village. The driver had his back to the closed door of the cargo area, holding his now-familiar sumo parade rest position.

The Alice Jones call two and a half hours ago kept plaguing her. She'd run the conversation through her mind numerous times and had yet to figure out what to do next. She should give her chief the heads-up that a troublesome phone call from the Santa Fe County Adult Correctional Facility could be forthcoming.

Cruz thankfully threw her out of the disturbing introspection when he said, "You're quiet."

"Thinking."

"Think out loud."

She gave Cruz her full attention, assessed him a moment, then blurted out words she didn't take the time to consider. "I screwed up, Cruz."

"Doubt it." When she didn't say anything else for a full minute, he said, "Tell me."

"Lefthand wouldn't authorize me go to Santa Fe . . . so I called Alice Jones."

Cruz stared at her. Stared some more. She imagined his heartbeat thudding beneath the Kevlar over his chest. Waited for him to cut her off, not wanting to know. But now that she'd started her confession she couldn't stop herself.

"Beyond foolish. Can't believe I did it." She dropped her head to study her boots in case Cruz's expression changed from emotionless to warranted disappointment. "I needed to find out what she knew about the 3D guns and somehow wound up telling her about Nathan's death. She totally manipulated me, which shouldn't be a surprise because she's wacked in the head beyond any scale of imagination."

"She's messin' with you," Cruz said. "Every charge against her is solid."

"Maybe. Maybe not. Nathan was the only witness. Charges for the drug dealer murders could be dropped. And could affect the Tonita, Kishi and Dora cases too." She turned to look at Nathan's coffin inside the hearse. "I really messed up. Need to tell the chief."

Then she chanced a glance at Cruz, who had diverted his complete attention away from her. He hitched his head and Eva turned around.

Her words, but not her worry, ceased as the same six elders who presented the empty casket earlier that morning emerged around the corner. They walked in pairs, two behind the next and the last. Heads up, focused ahead, hands clasping the ends of colorful shawls draped over their shoulders. Steps so smooth they appeared to float above the ground.

"We'll figure it out," Cruz said, although he didn't sound as confident as Eva had hoped.

Nathan's mother and father followed paces behind the chosen council members. Pabla popped to her toes, bent her torso to peer left, then right beyond the men. Gabriel clutched his wife's hand and looked only at the steps he would take ahead.

When the group reached the vehicle the driver remained in place, as if unwilling to relinquish his post. The lead elder laid a hand on the protective escort's shoulder and he reluctantly stepped away.

The Pueblo men took care unloading the casket, then they placed the bottom edges atop their shoulders. They took slow, short, precise footfalls in unison, a silent promenade. Before they joined the walk, Nathan's parents thanked Eva for bringing their son home safely. The young couple already looked exhausted and Eva prayed to the Creator to give them the strength to carry on.

Eva and Cruz walked a few paces from the young couple, who trailed after the wooden casket carried by the men, who would deliver their precious cargo to the next phase of Nathan's journey.

The walk felt ominous, so quiet without the excited chatter of tourists and visitors who normally gathered as respectfully as they could manage, at times large groups streaming from buses, or curious pairs who strolled hand in hand, taking tours led by teenage Pueblos well versed in the tribe's culture and traditions—and equally well taught what *not* to reveal about the private ceremonies and inner workings of the community.

The tribe couldn't keep secrets from each other, but few from the outside world knew about the rituals and rites of passage that had persisted unaltered for hundreds of years. Outsiders would never know the extent of the continual work during reigns of each governor and war chief to uphold the people's traditions and the right to observe Native spiritual beliefs in tandem with traditional religion.

Eva felt over one thousand years of spirits as they coalesced and surrounded her—their light and guidance matching her movements, reminding her to be vigilant. To protect. To banish outside influences that attempted to rip their youth from the protection of elders. A daunting task proving more difficult as technology advanced and the years zoomed by.

When they passed the San Geronimo Chapel, Eva caught the aroma of fresh bread baking in the dome-shaped adobe *hornos* that dotted the village, where round loaves cooked to perfection. All the trading shops were now closed, some of the artisans and residents standing outside the shops, waiting for the call to begin the ceremony.

The procession carried on until they reached the open area of the village. The chosen men halted their march outside the open door to one of the entrances of the North House, where a traditional, much-loved, faded and frayed blanket had been spread out to receive what they carried. They took their time to reverently lower the casket beside the wool cloth as long and wide as the box, as if it had been created for this very purpose.

Eva followed Cruz inside the first level of the house designated for where Little Bear's body would rest before burial, and looked up at the ceiling made of *latilla* and *viga* timbers from the nearby forest. The room still held the day's warmth in the clay and straw bricks covered in mud that created the two-foot-thick adobe walls.

Tables lined those walls of the open room, and soon they would be topped with various side dishes, slow cookers, and loaves of bread hidden under dish towels in baskets—the feast awaiting members of the community who would soon assemble in, around, and out of the house to mourn, celebrate, and give thanks throughout the night. The thought of the red and green chile stew and meat dishes to come caused Eva's stomach to growl and her mouth to water.

Flames danced inside the beehive fireplace at the farthest corner of the room. Piñon wood hissed and popped, the scent of sap mingling with smoke from bundled sage snaking to the ceiling.

Within an hour, visitors would begin to stream in and out of the house throughout the night as they paid respect, ate, sent up silent prayers, offered condolences. All sharing grief and shock for the bright light that would never represent the people, grow big and strong, make his parents proud as he graduated high school and maybe even college. Find a companion to share many years together. Hopefully stay on the reservation so he could teach younger members of the tribe, share his journey and tribulations and achievements and joy of a very long life lived in the traditions handed down over countless generations.

For now, only those close to the family waited in the room. They all looked nervous and cast quick glances at Pabla and Gabriel but didn't engage with the two. Eva figured, as like herself, none of them knew what comfort they should offer.

Eva felt uncomfortable being there out of uniform and under-dressed and grungy after the long day. She felt unworthy and judged, even though that most likely wasn't true. Everyone in the tight space at the moment cared about each other, wanted only to be there for the Trujillos and each other. Eva knew from experience that would soon change. Once the sun set and every member of the community began to line up, the energy would change. People would remember. Everything said or done. Any misstep would be relayed to those who weren't there to see it firsthand. She would be gossip fodder if she acted any way other than impassive.

She had attended many vigils on the Pueblo in the past—the most for those lost to COVID—and her grandfather's ceremony to this day stayed with her. She dreaded the next steps it would take to prepare the body of the little boy for the viewing by their people. Ancient customs, powerful magic of the *cacique* as he blessed the area, the family, then Little Bear.

Eva knew she should stay. Represent the law enforcement element along with Cruz, assure the members that this would be a peaceful gathering. But the longer she stood there the harder her heartbeats crashed in her chest. Her vision wavered, not from tears she vowed not to shed until alone and unwatched. She felt like an outsider. Merely one of the multitude of tourists who visited their land from every corner of the world over decades of time. She belonged, and yet she didn't. Couldn't relate to what was about to unfold. Certainly couldn't be a comfort to those who loved the little boy they mourned over.

The cloying fog of the smoke coated her lungs. Anxiety squeezed her heart, which threatened to burst from her chest. She panted, shallow and fast, unable to force the ability to control the breaths. Stuffed her trembling hands in her pockets to hide them. *Keep it together,* she inwardly warned herself, knowing that although fewer than ten people were in the room, she didn't want anyone to see that cowardice threatened to overwhelm her.

She leaned closer to Cruz and whispered, "I've gotta get out of here."

"Now?"

"Right now."

She felt the warmth coming off Cruz's arm, close to her own. Wanted to lean in, her chest to his, tight in each other's arms, tip up her face, meet his lips for minutes on end. But eyes were on them and those few words would have to do for now.

He said nothing else as he turned and led her out the open front door. She stepped away from those readying to prepare the body and a few more who had assembled outside, avoided everyone's looks as she pulled ahead of Cruz and strode toward the Beast.

She waited until after she turned the corner, out of view from anyone, then took in a deep breath and willed away the panic that continued to pursue her.

"First watch is on me," Cruz said. "Gotta stay. Will you be all right?"

Eva didn't realize he'd gone after her, didn't sense him behind her, and his words surprised her. She needed to get herself together. Needed to be more vigilant. Needed to ignore whatever was going on with her internally so she could present herself as the confident tribal officer for her people. But for now, she needed to escape for a while—even from Cruz Romero.

"Want me to stop by after?" he asked, keeping time with her rushed footfalls.

She stopped. Turned around to face him. "No. I *need* you to stop by," she said, wanting nothing more.

CHAPTER
FORTY-FIVE
KAI

Exhausted from the emotions he had dealt with all day, Kai thought he'd be able to nap for hours. Instead, he lay on his back, staring at his bedroom ceiling, replaying snippets of conversations and sights and sounds. Giving up on rest, he took up the ball and launcher from the tote bag near the door, snapped his fingers for Shadow to follow and they both sprinted through the house to the outside.

Dusk approached as he threw the ball to the Malinois until they reached the barn, then continued down the center aisle between the stalls. Kai greeted each horse by name as he passed, while Shadow stayed close, still unsure about the massive animals. Kai reached the stall where he kept his terrarium and halted, surprised to see someone there, knelt low to look at his collection straight on.

"What are you doing in here, Paco?" Kai asked.

"Looking at your plants. Never seen so many in the same place." He pointed from one plant to the other as he named them. "Cota for tea helps the kidneys, oshá for the ladies' cramps, rattlesnake broom . . . can't remember what that's for."

"Good for arthritis pain," Kai said, surprised by the man's knowledge. He told himself not to look too shocked. "You know plants?"

"The ones around here? Sure. My auntie made me learn them when I was a little kid. My brother wouldn't do it, but I liked going with her, way out to the mountain, sometimes Blue Lake. She'd point and I'd tell her what each one was."

"Who's your auntie?"

"Anita Barboa."

Kai's mouth dropped open when the man mentioned one of the most respected healers known to the tribe. "She was a good friend of my grandmother. You know Anita Barboa?"

Paco let out a belly laugh. "Dude, she's my *aunt* aunt. I live with her."

"Wow. Lucky. You can ask her about which plants to use for medicines any time you want."

"Sometimes. She's not doing much healing anymore. Her knees are bad. Can't bend down to harvest the roots and leaves like she used to. Makes her sad so I don't bring it up much anymore."

"She's got knowledge the tribe can't lose. It's important to remember everything she teaches you."

"Not like I'll take over for her . . . but yeah, I see what you mean."

Kai returned to his tending and pondered how he could ask Santiago's worker if he would introduce him to the healer. He had so many questions now that his grandmother had passed.

As if he'd read his mind, he asked, "You wanna meet her?"

"Absolutely!" Kai said, grateful for the offer so he wouldn't have to risk a rejection.

"I could make that happen." Paco nodded his head, big grin on his face. "Maybe then you'll talk me up to your mom?"

Kai returned the smile. "I could make that happen."

Paco moved closer when Kai reached into the enclosure and pinched off the ends of young leaves, diligent to remove two precise cuttings off each of the plants.

"Are you starting new ones to root?"

"No, but I should. There's a few in there I've only seen one place on the rez. Good idea, Paco."

He laid each selection on the table beside the glass enclosure, then took out two medicine bags from the pocket of his hoodie. Earlier that day, he had found a bigger leather pouch in the back of a dresser drawer in the bedroom he had yet to consider his own, and placed each of the items from his personal bag into the larger one. Then he put one set of the fresh cuttings into his old pouch, the rest inside what would now be his personal bag.

Paco pointed to one of the plants. "That one will bloom first, after the snow goes."

Kai took note of the goldweed that would be topped by bright-yellow blooms all over the plain when the weather turned warm. "Hopefully the winter won't be too harsh."

"Auntie says the white stuff will be here early. Need to get ready for it."

"What's going on out here?"

Kai and Paco both flinched at the booming voice.

"Hey, Uncle. Did you know Paco's auntie is Anita Barboa?" Santiago drilled him with a look, killing Kai's excitement. "Course you did."

Paco stepped to the mouth of the stall, careful not to get too close to his boss. "I've gotta go get cleaned up for tonight. See ya later."

"That was crazy!" Kai said after Paco hurried away. "Anita Barboa knows everything about plants and what they do."

"My mother taught her well."

The light bulb went off in Kai's mind. "You knew all along that I'd find out. Get to know Paco, maybe become friends. Meet his auntie someday."

Santiago shrugged. "Gotta pay attention. Can't always tell who someone is, or who they know, or may someday become." The uncle waited a beat, attention fully on the nephew. "Sometimes it does take two."

The wise tribal member turned and left Kai alone, convinced the man had a mad plan for everything and everyone, before they even knew one was needed.

CHAPTER
FORTY-SIX
CRUZ

Cruz decided to reset after Eva left. He needed to find patience for the long night ahead. He called out for the Creator to help him center, and found himself automatically heading for the embankment of the Rio Pueblo.

He kept thinking about what Eva had told him regarding the phone call with Alice Jones. He'd tried not to show any emotion—didn't want her to know how panicked he felt at that moment—but he wasn't sure he'd pulled it off. Her unwitting blunder could mean losing her job, even if nothing came of the prisoner's threats to contact her attorney and cause a whirlwind of doubt for the prosecution.

Cruz knew if Eva didn't tell Chief Lefthand about the unauthorized communication, he needed to. Going around his partner without her knowing could be a relationship killer. Eva would need to give him the blessing to speak on her behalf. For now he would wait for the spirits to guide him.

He crossed the short bridge made of thick wood planks and eased down the slope, lowering himself to his haunches in the tall grass. He unbuttoned and folded back the cuffs of his shirt, sending a prayer of thanks for the blessings he was about to receive. Then, he removed one handful of the cool, clear water after another to wash his hands, face and neck.

Afterward, he fashioned both hands into a scoop, dipped them in, and sipped the sweet, pure elixir that flowed from sacred Blue Lake, which originated in the mountains on the reservation, where only members of the tribe were permitted to visit and worship.

Leaves of the red willows and cottonwood trees rustled in the breeze, called to him. He looked up at the chirps of hidden sparrows and robins that had returned to their nests for the night. He heard a faint chatter that rivaled the birds and looked over his shoulder to see a group of Pueblo women walking toward him, each carrying a slow cooker or serving dish. One woman after another bid him a hello as they crossed the bridge in a single line, then made their way toward the North House.

Now refreshed and ready to meet whatever would come in the hours ahead, Cruz started a leisurely walk toward the mourning house, already missing Eva. She had looked tired and wrung out and he understood the need for her to flee. Worried this would all be too much for her, he wanted to join the woman who held his heart, but duty called.

Soon the *cacique*—the tribe's leader responsible for the spiritual and religious well-being of the tribe—would arrive and privately bless the boy and his family, and stay with them throughout the night.

The gathering would be sad. Tears would flow, but there would also be celebration. Friends and family would catch up and make plans for happier occasions to come. A sense of future and renewal occurred when death kissed one of their own. A reminder to hold those close to you closer.

When the sun fell below the horizon, children accompanied by their parents would giggle and chase each other on the plaza, food would be enjoyed and recipes exchanged, youngsters would gather around elders who shared tales in the oral tradition of storytelling. Drummers and singers would entertain to help pass the time, flames from bonfires would spark and zigzag to the sky.

A reprieve from the "real world" for a few more hours. A world where a bank robber roamed free, a police officer healed from the bullet that ripped into her, where someone in the region—maybe even on the Pueblo—created fake guns made to look real enough to cause a young boy to die.

Cruz "Wolf Song" Romero pushed the troubling realities aside, scraped the soles of his tactical boots on the mat before the front door of the mourning house, crossed the threshold, and got to work.

CHAPTER
FORTY-SEVEN
SANTIAGO

Fresh from a shower, dressed in comfortable clothing, favorite pair of moccasin boots laced up to his knees, hair pulled back and wound into tight folds and secured by leather tethers, Santiago draped the colorful handwoven striped wool shawl he had worn for luck to all his political engagements over his shoulders to cover both sides of his chest.

He left the house and took his time going back to the barn to gather his sister and nephew for Little Bear's viewing. As he walked, he mentally prepared for what the coming hours might present. He looked to the west, at the sunset he never tired of—sky of deep blues, to yellow, to rust at the horizon, streams of clouds stitched through the gradations.

He had decided it would be best for him, Paloma and Kai to make an appearance long after sundown, when many of those paying respects would have cleared out to spend time with their own families. Hopefully reflect on how fortunate they were for the people in their lives. How quickly their world might crumble.

The fragile couple who belonged to Little Bear had so far held up better than anyone expected. Santiago would gauge their endurance when he saw them again to decide how involved he needed to be for the next days of their mourning. Most likely it would be best for him to appoint an older woman to keep watch, act as a parent or auntie to Pabla and Gabriel. Someone unobtrusive and caring and kind.

Paloma immediately came to mind. The ideal candidate. *If* he'd be able to talk her into the task. Cajole her away from the gray stallion that had captured her entire attention for months now.

As Santiago reached the opening of his barn, Kai emerged from the farthest stall. The boy had spent many hours in the confines, tending to his plants. He missed hearing his nephew talk in low tones to the other boy who had many questions. Kai always had answers for Nathan. Santiago smiled, remembering. Smart. Super smart. Both of them.

Kai, now dressed in fresh clothes, gave Santiago a quick uptick of his head, put a finger to his lips, waved him to approach, pointed to the next stall over. He frowned, unsure of what his nephew called for him to see, took cautious steps.

Through the parallel slats at the top of the enclosure he saw Paloma. Her movements consisted mostly of arm movements, torso dipping and swaying, lips moving as she mouthed her step counts, eyes closed in concentration.

Dancing, he realized.

The scene took him back to more carefree days he thought would never end. Time spent watching his sister in her element, performing for crowds of admirers, some who had traveled hundreds of miles when they found out the famous "White Dove" would be appearing.

Kai joined him, open mouthed, looking as shocked as Santiago felt.

She fumbled her steps, nearly tripped. Santiago held out his arms as if he could catch her from twenty feet away. At the last moment she caught her balance and hopped on her good foot a few times, the injured leg held aloft. He heard the intake of air between her clenched teeth and he winced along with her. A few beats later she eased the foot to the ground, put more weight down, lowered and raised herself a few times, continued the steps—more cautious and less pronounced at first—and then gained momentum as her confidence returned.

Santiago couldn't remember when he had been more proud of the sister once lost to him.

He turned to Kai, who wiped his eyes with the sleeve of his sweat-shirt, fringe swinging from the medicine bag clutched in the other hand.

Tears wavered Santiago's view.

He trapped a grateful sob in his throat.

CHAPTER
FORTY-EIGHT
TOMÁS

No matter how many times Tomás washed his hands—water hot as he could stand, soap bubbles all over the counter at the kitchen sink and the front of his shirt and pants—he couldn't get all the residue off. The moment he'd arrived home, he had frantically changed his clothes and showered until the spray ran cold. Repeated the action every hour since, yet still felt the blood he was convinced had absorbed through the pores of his skin.

Or maybe what had him so freaked was the phantom sensation of the boy's hands as they gripped the gun that suddenly went off. And the surprisingly heavy weight of the motionless body as it bled out in his lap.

Salas was confident he hadn't been seen at the reservation. And he had heard gunshots numerous times before, while at his biological site. Probably kids aiming for rabbits or field mice, or hunters keeping their skills up by popping off bottles. Surely no one would question a single gunshot. Before he drove off he hadn't spotted a soul and figured no one had witnessed him, the tragic incident, or what he had done after.

He made a mental note of the tasks for first light in the morning. Burn the clothes, every stitch covered in blood and dirt, even the shoes. Go out of town to wash and vacuum the van. Ditch the shovel somewhere.

Plan figured out, he sat on his couch, remote in hand, trying to talk himself into or out of watching TV for an emergency bulletin. Deciding it best to remain ignorant of any possible developments, he tossed the remote aside and absently picked at one of the blisters that had raised from digging the hole that now cocooned the body of one of his students.

Although he didn't believe in evil spirits, he hadn't dared to speak the boy's name. Didn't want to tempt fate in case it was wrong *not* to believe. Wet warmth spread beneath his fingers. He looked down and he realized he'd popped the blister.

When he had arrived at the biology site on the reservation, he'd had twelve handguns in the back of the van—half older models, the others newly printed. Literally a fifty-fifty chance the one for Celio would be defective. But no, he had to choose one from the latest print run. If only he hadn't fixed the glitch Optum had told him about.

Restless from too much *if only* thinking, he walked from one room to the other, and wound up in the bathroom.

"Damn you, Optum," he muttered to the reflection in the mirror over the sink. "This wouldn't have happened if you'd just do your damned job and get me the money. Three hundred grand for the printing equipment and materials. Is that so much? Copenhagen investors. Yeah, right."

And where did Optum go every time he left Taos? Dozens of meetings after three years, each time a few days in town, max. Although Salas had tried to get to know his business partner, Optum always rejected the offer to go for a meal or a beer, even a cup of coffee. *Too busy. Gotta go,* the man's standard reply. Then, *poof.* Gone again, only to reappear in a week or a month or more.

"Promises, promises. Well, I'm sick of it!"

He stormed through the house, out the front door, to the detached garage, punched in the key code, stepped inside, hit the interior button.

As soon as the door hit the ground, he lunged across the open area, slid the secret door aside, went to the crate of pristine handguns that he had printed the night before. All assembled, only awaiting the rounds of ammunition from the box beside the gun bin.

Salas selected a handgun from the top. Took up a preloaded magazine. Shoved it in the handle. Pulled back the slide until the round found home.

He tapped the end of the barrel against his soaked thigh.

"Now what? You don't even know where Optum is right now. Where he stays when he's in Taos. Where he lives in Chicago."

And now a boy was dead. Because of him and his creations and his delusional need to make others' lives better. For praise or greed he wasn't sure. And for the love of a woman he most likely would never have a chance with.

Guilt punished him. Doubt and self-loathing overtook his desire for vengeance.

No longer concerned about his partner finding out if he'd opened the bag Optum had left in Salas's care, he tugged the zipper and looked inside. His eyes watered as he stared unblinking at his find, unable to move or fully comprehend.

Nine stacks of $20 bills bound in violet-striped currency bands. Quick math verified $18,000 total.

Money from the bank robbery. Had to be.

His business partner was a thief. And he shot a cop. Had duped Salas completely, putting his own livelihood and standing in the community in jeopardy. A terrifying thought came to his mind. What if he got caught with the money? The authorities would believe he stole the cash. Bank robbery was a federal crime. Attempted murder of a police officer might be an even bigger offense. He could spend his life in prison for trying to fulfill a dream.

Simon Optum's deception and lies felt palpable, a raw wound. A flurry of admonitions and curses spewed from Salas's mouth. How could he have been so entirely fooled for years by the partner who had vowed loyalty, assured him innumerable times that they shared the same vision?

"Celio is right, *Tomás*. You are stupid."

And then he remembered . . . Celio.

He had killed a boy. His student. A kid. It was his job to protect and keep him safe. And now he was dead because of a stupid accident that should never have happened. From now on he would be known as a child murderer. If anyone found out.

Right. *If* anyone found out.

He looked around at his machines and their movements that only halted when the spools of filament ran out. Ceaselessly churning, running on autopilot. Much like Salas's mind at the moment.

Salas listened to the machines' whir and pitches as they lulled him to a calm he knew he didn't deserve.

CHAPTER
FORTY-NINE
PALOMA

Paloma sat on the front porch of the family home, lightly swaying in one of the four rocking chairs, feet tucked under her, wrapped up in a blanket to ward off the night's chill. She massaged her leg, sore from the dance movements, a little worried she had worked it too much earlier.

Her mind drifted to the events of the viewing a couple of hours earlier. Paloma thought she'd have seen Eva there. Since then, she had left a few voice mails to see how her friend was doing—to check on her heart and her head—but hours later Eva had yet to call back.

Because of Santiago's status with the tribe, she and Kai and Shadow had followed him to the head of the line of mourners and walked through the door, where the Trujillos opened their arms and welcomed her.

Paloma had stayed at the perimeter of the room, queasy from the warm air and competing aromas of food simmering and burning sage, and the sight of the shell of a boy everyone in the tribe would lay eyes on and offer blessings to as the hours passed.

She forbade tears while there, willed herself to show no emotion, not an easy task because her mind kept flashing on the possibility that this could have been her own boy.

She had worried for Kai—that he wouldn't be able to face the body of his young friend. But as he often did, her son surprised her. He approached, without hesitation, tucked a medicine bag into Little Bear's small hand, whispered words she couldn't hear, nodded to the parents, left the house as soon as he said goodbye. Her heart galloped. Her pride swelled as she thought of how much her Single Star had become a man so like his father.

Santiago had stayed by them, their own shadow, like the dog, encircled them with his imposing aura. His mere presence parted the crowd of people, allowing them to pass, no displeasure uttered for jumping the line.

"What do you think was inside the pouch?"

"What?" She turned to the voice, forgetting for a moment that her brother had joined her and sat in the chair beside her own.

"The medicine bag Single Star gave to Little Bear."

"Oh. Leaves. From the plants in the terrarium the two of them were growing."

"Gonna miss seeing the little guy. Watching Kai teach him."

She heard a scratch, followed by a flame that lit up Santiago's face. He dipped a wooden match to the bowl of a pipe—something he rarely did. The tobacco leaves crackled in the bowl as the fire caught. Smoke drifted to her, sweet and comforting. The scent of her father. Tobacco—a mingling of fresh and smoked—that lingered on his clothes and hands no matter how often washed. The fragrance brought back fond memories. She closed her eyes and thought of him.

"Did all the stuff going on in Santa Fe make Eva want to go see her parents?" Santiago asked, wrenching her from pleasant memories.

"Don't know," she said. "Haven't talked to her. Why are you so interested?"

"Curious. Doesn't matter." Then he asked what he always did. "How many days now?"

Every day, sometimes more than once, the question seized her heart. The single thing that made her cravings intensify.

"Stop, Santiago," she said, her tone harsh so he would pay attention. "I need you to quit asking me that. When you do I think about it. Moving on is all I want. Not to keep track, or to report back." She reached out and squeezed his forearm. "No more micromanaging. Please, brother."

She was grateful she couldn't see his expression. Hurt or mad, she wasn't sure, but no angry energy sparked from him and he didn't shirk away from her touch. Instead, he took her hand and held it.

Stars winked in the black velvet sky, crickets made a racket under the porch, nightbirds argued in the willow tree near the chicken coop. No admonishment or disappointment came from her older brother. Paloma felt calm and maybe even accepted for the first time in 344 days.

"You don't have to prove anything to me, Paloma. And nobody expects you to be the person you were before all the bad happened. We just want you to be happy. I *need* you to be happy. And to know we're there for each other."

"Everything you've done for me and Kai . . . beyond family, and blood, and tradition. You're my savior, Santiago." She took her hand away and angled in the chair to look directly at him. "But don't for one—single—moment—think I won't take my son and leave you and the family home if you keep poking at me."

"Ha!" Santiago said, sounding amused rather than rebuffed. "Like Eva's parents. One day there, the next *poof.* Gone for good?"

He chuckled. No animosity lingered. Then *she* chuckled, relieved that no Santiago thunderstorm would crash that night.

"There's got to be a reason," she said. "Maybe same as what you and I are facing. Eva's grandfather and her dad got into it and neither would back down?"

"Takes more than that to destroy a family," Santiago muttered.

"Maybe Eva could ask Chief Lefthand for some time off. Go see her folks in Santa Fe. Try to make things right."

"No!" Santiago's roar echoed off the solid surfaces of the house and porch. "You will not talk about June Lefthand. To Eva or anyone."

"There you go again. Ordering me about what I can and cannot do." Paloma drew the blanket tighter around her body. "Why are you so touchy about Bobcat Leaps?"

He blew out a puff of air.

"I got her appointed chief of the cops. Why do you think I'd be against her?"

Paloma reared back, unaware, but not surprised by what she felt certain must be strictly confidential information.

Then he changed the subject and asked, "Have you thought about what I asked of you earlier? To watch over Pabla and Gabriel for a while?"

"How long?"

"Up to them. And you."

She shrugged one shoulder. "Think I would be helpful to them?"

"Yes. You more than anyone."

Paloma thought for a moment. Didn't trust her words, afraid they would come out harsh. A few minutes passed. Santiago didn't rush her. She silently weighed the good and bad. Getting too close to people since Ahiga's death, and most recently the murders of her cousin and two close friends, had cautioned her to guard her heart. *Don't let anyone in* had become her personal mantra. She had even rationed time to Eva in case anything bad happened to her best friend. That would surely be the final blow that would kill her.

"They won't want me," she said. "Because of what happened in their house."

"You didn't hold them hostage there."

"No, but I must have known they were in there somewhere, because of the boy."

"Did you know the boy was Nathan?"

"Not then. Not until much later."

"Did you ever see his parents there?"

"No. Never."

"Ever met them before? Know it was their house?"

"No."

"Then it will be starting fresh."

"Maybe," she muttered.

It had stunned Paloma when each of the parents had thanked her for being good to their boy when he would visit Kai, greeted her so warmly, held her tight, as if they didn't recall what they had been through. The shared circumstances that nearly caused all three of them to perish.

"They live close enough to ride Mako there and back each day," Santiago continued in his enticement. "You wouldn't miss out on the time with him."

"Don't want to mess up," she muttered.

Santiago tsked. "Not possible."

"I'm scared." The declaration sounded like a little girl's although she didn't intend it to.

"They need you. And maybe you need them. Their hearts are broken. Yours still is. You know what to say. To give them peace and to help them remember to keep going. Be strong. A reminder that they are not alone in their suffering."

Paloma gazed ahead at the darkness, then to the countless pinpricks of light in the black sky. In the distance, the direction of the barn, a horse whinnied. Faint but unmistakable. A callout of support from Mako, Paloma was sure.

"All right, Santi. I'll try."

CHAPTER FIFTY
DAMON

Midnight. Dark. A bazillion stars overhead. Damon's favorite time. Only creatures of the night out. Predators and hunters. Like him, and now the two losers beside him. The spirits would not be pleased about what he was about to do. If he believed in spirits anymore.

He kept alert, even though luck was with him so far—the cops on duty would probably still be keeping watch at the vigil for the dead kid.

"You were right about no one around," Manny said. It looked to Damon like the words hurt him to say. "Now what?"

"I know exactly what to do," Damon said. "But you and Cal have to follow what I say," he warned. "When I get the lock off, I'll go in and get the stuff. Me alone, got it? Stay outside."

"Oh, you're giving us orders? You're the boss now?" Sarcasm dripped from Manny's voice, a smirk on his face.

"Yeah," Damon said.

"No."

"Then I'm out." Damon gathered the straps of his bag of mismatched hand tools he'd taken from others over the years, rose, started to move away.

"Wait." Manny lurched for Damon, grabbed the back of his jacket. "We'll do it your way, okay?"

Damon considered a minute. Let the other guy sweat. Build the suspense.

Manny exhaled in relief when Damon shrugged and turned back. He motioned for the other two to follow his lead. They all crouched low, took slow steps toward the building and the contents that would save Manny's ass . . . if his contact could be believed. The guy lied all the time, but they'd been friends since each could walk. And Damon had absolutely no one else to rely on.

Thankfully he still knew his way around the reservation, where nothing had changed much since the last time he'd been allowed to set foot across the sovereign boundary line. Now here they were, behind the police station, a paper-thin plan in mind.

Damon stuck out a glove-covered finger and pointed to a door at the side of the building. "That's where we're going."

The trio bent lower and crab-walked until they reached the protection of the closest wall. Manny continued to look furious about his chickenshit brother still ghosting him as he tapped the barrel of his Beretta 93R machine pistol on the thigh of the jeans Damon was sure he hadn't changed out of for days. A waft of body odor hit him when Manny raised his arm to wipe away the sweat on his forehead, even though the temperature had dropped to fifty degrees. He swept back strands of his greasy hair and ran a hand over the stubble of beard he hadn't shaved away since he'd last changed into a fresh set of clothes. Everything about the man screamed "desperate."

Damon couldn't quite believe his own situation either. Standing outside the cop station, ten feet away from the brightest light on a pole he'd ever seen. Ducks on display for the killing. The single good thing was that he could see only one beat-up Chevy parked anywhere near the building.

Damon assessed the padlock that secured a solid security door shut, then unzipped the tool bag, took out a two-foot-long pair of bolt cutters, positioned the open blades against the shank of the lock, squeezed the handles. Time after time the lock slipped from the cutter's blades.

He repositioned and put all his weight behind his effort this time. Again the tool slid loose. Off balance, his body thudded against the door, the sound resonating in the night air along with curses from all three men.

"Cut through the body of the lock," Cal said.

Damon shook his head. "Can only do that with brass. This one's hardened steel."

Manny looked like he wanted to unleash his machine pistol, hit Damon and Cal until all the bullets in the extended clip ripped through them both, along with the door, find the fucking fake guns and get the hell out of there while they lay there bleeding out. He let out a frustrated sigh and hissed, "Would you two quit swinging your handyman dicks and get this damned lock open."

Cal nudged Damon aside to give it a try. He gritted his teeth, curved his back, grunted as he squeezed the handle grips. Arms shaking, face red from the exertion, he finally got the tool to cut through.

Damon slapped Cal's back in congratulations, stripped the hasp and tossed the padlock aside, wrenched the door toward him. He stood there shocked. A sheet of plywood over the opening halted his entry. Dread dropped to Damon's stomach. "Boarded up. Didn't expect that."

He turned to Manny, who had his jaws and fists clenched, breathing fast, nostrils flaring in and out, fury obvious. Cal inched a safe distance away.

"Used to be able to get in from the outside door," Damon said. "Must have a new entrance inside the building now."

"Get the screwdriver," Manny snarled.

The former tribal cop knelt down, studied the edge of the doorway, shook his head. "Won't work. Security screws. I don't have a driver bit for that. Anyway, probably secured from the inside too."

"Dammit," Manny growled.

"Someone's coming," Cal hissed.

They all turned to the sound of an engine that grew louder as seconds passed. "Shit, Tomahawk, you said you knew what you were doing," Manny said.

Damon got up from his crouched position, unfurled to his full height, stepped to within a foot of Manny. "Told you not to call me that."

He was a badass, but Manny was a desperate caged tiger with nothing else to lose. Manny raised the only remaining possession of value he hadn't hocked and laid the Beretta's barrel against his partner's chest. "Okay . . . what'll I call you? Loser? Failure? Idiot? Stup—"

"Okay, guys, knock it off," Cal interrupted. "We gotta go!"

Manny relented and turned to Cal, who pointed to a set of headlights that rose and fell ahead of dips in the road, getting brighter as the vehicle moved closer.

"This isn't over," Manny warned.

"Relax, man," Damon said. "I'll come up with another plan."

"No. You only get *one*. I'm done with you." Manny spun around to follow Cal, who had returned to the thick brush at the edge of the property. "Worthless Indian."

Manny had muttered the disrespect, but Damon heard every word. And he would not forget.

CHAPTER
FIFTY-ONE
EVA

Even the comforts of home hadn't calmed the unease tapping an uncomfortable rhythm in Eva's chest. She gave up on the interior of her house, and found refuge outside on the front porch. Finally able to breathe, she took in one lungful of the pine-tinged air after another.

Feeling more level, but always on duty even out of uniform, she made her way to the edge of the street to see if any anything amiss might catch her attention. At 10:30 p.m. most of her neighbors' windows were dark except for the blue glow of a TV at the house across the street.

Rio the Magpie came out of nowhere, dive-bombed her, screeched over and over, swooped again, landed on his fence post. "Hey, Rio."

She chuckled when the bird cocked its head, as if to say, *What are you doing here?*

"Shouldn't you be sleeping?"

Magpies didn't usually show themselves at night and she wondered if her self-appointed spirit animal had appeared for a particular reason. A warning maybe. Reminder to be cautious. Of what she wasn't sure, but there were a lot of options currently on the table.

She had made certain Nathan had been delivered back to his family, and she could now focus on what the morning would bring. For the moment, she wondered how the vigil was going. Cruz would call if there was a situation, and the chief or Ernie Mateo would let her know if she was needed. Still, she felt guilty for abandoning her post.

Too tired and wrung out, she had yet to return Paloma's call from hours ago. And she should at least text Andrew Kotz to see how he and Nadine were doing. She didn't know what to say to either of them because they both would want to know if she was all right. Was she? She wasn't sure.

She felt out of control, muscles coiled, unsurety her only guide. Sadness threatened to overwhelm her. When the spells came upon her she used to seek refuge at her grandfather's house. But even that was gone. A burnt-out shell that no longer soothed her.

As the panic started to ramp up again, headlights hit her. She jumped aside before Cruz's truck could clip the fence post she stood next to. She released a ragged breath at the mere sight of him. Rio rocketed toward Cruz when he got out of the pickup, chattering an admonishment for nearly plowing over her, and the bird's favorite perch.

She opened her arms and he enveloped her in his own. They stood there for minutes and when they separated she took hold of his hand and crushed his fingers until he let out an exaggerated shriek that sounded remarkably like Rio's. She chuckled when he flapped his hand in the air, tugged his sleeve, pulled him inside and shut the door.

The lovemaking had been satisfying as always. Slow and tender until precisely the right time. Both climaxes reached in tandem. Attuned to each other, as always.

And now, Eva's bathroom held a comforting scent of lavender and rosemary from the bubbles that billowed to the rim of her bathtub. The remaining exhaustion and fragility had subsided after fifteen minutes of soaking with Cruz.

Both crammed in together, facing each other, almost too tight for two. The porcelain tub was one of her favorite things about the rented house and she would miss it when she moved to the reservation. And the fireplace. Most of all, Rio the magpie. She'd have to see if one of the tribe's elders knew how to lure a bird to a new environment—maybe her favorite old-timer Torrie Lujan would know.

But first she would need to build the house, and for that she needed downtime. She would have none of that until the current cases were closed to her satisfaction.

"Longest day, maybe ever," Cruz said, voice calm and languid as he gazed at her.

"The past two days have felt like a month." She sank a little lower, blew at a peak of bubbles in front of her lips. "I'm gonna have a huge tub in my new house. Or maybe I'll take this one. Think the landlord would notice?"

"You'd lose your security deposit."

"It'd be worth it."

"And when is this new house gonna happen?" he asked.

She shrugged. "Good question. First we've gotta help find a bank robber and the missing money. Figure out who's making guns that are getting people killed. Pretty sure there's more stuff . . ."

"Yeah, but it's not all up to you. Plans going forward keep you sane."

"Going forward?"

"Something to look forward to," he said. "Beyond the job."

"Well, this is pretty nice."

"Yeah, it is." He let out a contented sigh, took hold of one of her feet and massaged the tight muscles.

She leaned back until her chin touched the surface of the water, and she let out a sigh of her own and closed her eyes to enjoy the company and the pleasurable sensations.

"Do you wish you could have gone to Santa Fe to see your folks?" he asked.

"Come on, Cruz, why do you keep bringing them up?" She sighed, weary all over again now that the frustration had been picked at. "Seriously. Stop. You're killin' the mood."

"Okay, okay."

"I should check on Kotz and Nadine. He's only texted a few times. Can't get him to answer his phone."

"Now *you're* killin' the mood," Cruz grumbled.

"Hey, we may need Andrew's help someday."

"Cousin Lily's avoiding me too. Sounds like she's not picking up for anyone." A frown wrinkled his brow. "It's not like her to ignore me. Let's go there tomorrow morning."

"All right. First thing, before we clock in," Eva said. "Enough shop-talk. All I want to do is relax and try to forget what's been going on for a while. Can you help me with that?"

"You know I can," he said.

She tugged his wrist until they were close enough to touch noses. "Then do."

Deep in the kiss, four hands roving slick skin, both of their cell phones, side by side on the bathroom counter, blinged text notifications.

"Leave it," he begged.

"You know I can't."

He growled his disappointment when she stood, stepped out of the tub, took the two steps to the sink.

She picked up the phone and glanced at Cruz, reclined lower in the tub, arms folded over his head, enjoying the view of the water sliding down her naked cinnamon-colored skin.

"It's from the chief," she said, clicking the text icon.

ATTEMPTED EVIDENCE ROOM BREACH. COME IN ASAP.

"Well, Hawk Soars . . . Our day just got longer."

CHAPTER
FIFTY-TWO
CRUZ

Cruz had been awake for hours. He'd caught up on his laundry, washed every dish piled up in his sink, ironed three uniforms that didn't even need the sharper creases, showered, dressed, checked all his LEO equipment on his duty belt, geared up. The entire time he tried not to think too much about the upcoming interview he hoped wouldn't be too painful for one of his favorite cousins.

Now he had been parked in front of Lily "Littlefeather" Bernal's house for ten minutes, waiting for Eva to join him. He checked his watch. 6:45 a.m. The sun barely peeked above the horizon, fifteen minutes early for the time Eva was to meet him there.

After last night's briefing about the evidence room break-in attempt with the chief and their colleagues, the two had solidified the plan to question the bank teller about what she recalled during the robbery.

Because the actual crime did not take place on the reservation, the case was a Taos PD and a federal matter, not tribal, so Cruz wasn't authorized to formally investigate. However, unaware of what had already been discovered by other investigators, he hoped Lily might recall something she hadn't yet shared, or might have been too hesitant to tell an outsider. Even the smallest clue had helped solve cases he'd been involved in before. Eva could then pass along their findings to city cop Kotz. A win-win situation . . . if the feds deemed the info serious enough to follow up on.

He hoped his cousin wouldn't feel ambushed by them showing up unannounced. Even if nothing came of their informal questioning, he needed to check in. Assure Lily she hadn't been forgotten and that her terrifying experience would not be taken lightly. The offender would be caught. He sent up a prayer that the promise would be convincing—at least to her.

Impatient to get this over with, worried that he and his partner would stir up memories his younger cuz would have preferred to forget all about, he leaned against his official pickup and thought about the cut padlock, the forced entry thwarted by the secured sheet of plywood behind the security door. Burglary attempt of what specifically, no one seemed to have a clue.

The outside door had been barricaded years ago and half the force didn't recall ever using that entrance. Lenny Ramirez, so furious and freaked out that someone had tried to infiltrate his hallowed domain, had gotten ready to load up the boxes of evidence into as many pickups as necessary and take them somewhere off-site. Offered to secure them in his workshop, stand over them, finger beside the trigger of a shotgun. Chief Lefthand had refused and, hours later, after her other officers had been released, had probably continued to talk down the beyond-vigilant cop.

His thoughts turned to another task that would need to be attended to. One more mission for Nathan "Little Bear" Trujillo remained. The saddest of all, as burials tended to be.

The 3D guns linked at least two crimes together—of that, Cruz and Eva were certain. The law enforcers needed to figure out how as soon as possible. The potential of another Pueblo in danger of more crime made his stomach churn.

Thankfully, before he could get any more worked up, Eva's matching pickup turned onto the lane and parked next to his own, then she took a massive hit from a to-go cup of coffee. When she flung herself out of the unit, she looked way more fresh and revived than he felt. Geared up and dressed in a crisp uniform, she strode to him and he wondered if this was her first, or third, serving of coffee for the day so far.

"Ready?" she asked.

"Think it's too early?"

She hitched her head at the front window. He turned to see a woman watching them from the front room window. "Littlefeather probably knows why we're here. Will want to get this over with as much as we do."

They took first steps to the door and Cruz resisted the urge to lean in and give Eva a proper hello. For strength or support, he wasn't sure. But she had her *All-business don't mess with me* face on, so he let her take the lead.

Before Eva could knock, the door opened a few inches. His cousin normally always gave him a vibrant smile, excited as a teenager whenever she saw him, but this time she looked hesitant and didn't invite them inside right away. From what he could tell, Lily had on a robe and slippers instead of the flowered skirt, colorful blouses and scarily high heels she usually wore.

"Hey, cuz. Can we talk to you for a few?"

Lily remained in place and Cruz cast a concerned look at Eva beside him.

"Won't take long, Lily," Eva said. "We need to get to the station."

Eva boldly took a step closer, crowding the entry until the door opened wide enough for both of them to step inside.

Rather than speaking a greeting, Lily waved them into the front room and sat on a leather couch that emitted a new-car scent.

"Don't know why you're here, Wolf," she said, her voice soft and quiet. "Already told my story a couple days ago . . . So many times. Taos cops, the FBI. Your chief even."

The information surprised him. He glanced at Eva and she looked equally confused.

"You're not going to work?" Cruz asked.

She shrugged. "I'm not going back. Ever."

"What will you do?" he asked.

"Work at the school maybe. Lots of youngsters to look after over there." She released a light chuckle. "Never thought I'd say that. Even think it."

"You have a good job, Littlefeather," he said.

"Not good enough to die for," the younger woman snapped. "I'm not police. Not brave. Not you. Quit making me feel like I shoulda done more, Wolf."

Tears beaded Lily's eyes and Cruz looked away to ease her embarrassment. He gave Eva the look for her to step in—see if the traumatized woman would open up to another female. He stepped back and Eva took his place.

"What else is going on with you, Lily?" Eva asked.

Cruz wondered too. The woman seemed preoccupied and distracted, not merely worried about what she had endured.

Lily lifted an open hand that noticeably trembled. "I was doing all right until you got me remembering again." She sighed and clasped her hands together. "Like I told the other officers, I didn't see the man more than two minutes. That's all it took to defeat all I've fought so hard for. A college degree doesn't prepare you for the darkness in people's souls."

"Nothing does," Eva said. "Except life and how you live it. You were working toward being the assistant manager. Doing so well. Cruz is proud of you—everyone is."

Eva stepped closer, stood before Lily, waited for Littlefeather to look up at her. "Don't give up on your dreams. Not for a piece-of-shit coward who had to hide behind a mask instead of facing a sister warrior who would have taken him down like the little bitch he is if he didn't have a gun."

The denouncement brought a slight smile to Littlefeather's lips.

Cruz covered his mouth to hide his grin, amused by the unaccustomed outburst of venom that flew from his partner's mouth.

"There is one thing we'd like you to try to remember, Lily," Cruz said when he'd recovered. "Has something else about the man come to you? Anything at all would help us out."

When she gave him a blank look, he attempted the tactic that had worked on city cop Kotz. "Walked with a limp? Tattoos? . . . Eye color?"

"Relax," Eva suggested. "Close your eyes. Take your mind back."

Lily took the suggestions. Less than a minute later, her eyes flew open. "Blue eyes," she mouthed more than said out loud. Tears beaded in her eyes. She raised a shaking hand to her mouth and trapped a sob.

"What, Lily?" Cruz asked.

She put a finger against her lips. Glanced over her shoulder. Spoke to Eva in a low voice, "You should go. I don't have anything to tell you. Can't remember anything else."

"Yeah, but—"

"We understand, Lily," Eva said, cutting him off. She snapped her head, took a few steps away.

Cruz cast a worried glance at Lily, then followed Eva, curious to know what he'd missed. Maybe a Native woman noncommunication he wasn't privy to, or would even understand.

Not much shocked him on the job. The females of his tribe were an altogether different matter. He rarely knew what was on their minds, and they probably would not share their thoughts with him anyway. Eva had a sixth sense when it came to reading people, one he never questioned. And so, unsure why, he prepared himself for the worst—because right now, Eva didn't appear at all unconcerned.

And that worried Cruz most of all.

CHAPTER
FIFTY-THREE
SIMON

Simon Optum woke up, at first unsure of where he was, or the time, or the day. He felt rested and let out a satisfied sigh, stretched his arms, rolled over on the comfortable mattress and thought about what more he could do with the bank teller.

Then potential loose ends to consider came to mind. His car was secured out of sight, SIG and the knockoff locked inside so Lily wouldn't accidentally find them. When he'd moved the Beemer that first night he'd checked everywhere for the elusive wig and hadn't found it inside the vehicle or in the trunk. All that worry for nothing. But it had all worked out because now he had shelter, food, company, and a new lover to add to his list of conquests.

He craved the coffee he smelled coming from somewhere behind the closed bedroom door and waited for his new Indian lady to bring him a cup. She would, he knew, because she had yet to deny him anything at all during his stay the past forty-one hours.

During that time, every now and then she would remember what had happened to her Friday morning, and the stench of fear would waft from her body when she'd recall the man with a gun who obviously wasn't afraid to use it because he'd shot a police officer. It hadn't taken much out of Optum to fake his concern as he held her while she occasionally cried, still terrified about what she had endured. What *he* had done to her. He would divert her thoughts while tight in his arms, then she would settle and he'd wipe away her tears and make her tea and pay extra attention to her and escort her to the shower and then return her to the now-familiar bed.

He kept waiting for her to somehow recognize him. Occasionally, while she slept, he ran possibilities in his mind about what he would need to do to her if or when she did.

He'd become comfortable in Lily's small, spotless house and considered how many more days he could get away with staying there. Before he could give that much more thought, he felt certain he heard something—voices from behind the closed door—and figured Lily must have turned on the TV. Maybe that was why she was dragging her feet about serving him the coffee. He plumped the pillow, crossed his arms behind his head and thought about which position they would try next.

His eyelids grew heavy. He blinked, each time slower, until they dropped shut. He drifted off, visions of driving his BMW, top down. Lovely Lily beside him, her hair blowing in the wind. His ticket out of Taos, and Get Out of Jail Free card. If he played the odds just right.

CHAPTER FIFTY-FOUR
EVA

Eva sensed something off. Maybe the way Lily avoided direct contact with her cousin, or kept glancing over her shoulder to the hallway that most likely led to the bedrooms of the house.

She leaned in close to Cruz when he joined her, and said, "I think someone else is here."

Cruz frowned, looked around the room, held his gaze on the hallway, dropped his hand to the butt of his gun. "Did you hear someone?"

"No, it just doesn't feel right in here."

"How do you wanna play it?" he asked.

"Keep talking to her. Nothing to upset her."

Cruz nodded his agreement and stayed put as Eva returned to the Pueblo witness. "Lily, do you mind if I have a glass of water?" Eva asked.

Lily made a move to get up from the couch.

"I'll get it. Sit tight."

She held Cruz's eyes a moment, then flashed hers to the opening that led to the kitchen, back to him. He gave her a slight nod in understanding, then he crossed the room so that Lily had to turn the opposite way of where Eva went.

Eva bypassed the kitchen sink and went to the back door. She peeked out the curtain that covered the pane of windows and saw a silver BMW sports car parked close to the steps that led to the house. She leaned in close to the glass, unsure at first if she had encountered the distinctive two-door before. It took only a moment to be certain, when she recalled the night of the robbery. Mind spinning from that open investigation, and the turmoil of Nathan's death, she hadn't been able to sleep and decided to see if anyone at the village needed anything to help prepare for Little Bear's upcoming vigil.

She'd been surprised to see so many cars in the lot at midnight and was drawn to the silver sports car. The very same vehicle she looked at now. At the time, she had assumed a tourist from Illinois had experienced engine trouble and had to leave the BMW there until they could get it towed for repairs. A somewhat common occurrence she had encountered, especially with the older-model vehicles on and off the reservation.

Alert for any sound or movement behind her, Eva ran options through her head. She opened a few cabinet doors until she located the glasses, filled two with water and returned to the front room with them.

"You must be doing really well at the bank." Eva handed one glass to Lily and set the other on the table in front of the couch.

The teller frowned in confusion and Eva hitched her thumb toward the kitchen. "The Beemer behind the house. Is that yours?"

"Uh—no." Lily dropped her gaze to her lap and fidgeted with the hem of her blouse. "No, it's a friend's."

Cruz instinctively caught on to what Eva alluded to. "Now isn't the time to make new friends. Better to rely on your family."

"Sometimes you can't talk to family. Too close. They get sad and don't know how to talk to me."

"Yeah, but—"

Eva held up an open hand, halting his words. "How about if we go for a walk? Get you out of here for a while?"

"Naw, I don't want to go anywhere."

Eva cut her eyes at her partner and he took the hint. "Won't go far," Cruz offered. "A little fresh air will be good."

Lily hesitated, then stood up to face the hallway. She held her gaze there for a full minute that, to Eva, felt like five. Then Lily sighed and moved to the front door.

Eva tucked up to Cruz when Lily exited the house, whispered, "Someone's definitely in the house."

He halted his steps, whirled his head to the hallway in clear view from where they stood. Hand on the butt of his holstered firearm, he looked ready to storm toward where danger might lurk.

Eva shook her head, listened for any sounds or indication they were not alone. Didn't hear anything. She hitched her head to the door and waited for Cruz to reluctantly follow her outside.

"I don't know anyone around here who drives a BMW," Eva said. "Do you?" When he shook his head, she said, "I saw the one out back parked at the visitors' lot on the rez Friday night."

Cruz dropped his eyes to Eva's hand on the butt of her duty weapon. "I'll take a look at the car and get a picture of the plates."

On the way to join Lily, she told Cruz, "I'll call for backup."

The officers split off—Eva remaining with Cruz's cousin as he rounded the corner of the house.

"I need you to get in my vehicle, Lily," Eva instructed, her voice calm so she wouldn't spook the other woman.

The teller's eyes widened, and she flipped her long braid to the front of her chest and held on tight to the weave of hair. "Why? What's going on?"

"You already know. I need you to step to the truck. You're not in any trouble. We want to keep you safe."

"From Simon?"

"Is that his name?"

"Yes. Simon Optum. He told me he's visiting from Chicago."

Eva put a gentle hand on Lily's elbow, ushered her to the DPS vehicle, stood at the open door until Lily slid in, then shut the door and positioned herself where she could safely keep watch.

Eyes on the front windows of the house, looking for any movement, she mashed the mic clipped to her shoulder. "Dispatch, I need backup at the Lily Bernal residence. Bank robbery suspect may be located. Need a lockdown on unidentified silver, later-model BMW two-door. All roads with access in and out of the area need to be blocked off both directions. Notify the chief. Copy?"

"Copy, Duran."

"ASAP, Dispatch. No lights, no sirens."

She dropped her hand to the butt of her Glock and unsnapped the holster's retaining strap over the trigger. Vehicle between her and the house, she leaned against the hood, the engine block in front of her body.

Cruz bent low as he charged from around the house to join Eva. Not even out of breath, the former sprinter checked Lily, then patted the air for her to lie down on the seat. He glowered at the younger woman until she complied.

"Didn't recognize the car." He raised his cell phone for Eva to check the photo. "Got the plate—sent it to dispatch. Think he's our guy?"

"Seems strange, doesn't it? An outsider getting close to a Native without cause."

"Maybe," Cruz said. "Just hope you're not rushing to conclusions. That car could belong to one of our people. Might be a used car— owner waiting for new plates."

"Lily's anxious enough to make me believe that's not true," she said. "Kotz and Lily both said he has blue eyes."

"That's not exactly need for concern."

"Do you want to be the one to tell the chief you blew off a possible suspect in a federal case?"

"Hell no. I think you're right. Just making sure we're on the same page when it comes to making our formal statements if this goes way wrong."

"Let's make sure it doesn't," she said. "Reinforcements are on the way. Told them to block off the roads. He won't get away this time, even if he bolts."

"Might spook him if our guys come in hot. What if he's armed?"

"Hopefully he kept his firearm in the vehicle."

"Nothing suspicious in plain sight so I couldn't check to see if it was locked."

Eva considered the options for a moment. "Let's see if Lily will tell me anything helpful."

She lowered herself and crab-walked to the rear passenger side of the truck. She opened the door to see Lily—rather than stretching out on the seat, she had curled up on the floorboard behind the driver's seat.

Eva laid a hand on the trembling woman's back. "It's going to be all right, Lily. Cruz and I need your help. You're safe with us. Can you answer a few questions?"

It took a while for Lily to raise her tear-streaked face. "I'll try."

"Good. That's all we want." She knelt low, got comfortable, held the other woman's eyes. "What do you know about Simon Optum?"

"Just met him Friday afternoon. Said he heard about what I was going through. Wanted to see if he could help." Her cheeks blushed red and Eva felt the young woman's embarrassment. "He brought me flowers. Made me feel special. Safe."

"Did you think that was unusual? A stranger showing up at your door?"

"No. He said he was a police liaison, with the city, there to help me with the shock of my experience. I believed him." Tears beaded her eyes. Her cheeks flamed redder. "He's the man who robbed the bank, isn't he?"

"I think so, yes."

"Put a gun in my face. Terrified me and my coworkers."

"Yes."

"I trusted him. Opened my home to him. My heart. He said he wanted to help me. We . . ."

Oh no, Eva thought. The man must be a consummate groomer to work so fast. A sociopath, at best. She didn't want to hear how far the stranger took the relationship, but guessed a romantic involvement.

"You don't need to say anything else." Eva stroked Lily's arm and walked away to let the younger woman begin to process her shame in private.

CHAPTER FIFTY-FIVE
EVA

The tribal police department was less than a quarter of a mile from Lily's house, and Eva knew it wouldn't take long for Chief Lefthand to arrive. Three additional TPPD units parked on each side of Eva's and Cruz's vehicles. The chief was first to slide out of the front vehicle, followed by their fellow officers, fully geared up in Kevlar, helmets and safety glasses.

Lefthand took the lead and bounded to Eva and Cruz, who continued to wait behind the protection of the engine block of Eva's truck.

"We're sure he's still in there?" the chief asked.

Eva nodded. "Lily left him sleeping in her bedroom."

The chief held her gaze on Eva. She nodded and when Lefthand closed her eyes for a moment, Eva knew her boss understood that the offender and his victim had become a couple.

"Was she in on the robbery?"

"No way in hell," Cruz snapped.

Lefthand looked again to Eva for verification.

"I'm with Cruz on that, boss. Lily only realized it was him when we spoke to her a little bit ago. Our questions prompted her to remember details she had pushed aside. The suspect's been isolating her from family and friends, gaining trust and controlling her. I get the sense she's been relying totally on him."

"Classic grooming behavior."

"Yeah. Completely manipulated her the whole weekend so he could hide from us."

"Why stay here?" Cruz asked. "Risk getting caught?"

"The whole city is locked down," Lefthand said. "Sheriff's department and Taos PD, even highway patrol's got a perimeter around the area. Could be he didn't get outa town quick enough and had no other choice. Found an opportunity."

The chief checked her wristwatch, craned her neck to see up the road. "All right. We've waited long enough."

Lefthand stepped away from Eva and Cruz and clapped her hands together. Once. Loud as a gunshot. "Everyone tuck in. Here's how we're gonna do this."

As if waiting for exactly that moment, clouds of dust tornadoed upward to the sky. One massive black SUV barreled their direction, followed by three city police cruisers, two sheriff's vehicles taking up the rear.

Eva's stomach plummeted to her toes, a visceral feeling of dread about who would pour from the vehicle.

"Shit just got real," Cruz muttered to Eva, confirming that her suspicions of what would come next would be all too true.

CHAPTER FIFTY-SIX
SIMON

Simon woke up unsure how long he had dozed. Hunger prompted him from the bed, even more than the curiosity to check the local news and see if the cops had given up on looking for the bank robber hiding where he knew they couldn't look. He knew all about escaping onto reservation land. Crossing over an invisible line to land where city cops couldn't follow. He'd heard that Indian cops were too busy busting their own drunks and wife beaters to care anything about a white man just passing through.

But he would stand out if anyone saw him with one of their own. It took no effort to convince the woman it was best for her to stay at home. To let him take care of her and keep watch to make sure she was safe.

He couldn't risk any of her friends or family knowing she had an unexpected visitor so he had kept Lily occupied. And he'd turned the sound all the way down on her phone and hid it inside a drawer in the bathroom. She had yet to look for it.

From the moment he walked in her house she had received his entire attention. Mostly in the bedroom, and shower . . . oh yeah, and on the couch in the front room. He wondered where they should get on it next as he got dressed, swiped a hand over his hair and opened the bedroom door to complete silence.

"Lily?" Optum said, buttoning his shirt. "Where are you? I'm ready for breakfast. Do you want to eat something first?" He smiled at his clever double entendre.

No voice answered. The place felt abandoned.

He went to the kitchen and poured a cup of coffee into a mug sitting next to the old-style percolator on the stove, took a sip, pushed the curtain over the sink aside to admire his treasured BMW.

He sloshed coffee on his shirt, dropped the mug to crash on the tile floor. Barely felt the sting of pottery shards and hot brew that had splashed on the tops of his feet.

He knuckled his eyes, thinking his vision must be deceiving him. Looked again.

A cop stood at the other side of his Beemer, rifle barrel resting on the hood, aimed directly at the kitchen window. At *him*.

"That bitch," Optum roared, and promised to take his revenge on the Indian chick who had betrayed him.

"Simon Optum," a distorted voice said from outside the front of the house. "Exit the house. Slowly. Hands on your head."

"Fuck that," he hissed.

He mourned the SIG that was secured in the glove box of the Beemer for fear of Lily finding it, to then realize he was the man who had held her at gunpoint.

He thought of his options. Limited at best. Wait for a bunch of swinging-dick cops to bust through the door? Or go out there first.

Neither scenario pleased him.

They could shoot him dead the second he stepped outside. Before they even knew he was unarmed, no threat at all. If he stayed inside it could get ugly. He imagined the door being forced open, a line of those fuckers rushing in, finding him, beating the shit out of him, then shooting him just because.

He paced the front room, hoping another option would come to him, and considered his odds. Dead, or in a jail cell waiting for his employer's consigliere to get him kicked.

He sighed, resigned to his only actual possibility. He would get out of this, as he always had before. His list of goals had only been half accomplished so far. Warehouse-size amounts of money yet to be made, even more to steal. Half the country he'd yet to visit, where he could practice his skills far from his home state. Women of every size and color to take as his own.

A photograph across the room caught his attention. He scowled at the Indian in the picture, wearing a graduation cap and gown. "This isn't over. I'll be back for you," he promised.

Then he smoothed back his hair, tucked in his shirt, folded back the cuffs to his elbows.

Stepped to the front door. Pondered the story he would tell to gain him the most favor. They would believe the rich white man over a naive Indian girl, without doubt.

He opened the door a couple of inches. Saw only faces darker than his own. Deep-seated terror rushed through his entire body for the first time in his adult life.

CHAPTER
FIFTY-SEVEN
EVA

Eva and Cruz hung back from a group of officers gathered around Chief Lefthand, brainstorming options. She looked at the sea of enforcers, surprised she didn't see Andrew Kotz. She thought for certain he would want to be there, but was probably forbidden so there wouldn't be any risk of tainting the ongoing investigation.

"Lily will never get over it if we ruin her house," Cruz said.

"Maybe he'll come out on his own."

Cruz looked around at the LEOs amassed around three separate areas. Some had guns in hand, others looked ready to do the same, everyone prepared for the worst possible scenario to play out. "Would you?" he asked.

"No. We're gonna have to go in and get him."

The front door opened. Everyone turned to the incremental movement. A man emerged, hands laced on top of his head. He took two steps, dropped to one knee, then the other, eased chest down on the ground.

"Go go go!" Chief Lefthand commanded.

Half the officers strode to the suspect, the others held position, all firearms aimed on the target. The first tribal officer to reach the man cuffed one wrist, then secured the other behind the man's back. A city cop and sheriff's deputy took an arm and scooped the suspect to his feet.

No words had been exchanged. The entire takedown had taken less than one minute. Many from the team looked shocked, others reveled in the capture, a few looked disappointed that they wouldn't be able to inflict some sort of violence as payback for the terror committed against the citizens and visitors of the normally carefree Taos tourist destination.

The detainee glowered at Lily—only her face visible behind the window where she remained inside Eva's vehicle. He bared his teeth, shouted curses and promises of retribution and filth and all the things he assured her would happen to her.

Eva sensed Cruz about to charge the monster who continued to terrorize his cousin. She reached out to block him from doing something that would put him in the cell next to the actual criminal.

The two federal agents rushed forward, elbowed the local officers aside. Each took hold of their captive's biceps, led him to their SUV, secured him in the back seat.

Eva hurried over to her chief and said, "Did you call them? Know they would take him from us?"

"No choice, Duran. He's a suspect, considered armed and dangerous. It's a federal crime investigation."

"Dammit!" Eva watched the black vehicle kick up dust as it pulled away. "Where are they taking them? Can we follow? We should at least be able to ask him about the 3D guns."

Lefthand launched to within inches from Eva, pointed a finger. "Enough, Duran. This is *not* the time."

Eva backed down. Heat rose from her collar as she cast a sheepish gaze around her. The remaining LEOs looked as distraught and let down as she felt.

The chief turned to Cruz. "What do you think, Romero? You've got the most experience dealing with the FBI on the rez."

Cruz continued to scowl at the vehicle growing smaller as it took away their only hope of closing the case on their own terms. "He's gone for good. We'll never see that guy again. Probably won't even know what happens to him, except maybe from the news."

CHAPTER
FIFTY-EIGHT
KAI

Kai thought he'd have trouble sleeping after experiencing and feeling so much the day before. Visuals of the long hours replayed in his mind the moment he'd clicked off the lamp beside his bed last night. Next thing he knew, morning's first light flooded his bedroom from the open curtain.

He'd awakened before Paloma and Santiago, got out of the house early enough to catch a ride with the neighbor he'd texted yesterday, and made it close to his favorite biological site on the reservation before eight o'clock.

Refreshed and mentally strong from the deep sleep, he raised a hand to the driver, who beeped his horn, then drove off, leaving Kai and Shadow to walk the last quarter mile to his destination.

He took the Chuckit! launcher from his backpack, loaded a bright orange and blue ball. "Wait," he told Shadow. The dog sat, crouched low, energy vibrating off his body in anticipation. Kai cocked his arm back, and flicked the ball to release and fly a high arc as he shouted, "Go!" The sprinting Malinois reminded Kai of the videos of greyhounds chasing a stuffed bunny around a track—his feet barely touching the ground as they propelled him forward.

He watched his companion and thought about Nathan's burial preparations that would begin in a few hours. By noon the little boy would join the remains of other members of their community who had perished.

Kai had been to a few ceremonies since the first grave had been dug and had started to fill up quicker than expected after COVID hit the reservation hard. His most recent journey there had been for his mother's first cousin Tonita Concha, a celebrated basket maker, and another fellow murdered Pueblo woman. Every time he realized his mother's grave could have been there too he shut down emotionally and it took him a while to pull himself out of the funk.

He appreciated reminders of what had motivated him from childhood. Why he wanted to stay on the land inhabited by his people for so many generations. This land. So he would come to this part of the tribal land for a much-needed nature reboot after a long week of indoor university classes under fluorescent lights that buzzed and flickered—he had begun wearing earbuds and sunglasses to buffer the annoyance during lab and study sessions.

He thought of Eva's dad and his potential success as an athlete. Understood why the tribe would have been upset about her father giving up on his dreams. Their dreams, apparently. Then he wondered if the final decision had been a difficult one for Benito Duran. Kai imagined Eva's father racing the area. The punishing workout it would have been, dodging desert cottontail and prairie dog holes, hurdling sagebrush, keeping watch for snakes, the plain solid under his feet.

Kai's first week as a high school freshman, he'd felt a connection with his biology teacher and decided to trust him with this secret location, where it seemed every indigenous plant thrived on a single plot of land. Within hours Mr. Salas and Kai had identified ten types of flora—twice that many more on the entire eight-acre plot that first day. The next week Mr. Salas had asked if he could take the biology class to Kai's cherished place, to help the non-Native students understand the ecosystem. He agreed, not wanting to disappoint his new mentor, but secretly wished he had never revealed the hidden location.

Kai kept his head down, thinking about last night, vision roving inch by inch in search of young leaves pushing from the soil. Anxiety and fear for the final goodbye to his young friend made it difficult for Kai to breathe.

He could still feel Little Bear's limp fingers when he pressed his old medicine bag containing cuttings from the terrarium plants that had originated on this very place where he stood. He had knelt down to sit on his knees beside his friend lying on his back, leaned in close to his ear, whispered, *"Don't worry, Little Bear. I'll look after the plants for you."* Then he got out of the mourning house before anyone could see his tears.

He wanted more time with the boy. In this spot where his teacher, and his grandmother before that, instructed and pointed out the flora that could heal—and even a few that could kill if ingested or prepared incorrectly. Holistic medicine could be dicey, even fatal, if not respected. Remedies he had hoped to pass down to Nathan.

Kai was all about respect for nature. Never more so than at this area. Shadow romped while the botanist traversed and discovered a few sprouts he didn't recognize. He took out his cell phone, aimed between his feet, clicked off a few photos so he could ask Mr. Salas about them.

Kai hoped to find his former teacher there as he often did on the weekends, and had been looking forward to talking more about his concrete houses idea, but neither Mr. Salas nor his big long van were anywhere in sight. He reached in the hoodie pocket for his new medicine bag and felt the outline of the plastic model Mr. Salas had gifted him.

Right away, Kai hadn't been sure the teacher's idea to build the cement 3D manufactured homes on the rez was a good one. Any threat to loss of work, even one job for one person, couldn't be a "good" thing for his people. And he didn't think the tiny printed representation looked much better than the lacking-of-character, everything-the-same HUD houses that already dotted the rez. But Mr. Salas had become a close friend and Kai didn't want to hurt his feelings, so he didn't say anything to lessen his mentor's ambitions.

Shadow's uneven movements caught Kai's attention, distracting him from his thoughts. The canine dropped the ball, nose to the ground, performed a figure eight, tighter each time around, a twist-and-turn search. Kai became as alert as the dog.

A blink later, Shadow started to dig twenty feet away from Kai. Not merely a curious swiping of feet, but an obsessive full-on rapid-fire excavation. Nose down, spiked ridge of hair along his spine, ears back, tail flicking. Dirt spewed, detached plant roots flew from beneath the canine as the hole got deeper.

Kai chuckled at the sight. "Did you find another toy soldier, boy?"

The dog didn't draw back or even hesitate.

Curious, Kai approached.

Shadow's insistent task grew more frantic. Kai's unease grew with every step.

"Stop, Shadow."

The dog didn't cease.

"Enough! Back!"

The dog's movements slowed to a halt. Reluctance evident, he woofed, spun 360 degrees, lay flat to the ground, keyed his entire attention on the hole.

Kai knelt to take a better look. Gaped—at first unsure if his eyes deceived him. His heartbeat pounded in his chest. Wide eyes watered. He dropped to the ground. Ass to the earth, heels kicking hard for traction as he scrambled backward.

He didn't trust his eyes. Flashed back on the bag of guns Shadow had found at the Trujillos' house. Shadow came to him, sat down, blocking the view. He let out a whine, held his master's gaze.

Kai fumbled for the phone in his hoodie pocket and redialed his most-called number.

The connection immediately went to voice mail.

"Oh god, Eva. Shadow found . . . You gotta get over here. Now! I'll text you a dropped pin."

He stood up, vision locked to the discovery. "Bring . . . Dammit, I don't know . . . Everyone!"

CHAPTER
FIFTY-NINE
EVA

Eva and Cruz stayed with Lily, who refused to return inside her house until he'd checked every room. Word spread fast, as always, and within minutes after the officers who had descended on the property drove away, three cars full of women arrived. They assured Cruz—who had shifted to ultra-protective mode—that Lily would not be left alone. All the women gathered the emotionally broken girl in their arms and began the necessary healing.

The front door closed and Eva could feel the sadness—heavy, as if a cloak had draped over her partner. She tucked her arm in his, led him to his vehicle, and followed close to his bumper as each drove to the station, where all their fellow tribal officers had assembled and waited for their boss to get off the phone.

Cruz walked in a daze to his desk and dropped in the chair. Eva rolled hers beside his and scanned the open room. All eyes were on the closed glass door to the chief's office instead of their work.

Her phone vibrated inside the sheath on her duty belt. The screen announced KAI. She sent the call to voice mail so she could concentrate on their boss, whose hand cupped her forehead, elbow resting on the desk, the other hand holding the handset of her desk phone. Eva couldn't read the expression, but she could feel the angry energy escaping from the one-inch gap under the door.

Lefthand spoke a few more words, listened, hung up the phone, stared at her desk. Stared some more.

Eva wondered if she was practicing in her mind the words she would say to the team, or if the usually calm Native woman was attempting to regain her composure after what looked to have been a contentious conversation.

A couple of minutes later, Lefthand stood outside her office and said, "All right, people, here's what I know." Everyone settled and lasered their attention on the top cop. "The FBI liaison assured me their lab would be checking ballistics to see if the round recovered from City Officer Tallow matches the handgun discovered in the vehicle parked at Lily Bernal's home. And now they can run sweat DNA recovered from the bank scene. Hopefully that will also be a match for the suspect who robbed the bank, and who Ms. Bernal had been . . . spending time with."

Cruz tensed beside Eva. Her colleagues shuffled in their seats and murmured to each other. She sensed that everyone was as uncomfortable as she was to know a criminal had manipulated his way into the heart of one of their people during the most vulnerable time of the woman's life.

The chief held up her hand to calm the group, then continued. "What they did verify is that our guy is Liam O'Banion, also known by more than a dozen identities. Thanks to Duran and Romero, the TPPD will be credited with solving the bank robbery case—as soon as the DNA connects the suspect."

Whistles and claps knifed the air and Eva did her best not to show her frustration.

Cruz leaned close to Eva, cupped a hand over his mouth and said in a low voice, "Yeah, right—those feds didn't even look over at us before they poached our guy."

Eva glanced around and sensed what her colleagues must be thinking. Investigating the crime they would *not* be tasked to undertake—Nathan's death—which had occurred in a different city, not on a reservation at all. That there would probably be no more vindication for the boy. Another insult and slight completely out of their hands. Two cases now.

She wondered what the point of being a cop was if their skills and the hours spent on the search and investigation were all for nothing.

Chief Lefthand looked directly at Eva when she said, "Solving crimes is a team sport, people. We did our part. Now it's time to let this go and get back to work."

"Ah, hell no," Eva muttered.

Cruz tapped her boot with his own. His eyebrows knitted together and he gave her a slight headshake.

Ignoring the silent warning from Cruz not to lash out, Eva said loud enough for the entire group of enforcers to hear, "So that's it? Our part is over? We caught the guy. Can we at least provide a list of questions? 'Cause I've got questions!"

Lefthand hardened her expression. "I'll see what I can do," the top boss said, no further attempt to quell Eva's agitation. "Lots of paperwork and follow-ups on open investigations have been put aside these past couple days," the chief continued. "Ramirez, I'm gonna need you to be on Little Bear's burial."

"Got it, boss."

"Everyone else—time to catch up and reset. Copy?"

All issued their own *Copy* replies and returned to their work.

Eva's phone buzzed a reminder, prompting her to retrieve the recording Kai had left.

She pinned the phone to her ear and listened a beat, unsure for certain what she'd heard. Stood up from her chair. Felt the blood rush from her body. Swayed on her feet. Grasped the edge of the desk to keep from dropping to her knees.

"What's goin' on?" Cruz asked, taking her arm to steady her.

She gaped at him. Stunned by the information she couldn't quite grasp, she said, "The shit just got real. Again."

CHAPTER SIXTY
EVA

Eva still felt pumped with adrenaline after the Simon Optum takedown. And she hoped she wouldn't still be rattled due to Kai's call by the time she arrived at the location he had texted her. The details from the panicked young man had been vague, but she had relayed what she could to Chief Lefthand, who right away started making her own urgent calls.

She needed to take a little time. Get herself together.

Twenty minutes later, Eva arrived to chaos.

She'd never seen so many official vehicles, marked and unmarked, in one place on this remote section of the reservation before. The sight reminded her of the Simon Optum takedown scene, but this one felt even more surreal.

Four of her fellow tribal officers, fresh off the Optum crime scene, stood at the periphery of the action. Cruz hustled to her after getting out of his own vehicle, but she didn't see the chief yet. She did spot a crime scene van, every door open, evidence cases ready to be accessed.

Chief Lefthand had provided Eva the approval to reach out to her former boss, Sheriff Clark Bowen, and he smoothed the way for the tribal department to secure Taos County's premier evidence technician, Lizbeth Herrera, and her team to process the scene.

Eva's favorite analyst, as well as her highly capable trio, wore full-body Tyvek coveralls, and each grasped nitrile gloves and booties. They huddled together as Lizbeth addressed her squad.

Cruz nudged Eva's elbow and she followed to where he hitched his head. Kai and Shadow stood apart from any of the professionals. He absently stroked his dog's head and kept his attention trained where Eva couldn't yet see.

Eva caught Lizbeth's attention and flashed her three fingers. The tech nodded and went back to her instructions.

"Let's talk to our boy," she said to Cruz.

"Shouldn't we wait for the chief?"

"I'm not waiting for anything," she snapped. "Look at him. He needs us."

She took off, Cruz one stride back.

"Thank you, Universe," Kai muttered as he spotted Eva. He reached out to hug her, but she held up an open hand, stopping him.

"Sorry," she said. "We need to protect anything you may have inadvertently picked up on your clothing or skin."

Kai tsked, a sound that reminded her of his uncle Santiago. "Guess I'm a suspect, right?"

Shadow tilted his head to look up, whined, scooched closer to his human.

"Who else knows about this place?" Eva asked, evading Kai's direct question.

"Lots of people," Kai said. "The Red Willow Center brings them. And when I was in high school, my biology teacher brought kids here to study the different plant species. He still does sometimes. Flora varieties here are unique to this area. I come here a lot."

"Tell us more about this teacher," Cruz said.

"Mr. Salas. Tomás is his first name. He was my mentor and adviser at Taos High. Helped me get into the university." Kai's mouth dropped open, realization coming to him. "No way he's involved in this. He's a good guy."

"Does he live on the rez?" Eva asked.

"No. He's not Pueblo."

"Mexican?" Cruz asked.

"I don't know. Hispanic, but we never talked about that. Hasn't ever been an issue. Does it matter?"

"It might," Cruz said, taking on his as-always suspicious stance.

"We'll need to talk to him," Eva said. "And have him provide a list of the kids who know about this place."

"I feel bad for Shadow. Uncle Santi joked one time that Shadow will be an excellent cadaver dog—that he could probably find any crime victim anywhere if they had a piece of plastic on them." He hitched a thumb where Eva assumed the body must be. "Check for something plastic. He's never wrong."

"Stay strong, Single Star," she said. "And don't talk to any officers but me and Cruz. Got it?"

Kai nodded. "When can I leave?"

"Gonna be a long day," Cruz said.

Kai's eyes filled with tears.

Eva gave Kai's arm a squeeze, then started toward Lizbeth, who knelt down beside what Eva figured must be the body discovery area.

"We're all gonna miss the burial," Cruz said, sidling up next to Eva. "Pabla and Gabriel won't be happy about that."

"Nobody will be happy," she muttered. "Another body on our sacred land. I can't believe this is happening again."

"At least he's not one of our kids."

She whirled on Cruz and shot him a scowl. "He's someone's kid. Won't hurt them any less than us."

Cruz raised his hands in surrender. "Just sayin'—"

"I don't want to hear it, Romero."

"Whoa, hang on—"

"Dr. Herrera!" one of her team members yelled out, waving her arms, smothering Cruz's admonition. "There's a dirt bike over here."

The discovery halted Cruz's words. He and Eva sprinted to the crime tech. "Kai has one just like that," she said, stopping up short of the discovery.

Cruz stuck two fingers in his mouth and whistled. He used wordless motions when he caught Kai's attention. Pointed to the motorbike, then to the young man. Kai shook his head, displayed two fingers in a walking motion.

"Not his," she said, "but I've seen several just like it."

"Where?" Cruz asked.

She didn't want to say. Feared the declaration would make the person in question a suspect. She bit back the words, thinned her lips.

"Duran, tell me," Cruz said.

"Santiago's. Same type of Kawasaki those drug dealers chased me on when I was looking for Paloma."

"Damn. This is bad."

"Really bad."

Lizbeth joined them, looked in the direction of the dirt bike, gave Eva a questioning look. "Got anything for me?"

"Pretty sure we know a connection to the bike," Cruz said when Eva didn't reply.

"Dana, shoot a photo of the VIN and plate, and a few of the cycle, for the officers so they can run the registration."

"You got it." The tech raised her Nikon, zoomed the lens, clicked off shots, trotted over and showed Eva the digital screen so she could take snaps from her cell phone.

Eva copied the photos in a text and sent them to Cruz. "I'll run it," he said. "Might be stolen, or maybe he sold it."

She crossed her fingers for Cruz to see.

"I've got blood over here!" another of Herrera's techs shouted from the opposite direction.

Eva and Cruz followed the lead tech, careful not to approach too close to the newfound evidence. Amid churned-up soil and tire tracks, ragged splashes of darkness crusted the dirt at least two feet in diameter.

"So this isn't a body dump," Eva confirmed.

"Unlikely," Lizbeth said. "Lots of blood. Incident most likely started here." She pointed to tire tracks. "A vehicle looks to have been parked here." Then she indicated dual indentations. "Altercation occurred, body possibly dragged in the direction of the recovery site."

The three watched one tech take photographs as another used a hand shovel to scrape away a scoopful of tainted dirt before placing it in a clear evidence bag. Another prepared a plaster of paris batch to make castings of the tire impressions.

"Can you walk us through whatever you've found out about the body?" Eva asked.

Lizbeth hooked an index finger for her and Cruz to follow.

Eva bit back the urge to let out a stream of curses when they reached the mound of dirt beside a partial hole. She took a final cautious step forward and took in the face of a soil-covered boy clad in an equally filthy dark sweatshirt.

Lizbeth pointed to a ragged hole in the cloth, where the left side of the covering was stiffer than the rest of the dark material, Eva suspected most likely from blood.

"Think that's a bullet hole?" Eva asked.

"I'm unable to confirm until the clothing is removed," the lead tech said.

"How old?" Cruz asked.

"Sixteen. We found a Taos High School ID. Celio Martine Novar."

Eva appreciated that Lizbeth didn't need to refer to her notes in order to recall the young man's name. She sent up a silent prayer for Spirit to watch over the lost soul of the boy who couldn't possibly have deserved the tragedy that had felled him.

She wondered about the young man's last moments—if he was scared, or angry. Did he call out for his mother or another loved one? If the event was an accident or planned from the start? Most of all she wondered if the boy knew his assailant. Maybe more than one.

So many questions. Most probably never to be answered.

Then something that didn't seem right caught Eva's attention. She knelt down to get a better look. "Is there something in his hoodie pocket?"

Lizbeth bent lower and took a closer look, then sat on her knees. Attention solely on the body, she held out a gloved hand and one of her assistants slapped a pair of needle-nose pliers in the proffered palm. Lizbeth widened the pocket with her empty hand and eased the pliers inside the hoodie pocket. A moment later, she withdrew an item and held it up for Eva and Cruz to see.

"Wait. Is that a Glock replica?" Eva asked. "3D printed firearm?"

"Looks real," Cruz said, sounding skeptical.

"They all do. Every single one we've recovered."

Lizbeth's second held open a plastic evidence bag and she secured the firearm inside.

"Why didn't they take the gun?" Cruz asked. "Seems strange, doesn't it? Best way to get caught, right?"

Lizbeth shrugged. "We don't know if this is a weapon used on the victim. If a firearm was used at all. Or if foul play is suspected."

Cruz tried again. "You're saying he could have shot himself? And maybe his companion freaked out, buried the body. Figured no one would find it way out here?"

"I'm not saying anything definitive, Officer Romero."

Cruz closed and opened a fist. "Yeah, but what do you *think*?" he asked, frustration raw in his tone.

"Look, I'm not going to speculate about what *could have* happened. There are numerous scenarios I could spew from looking at the scene. Only one would be correct. Let us do our job."

"Thank you, Lizbeth," Eva said. "We really do appreciate you walking us through the possibilities. We'll let you get back to it."

But Cruz hadn't finished poking, no matter how much Eva wished he would relent. "How long do you think he's been here?" he asked, eyes locked on the body, as if too mesmerized to look away.

"Best indicator is to find out the last time anyone was in contact with him," Lizbeth said. "From there we'll know a better timeline."

"Yeah, but what's your guess?"

Lizbeth stared at Cruz awhile, considering. After an uncomfortable silence she said, "I'm going to guess more than twelve hours, less than thirty-six. Mind you, that's a *guess*."

"Copy that," Cruz said.

"Too early to be sure," Lizbeth said. "However, that is a fair assessment of this scene at the moment. And before you ask, there's no way at this time to know for certain if this was an accident or premeditated."

Eva wanted to help out as much as she could. Needed not to feel so out of control of their situation and what would probably follow once the investigation undoubtedly grew beyond their small force. An idea formulated. Before she had a chance to second-guess herself, she said, "I'll try to get Dr. Mondragon approved to do the autopsy."

"Excellent idea," Lizbeth said. "You'll need him to work his magic on this one."

"I'll do my best."

She stepped away, took out her mobile, dialed the man she had relied on most during this seemingly endless journey for the truth, wondering if this would be the final request he would undertake. Or if he would deny the ask entirely. She had no idea who his contacts were, figured no one knew the full depth of his reach. But if you needed something done, fast and sure, Santiago "Hawk Soars" Mirabal is who you called.

And so she did.

He picked up on the first ring.

CHAPTER
SIXTY-ONE
SANTIAGO

Santiago sat at his kitchen table, hand on a legal pad covered in to-do notes, each chore crossed off, every task attended to. He looked off in the direction of the graveyard, where hundreds of people from the tribe would gather soon. He hadn't expected any calls. Assumed the day to come would be focused on the respectful and peaceful delivery of Nathan "Little Bear" Trujillo to his final resting place. A day of quiet reflection, full of community and remembrances, and yes, sorrow. He picked up his ringing cell phone next to his paperwork, the name EVA on the screen.

"Are you ready?" he asked. "Want us to pick you up, or meet us at the village?"

"We have a problem."

He did a quick scan of his memory. Nothing had been forgotten. He felt certain, then started to doubt himself.

Before he could inquire, she said, "Found a body on the rez."

"Who found a body on the rez?"

Hesitation too long for Santiago's comfort ensued. "Eva. Tell me."

"Single Star."

"Dammit!" he roared.

He cursed the universe, spirits, Creator, anything and anyone he could think of. His nephew had endured more than any man three times his age should have. Not even twenty yet and his life had been plagued by death and loss and turmoil that seasoned professionals, trained to psychologically withstand trauma, would have a difficult time overcoming.

"Actually, Shadow found the victim."

He would learn everything related to the incident soon, but not from her. She was a diligent officer, wouldn't risk misinformation that could hinder the investigation.

"I'll tell Paloma after the burial," Santiago said. "Hopefully the people with you will keep their mouths shut so we can put the boy to rest before all hell breaks loose again."

"Don't have to worry about the CSI team leaking anything. And Chief Lefthand will make sure none of our officers are spreading info."

"Might want to advise your boss to take all the phones. Photos speak louder than words. Never know who will leak something if it makes them feel important."

"Good idea," she said.

"What do you need, Eva? Or is Officer Duran asking?"

"Gonna need you to pull some more strings, Santi."

He sighed. "What now?"

"Dr. Mondragon. We need him for this."

"Couldn't get him for Nathan in Santa Fe. What makes you think I can get him for this?"

"Hispanic kid's body found on tribal land is a federal crime. The FBI would probably make the same request when they step up, but why let them have the glory? We need the best. No mistakes. I can ask Tavis, but he'll need approval higher up the food chain on his end."

The absolute last thing Santiago Mirabal wanted was to have federal agents crossing the boundary line, disturbing their sovereign land, getting in the way more than helping solve the crime.

Determination fired in his chest. "I'll make it happen."

Santiago clicked off Eva's connection and brought up the redial option for the statesman.

CHAPTER
SIXTY-TWO
TOMÁS

Tomás woke up in a panic, unsure where he was at first. He blinked, winced from the pain in his lower back when he tried to sit up, flopped back down. It took him another minute to realize he had fallen asleep on the row of seats he'd removed from the back of his van last month so he could bring home a few extra 3D printers he had purchased in Rio Rancho.

His first coherent thoughts turned to the boy who had died yesterday afternoon. Because of him. Killed at the site where he'd wanted to build his first 3D home—the location now forever tainted.

He glanced at his watch and couldn't believe he'd been able to sleep until 11:15 in the morning. Passed out more like it. Then winced at the funk of whiskey he rarely consumed, sour in his mouth. He eased his uncooperative body to a sitting position, elbows on his knees, hands cradling his head that thudded with each heartbeat. Replayed the events. A slideshow that flashed one horrific vision after another, that led to the fight over the pistol.

Tomás flinched at the remembered shot, louder than he would have ever expected.

The blood on his own hands. He rubbed them together, convinced the residue remained.

The boy's family would be missing him. His brother was violent, evident by the fresh cheek and lip injuries. If he did that to a blood relative, what would he do to a complete stranger who had betrayed him?

Lightheaded, thirsty as he could ever remember, the mere thought of getting up, crossing the garage, walking all the way to the house and to the kitchen for water exhausted him. More whiskey would have to suffice for now. He reached for the bottle beside his foot, and with an unsteady hand he unscrewed the cap, took a sip, winced. Tipped the bottle back for a longer swig.

Unexpectedly calmer now, he thought maybe everything would work out. Celio had told him his brother didn't know where the guns came from. Protected Salas for some reason. Maybe scared that Manny Novar would go after his teacher.

Salas remembered he still had the box of guns he was supposed to drop off, and now an envelope full of money. Someone would be looking for both. The worry sparked, ignited, took flame. If whoever was to actually receive the guns would be able to trace him, would they find a way to retaliate?

Salas had no idea how Celio had known who the distributor of the guns was, but his student seemed to. The contact never confirmed his identity, they had never met, only corresponded via texts. Salas never verified, but was pretty sure the party owned a gun shop in Albuquerque and also the private gun range there. Assured Salas every time that the printed guns were only used for teaching and example purposes. Didn't matter to the businessman and his clients if they worked or not.

If Celio, a kid, had been able to figure out the mechanism of the deal, surely a savvy businessman would. Manny too, probably. Who knows what clues Celio left behind at his house for his brother to find. Or in his locker—the student's counselor or the principal might allow officers to search for anything that might help find the boy. Salas would be fired for sure.

Something kept niggling him, certain he had forgotten an important element where the altercation had taken place. He searched his mind. Replayed minute by minute the events after the gunshot. Each shovel of dirt, dragging the lifeless boy to the hole as deep as he could manage to dig. Certain a heart attack would drop him alongside Celio's body from the exertion.

He stood up and the garage whirled around him. He lowered his center of gravity, held out his arms in front of him in case he did a faceplant to the cement floor, swayed in place until he felt confident enough to shuffle to the back room.

The comforting sound of motors and fans greeted him as he went to the worktable that held Optum's duffel full of the bank's money. Beside the bag sat the box of printed guns that were to be delivered and he now vowed never would be.

He made it to the stool at the farthest wall and had to sit there a moment. After he caught his breath and his stomach settled, he opened the cardboard flaps that had trapped the faint scent of spent gunpowder, then dug beyond the fold of blood-splotched money, and the flip phone he'd used to communicate with the person he now knew was Celio Novar.

He took out the pistol that had caused so much damage and studied the smooth lines of the replica that appeared as real as an actual semiautomatic, except for the blank plate under the barrel where a serial number would be stamped on a registered firearm.

When he picked up the box to make room for him to disassemble the pistol to clean, he thought the weight felt lighter than it should. Confused, he removed one unit after another. He stared at the pile lined up side by side and counted out ten.

Plus the one to be cleaned.

Eleven total.

Not twelve.

He dropped open his mouth, stunned to realize Celio must have taken one. He remembered only turning his back on his student for a moment to draw him away from the van. That must have been when the kid had taken it.

He counted again and again but his eyes and touch did not deceive him. Celio still had the gun on him. Buried along with his body. Or maybe dropped somewhere at the reservation site.

His vision went extra bright, senses ultra-sensitive. Because then Tomás remembered something else. An even bigger fiasco.

"No no no no *no*," he said, ramping up each repetition of the word's intensity.

The bright-green Kawasaki.

Still on the reservation.

He'd only seen it a moment. Hidden by brush. But if anyone found the ground disturbed and got nosy, they'd easily find the bike too.

He sat there, mouth hanging open, unable to believe how he could have been so careless. With the row of seats taken out there was plenty of room to put the bike back there—figure out what to do with it later.

"Oh god! And the kid probably had a backpack too," he yelled to no one but himself.

The series of blunders made him wonder if maybe he *wanted* to get caught.

He deliberated if he should go back and get the Kawasaki. Considered the foolishness a full five minutes before he reached for the remote on the workbench, clicked on the TV, searched the local stations for any news bulletins about a Hispanic boy's body being discovered in a shallow grave on the Taos Pueblo reservation. But as usual for a Sunday morning, Tomás found nothing but cartoons, infomercials and a church service.

He kept the set on in case a breaking news alert came on, and mourned as he imagined potential reporters and camera people there, disrupting the earth, uprooting his plants, defiling the sacred space.

Where he would never—ever—be able to return.

He picked up the gun the boy had lost his life over, cradled it in his hand, lowered his head and sobbed and sobbed. Fat tears splashed onto the grip and rehydrated Celio's dried blood.

A pool of crimson in Tomás's palm.

CHAPTER
SIXTY-THREE
EVA

Eva returned to Kai, who looked more perturbed than freaked out at the moment.

"They're trampling the plants," he said, leash in his hand taut, Shadow right beside him.

"Sorry, Kai. They need to be thorough. Can't risk overlooking any potential evidence."

"The flora here has a delicate survival balance. This very spot has been a gold mine of a find. So many different types of vegetation—some I've never seen anywhere else."

She wasn't sure if the outburst was due to the actual plants or a way to avoid what he and Shadow had discovered in his sacred place.

"They'll grow back," she said, all she could think of to offer.

"Maybe," he said. "Maybe not."

Eva was anxious to get back to her work, didn't want to miss out on anything Lizbeth and her team discovered as they processed the scene, but Kai looked scared and vulnerable, instructed not to leave the spot where he and Shadow had remained, going on three hours now.

She had asked him not to call his mom, to wait to alert anyone until after Little Bear's burial out of respect for the family and the tradition of the final steps for the boy. Eva stayed with him a little longer, unwilling to leave the young man alone and confused, unable to process the situation he'd found himself in. Again.

"I've been here forever, Eva. When can I go?"

"Not sure yet. Be patient a little longer."

He stood there and fumed before he said, "Is this gonna be my fate from now on? Finding dead people? 'Cause if it is . . ." Kai's words trailed off before he regained his thought. "We've both found two dead people," Kai said. "Some kinda sick club, right?"

Eva had actually discovered many more bodies than that since she'd started on the tribal force. And an additional twenty more as a deputy. Many of them victims pulled from traffic incidents, suicides, domestic incidents that went way too far. Tragically, an elderly couple found frozen to death in the forest—most likely a death pact so they could pass on together.

She didn't correct Kai. Didn't need to mention the obvious parts of being a cop at that moment, or that visions of corpses occasionally visited her dreams. That even during daytime hours flashes of murdered individuals and accidental deaths shook her to the core, left her puzzled and wondering why they decided to appear at that particular moment. She remembered every name, and unfortunately every face that gazed at her with their glazed-over eyes that would see no more, send up a silent prayer as she drove by their death sites whenever she passed on patrol.

A familiar pickup approached in the distance. More bodies and feet and potential DNA cross-contamination to worry about. She remembered what Santiago had warned—the danger of private pictures being leaked. It hadn't occurred to Eva that anyone on her team could be taking captures, other than shots to help process the scene. Suspicious now, she scanned her colleagues, didn't see anyone being devious.

"Stay here, all right, Single Star? I'll be back soon as I can."

"Tell them to watch where they're walking!" Kai said to her back.

The crowd of law enforcers and techs parted and a figure stepped through. Chief June Lefthand had arrived. It always amazed Eva how their boss could command an area without uttering a single word. Even Lizbeth seemed captivated and halted her work until the boss of virtually everything related to the scene and all beings involved swept the area with her astute eyes.

Lefthand stepped closer, protective booties stretched over the sharp toes of her cowboy boots, head angled toward the ground to make sure her approach would not compromise anything that could be tied to the incident, then stopped a few feet from the body's location.

Eva straightened her back, squared her shoulders, took on the professional attitude that conveyed her respect for their supervisor. Cruz and the other tribal officers gathered around the top cop.

Lefthand looked in the direction of the boy's body and said, "One of our people?"

"No, ma'am," Eva said.

"But he belongs to someone." The chief held her eyes on one of her officers after another as she scanned to make sure she had their full attention. "Highest level of care here, people."

In translation, Eva knew the chief meant nobody had better screw up. Keep your mouths shut. Figure this situation out. A shitstorm of finger-pointing and blame would undoubtedly be on its way.

"That's it for now," Lefthand said. "Assist the techs only if they ask. Don't get in their way." She flicked a hand and all but Eva and Cruz scattered.

"What about the burial?" Cruz asked. "Think we should postpone?"

The chief thought for a moment, then shook her head. "Ramirez will be able to cover it. The Trujillos said there would only be fourteen in total for the burial."

"Eleven now," Eva corrected. "Kai, Cruz and I were invited."

"Right," Lefthand said, then turned back to the immediate situation. "Who found the young man?"

"Kai Arrio."

If Eva had blinked she would have missed the downward twitch of Lefthand's brow, almost hear the inaudible *Oh no* the other woman must have been thinking.

The chief looked up at Cruz. "Do we know who this plot belongs to?"

He shrugged, so Eva answered, "Red Willow Center sponsors the area. Kai comes out here a lot. His high school biology teacher used to bring his class for field trips."

"Great. Hundreds of people have probably been here. Evidence gathering is gonna be a crapshoot."

Eva and Cruz waited for Lefthand's next thought while she went silent, studied the ground before she said, "What do we know about this teacher?"

Kai would be crushed if his mentor was involved in anything untoward, but she knew the chief's reasoning—everyone was a suspect until proven otherwise.

"Kai has only said good things about him," Eva said. "Don't recall any official complaints either."

"Novar's a Spanish name," Cruz said. "Celio too."

"I know what you're thinking—Hispanic body found on the rez," the chief said. "A Pueblo will be top on the suspects list for a potential homicide. Even if this turns out to be an accidental death, it could ignite racial implications of massive proportions."

"Hopefully Dr. Mondragon can do the autopsy on the boy," Eva said. "Prioritize whatever he can to rule out any of our people. He couldn't help as medical examiner with Nathan in Santa Fe, but Taos is his jurisdiction when he's not in Albuquerque. I asked Santiago Mirabal to pull some strings."

Lefthand didn't look pleased, and held her gaze so long Eva wasn't sure if she'd overstepped.

"Worth a shot," the chief said.

Eva had pushed aside the added pressure that, no doubt, the FBI would be rolling in, stirring up their own brand of shitshow. Soon. "How long until the feds cross our boundary?" Eva asked.

"Word's out," the chief said. "Left me a message an hour ago. Agents are waiting for me to offer the invite. Won't wait much longer. They're still in town with the bank robber. Their hands are full with that. We might have another day."

"Boss, they're not gonna share anything," Eva said. "Seems fair for us to be as covert as them for now."

The chief took a step closer to her officers. "Romero, Duran—shut it down before we're stuck in a pissing contest," their boss commanded. "Now."

"Yes, ma'am," Eva said, having no idea how to make the direct order actually happen.

CHAPTER
SIXTY-FOUR
PALOMA

Paloma stood outside the wall of the graveyard, cuttings of sagebrush and lavender wound in a light-blue ribbon clasped in one hand, cell phone in the other. The procession had reached its destination, Nathan "Little Bear" Trujillo carried by the elders the final steps to the hole that had been prepared the day before.

She had checked the screen often the past hour, waiting for word from Kai. Text after text and many calls later, still no replies from her son. Her mind spun—thoughts of what she would do if this were her boy going in the ground. Never to be seen or held or to hold ever again. The thought nearly broke her.

She nibbled her bottom lip, jiggled the raised heel of her moccasin, reminded herself to breathe.

"Are the cravings bad?" Santiago asked.

Paloma halted her frenetic movements. Shook her head, the response a lie she kept from him as often as he asked.

She hadn't realized her brother had joined her. He had been distracted when she saw him last, a couple of hours ago. Muscles sore from working them, she had moved slower than she wanted getting the kinks out when she woke up that morning. Earlier than necessary, Santiago had rushed her, goaded her to hurry up, had stood at the open front door, shaking his keys, tapping his foot in an impatient rhythm and had become flustered when Paloma told him she needed a little more time. She sent him on his way, told him Paco had offered to get her to the graveyard, and she would ride with him. That seemed to irritate her brother even more, but he agreed and off he went.

Now Santiago stood beside her, watching the procession's final steps, lips in a tight line, more anxious than before, angry energy vibrating off his body.

"What happened?" she asked her brother.

"Nothing. Ready to get this finished. Time to move on."

She furrowed her brow, upset that Santiago could be so callous. To rush the final ritual felt disrespectful and unfair to Pabla and Gabriel. She watched the little boy's parents—mother's arm looped in the father's, side by side, holding each other up as they stepped as one.

Paloma wasn't sure why they had requested her to attend. Pabla and Gabriel had both insisted she be there although others had not received the same generous invitation. She worried a little that she would be judged by those who had not been invited, or that this was a deceitful trick perpetrated on Paloma for her part in what had happened to the Trujillos in their home.

She chanced a look at the young couple. Pabla must have felt the connection—she raised her head, gave Paloma her eyes, held the gaze, seemed to take comfort in her tribal sister being there for her.

No longer uneasy, Paloma stepped through the opening in the short wall and entered the sacred space of those lost to the tribe, thinking one of the markers could have been for her. Or Kai. Eva and Cruz too, doing their best at their dangerous job to keep the people safe.

She had survived when only Eva and Kai believed she would.

Blessed with a new life, new beginning, new possibilities.

Paloma looked over her shoulder, where Paco remained, leaning against his auntie's Toyota parked in the dirt lot, waiting. Looking at nothing, and no one, but her.

CHAPTER
SIXTY-FIVE
EVA

Eva worried that Cruz might push Santiago too hard when he questioned the tribal councilman, alienate the one Pueblo who had been the most help to her in days. Last thing she wanted was to lose his favor.

Half the force needed to rest from the overnight vigil and she was the only officer who knew the medical examiner. She picked up her pace in the hospital corridor, looking forward to seeing her friend again, although the circumstances saddened her.

At the entrance that led to the morgue, she first took in a huge lungful of air, then another, preparing for the shallow breaths she would be taking during her time in the autopsy room. She pressed the buzzer for entry and a moment later one of the double doors swooshed open.

Her stomach roiled from the tang of chemicals and slight decay that hung in the tight space, grateful for the intentional chill in the air that ceased the perspiration that had beaded her hairline. She stepped closer to a body, draped waist down in a white sheet, lit by a round light fixture studded with six separate bulbs that hung above the stainless steel table.

"We appreciate you stepping in, Tavis," she said.

"Anything for my favorite former student."

She kept her direct vision off the victim. Every time she glanced at the lifeless corpse she saw Kai—imagined the implications if Paloma's boy had stumbled upon the same fate. If he had actually propelled himself off the Gorge Bridge, he would have been on the same table awaiting evaluation.

The previous dirt and muck and blood had been washed from Celio Novar's face and torso, which now looked gray and waxy. Baby-faced rounded cheeks, larger than average size, and underdeveloped arms and chest made him look impossibly young.

"What do you think, Doc?" she asked, turning her attention to the ME. "Premeditated or accidental?"

"Difficult to say." He used his pinkie to illustrate on the body's right wrist. "We've got faint bruising here. Could indicate that a struggle occurred."

"Fighting for the gun?"

"Perhaps."

"Any GSR present on the hand or forearm?"

"Ms. Herrera bagged Master Novar's hands at the scene, however GSR residue is fragile and most likely being covered with the dirt may have degraded trace residue. Samples were taken before we cleaned up the young man."

"Think he pulled the trigger? Suicide, maybe?"

"Trajectory of the fatal shot is not standard for suicide. At the moment I preliminarily exclude the fatality as self-inflicted. Whether or not another individual's hand also had hold of the firearm at the time of discharge is yet to be determined. Ms. Herrera was unable to verify that GSR was present on the entire barrel of the recovered firearm. Therefore, perhaps the slide was partially covered, which could indicate there was a struggle—if the recovered gun is indeed the cause of the fatality."

"Might never know about that though, right?"

"Quite subjective."

"Premeditated?"

"Unfortunately that will be for your investigation to determine. Ballistics will allow us to rule in, or out, the gun you have in evidence. In the meantime, scrapings from under the nails are being analyzed for possible skin cells. If he scratched a second party, this may provide further clues about a potential assailant."

Feeling stronger, stomach more stable, she glanced at the injuries she had spotted at the body recovery site. "What about the swollen cheek and split lip?"

"Older injuries. Not more than twenty-four hours before death."

A female, pristine white lab coat covering most of her petite frame, entered from around the corner of the autopsy suite and said, "Excuse me, Dr. Mondragon. Still no luck reaching the family. Taos PD said they'll keep trying."

"Thank you, Sheila. Eva, there's no need for you to stay. I'll let you know when we make contact."

"Keep me in the loop with your findings?"

"Absolutely. As much as I can."

"I realize . . . Confidential until facts are determined."

"Correct."

"But I can still check on you?"

"Please do."

She placed a hand over her heart and leaned toward her friend. "Thank you, Tavis. We're gonna figure out who did this."

"I know you will," he said, no doubt in his confident tone.

Mondragon draped the white sheet over the boy as he waited for her to leave. A kindness Eva never failed to appreciate.

CHAPTER
SIXTY-SIX
CRUZ

Cruz found Santiago Mirabal at the edge of the graveyard. The burial had finished, all the mourners gone. One of the most respected members of the entire Taos Pueblo tribe watched from the other side of the short wall. The last witness as workers shoveled remaining scoops of dirt on the grave of Nathan "Little Bear" Trujillo.

Cruz regretted the need to disturb the man, and although he felt certain Santiago knew he stood a respectful distance away, he waited awhile before he waved Cruz over.

"Feeling awful Kai and Eva and I missed the burial. Are Pabla and Gabriel all right?"

"What do you think?" Santiago replied, yet to look directly at Cruz. "Why are you here now? More favors?"

The lawman released a nervous breath and launched into what he knew would be an uncomfortable conversation—if the man decided to answer his questions at all.

"We found a green Kawasaki motorbike near the body found on the rez."

Santiago didn't respond or appear to be interested in the information.

Cruz took out his phone, accessed his photos, clicked on the first picture of the bike, flat on its side, beside sagebrush tall and wide enough to hide its frame.

He held the screen up for the other man to see. "Look familiar?"

No answer came from Santiago.

"It's registered to you."

"And?" Santiago responded, annoyed. "I have quite a few. Kai has one. I let my workers use them if they need transportation. Whatever it takes to get them to work."

"Why would it be abandoned on the reservation, Hawk Soars?"

"I don't know, Wolf Song. They're tools. I have many." Santiago rolled his open hand, a *Get on with it* motion.

Cruz showed another photo—the victim's school ID. "Do you know him?"

The other man bent closer to the phone. "Don't recognize the face . . . Novar. Never heard that name. Not Pueblo."

"No. Hispanic."

"Is he the boy you found?"

"Shadow found him. Then Kai."

"Yes, Eva told me. Was the motorbike near the boy?"

"The kid rode it there."

"You're sure?"

"Fingerprints all over the Kawasaki are a match with the body now in the morgue."

"Maybe the bike was stolen. I don't know. Haven't taken inventory on the vehicles in a while. Not interested in the Kawasakis. I'll ask my stable manager, Tommy."

"Better if I check with him, okay?" Cruz said.

"Why? Do you think I would be stepping in your way, Wolf Song? Wouldn't tell you the truth about what my man said. Am I a suspect in the death of that boy?"

"You know the answer to that."

"Yes," Santiago said after a beat, regret and sadness in the single word.

"Everyone is until the case is solved." Cruz took a step closer, then another, until they stood a foot from each other. "Even you, Hawk Soars."

CHAPTER
SIXTY-SEVEN
EVA

Impatient to get the most immediate evidence logged in, Eva personally took the bags that contained the 3D printed gun and Celio Novar's personal items recovered from the Taos Pueblo crime scene to the TPPD lockup. She used the backup key to access the door and left it ajar for Cruz, who had texted he would join her soon.

She looked at the boarded-up area in the wall and noticed that three times the original amount of screwheads now dotted the plywood, where the outside door once allowed entry. By Officer Ramirez most likely, who would be taking no further chances that someone would breach what he was tasked with keeping secure.

"No one's getting through that," she muttered, then placed the items on the table and got to work.

The plastic evidence bag crinkled as she took her time checking the knockoff firearm, barrel locked in the back position, magazine stripped from the handle. Then she snagged a pair of nitrile gloves from the wall dispenser, struggled them on and decided what she should attend to next.

Celio's school ID caught her attention. She turned the plastic rectangle face side up, shook her head, thinking about the loss of such a young kid, placed the credentials at the corner of the table to remind her the items she would reveal were once cherished.

Next she laid out a tactical knife—smaller but much like her own—recovered from the victim's pocket that had been fingerprinted and held no indication of blood on the blade or handle when processed at the recovery site.

His flip phone, Eva assumed to be a burner, was not password protected and contained only two phone numbers. The directory indicated twenty missed calls, fifteen voice mails and as many texts. She decided to hand off the task of delving into those correspondences so she could be more boots on the ground for the actual investigation.

The backpack, well worn, material supple from use, contained a notebook and seven various colored pencils, ends chewed, erasers bitten off. She flipped through the pages, impressed by the realistic drawings, and recognized the area where Celio's body had been recovered.

The two full and one partial bag of candy hit Eva especially hard. Treats for a little boy who looked to have often turned to sweets for satisfaction, maybe his only comfort.

Cruz joined her a few minutes later. He gave her a nod but offered no words as he took in the items laid out on the table. Eva began to worry that he hadn't yet said anything. Instead he took time putting together a cardboard evidence box and then wrote the case details on a sticky note. Eva thanked him for being mindful of the fastidious Leandro Ramirez, who would officially mark the box in his pristine handwriting when he came back on shift.

"How'd it go with Santiago?" Eva asked.

"Not sure you wanna know."

"Yeah, I do." She turned to Cruz, who studied his boots, looking guilty. "Uh-oh. What happened?"

"I guess I kinda called him a suspect in the kid's death."

"I'm gonna kill you. After Paloma, and Kai. Kill you dead." She planted her hands on her hips. "What were you thinking, Officer

Romero? You were just supposed to show him the pictures, find out what he knows about the bike, if he recognized the boy."

"Yeah, yeah. Don't think I don't already feel bad about this. We were getting along really good."

She pushed aside the personal and pivoted back to the job. "I want to check something before we put this away."

Ramirez kept the most recent dated boxes on one shelf, apart from the older cases, and it took only a moment to locate the evidence recovered from Nathan's dog's grave. She set the receptacle on a clear area of the table, opened the box, removed the bag of Glock replicas.

Next, she tugged free two more sets of protective gloves and tossed Cruz a pair to put on. Eva took up an indelible marker from a cup on the table, wrote her name, date, badge number on the sealed evidence bag, then unclipped the knife from her duty belt, flicked the blade open.

"What are you doing?" Cruz asked.

"We won't corrupt anything. Lizbeth already pulled the fingerprints. Only found Celio Novar's."

Cruz looked over his shoulder. "Lenny's gonna freak. He likes to be here to supervise anything done to his precious toys."

"He'll get over it," she said. "Sign the log on the bag as my witness."

He did as she instructed and said, "Just tell me what you're thinking so I can back you up."

She didn't reply, wanted to prove out her suspicions before she explained her actions. The blade sliced cleanly through the bag and released the smell of musty dirt. She withdrew one of the gun frames, then took out her Glock from its holster, ejected the magazine from her service weapon, pulled back the barrel and expelled the round. Then she studied the differences and similarities of the guns side by side, and assessed the weight of both.

Eva handed Cruz the evidence. "Feel it. The fake one's quite a bit lighter."

Cruz studied the replica, then hefted it a few times. "Gotta say, it's good workmanship."

"Don't 'gotta say' anything good about it, Officer Romero," Eva said, annoyed. "Copy?"

"Copy." He hung his head and set the pistol on the table. "You're right. Nothin' good came of them."

She felt guilty for snapping at Cruz—knew he didn't mean any offense. She'd wanted to bring him in on her earlier discovery, and thought this might be the only time the two would be in the evidence room alone.

She set her duty weapon on the table and made sure Lenny Ramirez hadn't clocked back in after his tour watching over the burial ceremony, then she hitched her head. "Wanna show you something."

Cruz rounded the long table, joined her at the farthest wall, looked where she pointed to the bottom shelf in the corner.

"Lefthand," Cruz said, reading the box. He turned to Eva. "Angel Simone? Related to the chief?"

Eva had assumed the same when she first encountered the notation on the box. "I guess. Common name, but maybe. I mean, the Lefthands go way, way back. Whatever the crime is, it happened a long time ago."

Always good at math, Cruz said, "Twenty-seven years ago."

She snapped her head to him. "Twenty-seven years?" She studied the date more closely and the realization hit her—just then realizing why the date seemed familiar when she stumbled upon the box. "That's when my parents moved away."

A look of concern creased Cruz's brow. "Do you remember the month?"

She nodded. "Remember the day, too."

After her long pause, Cruz opened his hand, prompting Eva to complete the thought she couldn't say out loud. She knelt down in front of the container, pointed at the date. Said nothing else. Didn't need to.

"You're sure?"

"Positive. Box isn't sealed," she said. "Should we open it?"

Cruz took her arm before she could reach for the lid, eased her upright, made sure no one watched them. "No case closed date," Cruz said in a low voice. "Guess it's unsolved."

Eva nodded her agreement.

"We don't know what this is," he said. "Not a word about what you found. Got it?"

"Maybe—"

Before she could convince Cruz to let her open the lid someone cleared their throat, and they both turned around. Chief Lefthand stood at the entrance, eyes going to where Eva and Cruz blocked. She didn't say anything, but Eva felt certain their boss knew they had spotted something not pertaining to their current investigations.

"All right, let's talk this through." Chief Lefthand reached for and put on the remaining set of gloves, then picked up the Glock replica recovered from the fresh crime scene. "Had about enough of these bogus firearms."

"Like the others we've recovered, the quality is exceptional. Professional," Eva said. "Wouldn't know it's not real to look at."

"They do look identical," Lefthand said.

"Real enough to get Little Bear killed," Cruz muttered.

"I've been doing some research and found out that ghost guns are easy to get," Eva said, relying on her recollection of the internet analysis she had performed over the past couple of days to get her through restless bouts of time. "Go online, place an order for a kit, pay for it, wait for the piece to be shipped. Lots of videos out there to show how to assemble them. No record of sales, no regulation at all. No background checks are needed. Kinda the same with what we're lookin' at here, except the frames and other plastic parts are 3D printed."

Cruz picked up Eva's real Glock from the table and the replica gun, turned both pistols upside down, pointed to the plates at the bottom of each barrel. "No serial number on the knockoff."

"That's what makes them untraceable and a big problem," Eva said. "Magazines and trigger, recoil springs and other items are purchased separately. Each unit only needs to be less than eighty percent finished to slide under the federal law."

"Allows open season for criminals and felons to purchase firearms," the chief said.

"And underage kids . . . like Celio," Eva said.

"All right, let's break this down," Lefthand said. "We have gun replicas from the Trujillos' property. That one found on Celio at his body recovery site. Also one recovered from Simon Optum's vehicle, which may or may not have been the one used during the bank robbery."

"And the one Nathan had when he was shot," Cruz said.

"Any word on the findings about that one?" the chief asked.

Eva shook her head. "Nothing yet. Santiago Mirabal has been helpful with the authorities in getting Nathan back here. I can ask him—"

"No," the chief snapped. "I'll reach out to the Santa Fe police chief and request photos."

"Copy," Eva said, taken aback by her boss's sharp tone at the mention of Santiago reaching out to help. He would want to. The request wouldn't be an imposition. If the tribal councilman found the request to be stepping over the line with his contacts, he wouldn't be shy about saying no.

"Every knockoff we have here look like duplicates," Cruz said, interrupting Eva's confusion. "That one probably does too."

"Would be good to know if we can tie all of this together," Lefthand said. "Stronger case if the evidence is proven to be related to all of the incidents when we catch whoever is manufacturing these damned things."

"*If* we find out," Cruz muttered.

"There's got to be something," Eva said.

As she was about to return the Celio Novar firearm to its evidence bag, something caught Eva's attention. She picked up her Glock, brought the fake one close, and barely made out an anomaly, almost the size of a pencil's eraser, etched in the plastic, below the magazine catch.

The face of a fox.

Curiosity pinged as she reached into the evidence box on the table, removed each 3D replica, set them out in a row, then studied one after another.

"What did you find?" Cruz asked.

No need for prompting, Cruz and Lefthand both reached for a different evidence bag and smoothed the plastic covering.

Eva pointed to a precise area, right side of the grip—first the knock-off, then the next, and next, to the last—and let the visual speak, louder than words. Cruz and Lefthand leaned in, noses inches from where she pointed.

"A fox head? I've never noticed that before. Is it on your Glock?" He took out his own firearm and studied the same area.

"No. It's part of the 3D design," Eva clarified.

The chief examined them so fast Eva wasn't sure she'd spotted the fox heads. Then Lefthand raised one of the replicas in her hand, studied it longer than the others, set the gun down, crossed her arms tight against her chest and glowered at every fake gun that looked all too real.

Sensing the need to clarify, Eva said, "Lizbeth Herrera told me about something a while back called a signature aspect. Something killers employ to claim their victims. Brand their kills somehow—a burn or tattoo or some sort of anomaly. Sometimes they take a personal item. A way to mark their territory, and to recall the memory. Whoever this person is uses the face of a fox to lay claim."

"Kinda like signing a painting or a sculpture," Cruz said.

"Exactly. Doesn't mean this person who manufactured them intended malfeasance, but it is suspicious."

The chief turned her full attention to Eva. "Tell me more about the gun found on our latest victim. Think his outcome is related to this?"

Unsure if the request was a test, or if her supervisor truly sought her opinion, Eva chanced her assessment. "Celio Novar's crime scene, and the knockoffs discovered from the Trujillo house—all involve 3D printed firearms. Gotta be related, right?"

"Gotta be," her chief concurred.

Relieved to have made the correct leap, she mirrored the chief's head nod. Eva waited, silent, lost in her own thoughts about implications, how to make the connection fit, prove their assumption with so many holes and unknowns and missing pieces to the puzzle.

"I'll find out if the replica recovered from Simon Optum's BMW matches the others," the chief said.

Eva realized how much pressure the chief must be under. The governor and the war chief and their teams, and the tribal council and various committees. So many with eyes on her. Waiting to see if the top cop would fail. Also people of the community, probably even her family members, wanted answers no one could yet give. All her responsibility.

"Chief," Eva said. "The same person . . . or people are making these things."

Eva recognized her boss's expression, a mirror to the one she had settled on her own face. Determination, fury, the need to unleash wrath. She felt the call to be the Pueblo warrior woman necessary to put an end to the instigators who, wittingly or not, had placed their community in peril. And needed to be stopped. Immediately. Whatever it took.

CHAPTER
SIXTY-EIGHT
KAI

Hours after Kai had been released from the crime scene, he still hadn't recovered from Shadow's discovery of the kid's body, and so he found solace, as many times before, with the plants he had selected for the terrarium. From the place he might never feel comfortable returning to. The realization left him sad and numb.

Taking in the comforting hay and alfalfa scents that hung in the barn, he thought about his mother. She had been unable to hide her emotions when he'd explained why he wasn't able to attend Nathan's burial. Santiago stood beside his sister, hands out to catch her when she swayed, hand to her mouth, face pale, eyes wide, probably imagining the horror he had seen firsthand.

She had wanted to forbid him from leaving the house, maybe forever, the only way to be safe. Santiago had stepped in then, reminded the overprotective mother that her son was an adult now, she had to trust him to make his own decisions, then led her away so Kai could heal along with Shadow.

In a way Kai thought she was right. Everywhere he seemed to go tragedy dropped in his path. And yet he'd been able to step around the obstacles. He looked at Shadow, filthy tennis ball between his feet. Patient, compliant, ready for whatever Kai asked of him. He had become stronger because of the Malinois. And the drive to help his mom get better. Be a good son, student, trainer. Learn what he could from others, figure out the rest on his own.

Paloma's favorite horse whinnied and he thought she had returned to baby him. He left the stall and stood in the open breezeway to wait for another plea.

Instead, Eva Duran walked his direction. Still in uniform, stride not as fast or confident as usual.

He sighed when she reached him. "Jeez, Eva, what now? Seems like every time you come here it's to tell us bad news."

She frowned, shrugged like she'd searched her mind for an instance when that hadn't been the case lately and couldn't think of a single time.

"Seems like bad news has followed me ever since I became a cop."

"Why are you here?" he asked. "More questions about what we found?"

"No, I need to ask you about Tomás Salas. We need to speak to his students. Hoping he'll be helpful with that."

"He's a good guy. I don't want you messin' anything up with him. You know how much he means to me."

"I realize—"

"What? You don't believe a non-Native wants to do good things for us?"

"I'm not saying that, Kai. But the boy you and Shadow found was one of his students. I need you to—"

Kai flicked his index finger to the ceiling and she quit talking. He reached into his hoodie, took out the medicine bag, unwound the drawstring, dug inside. The second set of cuttings he had pinched off for Nathan tumbled from the leather confines, drifted to his feet when he pulled out the item he wanted to show her. He rested the small plastic roofless house in his palm and held it out. "This is what Mr. Salas is doing . . . or plans to."

Eva picked up the item, frowned at the piece of plastic, turned it over to look at the bottom. He heard a faint gasp catch in her chest and he leaned in, unsure of what she'd reacted to.

"Where did you get this?" she asked, voice hushed.

"From Mr. Salas. He's gonna make these for us on the rez. 3D printed houses we can afford. He said as soon as he has the funding he'll get started."

"Where do you think he'll be getting this funding?"

"I don't know. Investors, I guess. He didn't go into that part."

"What else did he tell you about the money? Did he say exactly where he plans to manufacture the houses? Where is the equipment? Did he mention the names of these investors?" Eva rattled the questions off fast, not even waiting for him to answer a single one.

"I don't know," he said, frustrated. "Didn't ask. I was surprised that he wanted to help the tribe like that. Felt kinda honored, you know?"

"Interesting."

"Yeah, it is," he snapped, annoyed she didn't take his teacher's good intent seriously. "We need houses and don't have enough qualified people to build them. The ones he'll make will be made of concrete. Everything is automated."

Even to Kai the response sounded like a sales pitch, same as Mr. Salas presented. This time, the explanation rang hollow, and doubt began to creep up.

"Still need finish carpenters," she said. "Painters, roofers, plumbers and electricians, too, right? And the process sounds pretty specialized. Probably professionals familiar with the products and the equipment would need to be hired. Who's gonna pay for all that?"

Kai lowered his head and thought back on the conversation about Mr. Salas's plan, unaware if his teacher had taken everything into consideration.

"You weren't suspicious about how all of this would actually get accomplished?"

"No! Why would I be? He said he's got everything figured out, and I believe him. He's always been good to me. Taught me way beyond what he needed to. More than a teacher, he's a friend. He got me into the university."

"You got *yourself* into the university."

"He helped. Was there when my mom or Santi wasn't. *Or you.* For years he was the only person I could depend on. Who never left. Who cared a single shit to check on me."

Kai knew she probably wished his harsh declarations weren't true. But they were. Every single word.

She eased her tone and asked, "He hadn't mentioned his plans before now? In private or during a class?"

"No."

"Ambitious undertaking. You didn't think his project sounded a little odd when he told you?"

"No. Not at all. Quit questioning me like I'm one of your suspects!" he yelled. "I just figured he wanted his project to be a surprise for when he was closer to building the houses. I'm telling you, Mr. Salas isn't doing anything bad."

She looked to be considering how to deliver some sort of information.

"He's not!"

Eva didn't wait any longer. She blurted out, "Tomás Salas has been making the fake guns."

Shocked, he let out a burst of air, a single note he didn't expect to escape. "No."

Eva held her solemn attitude.

He scowled at her, so mad he wanted to run off before he said something he wouldn't be able to take back. "It's not him. You're wrong."

"I wish I was—"

Eva waited a beat, then reached for her cell phone, opened the photo gallery, swiped until she found what she hunted for, expanded the screen to make the image larger, handed Kai the mobile. "See that logo? Investigators and behaviorists call this a signature aspect. A criminal's behavioral way of claiming their acts of wrongdoing."

She swapped the model house for her phone and lessened the image to the original capture—the frame of a 3D printed Glock. "This is one of the guns Shadow dug up at Bonkers's grave. Do you see that?"

He barely made out the small face of a fox etched in the plastic.

"That stamp has been found on the frame of every 3D printed gun we've recovered." She dipped her head at his hand. "Look at the bottom."

Kai turned the little house over, raised it inches from his eyes, as if a closer look would change the vision of the same fox face. He trapped the plastic model in a fist so tight he thought blood would soon trickle from his palm.

Realization came clear—that his mentor had most likely printed and sold illicit handguns used to rob the bank, got that police officer shot, put his community in danger. The whole city too.

After a full minute, he found the words he needed to say most. "Was the stamp on the gun Nathan had when he died?"

Her jaw muscles tensed. She waited as if preparing for his reaction, then nodded her head—confirming that the matching fox face symbols proved Mr. Salas's involvement.

Kai's shoulders slumped. He wobbled on his feet. Opened his mouth but no words came out.

Shadow whined, attached himself to his master's side. Kai stroked the Malinois's face as realization slammed him in the chest and he found it difficult to take in a full breath. Eva took a step toward him and he held up a hand motion for her to stop. Last thing he wanted was comfort from the person who had revealed a truth he never would have wanted to know. Now convinced his mentor, teacher, person he turned to when no one else would listen had been a fake relationship—as inauthentic as the guns he made. The man who treated him like a son was actually a vessel of nothing but lies and deception.

Betrayal cut him. The wound deep and heartbreaking and unforgettable and unforgivable.

A devastating slash delivered by his most trusted friend.

The reason Little Bear was dead.

CHAPTER
SIXTY-NINE
DAMON

Damon sat in the back seat of the faded gold sedan and looked over the driver's shoulder to see the cell phone's screen Manny stared at, as if the info would change if he looked long enough. Forty-seven texts. Twenty-three missed calls. Eight voice mails.

The dude looked trapped. Damon could smell fear mingled with sweat and unwashed hair.

He knew Manny needed those guns. Or at least the money to give back to the weapons man who his friend had told him and Cal was even scarier than himself.

The three had been to Manny's house, out searching, back home, and out so many times Damon had lost count—looking for Celio, who hadn't come home yesterday, or anytime during the night. No sign of him this day either.

Now back at the house again, Manny slammed the car in park, headed for the front door. Cal looked like he didn't want to be there any more than Damon did, but they followed him anyway.

Manny pushed open the unlocked door, took the phone from his khakis pocket, looked at the screen. "Four thirty," he said, shaking his head.

Damon knew that Manny had come to the conclusion his brother had run away—with his money and the guns. The kid had the Kawasaki. Could be anywhere. Another state by now.

At this point Manny probably could have found a local kid with a computer and 3D printer and access to internet files to build more guns. Checked eBay or Craigslist, found someone to teach him how to get on the dark web to buy some. But he didn't have the brainwidth to try any one of those options. At this point the Spanish dude couldn't form a rational thought about how to get out of his situation. Damon suppressed a smile, knowing the idiot sure as hell wouldn't be able to figure out how to start all over.

Manny stood in the front room, Damon and Cal looking at him, nothing helpful to offer. Damon caught the smell of red pork *pazole*. Celio's favorite. Figured Manny did too because he charged to the kitchen, probably expecting to see the brother.

They only found his grandmother, alone at the table, still in the housecoat she hadn't changed out of all day, sliding the beads of her rosary between her fingers, lips moving in silent prayer.

"Where is Celio?" Manny roared.

His grandmother cowered, stuttered that she didn't know, same as she'd told him a hundred times already. Hadn't seen him since yesterday morning. Swore in the name of Jesus she was not lying—the only thing that saved her from a beating, Damon was sure of that.

The grandson flung one of the empty chairs across the room to smash against the refrigerator, stormed down the hall. Damon followed close behind Manny, who kicked in the closed door to Celio's room. Hands laced on the top of his head, he turned around and around. "Help me look!"

Damon wasn't sure where to start looking, or what to look for. For show, he peered under the bed, tore off the sheets and blanket, tipped up the mattress to check underneath.

"What are we looking for, man?" Cal asked, at the closet pulling down items from the top shelf to land on the floor.

"Guns, you idiot. Money. Clues where my traitor brother could be."

Room trashed, no indication about anything they searched for found, Manny dropped to the chair at the desk, gazed out the window. Damon looked through the glass, imagined the sound of the Kawasaki's *ree-ree-ree* up to the house.

Manny seemed to remember something and sat up straight. He reached for the handle beside him. The drawer stuck, so he gave it a tug. Pencils, pens and candy wrappers burst out of the compartment. Manny dug in and took out a notebook. Damon recalled that Celio had been drawing on something when Manny had told him to set up the money drop-off and guns pickup yesterday.

Manny flipped through the lined pages to the last one. Drawings of handguns, big and small. Some of the images realistic as photographs. Below the sketches, the name T SALAS written over and over took up the rest of the page.

Manny frowned, thought for a minute. Looked to Damon like the name seemed familiar but Manny couldn't place who the person was. Then he snapped his fingers—a signal of recognition. He reached for the stack of textbooks lined up next to the desk lamp, took up a math book, opened the front cover, fanned the pages, found nothing. Next was a biology book. Damon stepped closer. He knew that was Celio's favorite subject in school. He'd been with his grandma in the kitchen a few times when the kid couldn't stop talking about plants whenever she asked what they were used for as Celio showed her pictures.

Damon peered over the other man's shoulder as Manny opened the front cover, ran a finger over a handwritten notation.

CELIO—THIS IS MY NUMBER ONE CHOICE.

HOPE YOU LEARN A LOT FROM THESE PAGES

—TOMÁS SALAS

"Gotcha!" Manny tapped the inscription. "We start with this guy. He's Celio's biology teacher at the high school." He slammed the cover shut, got up, gave his boys a satisfied grin. "If he hasn't seen the little prick, we'll get the names of the kids in his class. He's gotta be hiding somewhere."

Damon thought the idea was a pretty good one, until Manny said, "Tomahawk, find out where this Tomás Salas lives."

"How am I gonna—"

Manny took a full stride to Damon, cutting off his words. Nose to nose, he roared, "You said you were a cop."

"Yeah, I got you, I got you."

"Prove it, *muthuhfuckuh*. You've got one hour."

One hour to make a miracle happen . . . Unless . . .

He wriggled his fingers at Cal—who knew what the action meant without words and handed over his phone.

He dusted off his investigatory skills, accessed the Taos County Assessor's Office, tapped in the teacher's name, waited for the result. The entire search had taken less than one minute. He smiled, held up the phone, pocketed the cell before Manny could snatch it away. Waited for the realization to sweep over Manny's face.

Then Damon beaded a glare at who had now become the *former* leader of their pack. "I'll drive," he said, finality in his tone.

CHAPTER SEVENTY
EVA

Eva drove the official vehicle closer to their location, a Taos neighborhood much like her own. Cruz, belted next to her, looked anxious.

Eva wasn't sure that what she wanted to ask her partner would relax him, but she couldn't hold back the question any longer. "Hey, have you noticed the chief gets kinda ticked off whenever I bring up Santiago? What do you think that's about?"

Cruz shrugged. "Maybe Lefthand doesn't want anyone to think Santiago's position holds more power than hers."

"To the tribe?"

"To anyone. I mean, how would you feel if someone looked only at me when you were the one asking questions? It's important for anyone involved to know she's the one in charge. In the loop about everything. If anything goes wrong in the investigation, she's the responsible party."

She gave him a sidelong look, and half kidding said, "You seem to be quite attuned to the inner workings of June 'Bobcat Leaps' Lefthand."

Cruz turned to look out his side window. "How do you want to play this?" he asked, evading her remark entirely.

"We're just gonna talk to Salas," she said. "See if he reveals anything that sounds off. Look for an opening that will allow us to search his place."

"Feels wrong doing this, Duran."

"Kotz should be there by now. He'll take point. We'll observe. Interject if he doesn't hit the objective."

"Be ready to hit," Cruz said, pointing to a police cruiser parked at the curb a few houses away from their target address, uniformed officer leaning against the rear bumper, facing their direction.

Kotz looked so innocent that Eva wondered how much experience he had questioning potential suspects. A wiz at the keyboard, researching, examining camera footage and running down leads, sure, but boots on the ground? She had no idea, and now felt nervous that the less-experienced city cop, who would need to take the lead, might hinder her and Cruz.

They both got out of the vehicle to stand with Kotz. "Should we let more of your people know we're here?" she asked Kotz.

"Just a conversation, right?" he said. "We don't want to spook him by bringing in a bunch a cops only to ask a few questions. Clear this matter up." He sounded less confident than his words conveyed.

Cruz looked over the top of his sunglasses. "And you don't want to be embarrassed if this doesn't turn into anything worthy of your fellow cops' attention . . . right?"

Kotz stared at Cruz a few ticks. Did not confirm or deny. Instead, he turned and took his first steps in the direction of the house they had verified Salas held the deed to.

Eva took hold of Cruz's sleeve to keep him there. "Stop it, Cruz," she whispered. "What're you doing? Why are you pushing him?"

"I wanted to make sure we won't run into any potential jurisdictional hiccups." Cruz repositioned his shades.

"Got it, but Kotz already looks nervous about this."

"He's Kai's mentor, right? If we need to prompt your buddy, lead with that."

Cruz picked up his pace to catch Kotz, Eva following at a slower stride and assessing the area as the residence came into full view. Multipassenger, faded maroon-colored older-model GMC van parked at the front of the house. Two-car garage detached from the one-story ranch-style in need of fresh paint. No vehicle in the driveway.

Eva studied Kotz, who looked more nervous as the seconds ticked off.

Cruz nodded toward the house. "We've got an opening," he said, big smile turning up his lips.

Kotz and Eva turned to watch as a man headed for the garage beside the house and proceeded to punch in the security code for entry.

"One problem solved," Eva said, thinking of the multitude of other situations that needed to go as smoothly.

CHAPTER
SEVENTY-ONE
TOMÁS

Unable to withstand the *not* knowing a single minute longer, Salas swept up his keys, locked the front door behind him. Mind and actions only on making sure the guns being printed and stored were secured, then head to the reservation to get the Kawasaki, *And look for that damned gun,* he thought. He rushed for the garage, punched in the security code, waited as the door whirred open, strode to the rear wall, pushed the rolling cart aside, opened the back door—

"Thomas Salas?" a female voice asked behind him. "All right if we talk to you for a minute?"

He was sure he hit the button to close the garage door. He slowly turned around and realized he must not have. Three police officers in uniform stood at the edge of his drive. One Taos city cop, two tribal representatives. They all stood looking at him, thumbs looped in their belts, hands close to the guns in their holsters. Real ones.

"I don't think we've met." She took long steps, entered the garage, closed the gap, held out her hand to shake. "I'm Eva Duran. Kai Arrio's godmother."

He took her hand, trying not to wince from her viselike grip. "Oh—hi—I'm—well, you know. To*más*, actually." He emphasized the correct pronunciation, something he didn't usually do but he felt the need for the tribal officer to get it right.

She hitched her head to the man behind her. "My partner, tribal officer Cruz Romero, and Taos police officer Andrew Kotz."

The other Pueblo and the redhead entered the garage, blocking Salas's ability to leave the garage. He felt trapped. Worse, he was unable to close the partially open door behind him—thankfully only cracked a few inches—the printers' cooling fans and whirring motors faint, but evident.

As inconspicuously as he could manage, he pushed the door shut an inch, then edged past the woman and took long steps until he reached the worktable in the middle of the space. She followed and he breathed easier, relieved to have guided her away.

"We understand you're familiar with a particular area on the reservation," Officer Kotz said.

"Umm . . . yes. I mean I don't know which particular area you mean, but in the past I've visited the reservation. For biological research." He turned to Eva, hoping to make a shared connection. "I had approval to be there . . . fully authorized by your governor's office. And the Red Willow Center, where I've taught agriculture and biology classes. Some of the kids I've mentored from there accompanied me to their—your reservation several times. I met with Kai quite a few times too."

You're talking too much, he screamed in his head. *You sound suspicious as hell. Stop!*

"When was the last time you visited that location?" Kotz asked.

Salas frowned, studied the floor, hesitated, pretended not to remember. "I don't know exactly when. Not for a while now."

"So, last month, year . . . Today?" the female officer asked.

Salas's heartbeat slammed in his chest. He turned his frown into a scowl. "I'm feeling uncomfortable. Do I need to call a lawyer?"

"No need for a lawyer, not at all," Duran cooed, probably an attempt to ramp down the intensity. "We can move on to something else. What do you know about 3D guns?"

On the edge of panic, he answered quickly. "Nothing. Nothing at all. Why would you ask me that?"

He tried to look as innocent as possible. Wasn't sure he was pulling it off.

"All right, I'll tell you." She leaned closer to him. "I think you know about some firearm replicas we've found in and around Taos. My colleagues and I believe you're more involved than you claim not to be."

Salas didn't have to hide his exasperation this time. Terrified they had found out his dealings, his mind spun, had to force himself not to sprint away fast as possible, get in his van. Go. Anywhere but here.

"How do you know this? Can you prove it?" Salas asked, unable to keep the belligerence from his tone. "Can you trace manufacturers of the filament printing material. *Prove* where they were made?"

She hesitated, then came back with, "We're working on that."

"Really? The Pueblo police force has that ability?"

Salas knew he shouldn't be so belligerent, stop being snide to the officers, but he couldn't seem to stop himself.

"Kai says you're a good man, Tomás," she said, getting the accent correct this time. "Help me believe that."

"What you're thinking about me is ridiculous. I don't even have access to the computer lab, where the 3D printers are at the high school. Students have to sign in and book appointments to print anything, and only those authorized have the door code to the lab."

The male Pueblo cop had a curious look on his face. He stepped closer to the back door. Looked at Salas. Took a few more steps.

"Wait . . . Don't go in there," Salas pleaded. He lurched forward, lost his footing, slammed against the back wall. The door popped wide open.

The officer poked his head inside, then ducked back out. Cut his eyes to his partner, then the city cop. Dropped his hand to the butt of his pistol, used his thumb to flip the strap that secured the weapon in its holster.

The other two spotted his action, did the same, all three now ready to pull out their guns and shoot if he did one single thing wrong.

The officer who made the discovery didn't enter the secret room, but took out his cell phone and started taking photos, then a video of the dozen 3D printers, all working to create the next batch of gun pieces in varying stages of completion.

One of the cops took in a shocked gasp of air. Another whistled, long and slow.

"I can explain," Salas tried.

The city cop moved so fast Salas didn't have a chance to react to his hand being seized, the feel of a cold bracelet going around his wrist, the clicking ratchet, pinch of skin and bone. He gaped at the police officer, pleading with his eyes as his second hand was captured.

Everyone turned to an engine's rev getting closer. A beat-up, nondescript, older-model faded-gold sedan, white smoke billowing as the rear tires skidded to a halt across the street from Salas's house.

Three of the doors flung open. Three men got out. They all had puffed-out chests, purpose to their strides. No fear at all on their faces.

A glint flashed in the late-afternoon sun. Unmistakable.

"Gun!" the female cop yelled.

CHAPTER
SEVENTY-TWO
EVA

Eva pinged on the well-built Hispanic man in front—long-sleeved button-down shirttails flapping, one arm hidden behind his back as he stormed their direction. A Native man followed two strides away from the man in front, gun up, pointed forward at head level. A step to the right, another male took up the rear, handgun lowered, no attempt to conceal it.

The leader looked directly at Tomás Salas, laser focused only on the teacher as he whipped a semiautomatic into full view, raised and held it straight out in a horizontal ninety-degree side grip. "Where are my guns?" he shouted.

Eva dove, pushed Salas as hard as she could. He propelled backward, staggered to catch his balance.

Bullets whizzed and pinged all around—distinctive three-shot bursts again and again, overlapping single shots from other pistols firing simultaneously.

In her periphery, Eva caught sight of a stream of white that poured from a paint can. Tufts of stuffing spewed from the row of vehicle seats along one of the walls.

In fluid motions, she spun, released the Glock from its holster, aimed.

Side by side, Eva and Cruz fired simultaneously—double-taps to body mass.

Bullets whizzed upward, they both ducked low.

The lead offender dropped to his knees, teetered, fell forward to land face down, a thud that vibrated Eva's tactical boots.

More gunfire followed, more shots, destruction all around, bullets piercing throughout the garage.

Kotz took a step forward, double-tap from his gun, swept his Glock a foot to the left, discharged again.

Eva's ears rang, a constant high-pitched scream she hoped didn't indicate a burst eardrum from the deafening discharges of six firearms expelling rapid-fire projectiles. Gun smoke tickled her nostrils, the garage seemed unnaturally bright, hairs on her forearms tingled, her right hand buzzed from the kick of her Glock and holding the grip so tight.

She took in and out long deep breaths, prayed for calm, assessed her body to make sure adrenaline hadn't masked the symptoms from a gunshot or ricochet wound. She kept her gun trained on the big man as Cruz rushed forward, kicked the extended-magazine handgun from the assailant's grasp, crouched down, held two fingers to the target's neck. He looked up at Eva and shook his head.

She holstered her weapon, stood across from Cruz, pulled out a wallet from the back pocket of the dead man's khakis, scanned the driver's license. "Manuel Novar," she said. "Lives in Taos."

"Novar?" Cruz said, hand held against his side. "Relation to the dead kid on the rez?"

"Maybe." She sorted through the other contents. "Two credit cards, thirty-seven dollars cash, gym membership card."

Cruz winced and said, "Explains the physique."

She found a photograph in a hidden compartment. "Got a photo." She studied the two figures, arms over each other, big grins, then compared it to the dead man at her feet, held it out for Cruz to see.

"Brothers," Cruz stated, verifying Eva's guess.

Cruz knelt down to take a closer look at the Native man on his back, legs and arms splayed at unnatural angles. "Aw, shiiit," Cruz said, drawing out the curse word. "That's Damon Sandoval. Used to be a tribal cop. Got fired for stealing evidence and selling it on eBay. Gambling problem. Couldn't shake it."

"Now we know how they knew about the evidence room door," Eva said.

"We sealed up the outside entry not long after the council booted him out," Cruz said. "Probably didn't know."

"Eva . . ." Kotz pointed.

She turned to Salas, on the garage floor, legs out, slouched up against the rolling cart.

The teacher clutched his stomach, best he could with both hands cuffed. A thick pool of blood on the floor where he sat grew wider with his every heartbeat. He kept his head turned toward the now fully open back door, watching the printers as they continued their endless advancement building up gun frames and various parts one miniscule line after the next.

She knelt down a few feet from the teacher, careful not to smear the blood. "Hang tight, Mr. Salas. Help is coming."

"Thank you for saving me," he said, voice faint. "Thank you," he muttered over and over.

For the briefest of moments Eva wondered if the teacher, who had been responsible for so much havoc on and off the reservation, would still be grateful for her and Cruz's intervention after his first days in a jail cell. Maybe the same facility as Alice Jones while he waited to be tried and convicted to serve many years in prison.

If he survived.

"I'm caught. That's for sure." He let out a chuckle and blood bubbled from his mouth. "Do you think Kai will come visit me in prison?"

"Don't know. I could ask," she said, now certain she never would. Moment by moment the man grew weaker and she realized she wouldn't need to.

He let out a relieved breath. "My wife left me a while ago. School has been my refuge. Taos High School Teacher of the Year three times." He wavered his head to look directly at her. "Did you know that?"

She shook her head and squeezed her hands shut so she wouldn't be tempted to reach out and clench his shoulder, assure him she was there for him. He wasn't alone.

"Tutored I don't even know how many kids who eventually graduated with honors and made it into good colleges. Even Kai. Best pupil I've ever had the privilege to share my knowledge with." His smile turned into a wince. "I hope he'll forgive me. Think he will?"

"Betrayal . . . is difficult to come back from," Eva said, not swayed at all by his story of woe.

The man reared back, as if her first word and its meaning had never occurred to him. Eva figured he probably didn't believe he'd deceived anyone at all.

"I was going to make the lives of your people better. Tell Kai I'm sorry. The house I wanted to build him and Paloma will have to wait."

The statement confused Eva but before she could ask him to clarify he coughed, spewing crimson mist, blood staining his teeth.

"How did you figure it out?" he managed to say, voice slower now.

"A little fox head told me."

"Damn," Salas whispered. "That was supposed to be my spirit animal. My protection."

Eva looked at Cruz and thought, *Turns out it was ours.*

"Your guns are responsible for two dead kids, and a shot police officer," Cruz said, his tone harsh and matter of fact.

Salas frowned, confused, so Eva clarified: "The initial one used for the bank robbery was the impetus for the officer getting shot."

"I don't know anything about that bank robbery," Salas said. "Nothing. I promise. I've got nothing to lose or gain by lying to you about that."

"Fine," she said. "What about the replica a young boy had in his possession? The one responsible for his death. The lure of a firearm can make people do things they normally would not even think of. Bend their nature. Make them someone they don't recognize."

"Did you say a young boy found one of my replicas?" Salas asked.

"Nathan Trujillo. Taos Pueblo Native. Eight years old. Shot while holding one of your knockoffs."

"That was him on the news?"

She didn't answer, locked her attention on his horrified eyes.

"No, no, no," Salas muttered. "That can't be. My guns didn't even work . . . Until . . ." He didn't finish the thought.

"Tell that to the kid on the reservation," Cruz said. "Worked fine for killing him."

"He was one of my students. I didn't know he was doing the pickups. Leaving me the money. The mastermind of the whole operation. His brother was only the middleman."

"Must have figured out you were making them," Cruz said, more to himself than Salas or Eva.

"But who's selling them?" Eva asked Salas. "Manuel? Celio? Someone else?"

"I . . . I . . ." Unable, or unwilling, to say more, Salas lifted one shoulder a few inches—an *I don't know* or *I won't say* motion. Eva wasn't sure which.

A long exhale wheezed from the man's mouth. His hands went slack, head lolled to his chest, shoulders slumped lower. No rise or fall from his chest.

Eva eased the teacher's lifeless body to rest on his side, looked up at Cruz, who didn't look quite right—face pale, listing to the right. The Glock, held barrel down, twitched in his grip. She frowned, scanned her eyes down his body.

He looked where her eyes stopped roving—at his side, above his duty belt. "Yeah, someone got me," he said, let out a light chuckle, wavered, sat down hard on the cement floor.

"Ah shit, man," Kotz said. "Not again." He grabbed a length of material from one of the shelves, hurried to the other two, mashed the cloth against Cruz, soaking up blood that saturated the side of his shirt and upper portion of his pants. "Hang on, buddy."

"All right, that's enough," Cruz said, wincing. "You gonna kiss me next?"

The unexpected humor caused Eva and Kotz to let out surprised chuckles.

"Doesn't look bad," Kotz said, although he wasn't actually able to look at the wound.

"Is that what you told your girlfriend?"

Kotz snarled.

"Too soon?" Cruz smiled, lessening the dig.

The whir of a single siren grew louder as it approached their location. Then another and another until the block was choked with official vehicles, emergency lights flicking their reflections from the front windows of every house on the neighborhood street.

CHAPTER
SEVENTY-THREE
EVA

An hour later the coroner's van rolled up and backed into Tomás Salas's driveway. Eva and Cruz watched from the sidewalk, outside the kill zone. Out of the way as the city force took point, but close enough to watch everything.

The moment Lizbeth Herrera arrived on scene she had ejected the three officers from the area, warning them to be cautious not to displace the forty or more spent casings that littered the driveway, and from the police-issued firearms on the cement floor of the garage.

The first paramedic on scene had patched up Cruz, who declined further immediate treatment. Eva and the medic shook their heads as her stubborn partner signed the waiver for refusal of transport that released the city from negligence if he dropped dead instead of going to the hospital. Thankfully the shot had been a clean through-and-through above his left hip, no organs hit, and minimal bleeding once the attendant tended to the wound, applied sterile dressings and adhesive bandages.

Investigation fully underway, Eva stood beside the cottonwood tree Cruz sat against, legs crossed as he cradled his side. Out of the way, but close enough to watch Lizbeth Herrera and her team put their full attention and expertise into assessing the scene. One of the techs, camera focused tight, took shot after shot of the offenders' firearms that Eva and Kotz had lined up on the worktable in the middle of the space.

In the back area of the garage, another tech cataloged the array of 3D printers that continued to spew filament, replica guns growing as the minutes ticked off.

The bodies of Manuel Novar and the other as of yet unidentified offender remained face down on the ground, wrists secured behind him—*just to be sure*, Eva had muttered out loud when she ratcheted the handcuffs.

She tried her best to avoid looking at Tomás Salas, where he had taken his last breath. Kai would be devastated about the loss of his mentor. She had no idea how to give him the news, but knew it should be her.

She turned her attention to Kotz, who stood at the edge of the street, leaning against one of the TPD cruisers. His sure shots of Manuel Novar's two henchmen seemed to have redeemed him as a competent law enforcement officer in the eyes of his supervisor and colleagues, who rallied around the LEO, full solidarity in play.

"That was one badass gun," Cruz said, interrupting her thoughts. She frowned at him, confused by the statement.

Cruz nodded toward the table. "The Beretta. Never seen one like it."

"Good thing the piece only deployed three rounds at a time," Eva said. "Fully automatic probably would have taken the three of us out."

"Firing it gangster-style helped us too. No way for an accurate shot," Cruz said. "We lived a blessed life today."

"We were lucky, Cruz. And we still don't know who Salas was making the guns for."

"Boss will understand, if that's what you're worried about. We came here for a conversation with—"

"And got into a shoot-out! Look around. One stray bullet from our guns and a civilian could have been hit. Or worse. We're *waaaay* out of our jurisdiction here. Lefthand is gonna have our butts."

"We'll be all right, Lightning Dance. The chief wanted an end to this." He pointed at Salas. "That's the end."

Eva hoped his reasoning would be convincing to their supervisor. She wasn't sure it would be enough to keep them out of an inquiry headed by the Taos PD. Maybe even the FBI. Or ATF. She shut down the mind-numbing possibilities, which would probably haunt her the moment she shut her eyes for the night. If the endless day ever actually ended for her to do so.

Exhausted now that the adrenaline had fled, she propped herself against the tree, put the worries aside and asked Cruz, "Does it hurt?"

He looked up at her, shrugged, then winced and took in a wheeze of air between his teeth.

"That's a yes," Eva said, mad all over again. "Hospital next, Officer Romero."

"We're gonna be here awhile. Maybe Chief Lefthand will bring us sandwiches."

"Uh-huh. That's gonna happen."

"Keep thinking about what Manuel Novar said," Cruz said. "He asked where his guns were, but not about his brother."

"When I met with Dr. Mondragon, his assistant said TPD were having trouble contacting the family. Maybe he didn't know his brother was dead."

"Still . . . I wonder if he would've asked if he knew. If the guns were more important to him."

She focused on the brother of the boy who had perished on the rez. "We'll never know."

Cruz locked his eyes on Tomás Salas, awaiting the body bag beside his now-prone form, and said, "And *that* guy. Wanted to build houses on the rez." He tsked. "To *help* us."

When Eva didn't respond he bumped her boot with the side of his fist. "Remind you of someone?"

Eva knew he meant Alice Jones. She stayed quiet. Wouldn't give the psychopath the satisfaction of speaking her name out loud.

"Why do these non-Natives want to try to help us?" Cruz continued with his rant. "We need nothing from them. All we really *want* is to be left alone to deal with issues on our own. Like we have for a thousand years."

She tuned out Cruz's complaints and turned to look at the third member of their unfortunate trio. Andrew Kotz looked uncomfortable surrounded by his people, his smile ringing insincere to her, as if he was trying to appear unaffected. Glock stripped from his holster. Again. "Feeling bad about Andrew," she said.

"He'll be fine. Probably get a medal. Double ceremony—one for him, one for Tallow."

"That Pueblo Kotz got," she asked. "Sandoval. Did you know him?"

"Naw. Cop before my time."

"Between you and me . . . it looked like Sandoval was aiming his piece at the back of Manuel Novar's head. That he was his target, not at Salas, or Kotz, or us."

"Looked that way to me too," Cruz said.

"What do you think that was about?"

"We'll never know. Hey, at least we didn't kill one of our own."

Eva nodded her agreement. "The *one* good thing."

"The spirits would not be happy."

She extended her hand to help Cruz stand up. "Or kind," she said, finishing Paloma's favorite saying.

CHAPTER
SEVENTY-FOUR
EVA

One month later

The turnout of people on the expanse between the North House and the Rio Pueblo surprised Eva. She had thought the weather would keep most inside their homes, and was pleased to see so many from her community there to celebrate the life of Nathan "Little Bear" Trujillo.

Eva caught snippets of conversations as she walked past. The first week of October brought unexpectedly frigid temperatures, and the month continued to remain unseasonably chilly. Many grumbled about the cold, snow would be coming soon, time to get more firewood and provisions before they couldn't get to the main road. She shivered, zipped up her jacket as far as the pull would go, looked up at the sky that had darkened since she'd arrived.

She spotted Cruz and wound her way around men who wore elaborate beaded headdresses, eagle feathers in the crowns and fringed dresses of the women—outfits designed and stitched and beaded by their own hands. She smiled at a group of tiny children dressed in full regalia, miniature versions of what their parents and aunties and uncles wore.

She gave Cruz her eyes and they needed no words to convey the pride of their people. "Have you seen Kai?" she asked him.

He pointed to a group of youngsters at the edge of the gathering, all circled around the teacher and the four-footed companion at his side, the center of their attention.

"Kids from the Red Willow Center," Cruz said. "Some are from Nathan's class. Kai started teaching them about the plants." He pointed to one girl in particular, the smallest, head held back all the way so she could watch Kai. "That's Betty. Nathan's best friend. She saw what happened to him. Kai's taking special care of her."

"Nathan would appreciate that," she said, voice cracking from the emotion she promised herself she would not allow on this day.

She caught Kai's attention and waved him over. He wore a leather belt adorned with bells that jingled as he stepped and Eva thought Shadow looked very proud of the matching version strapped around his neck.

"Exciting, isn't it? Look at all the people here for Nathan," Kai said, beaming, eyes shining. Shadow did a quick spin, as if seconding his master's statement. "What's gonna happen next?"

Santiago, striped shawl woven in the colors of the Taos Pueblo flag draped over his chest, appeared beside them and said, "Watch. Regale. Remember."

Six Pueblo men, young and old, sat around a five-foot-diameter drum, leather-covered mallets resting on the taut skin tied to a willow tree frame. They waited for the leader's head motion, then all simultaneously raised their sticks and struck the first blow. Lightly at first, gathering momentum and intensity as each beat progressed.

Across from the drummers, a group of females dressed in performance attire gathered in a tight circle. All dipped and bobbed, slight motions in time with the drumbeats. As the momentum intensified, the ring of dancers stepped another revolution together, then spread out, the circle growing wider. One end opened and a single dancer emerged from the others. Head held high, hands on hips, eyes to the horizon.

The one. The only. The chosen. Paloma "White Dove" Arrio pranced as the other women lessened their movements and allowed their sister the spotlight.

Dressed in full traditional regalia, colorful beads adorning her outfit shimmered in the sunlight. A single eagle feather stuck in her beaded headband bobbed as she stepped. Triangular cone jingle bells affixed to the long fringe that ran the length of the cloak she clasped in her hands tinkled with every jolt of her body.

A breath caught in Eva's chest. She reached for Cruz's hand and they held on. Kai edged closer, his arm next to her own, entranced by the sight the entire tribe believed would never be witnessed again. The gift to and from the most famous hoop dancer in four states.

Eva recognized the white knee-high leather moccasins, fringe stitched along the back seams. Her best friend had worn them only one other time—for her wedding ceremony. The strands whipped and twirled, propelled by each rise and strike of the shoe, keeping perfect time as each musician's mallet hit the drum.

Rather than a hoop dance Paloma had been famous for, she performed a traditional fancy shawl dance revered by the people of many tribes. White Dove spun, whirled her arms, held her body low and then rose, one foot hitting the ground as the other lifted, toe tap to full foot on the ground, the movements exquisite and dramatic.

Eva thought her best friend could take flight at any moment. Tears coursed down Eva's cheeks as she nodded her head in rhythm with every strike of the drum.

The beats grew intense, each more forceful, the drummers' voices rising in crescendo. The leader held a wail, the highest note Eva had ever heard.

She scanned the crowd, pleased to see awe on the faces of her people. Some dabbed at tears, a few held hands over their mouths, fascinated by every movement. Mesmerized. Stunned to silence. A few elders placed tented fingers under their chins, lips moving in prayer as they gave thanks for the miracle no one thought possible.

Their White Dove danced and danced and danced.

Santiago swiped his face with a red, white and blue bandana, then handed the cloth to Kai, who did the same.

Eva caught a quick movement as the crowd directly across from her split and Paco Barboa shouldered his way to the front. He stood at the edge of the performance circle, eyes locked on Paloma. He watched her every maneuver, dipping and swaying in place. So entranced Eva thought he might reach out to her. She prepared to warn Cruz about the potential security risk. The concern lasted only a moment when she remembered that the kinder, gentler, quieter of the twins couldn't possibly be a threat. Paco stared at her friend, attention locked, goofy look on his face, and Eva realized the younger man had fallen in love.

The former hoop dancer, who now danced again, whirled, motion growing faster after each spin.

For three full minutes.

White Dove stuck the landing at the final strike of the drum. Perfect unison. She held the pose—head up and off to the side, one foot crossed in front of the other, one arm raised to the sky, the other to the ground, shawl clasped in her hand—splayed to resemble a hawk's wings soaring on an air current.

Silence enveloped the crowd. Not a single baby cried. No murmurs of approval or dissent came from the ring of watchers.

Paloma held the pose.

No reactions came from the mute observers.

Eva caught the slight shake of her friend's injured leg. Inwardly she urged Paloma to release the stance.

And still Paloma held the pose.

An endless time later, Kai lifted his strand of bells and gave one resonant shake. The rattle echoed and lessened. A beat later, he issued another shake, harder. He took a step closer, broke the invisible line of the dance circle, took hold of both ends of the bell belt and shook it over and over and over. Shadow jumped and popped up and spun, making a clatter from his own bells.

Finally, at last, the people clapped—cautious at first, then more confident, the noise growing louder. The drummers joined in, a steady beat. Chants and cheers and high-pitched yips rose up that sounded like Shadow's expression of excitement.

Gentle flakes of snow floated from the sky, blessing the people, and the performer with white halo crowns.

At last Paloma lowered her arms, head, uncrossed her legs and bowed to Kai. Then she kissed her palms and extended them to her people time after time as she turned in each of the four direction quadrants. Lastly she again kissed her palms, raised them to the heavens and mouthed the words *We will always remember you, Little Bear.*

The touching tribute caught the breath in Eva's lungs.

CHAPTER SEVENTY-FIVE
EVA

The next morning, Eva parked the Beast next to where the front of her grandfather's house once stood. She got out and assessed what would one day be the site of a new house that would become her home—if she ever found the time to get started. And the extra funds. And the manpower . . . The mere thought of what it would take simultaneously caused her hands to itch to get busy and her mind to shut down from exhaustion.

She had continued to heal from the altercation at Tomás Salas's garage, and the aftereffects of the bank robbery and 3D gun investigation. Some nights, sleep evaded her, and when she did finally drop off flashes of gunshots and blood and noise and chaos wrenched her awake.

It helped to be outside. To focus on something other than police work and cases that would most likely never be solved to her satisfaction, all the unasked questions that wouldn't be answered.

Thankfully she had an outlet to keep her busy, and now the burnt studs and other detritus had all been removed. Only the foundation remained, and the water from the well tasted sweet. Settling in the very spot where she stood tapped a pleasing rhythm in her heart.

Snow had fluttered from the sky overnight and now an inch of white stuff clung to the foundation. Black clouds low to the ground threatened more weather, weeks ahead of season.

She opened the rear door of the Rover and took out a broom from the cargo area. She stepped to the middle of the slab her grandfather had poured and leveled sixty years ago, took up the broom and swept snow off the concrete—slow strokes, more of the bare concrete revealed after each swipe.

The monotonous calming motions allowed her mind to wander and she thought about the bank robber and how that person had evaded local police and the feds as well. Salas had been convincing that he wasn't involved in the actual robbery, even though an officer from Kotz's team had found the stolen money in Salas's garage, still bound in straps, in a bag along with another $2,400 inside an envelope, stained with what turned out to be Celio Novar's blood type. Eva was also convinced the meek schoolteacher didn't have it in him to intentionally shoot anyone—especially not Celio Novar.

She regretted that she'd never gotten the chance to get out of Salas who the party was who actually purchased the 3D guns from him. The distributor's identity still remained unanswered, in the grave with Salas's body.

Somewhat redeeming himself, Tomás's last words were about teaching and how proud he was of his students—especially Kai—rather than the 3D homes he wanted to build.

The entire three-day life-altering journey had continued to take a toll on her and everyone in her orbit. Most terrifying had been Cruz getting shot. Nothing serious, thankfully a through-and-through bullet wound, but she felt faint every time she thought of how close they had come to being killed along with the teacher.

Nadine Tallow continued to heal from her brush with death, aided by Andrew Kotz, who had moved her into his house so she would have the care only he could provide. Eva figured wedding bells would ring for them within a year—if Andrew didn't hold on to Nadine too tight.

Something curious continued to baffle Eva. The last time she'd entered the evidence room, out of habit now, she had glanced at the shelf that usually held the Angel Simone Lefthand evidence box that featured the date her parents had abandoned her twenty-seven years ago. She stood there, slack jawed, stunned to see a different receptacle in its place. Figuring what she looked for must have been shuffled around, she scanned every row, the front of every box. Didn't find it anywhere. She wondered if she should talk to Lenny Ramirez about it, but didn't want any red flags to go up.

Eva had yet to see that box again, and contemplated more than a few times what harm it would do to ask the chief directly. But something told her not to pry. Not her business.

Movement at the top of the lane caught her attention and soon she recognized Santiago's truck ripping up the snow residue behind its massive tires. Kai, Paloma and Shadow got out of the king cab and Eva gave the young man a wave he returned with a mere upward nod of his head.

She and Kai had yet to spend any time alone since she'd told the student about his mentor. She had crushed his respect for the man and she had so far been lacking in how to repair their relationship. She missed the boy and his dog, and their adventures together. Paloma told Eva he would move beyond it—after he got over the embarrassment and shame that he had been so naive to be fooled by someone he thought he knew so well. Still, Eva felt a piece of her had been torn off.

Paloma and Santiago joined her at the Beast, while Kai split off and threw the ball for Shadow—all four paws kicking up puffs of white, claws raking sharp impressions as he sprinted.

"Hee-yah-ho," Santiago said.

"Hey to you too," Eva said. "What're you doing out here?"

"Wanted to see how much progress you've made."

"Pretty proud of myself. See?" Eva swept an arm to the six-foot square of cleared concrete.

Paloma and her brother chuckled.

"Hear *you've* been busy," she said to Santiago. "3D houses, huh?"

"Yep. Pretty damned good idea. Wish I'd have come up with it."

Eva unfolded a blanket in the back of the Rover, popped up to sit on the bumper, then patted the covering for Paloma to join her. It took time, but Eva sat on her hands and let her friend manage on her own.

"I checked out one of the machines that just came in at a builder's site in Santa Fe," Santiago said. "An automated arm lays out perfect rows of concrete, one on top of the other. Fascinating. Mesmerizing, like a midnight campfire."

"Thought you were all about keeping workers on the rez," she said.

"All of our carpenters are in Albuquerque or Santa Fe. Gotta be creative," he said.

"Paco and Navi Barboa are going to help," Paloma interjected.

"That's good," Eva said. "Maybe that'll keep them out of trouble."

"I'm sponsoring a few classes at the Red Willow Center," Santiago said. "Got some professional electricians and plumbers lined up to teach. Figure that's the only way to keep the young people here on the land—make an opportunity for them. Some of the classes will be only for women."

She reared back. "That's progressive."

"Maybe."

"Gonna piss off some warriors."

"They'll have their own classes."

"Kai could teach landscaping with indigenous plants," Paloma offered.

"That is a great idea." He pulled out the palm-size notepad and a pen from his back pocket and jotted down his sister's idea as a reminder. "I'll add that to the instruction list for tribal government approval."

"Always looking out for us," Eva said.

He shrugged. "It's what I do."

Eva reached out and patted his shoulder. "You're a good man, Hawk Soars."

He shrugged again, leaned in close to Eva and whispered, "Don't tell anyone."

"Cement houses. Really is a very cool idea."

"Very cool," he muttered. "You sure you don't want me to construct you one?"

"Nope. Need to build it by hand, just like Grandpa did."

Kai and Shadow trotted over, both panting. Kai, face flushed, hair windblown, tears from the crisp air glittering in his eyes, looked happy as Eva could remember. She cooed to Shadow and ruffled his neck.

Kai unzipped his jacket, reached inside the front pocket of his hoodie, took out a black velvet pouch, handed it to her. "Keep forgetting to give this to you."

Eva untied the strings and knew right away what her fingers touched before she tumbled the item into her palm. "You don't want to keep this?"

"No, I got it for you. To remind you of your magpie when you move away from the city to live here." He nodded to the bracelet. "That's so maybe you won't miss Rio too much."

Eva admired Ricky "Singing Elk" Soto's beaded representation of a magpie in profile. The custom silver cuff felt comfortable the moment she positioned it on her wrist, as if it had been made for her alone.

"Thank you, Kai," she said. "This is very special."

"Wouldn't it be cool if Rio came with you?" Kai asked. "Maybe we could catch him." He turned to Santiago. "Think it would work if we're careful?"

Paloma shook her head. "Don't think you're supposed to do that, son."

"Magpies are smart," Santiago said. "Maybe he'll be like Shadow and sniff you out, Lightning Dance."

"Yeah . . . if I was made of plastic," Eva said.

The four laughed. Shadow yipped.

Movement caught her attention—another pickup headed their direction.

"Is that Cruz?" Eva asked. "What's going on? Why are you all here?"

Santiago clapped his hands and rubbed them together. "Ah, now we start," he said and then waved for the group to follow him to his pickup.

Cruz parked and hurried from behind the wheel, hurried to join everyone, pulled Eva close, gave her a quick kiss and pulled back, grin on his face that confused her.

"All right, spill it," she said.

Santiago pointed to the back of his four-by-four. She popped to her toes and looked over the side panel. Lengths of bare lumber, boxes of nails, milk crates full of various tools and other building necessities filled three-quarters of the bed. She turned her attention to her companions and held their eyes one after the other.

Eva's heart surged. Emotions flooded over her. Tears wavered her view of the people she held dearest. She didn't need to reconnect with the people who gave her life. All the people she needed or wanted to belong to were right there. Now. In the place she loved most.

"My turn," Cruz said, motioning them to join him at the back of his truck. "I've been hiding this at my place for months."

Her love and light dropped the tailgate, whipped aside a tarp, revealed a blinding-white claw-foot porcelain bathtub.

Big enough for two.

ACKNOWLEDGMENTS

First of all, great big thanks to those who discovered this book and allowed the words into your heart.

Hugest appreciation to my quite brilliant agent Liza Fleissig, head honcho at the Liza Royce Agency, who was instrumental in securing Liz Pearsons, the most amazing acquiring editor any writer could dream for. I couldn't be more proud to be on this journey with you ladies.

Cheers also to the numerous Thomas & Mercer teams who worked so hard to release the most glorious end results for the Eva "Lightning Dance" Duran books. This one took a bit of doing, and development editor Jon Reyes kept me on task yet again with his wise eyes and excellent suggestions. For the line and proofreading edits, Stephanie Chou and Bill Siever caught all my annoying blunders. Also kudos to all the other editors and blind readers involved, as well as so many other behind-the-scenes folks at T&M—you have my appreciation for life!

Out of my deepest respect for the culture and traditions, hours beyond counting have gone into researching the Native American elements featured in my books set on the Taos Pueblo. Since 2007, I have depended on Floyd "Mountain Walking Cane" Gomez and other members of the Taos Pueblo tribe to help me get the details correct. As well as taking advantage of their personal assistance, I have spent much magical time on and around the reservation, taken many tours over the years given by Taos Pueblo community members, reveled in stories told, and performed online searches to help me remember the thousands of details until my eyes bled. Any and all mistakes on these pages are my own.

I researched the character names used in *Havoc* and the previous book, *Redemption*, many of them drawn from the 1929–1940 Census Bureau rolls. Although first and last names remain current, no actual individuals are represented in my books. As of this writing, the Taos Pueblo Police Department has a female police chief. That said, even this character is purely from my imagination.

Tracie Paolillo came through once again to help me represent the forensics and crime scene elements correctly. Tracie, your humor and joy for life make learning about death and darkness less of a bitter pill to take in.

Bestselling and massively talented author Isabella Maldonado is my past and present go-to for insights into the law enforcer mindset, and . . . just about everything related to this roller-coaster ride of publishing experiences. Above all else, your friendship means more to me than you could possibly know.

Stacie Strauss, dog trainer extraordinaire. Thank you for your expertise over the years, so important for the doggie obedience and handler details for this book. Also kudos for training me to wrangle our Ausky, Roo—a.k.a. the Dragon.

It takes a *lot* of people to birth a book, and a plethora of fellow writers and professionals, friends all, helped keep me focused and shared their knowledge and expertise so I could present the most true-to-life experience for you, kind reader. Those who answered the call for this book include Dr. Jennifer Hartmark-Hall, Paige Johann, Rebecca Cantrell, Chuck Miiller, and John Mullaney. These are fine and brilliant professionals who constantly give me their time and knowledge at the drop of a hat. I couldn't appreciate you more. Again, any mistakes are mine alone.

A lot of brain power was necessary for *Havoc*, therefore too many people were neglected. Shout-out to those closest to my heart. You know who you are. I will try to do better next time.

Last mentioned but first in everything, hubby John. My love, light, joy. Ahhhh, John. You are every reason these words have been released to the world.

About the Author

Photo © 2022 Ted Stratton

Deborah J Ledford is an Agatha Award winner, three-time nominee for the Pushcart Prize, two-time finalist for the Anthony Award, and the Hillerman Sky Award nominee for best mystery writer who captures the landscape of the Southwest. She is the author of the Eva "Lightning Dance" Duran series, including *Redemption* and *Havoc*, the latter her sixth crime fiction novel. Part Eastern Band Cherokee, Ledford lives in Phoenix with her husband and their awesome Ausky. To find out more, visit http://DeborahJLedford.com.